LOVE AT CA

LOVE AT CAFÉ LOMPAR

Anna and Jacqui Burns

HONNO MODERN FICTION

First published in Great Britain in 2021 by Honno Press
'Ailsa Craig', Heol y Cawl, Dinas Powys, Vale of Glamorgan,
Wales, CF64 4AH

2 3 4 5 6 7 8 9 10

A catalogue record for this book is available from the British Library.
Published with the financial support of the Books Council of Wales.

ISBN: 9781912905379 (paperback)
ISBN: 9781912905386 (ebook)

Cover design by Anne Glenn
Text design: Elaine Sharples
Inside cover design: Mad Apple Designs
Chapter heading illustrations: Shutterstock
Printed in Great Britain by CPI Group UK

For Carole Cox,
Who taught us the importance of love, family
and food!

PROLOGUE

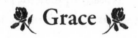 Grace

It felt like falling without a parachute. Hurtling through a void. That's the only way I can explain the shock of losing Dan.

He had a heart attack, brutally sudden. I'd been shopping in town and when I got back to my car I saw fourteen missed calls on my phone. Several from Dan's colleague, Will, and the last five from my daughter, Kat. When I listened to her voicemail, Kat was sobbing and I could only just make out her plea: 'Call me now.'

Dan had the heart attack at work, and had been rushed to A&E. I didn't know until I reached the hospital that he'd already died. Kat and I held onto each other, grief overwhelming us. He was just fifty-two.

I was enveloped in kindness at first: cakes and stews donated by well-meaning friends and neighbours; my sister Claire patiently listening to me sob on two a.m. phone calls; cards with poignant messages from his colleagues.

But four months later, most people had moved on. I still got the tilted heads in Waitrose from acquaintances, with a concerned, 'How're you keeping?' Claire, of course, would always be there and Kat wanted to talk about Dan as much as I did. But she lived over a hundred miles away in London, juggling a demanding career with an even more demanding boyfriend.

1

I'd finally tackled Dan's wardrobe last week and sent his clothes to the charity shop, keeping only the silver cufflinks I'd bought him for our twentieth anniversary and a pair of flannel pyjamas. His smell still lingered on them when I buried my nose in the folds. Today I was really ripping the plaster off. I was going to sort out Dan's study at the back of the house: clear out his drawers and send his books back to the university.

Soft, buttery morning light filled the room, dancing across the bookshelves, highlighting just how much stuff was in here. The shelves were bursting with everything from American and European politics, history and economics to the thrillers he devoured in his spare time. On the bottom shelves were his DVDs: Dan loved old British sitcoms like Fawlty Towers, Dads' Army.

The east-facing study looked out at the garden and I stopped to gaze at the lilac delphiniums towering against the stone wall and the blousy pink and white peonies in the farthest bed. The garden was my territory, my escape, but today I mustn't let it distract me. I had to face my memories.

Dan's earnestness was what first drew me to him. Well, that and his unruly hair and dark, serious eyes. He was a Heathcliff, intense and passionate. He used to laugh a lot in those early days, and he could make me feel I was the most important person in the room. He was a third-year politics and economics student at Bristol, and I was first-year English literature. We met in the students' union's crowded, smoky bar. I had gone with a friend, ignoring the essay I had to hand in the next day on the Romantics.

I ended up sitting next to him, Tears for Fears thumping in the background. When his arm brushed against mine, it felt electric. Two years older, he seemed so knowledgeable and sophisticated. His name was Danilo Milovan Lompar and he was from Montenegro, which sounded so wildly, impossibly exotic to me then.

'A tiny place called Perast in the Bay of Kotor,' he said, in that precise way I came to know so well. 'It is very beautiful.'

His family had moved to Britain when Dan was a child, but he still had an aunt there. Dan's parents had died in an accident just before his A-levels. Outside the bar, he kissed me, his hand in my hair, pulling me towards him. He stayed that night, the next, and barely left from then on.

The phone rang, bringing me back to the present. It was Claire. I pressed speaker phone as I sat in Dan's office chair, unlocked a desk drawer and began pulling out receipts and letters.

'Morning, hon,' Claire trilled. 'Now before you argue, I've booked brunch in Giovanni's. I'm picking you up at eleven-thirty. I've got to get out. The twins are driving me nuts.' She sighed. 'Laura is stressing about her mocks and Liam hasn't a care in the world. They're chalk and cheese, honestly!'

I picked up a photograph in a silver, heart-shaped frame Dan had kept on his desk: the three of us at Bristol Zoo. Two-year-old Kat clung onto a fluffy giraffe as if her life depended on it. With her other hand, she held Dan's. She had always been a proper daddy's girl and I tried not to let it bother me. It really didn't – I loved them being so close.

'I'm just making a start clearing up Dan's study and I'm not sure I'll have time...'

3

'Come on, Gracie, it'll do you good to get out for a bit.'

As she spoke, I rummaged in the drawer, pulling out sheaves of paper, pens without their lids, old notebooks. I'd forgotten how chaotic Dan could be – my task seemed mountainous. I tugged at the drawer, but something was jammed. I half-listened to Claire.

'I've got that wedding at the end of the month. A cousin of Stu's. Did I tell you?'

'Hmm,' I muttered, trying to sound interested. My fingers grasped something wedged in the back of the drawer. I gave a hard tug, the drawer shot forward and the whatever-it-was came away in my hand — an old envelope. 'Ouch!'

'Are you OK?' Claire asked.

'Sorry, I just broke a nail.'

'Anyway, I was hoping we could visit the High Street afterwards. I'll pick you up, OK?'

I mumbled something and Claire rang off.

I turned over the envelope, intrigued. In Dan's small, sloping handwriting was written: 'Rosa and Luka'. Nobody I knew. The hairs prickled at the back of my skull as I slid three photographs out of the battered envelope. Something didn't feel quite right.

The first picture was of a young, attractive woman, all voluptuous curves and long dark hair. Rosa, presumably. She and a younger Dan were standing outside a modest villa, cerise bougainvillea snaking around the entrance. She wore a tight-fitting dress stretched over a noticeable bump. Dan's dark fringe flopped down his forehead, and his arm rested territorially on the woman's shoulders.

The second was of Dan and a little boy, about four years old.

Maybe he was a relative of Dan's I had forgotten about – they looked so alike. An azure sea shimmered behind them.

The last was a more recent photograph. The boy was at least fifteen and Dan's hair was beginning to grey. Happiness radiated from them. I hadn't seen that smile for a long time. At the bottom, someone had written, Dan, Rosa and Luka. Perast. May 2016.

On the back was a message in handwriting I didn't recognise.

'A perfect day with my gorgeous man! I love you, darling. Counting down the days until we're together again. Rosa xxx'

The shock hit me like a punch to my stomach.

PART ONE – MONTENEGRO

ONE YEAR LATER

CHAPTER ONE

🌿 Kat 🌿

I pushed through the crowded arrivals lounge at Dubrovnik International, heading for my mother. Her new sunhat shone out across the crowds of people in all its yellow glory. If there was a way to stick out more as a tourist, I couldn't think of one.

'Ryanair is right when they talk about no frills flying,' I said, as I joined her at the desk and sniffed my T-shirt. 'I was sitting so close to the man next to me, I think I've caught his B.O.'

Mum sighed, rifling through her hand luggage. Some of its contents spilled out on to the desk.

'I can't find it,' she muttered, stress creasing her brow. 'I could have sworn it was in here...'

I looked up at the car rental clerk. He gave me a disinterested smile before turning back to his computer.

'What have we lost?' I asked, reaching out to hold her bag open for her.

'They need my driver's licence, and I can't effing find it.' She paused to lift her hair off her neck. 'It doesn't help it's so bloody hot in here.' I knew stress levels were high when Mum started swearing.

'Have you looked through your purse?'

'Of course I have!' she bit back.

'Why don't I go through it again? Fresh pair of eyes?'

Mum continued searching through the handbag's deep pockets, moving crumpled tissues and receipts so worn you could no longer tell where they came from.

I carefully searched her purse, thumbing through shiny cards and more receipts, but no tell-tale pink plastic driver's licence.

I found a picture of Dad at the back and stopped. A three-year-old me sitting proudly on his lap at the top of a slide he was clearly too big to fit down. Emotion welled up in my throat. I was still so close to tears at any moment. Would this feeling ever pass? A year had gone so quickly.

'Shit,' Mum said, looking up. 'I can't remember the last time I used it.'

'And you didn't check?' The question came out more angrily that I'd intended.

'I thought I had it.' She looked lost. Normally Mum always checked everything — but there was nothing normal about this trip. I needed to remember how hard this was for her.

We heard a groan from the growing queue of tourists behind us and the man at the desk cleared his throat.

'You can't hire a car without a licence,' he helpfully reminded us.

'I know,' Mum said between gritted teeth.

'Let's just use mine.' I flicked through my purse for my licence card. We had to pay an extra seventy quid because I was under the age of thirty. I swore under my breath as I handed over my brand new kuna currency. It felt as if we'd been at the car hire desk for hours by the time we were given the keys.

'Do you know I've always liked a Nissan Micra?' Mum said, as we wheeled our suitcases towards the car depot.

'Dad would kill you for saying that.'

'Him and his Audis.' She gave the first real smile I had seen from her in months.

'Right, Kat, just remember, deep breaths, no need to rush,' Mum said, more to soothe herself than me.

The little car juddered to life. Our route had already been planned, printed and highlighted by Mum. I didn't point out how unnecessary this was with satnav. I knew she'd say, 'It's nice to have a printed copy to fall back on.' The catchphrase of my childhood.

We headed for the roundabout, my foot pressing a little too hard on the accelerator. I was a bit out of practice – I barely needed my licence since moving to London; the restaurant where I worked was only a tube stop away. But it was all coming back to me and driving in London taught you to be aware and ready for anything.

Mum's foot pumped imaginary brakes as we approached.

'You don't need to do that.'

'I'm sorry. I'll try not to.'

We looked at the road sign. Zagreb, Hvar and Split, glamorous locations I'd seen on Instagram. We were going in the opposite direction. Montenegro, Kotor and Perast. Equally lovely, I was sure, but we weren't going for the glamour.

Rosa and Luka.

For a second, I considered turning the other way. A week on the beach in Split. Reading books, dipping our toes in the crystal sea, drinking cocktails. I worried for the thousandth time that I wasn't strong enough to support Mum through this.

The pain of losing Dad had suffocated me, like walking through life with lead shoes on. Finding out he had another woman, another family, was a betrayal I would never have thought possible. My beloved father had kept this massive part of himself hidden from us. Had he felt the same way about them as he did for us? Did he think about Luka every time he hugged me? Questions I could never answer. The wound was still raw.

I looked across the car at Mum, who seemed far away, and wondered if she was thinking the same things.

'Here we go.' I pulled out onto the roundabout, after waiting too long for the road to completely clear. I counted my breaths, one, two, three, to keep them steady. All I had to do right now was concentrate on the road. I couldn't think about what would happen tomorrow. Google maps reckoned it was just an hour and a half to Kotor. I added on another twenty minutes for my snail's pace driving.

'I'm proud of you,' Mum said, patting my knee a little patronisingly as we pulled out on to the open road. I chose not to bite. I felt shackled to the slow lane, as faster cars pulled past.

We turned a corner and suddenly we were a world away from the busy airport.

'Look at that,' I breathed. The coastline spread out in front of us, the hyper-blue sea dotted with luxury yachts and bordered by endless sand. 'It's a wonder Dad wanted to stay in the UK when this was his home.'

'Makes a difference from rainy Bath.' Mum gave me a tight-lipped smile, one I had come to recognise when she was thinking of him.

Small talk had become our comfort blanket since he'd died, muffling anything deeper. I felt we communicated more through what we didn't say.

Dad and I had had a private language since I was a child. He'd tell me stories of his old best friend, how they'd sneak to the front windows of their homes, across the street from each other, to send secret hand signals when they should have been in bed.

'Show me,' I'd asked, enraptured by his imagination. We were a little team, on a covert mission, making signals at the kitchen table behind Mum's back.

'Give me your peas,' he'd sign, knowing I didn't like them, saving me from another telling off. She could never understand why we giggled so much at dinner time. The memory hurt now as much as it had made me laugh then.

We drove in silence for a while, Mum apologising when she clutched the door handle as another car pulled out in front of us. A sign welcomed us to Montenegro as we crossed the border from Croatia. We'd never been here before. We'd been to Italy more times than I could count on both hands but Dad had always chosen holidays to Italy over his home country. We knew why now, of course.

Thick, lofty trees shaded the road from the insistent sun, beating hard on the roof of our Micra. I could feel my right arm burning through the small driver's window.

'You could do with some sun on you,' Mum said.

I was well aware of my ghostly complexion. My skin hadn't

had a hint of a holiday glow for years. Ever since I'd joined the kitchen at Truffles, in fact. Working unsociable hours six days a week didn't leave me with much time for sunbathing. I slept in until eleven A.M., then headed back to the kitchen, and my annual leave was usually spent researching new recipes for the menu. I'd only been allowed to take this time off because I'd promised I'd send any recipes I could find back to Mark, the head chef. He fancied the sound of Montenegrin fusion dishes.

'No one else is doing that right now, are they?' he'd said, always seeking the next new thing. He was obsessed with bettering the restaurant, evolving the menu.

In truth, I was exhausted. I was back in the kitchen exactly a week and a half after Dad died. Mum had been aghast, but it had given me a solid excuse to duck out of funeral arrangements and sorting through his stuff. Any guilt I felt was nothing compared to the grief of losing my best pal, and I could work my feelings out on the appetisers' section of the Truffles' menu.

I needed a holiday. So did Mum. We needed this together.

The sun was falling sleepily down the sky by the time we arrived in Kotor. I recognised the walled city from pictures in my guidebook. The impressive facade stretched up to the surrounding mountains. The bay was even more beautiful than I'd expected, and as dramatic as a film set. I thought of the clothes I'd packed. My supermarket shorts and t-shirts weren't going to be anywhere near glamorous enough, judging by the flocks of tourists strolling around the city walls.

This was a place for love, for proposals and weddings, couples and happy families. Our hurting hearts were awkward and out of place.

'This is it,' I said, pulling up outside the white-washed villa we'd chosen on Airbnb. Mum leaned across me to take a look.

'It looks smaller in real life, more ... lived-in,' she said, taking time to choose her words, her eyes scanning the overgrown path, crumbling garden wall and worn doorway.

'Well, this is it for the next two weeks,' I countered. 'Home.'

CHAPTER TWO

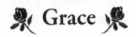 Grace

We'd booked too late to get a sea view. The little Airbnb was deeper into the old town than I imagined, up steep, stone steps. There was a tiny terrace at the front, with a small bistro table and two wrought-iron chairs. A wooden sign, 'Apartman Nina', hung drunkenly by the front door.

Even after eight o'clock, it was stiflingly hot, and my face felt flushed. I wrestled the cases out of the car and saw Kat on her phone, again! She was always on that bloody phone.

'What are you doing?' I asked.

'The owner has sent a code for the front door. Let's get in. We can sort the cases once we get inside.'

'Sorry,' I mumbled.

Kat was always the practical, capable one. Nothing fazed her. She could put together an Ikea table without breaking into a sweat. I watched her frown as she punched in the code to open the key-box. It made me catch my breath, how much she looked like Dan. Her long hair was tied up in a high ponytail, tendrils framing her heart-shaped face, and her intense eyes were almost identical to his. She was tall, with long, slim, athletic legs. Sometimes it was difficult to see anything she had inherited from me.

'Home sweet home,' she smiled, letting us in.

'Well, it's … bijou,' I tried to make light of it, as we walked through the compact living and kitchen area. The orange kitchen units were tired, and a small table and chairs had been squeezed in next to a grey corner sofa that took up most of the room. We'd be on top of each other for two weeks. 'It looked a bit brighter in the photographs.'

'There's just one bedroom, but I think this is a sofa bed. I'll sleep here,' said Kat, flopping onto it. She scanned the booklet left for us on the coffee table. 'There's WIFI, thank God.'

'Let's get the rest of the stuff from the car, and then we can grab a bite to eat,' I said, my stomach groaning right on cue.

After a quick shower — a grumbling, spluttering contraption— we set off to explore. Walking towards the lilac and crimson sunset, we headed for the square, wandering through labyrinthine lanes of bustling bars and tavernas lit by tiny fairy lights in fruit gum colours draped in hedges. We chose a small taverna in a street just off the main square and watched the souvenir shop owners pack up their displays and roll up their rainbow-coloured awnings. Exhausted, we shared a bottle of local wine in silence as holiday makers strolled by.

'What shall we order?' Kat asked, perusing the menu. 'Hmm, I think I'll have sarma. Sauerkraut rolls filled with minced pork and rice, served with mashed potato,' she read out loud. 'It sounds delicious.'

'Grilled tuna salad for me.' I wanted something familiar. I was too tired to pretend this was a holiday.

'Ispod sača sounds incredible, and the black seafood risotto. I'm going to have to taste some of these dishes before we go

17

home.' Kat's eyes lit up. 'We're always looking for something different at the restaurant. I promised Mark I'd check out some of the local recipes.'

Music drifted over from one of the bars in the square, cutting through a symphony of cicadas.

'I can't believe this is the first time I've visited,' Kat said, sipping her wine.

'Dad never seemed that keen. He said that he didn't remember much of the country as they moved to Britain when he was five. Then losing his parents – I just thought it brought back unhappy memories.' I paused. 'I guess it makes sense now. I'm seeing everything differently.' I let out a long breath. 'Tainted, somehow.'

Kat winced. I knew she still wasn't prepared to say anything negative about Dan, but it all hurt me so damn much. He had betrayed both of us, not just me.

I went on, 'He did all those lectures and conferences abroad. Perhaps that's when he visited them, his—' I caught my breath. 'His other family.' I closed my eyes.

The waiter came over to the table, his eyes fixed on Kat as he laid the plates in front of us.

'If you need something, you call,' he said in broken English, smiling at her. He was very handsome, tanned and blue-eyed. He proceeded to pour her some wine, flicking his wavy hair from his face, and then filled my glass as an afterthought.

'It's good to see my invisibility cloak is still in working order,' I said as he left.

Kat smiled at the familiar joke.

'What did you tell Adam about our trip?' I asked.

'Just that we needed to spend some time together, which is true. And that we were going to see where Dad first lived as a child. Again, true.' Kat looked directly at me. 'I didn't tell him all the other stuff. Too awkward, to be honest. A bit raw, too.'

A young couple passed, hand in hand.

'Adam would understand, but I'm just not ready to share this with anyone yet.'

'Shall we stay around the bay tomorrow?' I asked. 'Perhaps we can visit Perast on Saturday. Find our bearings, relax a bit.' I wanted some time to pluck up courage first. Or was I just putting it off?

'Sounds like a plan,' said Kat. She stopped eating. 'Do you have any idea where they live?'

'No, but it's a tiny place. We'll find them, I'm sure.' I gulped some wine. 'What we'll do then, I don't know.'

The sun was streaming through the window the next morning. My legs were twisted around the thin cotton sheet. Half-asleep, I dreamt I was in our bedroom at home and Dan was beside me. I could feel the heat of his body. I reached out, but the movement woke me. The bed was empty.

I lay there. I couldn't face Kat yet. I could hear her in the other room, chatting to Adam. Her voice was light, singsong. Kat was the only person who could understand how I was feeling, yet somehow we couldn't reach each other.

When the phone call was over, I wrapped my thin dressing gown around me and went through.

'Morning, sleepyhead,' Kat said. 'Sleep well?'

'A bit,' I yawned.

'Well, I beg to differ,' she laughed. 'I'd say it was like crunching gears. No, more like a pneumatic drill. The walls were shaking.'

'Cheeky,' I grinned. 'Your dad always said I snored.'

The light moment was gone at the mention of him.

'I've picked up some Danish pastries and coffees from the café on the corner,' she said, standing. 'I've put them outside. Let's enjoy our breakfast watching the world go by.'

After eating and dressing, we bought some cheese rolls and bottles of water and hiked up the Ladder of Kotor. I felt we deserved to be sightseers, just for today.

'It's only four miles along this winding trail,' Kat breezed, reading the guidebook.

'Is that all?' I asked, sarcastically.

As we followed the trail zigzagging up the mountain, my calves burned and I regretted the Danish pastry, feeling cumbersome and unfit. As we went higher, the ground was rocky and uneven, and my leather sandals were not up to the job. A family with three children swept past us, and the embarrassment gave me a fillip to keep going.

'The views are spectacular from up here,' I wheezed.

'Let's stop for five minutes.' Kat paused and sipped her water.

We could look down at the terracotta-roofed villas of the small town and the skiffs and fishing boats bobbing in the horseshoe bay. A huge cruise ship was moving into the harbour, a monolithic city, like a sparkling cathedral at sea. Opposite, cottages and villas clung to the shore and the valleys stretched into the horizon. The cobalt water glittered in the midday sun so brightly I had to shade my eyes.

'It's beautiful,' Kat said, snapping shots with her phone, and taking the requisite selfie. 'Come on, Mum,' she laughed, slipping an arm over my shoulder. 'If we go to the right, we'll come to the Fortress of St Ivan. We can eat lunch there.'

I rallied at the sound of lunch, more interested in that than the fortress, or even the attractive little chapel nearby. I enjoyed the small hiatus before we started back to the town, grateful to be heading downhill.

In the afternoon, we visited Kotor's famous cat museum, the Museo del Gatto di Cattaro, a small stone town house with photographs of cats littering the walls and newspaper articles about cats in the town. Even for cat lovers, there wasn't a great deal to see, but it was a welcome respite from the afternoon heat. According to the temperature display on a clock tower, it was 40° and I was wilting.

'I'm going back to the villa,' I told Kat. 'I'll have a little siesta before tonight.'

'All right, Mum, I'm going to do some exploring. There are some restaurants along the front and I want to see what seafood they serve. I won't be long.'

'Take your time, love.'

I trudged back, vowing to put a plaster on my little toe, which felt blistered. My phone rang as soon as I put the key in the lock at the villa. I picked up, cradling it precariously between my neck and shoulder as the door swung open.

'Hi, Claire,' I said, collapsing on the sofa.

'Hi, hon. How's it all going? How's the Airbnb? Liam, look at the bloody mess in this kitchen,' she bellowed suddenly. 'Sorry, Gracie, but he's unbelievable. He made a sandwich for lunch and there's crumbs everywhere. Honestly, how hard is it to clear up after yourself?' She sighed. 'Anyway, you were saying?'

'Everything is fine here. Well, not fine, but we're coping.'

'So when are you going to see his family?'

'Tomorrow, I think, but I'm nervous. What do I say to them? "Hi, we're Dan's wife and daughter, his first family. And you must be Rosa, his mistress. Only he didn't tell me anything about you and Luka. Did you know we existed?"' I bit my lip.

'I can't imagine how you're feeling. I just never thought Dan could be capable of doing something like this, so underhand and hurtful.'

'You and me both,' I agreed.

'What does Kat say?'

'We've hardly spoken about it. We'll have to, of course. I don't know, Claire, she idolised him. It's so damned painful. Perhaps we should never have come here.'

'About bloody time!' Claire yelled, not at me. 'Have you seen the mess of this kitchen? Sorry, Gracie, I'll phone tomorrow. I'm thinking of you both.' The phone went dead.

My heart was weighed down with the thought of the next day. Even the Montenegrin version of baklava I'd bought earlier, with sticky raisins and walnuts, didn't comfort me, the syrupy pastry cloying in my throat. Each second, each minute, brought me closer to this momentous meeting and I had no idea what to expect.

But we'd come all this way, we had to go through with it.

CHAPTER THREE

🌿 Kat 🌿

The sunset across the bay of Kotor cast an almost pink haze across the town. It was hard to keep in a straight line as I strolled along the sea front. There was simply too much to look at: the city walls, the dramatic mountains and the glittering turquoise sea. If Adam were here, he'd be stopping to snap pictures for Instagram every few metres.

I meandered along between the street stalls selling tourist fridge magnets and cat-printed bags, and the restaurants, where waiters were laying the tables for evening service. They reminded me of Truffles, only here I could enjoy myself. It felt like paradise, as I stopped to inhale the heady Mediterranean cooking scents of garlic, lemon, chilli.

A cat brushed past my legs, all white fur and whiskers, begging for attention. I bent down, my fingertips grazing the length of the small creature's back. He turned and circled back past my hand.

'You're a cutie,' I said, smiling at his purr.

I'd read about the famous cats of Kotor on the Lonely Planet website, but I didn't realise quite how many there would be, winding their way down the old town's streets and alleys, watching the throngs of people walk by. I liked cats and wanted to get one at home — a furry friend to stroke after another arduous shift — but Adam was allergic to them.

'I've got no food for you, I'm afraid,' I whispered to my new friend, but he didn't seem put off, following me for a few paces along the street, before running on his way.

If I told Mum about him, she'd be back the next day with little morsels of food; she was such a softie. It's a shame she'd gone back to the villa tonight. She'd claimed a headache from the sun, but I thought it was more likely to be the white wine this afternoon. Still, I had to admit it was nice to have a breather. I don't think Mum and I had spent this much time together since I was a teenager and it was intense. Seeing the pain Dad had inflicted on her was stifling, like breathing through cotton wool.

'Looking for somewhere to eat?'

A waiter on the doorstep of a seafront restaurant was beckoning me in.

My instincts were to find somewhere myself, taking the time to study the menus first, but my feet were tired, thanks to a new pair of sandals I'd hastily chosen for this holiday. I could do with a rest, and I had promised to call Adam.

I let the waiter lead me to a table close to the water's edge. If I slipped my sandals off, I could probably soothe my feet in the Adriatic.

'Glass of wine to start?' the waiter asked, a glint in his eye. He was handsome, in a classic European way, all dark curls and toned, tanned skin.

'Go on then, surprise me,' I smiled. I was on holiday after all, even if that wasn't really why we'd come.

'I know just the thing.' I'm pretty sure the waiter winked

before placing the menu down and walking off. The gesture was cheesy, but I surprised myself by smiling back.

It was fun to have some male attention. Adam and I had been together since the first day of catering college. I appreciated having someone who understood the pressures of being a chef, and we shared a love of food so intense, I doubted anyone else could understand. That was the DNA of our relationship, all six years of it. I knew Adam loved me, but sometimes I struggled to think of a meal we'd eaten together where he'd taken more notice of me than the food.

I spent my life around spitting oil and burning hot ovens, alternating between chef's whites and pyjamas. I could probably count on one hand the number of times I'd worn anything else in the last five years. It was nice to feel like a proper woman again in my cotton sundress and curled hair. I felt pretty, almost desirable.

I looked up to see the waiter coming back and felt almost shy. He was boyishly good-looking, although probably not a day over nineteen. Why were Mediterranean men so attractive?

'Someone like you can't be alone here, can you?' He placed the wine down. It was such an old line, I couldn't help but laugh.

'No, I'm with my partner, but he's back at the hotel.' I don't know why I said that. I knew this was only a harmless flirtation.

'Shame,' he joked.

'What do you recommend on this menu for someone who wants to try the best food Montenegro has to offer?' I asked, changing the subject, looking down at the choices in front of me.

'Well, you are on the coast.' He swept his hand around as if I hadn't noticed the scenery. 'So you must have the best seafood dish we have: buzara. It's prawns, shellfish, all the little fishes, cooked in white wine in a pot. Very delicious.'

I tried not to smile at 'little fishes'; it was charming. Buzara sounded perfect for a lazy evening in late May. I knew I'd been drawn here for a reason.

Dad had never talked much about Montenegrin food. Although I'd often asked what kind of meals he'd had growing up in Kotor and Perast, he dismissed the cuisine simply as similar to Italian or Greek cooking. In fact, he never seemed to give concrete details about this place. I wondered now if that was all part of the cover-up.

I pushed the thought of Rosa and Luka away before it could cloud my good mood. Today was for exploring, getting to know the place Dad had called home for the early part of his childhood. And I needed to call Adam. I'd spoken to him that morning to catch up, but the connection hadn't been great. Now it rang for a while before he answered, his smiling face coming up on FaceTime.

'There's my little runaway,' he said, as my face showed in the top corner of the phone screen. I rolled my eyes. Adam was having a dig at how quickly we'd booked this trip again.

When Mum first found the pictures, we didn't know what to do. I'd got to Bath as quickly as I could, luckily my only day off that week. We'd sat in silence around the kitchen table, dumbfounded, the pictures spread out in front of us. The man we knew and adored with his arms wrapped around someone else, gazing at her in wonder. My mind couldn't process it. I tried suggesting other explanations – relatives, friends – but neither of us believed that. Why keep them a secret? I could do nothing but stare at the face of my brother, the same giveaway dark lashes and set of our faces. These two strangers didn't seem real, but at the same time, the pain was searing.

I'd spent the next few months searching the internet for various combinations of 'Rosa', 'Luka' and 'Perast', afraid of what I would find, but nothing came up. Mum went through Dad's bank statements and found monthly payments to an account she hadn't seen before. Clearly, he'd been supporting them. Dad was on good money as a university professor, but keeping two families? Mum had her own bank account. She'd run a garden nursery business when I was very small and had sold it for a good profit. She only worked part-time now. How had he managed to hide all this from her, from us, for years? I would never ever have believed him capable of it.

With time, our hunt for information lost momentum. Work got so busy and I buried my feelings inside. Mum left me a voicemail one day that said, 'Let's just ... forget about this. We don't really know the truth. We need to let it go for our own sanity.' It seemed like the best option. There was nothing like denial for an aching heart.

But it would not go away. I had a brother. I turned up at Mum's, one day in April, to tell her what I knew we had to do.

'We have to go to Montenegro,' she said, taking the words out of my mouth.

We knew we had to find Rosa and Luka, and we had to do it before we could chicken out. We didn't discuss what would happen once we met them, didn't think about it, so we couldn't change our minds again.

I went straight home, telling Adam we'd booked flights to Dubrovnik and the little Airbnb in Kotor for two weeks. I said we wanted to get closer to Dad and see where he was born.

I intended to tell him about the other family, I really did, but the day we made our discovery changed me forever. I was a new person with a secret etched in her like a ravine on a mountain side. When I began to tell Adam how Mum was coping, he'd nodded and started talking about his current job, problems with the event he was catering. After that, somehow, I just couldn't tell him. I didn't want to admit, 'My dad was having an affair.'

'Hey, stranger, look where I am.' I flipped my phone camera around, dodging the other tables and showing him the water's edge and surrounding landscape.

'Don't make me jealous, Kat! Look where I am.' He turned his phone around, showing me the bins that lined the little yard outside his test kitchen at work. I laughed. I must have caught him slipping out for a cigarette. He confirmed my suspicions, the lit end hanging casually from his mouth when the camera focused back on him.

I always got on at him to quit smoking, hating the way the smell permeated every fabric we owned. Mostly, he agreed to try, but on a bad day he'd sometimes say, 'Don't be so prissy, Kat. You started before me in college.'

I chose not to comment on the smoking today. I didn't want to ruin the serenity I felt here.

We chatted about the upcoming wedding he'd been trialling dishes for. He told me about the bride sending back plate after plate and huffed about choosey customers. I only half-listened, half-watching the waiter walk a group of four young women to the table next to me, all bare-legged and long-haired. They were lapping up his cheesy lines and giggling like girls in a school playground.

I told Adam about the cat museum and the little one that had followed me earlier.

'Don't be on at us to get a cat again, darling, you know I can't. Now if you said a dog...'

'We don't have time to look after a dog. I wish we did. It would be cruel.' We'd had this conversation a hundred times.

'All right, all right,' he said good-naturedly. I heard someone call Adam off-camera. He looked back at me, the camera blurring the stubble on his jawline. I remembered the days I used to kiss along that jaw, the tickle of the hairs against my skin. That felt a whole lifetime away now, another country, another couple, unburdened by this secret between us.

'Apparently, the bride wants to try the beef with a different sauce this time.'

'Knock 'em dead,' I smiled, although we'd been talking barely minutes. 'I love you.'

'You too.' He clicked off.

I looked out to a passing boat, carrying buckets of fish and a team of men. I wondered if they hung up on their wives and girlfriends with a casual 'you too'.

I was being sensitive. I looked up to see my buzara arriving, brought by an older, slightly wearier waiter. The smell was delicious, summery and light. He asked how long I was staying in Montenegro and what I planned to do.

'Perast is very beautiful. You must go to Rocco's while you're there — best homemade baklava in the bay of Kotor.'

I agreed to try it. I wondered if Dad had ever been to Rocco's. Was that where he met Rosa and Luka? Would we be able to find them?

Did we actually want to?

CHAPTER FOUR

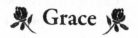 Grace

I had another restless night, which didn't surprise me. My stomach fluttered with nerves. The more I thought about the day ahead, the more I realised what a stupid idea it had been to come here. What could Kat and I possibly gain? Did Rosa and Luka know about us? Did they even know Dan had died? If they didn't, how could we tell them? I couldn't face it. And yet a small part of me wanted to hurt this woman, who had caused me so much pain.

I was bloody angry. I kept going over everything Dan had hidden from me for so long. He had spent about three months a year out of the country. Work related, he told me. It was part of the pattern of our married life.

He was a well-respected politics and economics professor and gave conferences and lectures in Britain and abroad. If I was honest, I basked in his success. I was proud to tell people what he did. He earned a good salary and we had a gorgeous limestone house in Bath. It was a mess when we first bought it, almost falling down, but we were young and blithely optimistic and we'd done a lot of the work on it ourselves in the early days. God, it was hard, but those times were some of the happiest of our marriage. When he became more successful, I had to get used to him travelling for work. I never even questioned it. I convinced myself, and others, that it was part of the reason our marriage worked so well.

'Do you miss him?' Claire asked me once, when we went to see a film in town and had a meal in Ask Italian afterwards.

'Only when a light bulb has blown,' I said, smiling, as I twirled pasta around my fork. 'Seriously, it's exciting when he comes home. It keeps a little spark between us.'

'I'm not sure how I'd feel if Stu was away so much. I'm not sure I'd trust him.'

'You would,' I insisted. 'I trust Dan. He's never given me any reason not to. And he's always so darned pleased to get home.'

Claire laughed, 'Well, he certainly brings a smile to your face when he does. You've got a good one there.'

I sipped my wine. I'd only admit it to myself, but I felt a bit smug. Stuart was in IT and I saw Claire's eyes glaze over whenever he spoke about his work, even more so when he talked about his various ailments. Dan could be morose at times, distracted, but he was exciting, fascinating. People admired him. He'd even appeared on Question Time once. And some of that glory rubbed off on me.

But did I ever really know him at all? That was the hardest question. If he hadn't died, would I have ever found out about Rosa and Luka? Had he ever considered telling me?

What about Rosa? She'd had Dan for just three months each year. Snatched moments in time. Was that enough for her? Where did she think he was the rest of the time? How could you be close to someone when you saw them for just a fraction of the year? Didn't she mind having to share him? I couldn't imagine her knowing about us, yet at the same time, I had a funny feeling she did.

The questions wouldn't stop and each one tore me apart.

I crept out of bed. It was only 5.30. Stumbling around the living room, I tried not to disturb Kat. She was sleeping with her back towards the kitchen, and I could hear her rhythmic breathing. I was relieved. She deserved a break. She worked so hard at the restaurant and this had taken an emotional toll on her as well as me.

I made myself a cup of coffee and, wrapping my dressing gown around me, went outside and sat on the tiny terrace. Streaks of light shone between the buildings and I could hear a dog barking in the distance. The town was just stirring awake, its bones creaking slowly to life. A small delivery van stopped outside the bar on the corner and the driver left some boxes outside, bottles tinkling as he placed them down on the cobbled street. I could hear his radio playing softly, the music strange and unfamiliar.

I thought back over last night's phone call with Sylvie. She was the manager of the charity I worked for, Project Child UK. We raised money for children from deprived backgrounds, giving them opportunities to go to summer camps around Britain and collecting money for toys and books for birthdays.

I was passionate about it. I remember when Kat was in infant school and I saw other children with thin, grubby coats too short at the sleeves. It made me feel guilty that Kat had so much.

My work was mainly arranging events and phoning businesses, pleading for donations. I worked there just two days a week and the money was abysmal, but after I'd given up the garden nursery, I felt at a bit of a loss at home.

The garden nursery just outside Bath I'd started when Kat began school had taken off more quickly than I could ever have believed, but it was also more work than I'd expected, and the strain of being a mother and being solely responsible for a business had burnt me out. I only realised how tired I was after I stopped. When a company with several garden centres offered me an enormous cheque for it, it was a no brainer to accept. I needed a change, and their cheque paid for a lot of work on the house. But that didn't mean I wanted to do nothing.

The charity work gave me purpose, even if I could do some of the tasks with my eyes closed. There were only three of us working there, Sylvie, Harriet, also part-time, and I. I had taken two months off work when Dan died and had asked Sylvie for two weeks' unpaid leave for this trip.

'Hi, Grace. How are you?' she'd asked last night.

'Fine,' I replied, keeping my voice light. 'Are you managing OK? I know the fundraiser is causing a few headaches. I'm sorry I left you in the middle of it all.'

'You need the break, Grace. Two weeks in the sunshine will do you good. You've got to treat yourself, be kind to yourself. And it must be lovely to spend time with Kat.'

Sylvie was a gentle soul, just right for charity work. She'd give you the coat off her back if you needed it. She lost her husband ten years ago. A widow. Now I had joined the club that no one wanted to be part of. We chatted for a while about a recent donation PCUK had received from an anonymous source. 'Quite mysterious,' Sylvie said.

'Have you managed to secure a venue for the fundraiser,' I asked.

'I think so. We even considered the golf club at one point, but the rental is too high. That handsome Neil Hadley came in. You remember him? He was asking after you, Grace.'

I did remember Neil Hadley, a tall, good-looking golfer, who'd donated to Project Child more than once. He had kind eyes and was charming to everyone.

'Anyway, I've got a few phone calls to make this evening,' Sylvie said, 'so I'll let you have some peace. Enjoy your time with that lovely daughter of yours.'

A woman in an apartment opposite shook her rug noisily against the railing of her balcony, oblivious to the early hour. I watched one of the town's cats trot purposefully along the pavement, then I scrolled through Facebook to take my mind off the day ahead. There were the usual birthday alerts, posts about children and grandchildren, messages of support. Everyone's best versions of themselves.

'You OK, Mum?' Kat's voice startled me. 'Bit early for a Facebook scroll.'

'I couldn't sleep.'

'Me neither. I can't help wondering what we'll say to her. What she'll say to us. What we'll find out.'

'I know.' I nodded. 'Me too. Come on, we'll have some breakfast and a coffee at the harbour. We've come all this way, so we'll have to see it through,' I said with a resolve I didn't really feel.

I saw Kat give an odd look at my sunhat as I was getting ready. I'd spent ages deciding what to wear and opted for a white T-shirt and navy linen culottes, which I was beginning to regret as they were already crumpled. I wanted to look effortlessly stylish and I thought the yellow sunhat was a fun, frivolous touch, but was it too much? I was at least ten years older than Rosa, judging by the photos, and the last year had given me more lines and dark eye-bags than I'd ever thought possible.

The morning was hot, and it was just after ten o'clock when the tourist boat stopped off at a Catholic church on Our Lady of the Rock. The small islet was already crowded with tourists slurping ice creams and taking selfies. Kat and I found a bench and gazed at Perast on the opposite coast.

Perast nestled in a niche at the bottom of a towering valley, a small village filled with elegant villas and Baroque churches. There were a few boats along the rocky shore and the Adriatic Sea glinted in the midday sun.

'Do you think we'll find them?' I asked Kat. 'The last boat leaves at five.'

'Yes,' she said with conviction. 'There are less than three hundred residents. I should think it's the kind of place where everyone knows everyone else.'

Our boat was ready to take us across the water. Ten minutes later we disembarked in Perast, a pleasant surprise after the more touristy Kotor. There was one main street along the seafront and steps led up from the square to villas and hotels behind it. Seafood restaurants lined the shore, their snow-white awnings rippling in the breeze. We decided to eat in one and ask if anyone knew Rosa and Luka. We had the photo ready to show people.

The plan was fine in theory, but now we could actually ask someone, our courage deserted us. We both picked at a salad half-heartedly and Kat asked for the bill.

When the older waiter brought it to our table, Kat stopped him. 'Excuse me, can you help us?' she faltered.

'Do you know these two people?' I asked, picking up where she left off, holding up the photo. 'They are relatives of ours.'

The waiter stared at the picture, putting our plates back on the table. After a minute, he shook his head.

'No, sorry,' he said. 'Ask Ivana. In pharmacy.'

We both sighed, but to be honest it was with relief. We paid the bill and left. I was shaking as I picked up my bag and followed Kat into the street.

'I almost didn't ask then,' Kat admitted sheepishly.

'I know,' I agreed. 'This is a terrible idea.'

However, without saying anything, we headed for the pharmacy. The familiar green cross could be seen from the shore. We waited to cross the street, a lone motorcyclist wheezing noisily past. The sun struck my head. We walked over and went in.

The pharmacy was empty of customers. A young, dark-haired woman at the till looked up as the entrance bell tinkled.

'Ivana?' I questioned, before my nerves could desert me.

The girl shook her head and mimed, pointing to my watch, 'One hour.'

'This is hopeless,' I whispered to Kat as we sat on a bench opposite to wait. It was agony.

After an hour, an older woman came out of the back room. We hurried inside. The young girl we spoke to earlier nudged the new woman and spoke to her in Montenegrin.

'Me Ivana,' she said, puzzled.

I retrieved the more recent photo of Dan, Rosa and Luka.

'Do you know these two?' I asked, pointing to the mother and son.

She shook her head, 'No.' After a pause, she asked, 'Names?'

'Rosa and Luka.' I took a wild guess and added, 'Lompar?' Maybe people around here had known Dan.

The young girl looked up at the mention of the names and seized the photographs from Ivana.

'Lompar?' the old woman queried, and they spoke to each other, excluding us completely. It was obvious she recognised one of them. She turned to me. 'Tivat.'

'Pardon?'

'Tivat! Tivat!' she repeated impatiently.

Kat and I looked uncomprehendingly at each other.

She reached behind the counter and brought out a folded-up tourist map. Opening it, she pointed, 'Here. Tivat.' Her finger traced around the bay of Kotor. 'Café Lompar.'

I muttered my thanks and stumbled outside. Moving from the air-conditioned pharmacy to the hot street took my breath away.

'It has to be them,' Kat said, as shaken as I was. 'The name of the café.' Dan's surname. Our surname.

We went back to the shore to catch the next tourist boat heading to Kotor Town.

'We'll go tomorrow,' said Kat, as we clambered into one of the boats, a bigger one than we'd taken earlier. I couldn't wait to get back to the Airbnb and barely looked at anyone as I mumbled my thanks to the young man helping me down the steps.

Kat joined me a minute later, her face ashen.

'Are you all right?' I asked. I turned to look where she was staring: the handsome, dark-haired man helping tourists into the boat.

'It's Luka,' she said.

CHAPTER FIVE

❦ Kat ❦

I've always had a fascination with those television shows that reunite long-lost family members: parents and adopted children, sisters separated by war, twins forced to live apart. I used to watch in amazement, eyes brimming with tears, as they walked towards each other with arms outstretched. How must it feel to see someone bonded to you by blood and such deep ties, who you'd never met before? I couldn't imagine it feeling anything other than joyous.

This felt like being winded.

I sat next to Mum on the boat, bobbing up and down, surrounded by tourists enjoying their day of exploring. I felt sick.

'My God,' Mum breathed. 'It's got to be him.' She reached into her bag to get the pictures, the edges now worn, but I needed no confirmation.

I watched Luka help the last remaining tourists hopping down the small steps onto the boat. He looked natural, clearly accustomed to life on the water. He was tanned and curly-haired, a similar height to me, and unmistakably my father's child. The curve of his chin, the dimples either side of his mouth: it was him. My half-brother. Flesh and blood.

A total stranger.

Among the small collection of pictures Dad had kept hidden, we'd found a more recent looking one of Luka standing with his arm slung around Rosa in a garden, the lawn dry and threadbare. He was smiling in the picture, a smile that reached out to the camera and crossed oceans, as if it was meant for me. He looked just the same now as he untied the boat from the small pier, his foot confidently anchoring it to the side as he finished untangling the rope. He seemed relaxed and self-assured.

I thought I had prepared myself for seeing my brother, reminding myself that none of this was his fault, that Luka had nothing to do with Dad's affair. But he was inextricably linked to it all, a product of our pain.

We both stared at him, paralysed. I had made peace with our unsuccessful day's searching, exasperated and relieved that we hadn't found them. The nugget of information we'd gained – 'Café Lompar' – was enough to keep me going until tomorrow. I couldn't believe Luka was actually here, and we were confined on a boat with him for the next hour.

'What should we do?' I asked Mum.

She squeezed my fingers. I didn't know when we'd last linked hands, but it felt comforting. We needed each other.

'Should we talk to him?'

'I don't know if I can,' I stuttered.

'Me neither. What the hell would we say? "Hi, this is your half-sister and I'm your dad's wife in England?"' Mum's voice was thin with tension. She spoke quietly but still drew a confused look from the couple sitting next to us.

Luka was oblivious to our focus on him, moving to speak to the captain of the vessel.

The afternoon sun blared down on my scorched shoulders. The gentle spray of the passing waves was soothing as the engine fired up, ready to carry us back to Kotor and the safety of Apartman Nina.

Luka turned around, shielding his eyes from the sunlight. I swear I stopped breathing as his gaze crossed us, probably counting the number of tourists on board. He turned back to say something else to the captain, inaudible over the growl of the engine. I was glad the boat was so busy; we could blend in with the crowd.

'I don't know, I don't know.' I heard Mum talking under her breath, as she fiddled with her star necklace, moving the pendant back and forth on its silver chain. Dad had bought it for her for Christmas. Something about the movement was disconcerting, a reminder of Dad.

Could we talk to Luka? Should we talk to Luka? What if he knew nothing about us? We could be ruining his life unnecessarily, and what would we gain?

'Excuse me, do you mind taking our picture?' A group of Americans sitting opposite thrust a camera in my face. It felt unfair. I wanted so desperately to stare at Luka. I resented even a moment's distraction. I tried to take the picture as quickly as I could, not caring if I caught all five of their smiling faces in the frame.

When I looked back, he was making his way down the boat. There were two aisles between the passengers, and luckily, he chose the other one. Mum and I watched in silence. I realised I was clenching my entire body, my breathing shallow.

At the back of the boat, he circled round and came down our

side. Oh my God. He was so close now, I could make out a scar on his jaw. He looked more like Dad the nearer he came. I was absolutely certain it was him.

He smiled at the couple seated next to us and asked them if they could move down the boat. He reached up to fiddle with the roof rack above the vacated seat, shading us from the scalding sun.

Mum turned to me. She looked nervous, but something else. Excited?

'Excuse me?' she said to him.

I didn't expect Mum to be so bold. Luka turned to smile at her, a confident dimpled smile that had Dad written all over it. God, he was one hundred percent a Lompar. Just like me.

'How long will it take to get back to Kotor?' Mum asked, gesturing towards the sand-coloured stone town some distance along the coastline.

'About forty minutes,' Luka said. 'Although Akso did have a few rakijas with lunch. He struggles to steer in a straight line at this time in the afternoon.' He mimed drinking the popular Montenegrin brandy, then laughed to show he wasn't serious.

I exhaled. The ice had been broken. It was perfect.

My brother was perfect.

Mum laughed. 'Do you live in Kotor?' I was glad she had plucked up this courage from somewhere. If it had been down to me, I'd have gawped at him open-mouthed the whole journey back. I looked at her friendly face. This was the son her husband had produced with another woman. I felt ... proud of her. Amazed, actually.

If Luka was surprised by the question, he didn't show it.

'No, no, not Kotor. I live in Tivat with my mother. It's a town further down the coast from here, very beautiful. Although I grew up in Perast.'

'Really? You must be very close?' Mum said.

I squeezed her elbow, not wanting to scare him off.

'Your English is perfect,' I said, before realising I sounded equally as mad.

Luka didn't let a beat pass before answering me. 'Thank you very much. My father lived in England and I used to love practising my English with him. Very useful in this line of work.' He gestured to the tourists.

I heard it. The past tense. My father lived in England, used to love... I noticed the dark skin under his eyes, that familiar look of grief, of being a ghost in your own skin. He knew what happened to Dad then. I didn't know how he knew, but I felt connected to him in our sadness.

'Have you ever been to England?' Mum asked. I wondered if she had picked up on it too.

'Just once, maybe five years ago,' Luka nodded. 'I went to London. It was cool but too built-up for me. This is what I love.'

The bay was beautiful, the sea a vivid blue, reflecting a cloudless sky as we sped along.

'I can see why. It must be hard to leave?' I was talking rubbish, but I couldn't control my excitement. I was speaking to my brother.

'Yes, although I will be moving to Berlin in a few months for university, to study Law.'

'Wow!' Mum and I said at the same time. We sounded like a pair of old women, who delighted in gossip. Luka didn't seem to

44

mind. He spoke fluently and with a charisma that felt familiar, like Dad.

Luka talked to us for much of the journey back. We learnt he'd worked for this tour company for the last few summers, making some extra money while working towards his law degree. He also told us about Café Lompar, a little beachfront diner serving ice creams and Montenegrin nibbles, owned by his mother, who worked front of house. He helped out in the restaurant now and again, but got under his mother's feet.

'She loves chatting to the customers. My mother can talk and talk.' He elongated the word loves and rolled his eyes. I wondered if she'd love talking to Mum and I as much.

'My name's Grace and this is Kat,' Mum introduced us. There was absolutely no flicker of recognition at the names. Mum glanced at me. So they didn't know about us then.

'Luka,' he smiled, just as he was called back to the front of the boat. The ancient city walls were drawing closer; we were about to moor.

This was our chance to tell him. Maybe our only chance. Would we see him again?

'I can't do it, Kat,' Mum whispered.

I thanked her silently. I couldn't do it either. It had been so lovely talking to him, getting to know my half-brother as a passing stranger, one of the thousands of visitors he helped to transport across the bay every summer. No weight of family, betrayal or scandal. It felt wrong to tarnish such a perfect Montenegrin afternoon.

We nodded our goodbyes to Luka as we disembarked, and he raised a hand to us. But as we paused to let the crowds of other tourists pass, I hesitated. Would this be the last time I saw him? Mum looked equally ambivalent. She turned to look at him one last time, then touched my arm.

'Come on, let's go back to the apartment.'

We fell into step following the stone wall of the seafront. It was the right thing to do. We needed time to think, to work out our next move.

Meeting Luka was strange. I wondered if I should feel more whole, complete, having found a missing piece of the jigsaw of my life: my half-brother.

'You're quiet. Everything OK?' Mum asked.

'Yeah, I think so.' A wave of exhaustion washed over me, and I tried to shake it off. 'I need a glass of wine.'

CHAPTER SIX

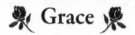 Grace

As Kat and I headed towards Apartman Nina, the bars and tavernas were bustling with waiters collecting the crockery and glasses from the afternoon diners and laying out pristine tablecloths for the evening's service. In her floral, halter-neck sundress, Kat's shoulders looked flushed from the afternoon sun. We were both silent, locked in our own thoughts. We picked up bottles of water, teabags and some brioche rolls for breakfast in one of the local supermarkets and I sighed with relief as we entered the cool of the apartment. Kicking off my sandals, I flopped on the sofa.

'What a surreal afternoon!' Kat said at last. 'He was nice, though.' She met my gaze.

'Hmm, he was,' I admitted. Her eyes glittered with excitement and I was lost for words. How could I tell her how I really felt?

'There was no mistaking him,' she went on. 'He has Dad's unruly hair and those dark eyes. The Lompar dimples. It gave me goosebumps. It was like looking in the mirror. A male version of myself. God!' She stopped suddenly and shook herself. 'Unbelievable! Did you hear him say he'd been to London?'

I nodded.

'And I think he knows about Dad. About the heart attack, I mean. But I'm not sure that he knows about...'

My phone vibrated on the kitchen counter.

'You get that. I'm going for a walk. I might try and catch Adam.' And with that, Kat was out of the door.

Claire's name lit up on the screen. 'Hi, hon,' she said, and without any preamble, 'How's things going? Have you found out anything yet?'

I settled back down on the sofa, curling my feet underneath me. 'Well, we went over to Perast. It's a tiny place, beautiful. Couldn't find anything out at first. Then we met a woman who knows them, and they've moved to another town.'

'Ooh, frustrating!' Claire sympathised. 'So, what are you going to do? Are you going there?'

'Wait, the best is yet to come. We met Luka on the boat back!'

I could hear Claire gasp. 'Oh, my God. What's he like?'

'He's Dan's, all right. No mistake. The same stature, hair, eyes, everything. We chatted to him.' I stopped as Claire gasped again. 'But, no, we didn't say anything.'

'What does Kat think?' Claire asked.

'That's the thing.' I paused. 'She's excited. I can tell. And trying desperately to hide it from me.'

'I can understand,' Claire said. 'He's her brother, well, half-brother.'

'Exactly. To me, though, he's nothing, really. Dan's love child. I don't know what to think. But with Kat, this is the start of something.' I sighed. 'And now we've come here, she'll want to keep in touch. We're linked to this family of Dan's, whether I like it or not. This other family.'

'It must be so strange for you,' Claire said soothingly.

I caught sight of myself in the television set opposite the sofa

48

and grimaced at the woman staring back at me, slightly crumpled and carrying too much weight, a body fighting and losing the onslaught of age. 'They've moved to this place called Tivat, on the other side of the bay. It's a bigger town but they've got this café or restaurant place called Café Lompar, so it should be easy to find.'

'Will you go there?'

'Probably. Kat and I will decide tonight. God, how could he do this to us?' I wailed.

'He was an out-and-out bastard, that's how!' Claire said in a show of support.

'It's indefensible. I can't excuse what he's done. I can never excuse it.'

'The age-old story of trading in his wife for a younger model. It's all about sex.' She paused, before saying philosophically, 'Men are simple creatures.'

I nodded. 'Rosa is impossibly glamorous! You've seen the photos, Claire.'

'All melon-tits, tiny waist and teeth,' said Claire.

'Don't forget the long, dark hair, the endless legs, the flawless, olive skin.'

'What a bitch!'

We both laughed, something I'd forgotten to do in a long time. 'I don't know what to do, Claire. Tell me what to do.'

'Talk to Kat tonight. She's a sensible girl and whatever happens, she's your daughter and she loves you.'

'We're finding it hard to communicate at the moment. We're tiptoeing around each other. Both afraid to hurt the other.'

'You'll find a way through this, I know you will.'

I sighed. 'Come on, let's talk about something else. How's school going?'

'Well, the Head is convinced we'll have the Ofsted inspection this half-term. They only give you two days' notice these days. It's stressful as hell. And it doesn't help that I teach in the same school as Laura and Liam. I'm about as welcome as a dose of chlamydia when they see me in the corridor. They both say they avoided history GCSE just so I wouldn't teach them.'

'They're just typical teenagers,' I said.

'I tell you what, though,' Claire went on, 'I think Laura's got a boyfriend. She's all secretive about it, but I saw his text to her yesterday.'

'Gosh, how?' I asked.

'When I picked her phone up and scrolled through her messages.'

'You're shameless.'

'It's not good to have secrets...' Claire began, and then realised her mistake. 'Oh, sorry, Grace, I didn't mean anything.'

'It's OK, honest.'

We chatted a few more minutes and then I showered. Kat returned later with some pitta bread, salad and lamb pieces.

'It's prepared with kajmak,' Kat explained. 'I've been wanting to try it. It's braised in milk. Sounds icky but it looks and smells divine. And I thought neither of us would feel like going out tonight. I've picked up some wine too.'

As we sat in front of the television, eating the lamb pittas, we scrolled through channels trying to spot BBC News. Instead, we flicked through endless game shows, and a Montenegrin soap with families shouting at each other.

'You don't need to speak the language,' Kat laughed. 'He's having an affair with the receptionist and his wife is seeing her personal trainer.'

'It's not just us with the chaotic personal lives, then,' I said, a little too sharply.

'We're not the only ones, Mum. Adam's mother has been married three times and he has two half-brothers and a stepsister. He's never even met his father. He hasn't once tried to get in contact with Adam.'

'I suppose,' I said.

'At least Dad tried to be there for us. But it's pretty shit what he's done to us.' She took a gulp of wine. 'I try to think of excuses for him. Like he hated confrontations. Or he loved both families and couldn't bear to give any of us up. I wonder if he ever came close to telling us.'

'You mean he wanted to have his cake and eat it! No, I doubt if he ever thought of telling us.' I couldn't keep the bitterness out of my voice.

Outside it was dark and the deep, charcoal sky was freckled with stars.

Kat turned to me. 'I think we should go to Tivat tomorrow. We have to face this.'

I nodded slowly.

'I've been looking at the map. It's only six kilometres away. I've even looked at Café Lompar. It's on the promenade by the harbour. Double-fronted. It seems quite popular.' She showed me her phone.

And there was Rosa, all smiles, standing outside Café Lompar. A huge sign with the words 'Grand Opening' was draped across the restaurant. She was breathtakingly gorgeous. Successful and beautiful. I was the faded wife, working for a charity, ambling through life without any particular aspirations. I'd been quite content with our cosy, comfortable life as a unit of three.

Yet two decades ago I too had been running my own successful business. Where was that woman now?

Kat continued, 'I think we should hang around the town here tomorrow and then go over late afternoon when it will have quietened down. It's not going to be easy, Mum. But she should know about us. He's betrayed all of us, really.'

'Somehow I don't think we'll bond over that. If she doesn't know about us, she'll be shocked and angry. No angrier than me, though. It's so bloody hurtful.' My voice dropped. 'He obviously didn't love me at all.'

'I don't believe that. I used to tell Adam that you two had the perfect marriage. I know Dad could be moody at times but you were affectionate and teased each other.'

'Appearances can be deceptive. I loved him, though. It was real on my part.'

'I know. You don't have to say that.'

We lapsed into silence. Kat yawned. 'I'm shattered. Do you mind if I go to bed?'

In my room, the long voile curtains hung limply in the still air. I opened the window on the furthest latch and switched on the air conditioning. I lay awake gazing at the huge ivory moon suspended in the inky sky. I wiped the tears from my face, grieving the marriage I thought I'd had, that Dan had made me believe we had. Then I tried to read for a little, to take my mind off the whole thing before I fell into a fitful sleep.

In the middle of the night, I became aware the door was standing ajar. I was startled, but then saw Kat's silhouetted figure.

'Can't sleep?' I asked.

She nodded and then slipped into bed next to me without saying a word. I stroked her hair, as I used to do when she was ten and had a nightmare. Her face was damp. It didn't take long for her to slip into sleep. I lay awake, watching the sunrise cast a peach paint stroke across the dawn sky.

CHAPTER SEVEN

🌿 Kat 🌿

I rolled over in bed, wincing at the friction of the crisp sheets against my sunburnt shoulders. The light was streaming in through the curtains, making me squint. It took a moment to realise I was in Mum's room. There was something comforting about it; the floral scent of Mum's perfume on the bed linen made me remember when I'd sneak into my parents' bed as a child on weekends and holidays, hoping desperately they'd wake up and start the day, not caring what time it was. I'd snuggle down between them and breathe in the familiar aftershave Dad wore to university every day, and Mum's smell, so delicate and feminine.

I heard the trickling shower in the next room, and checked the time on my phone's screen: seven A.M.

I kept playing the conversation with Luka over and over in my mind. I wondered how he'd have reacted if we'd said who we were. I was desperate to be able to tell him, to hug him, call him my half-brother. It was a bond I'd never felt before. If only I could fast-forward through the pain it would cause, I was sure we could build a relationship.

I knew Luka would be a part of my life forever.

My phone rang, the clinical sound piercing through the

synchronised cicadas outside. It must be Adam. I picked up my glass of water and headed for the kitchen. I could make a pot of coffee while I talked, ready for when Mum came out of the shower.

Only when I went to answer, I saw 'Mark' flash up on the screen. His name was an anchor, weighing me down, dragging me back to my real life, with no Montenegrin sunshine, no Luka. What did he want?

'Hello?' My voice sounded overly formal, filling the small space of the kitchen.

'Kat, hi. It's me.'

I calculated it was six A.M. in the UK. The man had no concept of sociable and unsociable hours. Head chef Mark Douvall owned his employees' freedom and time. That was the price you paid to work in a Michelin-starred kitchen. It was a drag. Life out here seemed slower, more relaxed. I doubted the head chefs at Authentika, Rocco's or Café Lompar would be calling employees at this time of morning. And he knew I was on holiday.

I was struck by the memory of Dad's fiftieth birthday party, the fancy party I'd planned with Mum for a small collection of his favourite people. I'd made an ornate cake, topped with a tiny stack of books and pair of glasses made of fondant, and piped with a toffee buttercream that shimmered like liquid gold. We'd even made a slideshow of our best pictures of him, to play throughout the night. I'd told everyone at work my plans and booked the time off months in advance. But an hour into the party, I checked my phone and saw ten missed calls from Mark, and a 'Ring back NOW' message.

'You need to get back asap, Kat,' he said. 'Anton's called in sick, and I've just seen fucking Grace Dent walk in with a group of fifteen. Grace Dent! It's a fucking nightmare.'

I'd tried to argue – we'd had high-profile restaurant critics like Grace Dent in Truffles before – but he wasn't having it.

'Think very carefully about your priorities here, Kat. You turn me down now and you'll be flipping burgers in McDonald's for the rest of your life by the time I've written your reference.'

I walked back to Dad, tears in my eyes. I think he saw how distraught I was. He was as gentle and understanding as ever.

'Listen, you've got to do what you've got to do.' He'd put his big hands on my shoulders and squeezed them. 'This is the best present I could have ever asked for anyway.'

'I'm glad you like the party, Dad.'

'No, I meant having a daughter as lovely as you. Now go on, Kit Kat, knock 'em dead.'

Mark's voice on the phone pulled me back to the present, 'Can you hear me?'

'Yes. Is everything all right?'

'Yeah, yeah... Well, actually, no.' I could hear the stress in his voice. 'We've just had a shit review in the Guardian. The Guardian, of all papers! Listen to this: "Floundering chef Mark Douvall might think he's being original with his blue-coloured broth for the Lac Delphine, but the actual flavour of the liquid is so bland I could cry." Can you fucking believe it? And then it goes on...'

I zoned out as I filled our cafetière, considering how much better this conversation would be if I were already one cup in. Mark was talking so fast, he sounded like he'd downed ten coffees already.

'So what?' I said when he'd finished talking.

Mum came into the kitchen in a lemon-edged dressing gown, her damp hair falling at her shoulders. She looked young, fresh. I smiled at her and rolled my eyes indicating the phone and mouthing, 'Mark.'

I said, 'One bad review doesn't make a difference. Remember the review Restaurant Eleven got in there last year, and they were given their third star a month later?'

'Yes, but they changed their game. We need new dishes, Kat, a new menu. Something no one else is doing. I need you back here next week to help out.'

I realised I was chewing my lip. How could he be doing this to me again? I never took annual leave, never left the country, didn't even take a proper break when my father died. The man had no respect for me, and I was furious. I walked into the bathroom, not wanting Mum to hear my conversation.

'Mark, you know I can't do that, I've got another ten days here. You said it was OK.' I tried to sound firm, but suspected it came out as pleading.

'That was before the Guardian got involved. This is the Guardian. We need to be on our A-game, and I don't have a fucking sous chef this week!'

I picked at my sky-blue nail polish. There was no use arguing with Mark. The guy was like a spitting bulldog when he wanted something. Maybe I could buy more time?

'Please, Mark. I can't get back anyway, at least not until the weekend. But I've seen some ideas for recipes here that would be seriously game-changing.' I was bluffing, but what else would stall him? 'We're going to a little café today in the next town along.

It's meant to be the best on the Adriatic coast. Let me try out a few things in the apartment tonight. I'll send you the recipes as soon as I can, maybe tomorrow?' I could tell this had caught his interest.

'Fine, and you can look for flights back next week?'

'I guess I could have a look,' I conceded.

'What's the café called anyway, see if I've heard of it?' he asked.

'I have to go, the taxi's here.' I hung up.

'Everything all right?' Mum was lingering in the cramped hallway.

'Just Mark.'

She tutted, knowing what he was like. 'You shouldn't let him run your life like that.'

'I know, I know.' I chose not to tell that I'd 'agreed' to look at early flights home. I had no intention of doing it. I'd had enough of Mark, but I would need to keep him off my back.

'Shall we have breakfast?'

'I've got the oven on,' Mum said. 'Anyway, serious dilemma. What the hell am I going to wear today?'

'Ooh, what have you brought with you? It has to be something killer for meeting your husband's other woman, something ... intimidating,' I said, trying to keep things light-hearted.

Mum smiled. 'Are we masochists for doing this to ourselves?'

'I don't know,' I sighed. We looked at each other for a moment before Mum's smile broke, and we both burst out laughing with the absurdity of everything.

I felt more confident as I drove the tomato-coloured Nissan today, a little more familiar with Montenegrin road signs. The journey was only fifteen minutes. We'd decided to take the scenic route to Tivat, following the road as it hugged the coastline. We passed several wedding parties posing for pictures with the sea as their backdrop.

'I didn't realise this was such a popular place to get married,' I said, watching one bride throw a bouquet over her shoulder into the Adriatic.

'Do you think that'll be you and Adam one day?' Mum asked, looking out the window.

'I don't know.' It was the honest truth. Adam and I had been together so long, our lives intertwining threads of a canvas. But I'd never pictured us marrying. Never imagined him crisp in a suit, laughing with 'the lads' about something foolish that happened on his stag do. I'd never been that interested in wedding dresses, mocking the brides that invested so much money in a fluffy white meringue they would wear for one day and then never take out of the box again. Early in our relationship, Adam and I had revelled in the fact we both felt the same way about weddings, feeling secretly superior as our friends and colleagues 'tied the knot'.

But lately it felt as if there was another reason we didn't marry, something much harder to put my finger on.

Was Adam the one for me? Could I really spend every night coming home to him? See his hairy back in bed next to me every morning? And if he really was 'The One,' why hadn't I told him the real reason we were in Montenegro?

'Oh no, we're here already,' Mum said, as the passing buildings and dark blue sign told us we had arrived in Tivat.

I could see why Luka spoke so fondly of it. The town was

gorgeous with its palm-tree-lined seafront and harbour filled with yachts. The sky had a handful of clouds and a cool breeze blew through the car window, pleasant after the stifling heat of the last few days. Tivat was more modern and cosmopolitan than Kotor, with a long promenade of bars, restaurants and supermarkets, visitors milling about, and the odd cat languishing in the cooler air.

'This is it then,' I said, getting out of the car.

We'd pulled in at possibly the most scenic car park I'd ever been in, the sweeping view of the narrowing bay a far cry from the concrete my Hackney flat looked out on.

'Ice cream and a stroll along the front?' Mum asked, casually.

'Delaying tactics,' I put my sunglasses on. 'I like it.'

CHAPTER EIGHT

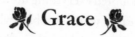 Grace

Tivat was a bustling, harbour town, with glass-fronted boutique hotels and traditional, stone buildings with wrought iron balconies and shuttered windows. Pizzerias, steakhouses and Montenegrin restaurants vied for the tourists' attention, offering cut-price lunches and three-course dinners for fifteen euros. There was an air of sophistication and a vibrancy about Tivat that seemed a world away from the cobbled streets and charming narrow passages in Kotor.

As we strolled along the promenade, Kat pointed upwards. 'That hotel's got a roof pool. You can see why Rosa moved here. Makes much more business sense.'

Yachts lined the harbour, basking in the afternoon sun, testament to the affluence of the town, their masts towering into the sky. We did some window-shopping, gazing at the haute couture, the art galleries with displays of Murano glass, and the jewellery shops with their platinum bracelets and diamond earrings draped artfully on white columns.

'There's no prices on these, which means they're out of our range,' I said ruefully and a little too loudly. Inside, the glossy-haired shopkeeper sniffed and returned to reading her book. Clearly, she could tell she didn't need to turn on the charm for our benefit.

'Remember that eternity ring Dad brought back from Vienna?' I reminisced. 'It was beautiful.'

Kat winced and I knew why. Every memory seemed tarnished. Had he only given it to me because he felt guilty? Had he really been in Vienna? I doubted everything now.

We bought ice creams, which dribbled white rivers down our hands, and Kat stopped to read the menus of the seafront restaurants, snapping shots with her phone when she liked the sound of something.

'I'd like to try some of these, Mum,' she said. 'Priganice. It's a type of doughnut that can be made sweet, or savoury with cheese.' Her eyes lit up whenever we talked food. It was her passion. I could barely concentrate, though, dreading the confrontation to come. Would it be a confrontation? I had no idea what I would say to Rosa or how she would react to us.

A few steps later, we saw the sign: 'Café Lompar.' It stood at the end of the promenade, a well-established place, its large, double-fronted windows bolted open, facing the shimmering, cobalt Adriatic. We stopped in our tracks. I felt Kat's almost imperceptible intake of breath.

It was a more traditional place, with rectangular oak tables and painted grey chairs. Inside they had a stone bar, and blackboard menus lined the upper walls and the bar, covered with offers: 'Handmade bread,' 'Fresh seafood caught daily' and 'Craft ales and tapas.'

We hovered outside. A young waitress in a red apron was taking orders from one of the tables lining the front terrace. Inside, we could see two other waitresses clearing tables and a young waiter opening a bottle of Prosecco at the bar. My neck prickled with heat.

'What shall we do?' asked Kat. 'Shall we order some lunch?'

'Yes,' I stammered. 'Let's go inside.' I looked frantically for Rosa, but I couldn't see her.

A young waitress gave us two menus and we said we'd prefer to sit inside. Kat faced outwards towards the sea and I placed myself opposite the bar and the door to the kitchen.

'My name is Maria and I will be your waitress. Would you like a drink?'

Kat ordered a Peroni, but I wanted to keep my head clear. 'A diet Pepsi, please.'

'Perhaps she's not here,' Kat said, when the waitress retreated.

I tried to concentrate on the menu, but as the waiting staff entered and returned from the kitchen, my head shot up every time the door opened.

'Shall I order two palačinke for us?' Kat said. 'Pancakes with savoury fillings?' I nodded. I didn't care what I had.

And then Rosa appeared.

A slender woman with thick, black hair. Unlike the other staff, she wore a black apron. She laughed with some customers, offering drinks and topping up wine glasses. She exuded charm and confidence and obviously knew her regulars. Her eyes flitted across to us, and then she looked at the customers outside.

Kat turned to see what I was staring at, and her eyes widened.

'That's her then. She's not as tall as I imagined. Well, I don't know what I expected,' said Kat.

I felt as bewildered as she did. I didn't know what to think. I kept catching Rosa's eye and shifting my gaze away quickly.

I could see what Dan saw in her. She was lovely. I felt very self-conscious, pulling my T-shirt over my floral M&S skirt, wishing

I'd worn something a bit less conspicuous, a bit more under-stated.

It was past three o'clock and Kat and I were still pushing our food around our plates. Other diners had trickled out onto the hot pavement outside. There was only one other table left, a family of four, and they were paying the bill. In the corner of my eye, I saw Rosa clearing tables.

Kat said, 'It's now or never, Mum. Look, it's better I wasn't here. I'll wait for you outside.' We had tentatively agreed this plan on the way over.

A strange feeling of calm washed over me. As Kat slipped outside, I waved for the bill and Rosa walked over, as if in slow motion, holding my gaze. As she stood at the end of the table, card machine in hand, I swallowed hard.

'It's Rosa, isn't it,' I said, more of a statement than a question.

'I know who you are,' she said flatly. 'Grace.'

Her directness startled me. 'How? Uh – how?'

'I knew you would come. I have been waiting for you.' She pulled out a chair and sat down. 'What do you want?' Her unwavering gaze was disconcerting.

What did I want? I had come nearly two thousand miles and now I had no idea what to say.

Up close, she was even more beautiful. Her face was lightly lined, but her eyes were a deep brown with coppery flecks, large and expressive. She flicked her hair from her shoulders, a habit I had observed several times as I'd watched her over lunch.

'You know about us?' I asked. 'When did you find out?'

'I was pregnant with Luka,' she began, looking down. 'It is a cliché. I saw your messages when he was in the shower.' She shrugged. 'It all made sense. He was never with us too long, always worried about getting back.'

'But you stayed with him. How could you? He had a family!' I shook my head with disgust.

'It was too late. I loved him,' she said simply with a shrug. 'I was carrying his baby. He begged me to stay.' She twisted the bottom of her apron in her hands. 'I don't expect you to understand. I just couldn't walk away. I wanted to ... but I couldn't.'

I began to falter, 'You know he's dead? It happened a year ago.'

She nodded. 'Yes, a friend of his in the university, Will, called me the next day. It was a shock.'

Will told her? I felt the ground shift beneath my feet. I considered Will a friend. He and Sarah had been around for dinner dozens of times. They were godparents to Kat! Yet, all this time, he knew about Dan and Rosa? Did Sarah know? I was a bloody idiot. How many people knew that Dan was screwing around? I was trembling with anger.

Rosa said, 'I thought about going to the funeral, but it was better I didn't. It was better to leave things as they were. Luka was desperate to go.' After a pause, she murmured, 'So how did you find out?'

'I found some photographs. Of you and Luka.'

She nodded, 'A pity. Inevitable, perhaps. It has been a secret for too long.'

'What about Luka? Does he know?'

She sighed. 'That has been the hardest part of all this. Danilo found it easier to lie than I did.'

I winced as she mentioned his name. I never called him by his full name, or only when I was teasing him.

She gazed out at the sea. 'I told Luka when he was ten. He wanted to know why his father was never around like his friends' fathers. It wasn't fair on him.'

I had imagined shouting at this woman, swearing, even screaming at her. But now she was sitting in front of me, I couldn't. It wouldn't solve anything. It wouldn't even make me feel better. I just wanted answers.

'You were prepared to share him all those years? I don't understand. I couldn't have done that. You can't have seen him for more than three months a year.'

'It was hard, I admit, at first. We fought. We split for a while,' she said, shaking her head, flicking her hair from her face. 'But I was pregnant, and life is different here. A woman on her own. I even took his surname. People in Montenegro have old-fashioned values.'

'But you were willing to accept that he was married to someone else? I would never have done that.'

'You have no right to judge me!' She flared up. 'He was the one who cheated, not me!'

'He wasn't yours to have,' I said, a bit louder than I expected. The waitress, Maria, looked over quickly.

'What can I say? Both of us were hurt. It is not a competition.' She looked at me steadily. 'There are no winners in this.'

Another waitress was leaving. She shouted over in Montenegrin and Rosa waved.

'I threatened to leave him many times,' she continued. 'Then I think perhaps I got used to him coming and going. I have always been independent, and he never gave me that much help financially. I started this business a few years ago. It kept me busy.' She sighed. 'In the last two years or so, he visited less often.'

66

'You've had time to process this,' I said, my mind in turmoil. 'He was not the man I thought he was. I trusted him.'

We were both silent.

'He was a good father,' Rosa said eventually. 'At least when he was here. He loved Kat, and you.'

'Yes, he loved Kat,' I admitted, but I couldn't believe that a man who cheated for so many years, who lived a double life, was sincere about love.

'Men are selfish. He told me he was going to leave you many times.'

The words were a kick to my stomach.

If Rosa realised this, she didn't show it. She went on, 'I believed him at first. I was a fool. Eventually, I lost hope. He said it too many times.'

She gazed out at the sea. 'And do you know what?' She paused. 'If I am honest, as time went on, I didn't want him to leave you. I got used to it, being on my own.' She smiled wryly. 'I think I had the best of him.'

The cruelty of it was breathtaking. But then I remembered telling Claire once that I had got used to him leaving. I coped, perhaps even liked him being away. Sometimes it was harder when he was at home.

Like me, I realised, Rosa had given her best years to this man. Were we so different? I couldn't empathise with her, though. I wasn't ready to let go of the myth of the femme fatale who had stolen Dan from me.

'So, where do we go from here?' I asked.

'Well, Luka and Kat, they are brother and sister. They deserve to know each other. Luka is a good boy. I am sure they will get on. After the summer, he is going to university.'

I nodded, 'I know. We've met him.'

Rosa was now on the back foot. 'Ah, I see.' She looked annoyed, but covered it quickly.

'He didn't know who we were. We didn't tell him. He was on the boat over from Perast.'

'Yes, he sometimes helps his friend, Milo. It is better I tell him.' She reached into her pocket and wrote down her number and passed it over to me. 'How long are you staying?'

'Another week, I think.'

'I have to go.' Rosa stood up abruptly. 'We have to clear the tables for dinner service.'

I reached for my card to pay the bill.

She dismissed me with a wave. 'Call,' she said.

CHAPTER NINE

🌿 Kat 🌿

Mum was quiet on the drive back from Tivat yesterday, passing the conversation with Rosa off as 'fine'. We travelled in near silence as the laidback palm trees of the town gave way to the more traditional olive groves that dotted the hillsides.

Was she mad at me for leaving her? We had agreed beforehand that I would give them space, let them talk it out. I did feel uncomfortable when I left her though; she needed my support now more than ever. She'd looked so fragile as I walked away, and for the first time in my life, I hated my Dad.

I didn't know what to expect from Rosa. Obviously, I'd seen the pictures, and knew the olive-skinned, long-haired goddess that was waiting for us. But in the pictures, she seemed so young and perfect that she wasn't real, like a model from a magazine. Seeing her in the flesh, older and a little more tired, was painful.

How dare Dad break our trio? It had always been the three of us, our perfect unit. They were my shield from the world, my comfort blanket when times were tough. And yet he'd had this whole other life. It didn't make sense. I wondered, as I often had, whether he compared us to them, whether he thought of Luka every time he hugged me. I wondered if he felt like a fraud, or if he was happy to live these parallel lives, confident we'd never find each other.

Mum started to open up back at the apartment. As she went through their conversation, she told me that Rosa knew about us all along. I couldn't believe it! How could this beautiful woman be happy with a husband she had to share, and only saw erratically, three months out of twelve? Happy with my dad, the man I'd made my first mud cake with on the banks of the Bristol Channel? The man who called me Kit Kat and learnt the dance moves to the Spice Girls with me? Yes, he was solemn and earnest in work, but at home he was my goofy, fun-loving dad. Mine.

And yet all my confusion and hatred didn't change the fact that I had a brother. All my life I'd revelled in the spoilt, hand-me-down-free childhood of being an only child. I'd always made out that I was happy having Mum and Dad to myself, that I didn't want a protective older brother or sister. And now I had a half-brother.

I turned the strip of paper over in my hand as I looked out to sea from our balcony. Mum had given the phone number to me on the journey home. I'd stared at Rosa's neat, measured handwriting, wondering what to do. I had to speak to Luka again. I wondered if he would be so friendly now he knew who we were.

'Are you all right, Kat?' Mum asked, joining me.

'Just daydreaming.' I shrugged.

'God, you've caught the sun. Get some cream on you. Do you want me to do your shoulders?'

I batted her hand away but smiled.

'You looked just like him then,' she said.

'Dad?'

'No.' She winked. 'Luka.'

'Mmm, paradise.'

I kicked off my flip flops and lay back against the marshmallowy cushions of the sun lounger. 'Now this feels like we're on holiday.'

'I just wish I hadn't eaten so much,' Mum said, unbuttoning her shorts. 'Do you think Rosa would have eaten a three-course meal for lunch?' She mimed Rosa's tiny waist and flicking of her hair.

'Please, Rosa's probably never seen a carbohydrate in her life!' It felt nice to giggle, even if it was at catty jokes.

Both of us fell into silence as we admired the view from the beach. We'd decided to spend the day in Budva, an escape from the Bay of Kotor and anything that reminded us of Rosa and Luka. A Google search of 'best beaches in Montenegro' suggested this coastal town, which promised secret coves, sand and stone buildings that looked like images from a glossy holiday brochure. Budva didn't disappoint; despite the bigger hotels that lined the beachfront with their neatly clipped lawns, symmetrical rows of loungers and marble entrances; the azure waters of the Adriatic gave everything a serene feel.

We'd spent the morning exploring the cobbled streets, admiring how clean and pristine the centuries-old town looked. We'd pitched up at a seafood restaurant for lunch. The place had no menu, as they served only fresh fish, whatever had been caught and brought to shore that morning — foodie heaven!

I was glad I stopped after one glass of wine, my head slightly woozy in the midday sun. We were planning to join a tour that afternoon, walk across the small concrete strip of land that led out of the bay to Sveti Stefan, a private island with red-roofed buildings and a five-star hotel that had boasted a wealth of celebrity visitors. But once we'd got up from lunch, we both decided we were so wiped out, we needed to flop on a beach.

'I just need to feel like an ordinary woman on holiday,' Mum said. I knew what she meant, I felt drained too. My head was spinning from the events of the last few days, of Rosa and Luka. I needed time to decompress.

It was nearly eight o'clock by the time we got back from the beach.

'Damn, I promised I'd call Claire to check up on her after Laura's date,' Mum said, clutching her phone.

I'd heard all about Laura's boyfriend and Claire's snooping. I hoped Mum never did that to me; I'd die if she'd seen some of the things I'd sent to Adam when I was in college.

'I'd better ring now.' She darted off to the bedroom.

I slung my bag down on the kitchen counter. What now? Should I have a shower, wash the gritty sand from between my toes? Start planning some meals for Truffles?

I knew they were all delaying tactics. The phone number was nagging at me. It was now or never.

I walked out to the balcony. My hand shook as I got out the number. I puzzled over the area code, wondering if it was a landline or mobile. Would I reach Rosa or Luka? With a bit of luck no one would answer. Then I could take the coward's way out and leave a voicemail.

I triple-checked the string of numbers on my phone screen, before taking a deep breath and pressing call. I could do this.

A few static-filled rings, then a husky-voiced man answered in

Montenegrin. I didn't know who it was, but I could tell it wasn't Luka. I lamented my poor knowledge of any language other than English.

'Hello, I'm trying to reach Rosa Lompar? Or Luka? If either of them is there? Luka Lompar?' I sounded terrified. Like I was being interrogated.

The man on the other end of the line hesitated. 'Luka? Yes, Luka is here.'

I heard something being said in another language, before the word 'English', and then a reply from Luka. Thank God.

'Is this Kat?' He sounded as shaky and unsure as I did. I didn't want to surprise him, for him to feel uncomfortable. Especially after our easy conversation the other day.

'Yes,' was all I could say.

'So, I finally learn who you are.' I was struck again by how perfectly he spoke my language. I wondered how much Dad had helped him. 'My mother told me it was you on the boat the other day.'

'I'm so sorry we didn't tell you straight away. I wanted to but I ... I ... couldn't do it.' I hoped he wouldn't hate me. 'We weren't trying to hide it from you.'

'I get it,' he said. 'It's hard. Meeting family for the first time.' I could hear the smile in his voice. Relief coursed through me.

Family.

It was such an odd word.

'Yes, well, I think ... I was wondering if we should meet again. Now we both know who we are. I mean ... what do you think? Do you want to?'

God, I couldn't string a sentence together. I hoped he didn't think I was stupid. I wondered how much he knew about me. How much Dad had told him? Was I what he expected?

My brain whirred with so many questions, I almost didn't hear him answer.

'We could…' He paused.

I waited, picking at a thread on my denim shorts. I'd have none left by the end of this conversation.

'I guess it depends,' he said.

'OK. Depends on what?' The thread unravelled some more.

'On what you have planned. You've been on my boat. And your mother. Now you can take charge.'

I realised I was grinning hysterically. So Luka was a joker? Just like Dad could be with me. I could hear him laugh on the other end of the line.

'Well?'

I had no idea what to say. Tour of Apartman Nina? Road trip in the Nissan danger mobile? Then it came to me.

'I could do with some help. But it depends…'

'On what?' He sounded intrigued.

'Are you any good at cooking?'

CHAPTER TEN

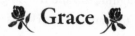 Grace

Not for the first time, I berated myself for forgetting to bring my driving licence. I sat in the back of a taxi on my way to Cetinje, which was about forty-five minutes from Kotor Town. It was up in the mountains and the scenery was breathtaking. I knew that Montenegro was popular with skiers in the winter. The rugged promontories formed a dramatic backdrop to the serpentine road leading to the small city.

I was on my way to see Sofija, Dan's aunt. He fondly called her Aunt Sofija, so I always did the same, even though I had met her once only, at our wedding. She was a diminutive woman, with a wide smile and shoulder-length, greying hair. I'd been delighted to meet her, the only living relative Dan had. She'd wrapped me in a warm hug the day before the wedding. I had taken her to a local hotel to have afternoon tea. Dan had a few things to take care of at the university and I seized the opportunity to get to know her better. We'd taken a seat in the window, overlooking the lawn. It was early May and the apple trees were in full blossom, shedding their delicate confetti in the gentle breeze.

'You have made Dan so happy,' she'd told me. 'He deserves happiness.'

She laughed as the tray of sandwiches and cupcakes, scones and brownies were brought to the table by the assiduous waitress. 'This is the first time I have had tea in the afternoon,' she said, her eyes lighting up. 'Is this all for us?'

'Yes,' I had said, laughing too and reaching for a sandwich. 'We can take some home to Dan. I am sorry this is the first time we're meeting.'

'I hate flying,' she said, 'but I couldn't miss Danilo's wedding. I am all he has since my husband, Aleks, died three years ago.'

'What were his parents like?' I was desperate to learn more about them. I often tried to ask Dan, but I was afraid I would open old wounds.

She'd nibbled her sandwich. 'They were very loving parents. Adored Danilo. They were always active, kayaking, skiing. My sister Jovana stayed at home to look after Danilo. Stefan was an engineer.' She paused, gazing at the lawn, lost in thought. 'I missed them terribly when they moved to the UK, but I could understand why.'

As the taxi climbed higher into the mountains, I could see what Aunt Sofija meant. The scars of war were still visible. Abandoned stone houses dotted the landscape and wooden crosses marking graves were everywhere. We passed thick forestry, the glittering Adriatic far behind us.

I had phoned Aunt Sofija the night after Dan died. It was the hardest phone call I'd had to make. Kat sat beside me, and we held hands as I broke the news. I was painfully aware that she was alone, and I promised to visit her as soon as I could.

Last night Kat had spoken to Luka. She'd gone outside as I spoke to Claire in the bedroom. I thought it was Adam she was speaking to, but then got caught up in Claire's phone call. She had, of course, been desperate to find out about my meeting with Rosa.

'So, what was she like?' she asked.

'Well, she knew all about Kat and I.'

'Bitch!' said Claire.

Her unquestioning support was a comfort, but I shook my head. 'I honestly don't know what to think. She said she tried to break it off with him but couldn't. He'd lied to her, too. Will and Sarah knew all about it, or at least Will did. He was the one who told her Dan had died.'

Claire was as taken aback as I was. 'I bumped into Sarah last week in Waitrose. She'd just come from yoga.' I could picture Sarah in my mind. Skinny as a bread stick and always on the way to or back from the gym, her yoga mat curled under one arm, ponytail bobbing as she spoke animatedly about hot yoga or some other new workout. 'She was asking how you were, all concern and sincerity,' Claire went on. 'I can't believe it!'

Her indignation fired me up again. I'd heard in divorces that married friends often chose sides, abandoning one half, and this felt a bit like that. I had trusted Sarah, counted her as a close friend. I swallowed hard.

'How did you leave things with Rosa?' Claire asked.

'She gave me her number so that Kat and Luka could stay in touch.' I didn't want to discuss that. 'How are things with you?'

Claire sighed, 'Well, all hell has broken out since I last spoke to you. This boyfriend of Laura's is twenty-one. Bloody twenty-one! He's a second-year art student.'

'What's he doing with a sixteen-year-old?'

'Exactly. We had this blazing row. It all came out. She's been seeing him for the last three months.'

'Oh, God!' I said, in sympathy.

'She's on the pill. Stu was horrified when he found out. His little girl on the pill. Having sex. Until I told him it would be worse if she wasn't — that stopped him in his tracks.' Claire sighed. 'It didn't occur to him that when we met I was only fifteen and we were having sex then ourselves. Anyway, the atmosphere has been awful. I want to forbid her to see him. I can't, though. She's sixteen, as she keeps telling me. I'm an adult, I could get married if I wanted. You can imagine — I told her, Over my dead body.'

I resisted the temptation to giggle.

'You never had this with Kat, did you?'

'Not that. She did go out with some horrors though. Remember Ezra, the traveller?' I shuddered. 'I thought she was going to run off to Ireland with him in a caravan. And Dan took it badly when she didn't want to go to university. He thought catering college was second rate. He wanted his daughter to have a career in academia.'

Claire laughed sardonically.

'It took him an age to come to terms with it. Then she began winning all those awards and he could see just how passionate she was about cooking. I still worry she works too hard. It's a gruelling life and that boss of hers is a pillock.'

'Well, there's an awful lot of those around. Anyway, we've agreed Laura can still see River...' Claire broke off. 'What a ridiculous name! On the condition that we meet him. So he's coming around for Sunday lunch. Would it surprise you if I told you River is vegan?'

I laughed.

When I rang off, Kat was preparing dinner. 'We're having buzara,' she said, 'a seafood stew.'

'It smells delicious.'

'There's bread in the oven, too.'

'Have I told you lately that you're a genius?' I said, pouring wine for us. 'How's Adam?'

She paused, 'It wasn't Adam I was speaking to. It was Luka.'

'Ah. So what did he say?'

'Oh, he's great, Mum. Really funny. The thing is, he wants to meet up and he's only free tomorrow, as he's working on the boat for the next few days.'

'Of course, you must meet him. It's fine. I'll explain to Aunt Sofija. I'm sure she won't mind.' I could see the relief wash over her. 'It's better that you see him alone first. Get to know each other.'

She kissed my cheek lightly. 'Thanks, Mum.'

Kat had taken the car, as she was picking up Luka, so the taxi was the only option I had to get to Cetinje. The mountain scenery turned to the terracotta roofs of houses. The taxi driver glanced at the sat nav and turned to me. 'Two kilometres.'

Sofija lived on the outskirts of the city. We passed elegant, faded villas, theatres, churches and museums. A large mural covered one wall, a celebration of the Cetinje-born artist, Dado. I was reading about him last night. Sofija's house was a single storey villa, with a wide porch across the whole front of the building. The taxi driver agreed to pick me up in a few hours.

Sofija must have been waiting for me as she rushed out to greet me.

'Grace' she smiled, enveloping me in an embrace. She was much frailer now, her hair wispy and completely grey, her frame thin beneath her floral pinafore. 'At last you are here.'

'Aunt Sofija, it is so lovely to see you.'

She looked behind me, 'Kat?'

'I'll explain later,' I said, unsure how much she knew, if anything at all. I dreaded what I'd say, hating being dragged into Dan's lies. I felt a raw ache inside me.

'It's a lovely house,' I said, as I looked at the view from her kitchen. It was on an elevation, with views of the higgledy-piggledy roofs of the town and the voluptuous curves of the mountains in the far distance.

'I have lived here all my life,' she said, 'and I never get tired of that view. Now, have a seat and please drink some lemonade. It's chilled.'

We talked about Kotor and Apartman Nina and what Kat and I thought of Montenegro. 'I'm sad that this is the first time I've been here. I don't know why. Dan never seemed to want to come and I don't know why I didn't insist.'

She covered my hand with hers. 'You are here now. And you will come again. Dan came a few times but I understand he was a busy man.'

I nodded, not trusting myself to speak.

'I am sorry I did not come to the funeral,' Sofija said. 'I am too old to travel now, and I hate flying, as you know.'

'I know,' I soothed.

While she bustled in the kitchen, I looked at the photographs on her sideboard. They were of her and Aleks on their wedding day and another of them picnicking in a forest. One was of her in uniform when she was nursing in the local hospital. There was Dan at his graduation. He was smiling, his untameable black hair falling over his forehead.

'We could never have children, Aleks and I,' Sofija said. 'We tried for many years, but it wasn't to be. Danilo was like a son to me.' She carried in a tray with hams, cheeses, a tomato salad and bread.

'You shouldn't have gone to any trouble.'

'It's nothing.' She dismissed this with a wave of her hand.

We spent the afternoon talking about my work with the charity, Kat's job in Truffles and Dan. I showed her photographs of our house in Bath.

'Would you like to see some photos of Danilo with his parents? They were a beautiful family.'

I nodded eagerly and she pulled an album from the sideboard. Dan was more like his mother than his father. In one photograph she was about Kat's age, lying on a beach. He had the same intense eyes as her. It reminded me of a poem I'd once read, and the lines: 'Not yet my mother, although I was clearly already your child.' It was an odd feeling, looking into the eyes of this stranger, who was so familiar.

'Danilo was so like Jovana. She had this fierceness about her and yet she was very compassionate. Loyal. They were very close,' Sofija said.

'The accident must have been a terrible shock.'

Her face clouded. 'You never get over something like that, losing a sister and a brother-in-law. Cut off so young. A lorry ploughed into them. Danilo was in school studying for his A levels, as you know.' She shook her head. 'Terrible. Terrible for him.'

I shivered despite the warmth of the afternoon. 'Dan rarely spoke of it and I didn't push. Did he ever want to return to Montenegro?'

'Aleks and I wanted him to live with us, but he was determined. He was very strong-minded.'

We both stopped talking, wrapped up in our memories of Dan. It was now or never.

'Dan had another family,' I blurted out. 'He has a son and another woman. Here in Montenegro.' I couldn't think of any way to soften the blow.

The horror on her face told me she'd had no idea.

'Where?' she asked.

'In Tivat. It has been going on for a long time.'

She touched my hand for the second time that afternoon and my heart went out to this compassionate woman who had suffered her fair share of grief.

'Danilo ... I have no words,' she trailed off. I realised how hard it was to face the failures of someone you loved.

I told her about Luka and Kat meeting. I said very little about Rosa. She listened quietly, a look of understanding on her face.

Later, we spoke about safer subjects. Sofija told me about her bridge afternoons with her neighbours and her love of the garden, something we shared. Outside, she showed me her herb patch, with oregano, rosemary and lavender.

'Lavender grows well in the rocky Montenegrin soil,' she explained.

Kumquats, like bright orange pendants, hung in a shaded section of the garden. In ceramic pots, white and lilac rhododendrons were offset with delicate-pink, diaphanous azaleas.

The afternoon flew by. I found it hard to shake off the guilt I felt for not visiting Aunt Sofija more. She deserved better and I vowed I would keep in touch with her, a promise I repeated, as the taxi drew up.

I was grateful the surly taxi driver spoke little English as he sweated in the front seat on the way back. It allowed me time to process all I'd heard about Dan and his childhood.

When we drew up outside Apartman Nina, the Nissan was parked outside. I could see Kat in the kitchen window and I realised she was talking to Luka. He was still there. They were laughing like old friends and my heart gave a jolt as I faced yet another ordeal ahead.

CHAPTER ELEVEN

🌿 Kat 🌿

'Wow, I have never seen anyone make pastry this quickly.' Luka took a bite of the doughnuts we'd made earlier. 'Like lightning.'

'Tricks of the trade,' I said, brushing a quick egg wash in between the layers. 'The longer you take, the more the butter melts and the less flaky it will be.'

'Mmm, you do need it to be flaky. My grandmother used to make the best baklava ever. You would love it. My grandmother on my mother's side.' He gave a small, awkward smile.

The timer started to chime on my phone. 'The bureks must be ready.' Luka took his cue to get the pastries we worked on out of the oven. The cheesy smell of the Balkan breakfast dish was out of this world.

'To a Montenegrin, there is nothing better than a warm burek,' Luka said, moving the crumbly pastries stuffed with mince meat, cheese and pepper onto a plate. 'They're best warm, try one.'

I took a bite, relishing the filo as it melted on my tongue. Luka watched me with a smile on his face.

'That is incredible.' I had to hand it to him.

'And you thought I couldn't teach you anything,' he teased. 'My sister, the chef.'

I flicked at him some of the water I was using to seal my

baklava. I was surprised at how easy it was to joke around with Luka. To enjoy myself. The afternoon had been like hanging out with a best friend. I'd worried we'd have so many uncomfortable silences, I'd be permanently clock-watching. In fact, I hadn't checked the time once, hadn't picked up my phone, usually an extension of my right arm.

I'd picked Luka up earlier from Café Lompar. I dreaded having to make small talk with Rosa, but luckily the restaurant was closed and she was nowhere to be seen. I couldn't help glancing around like a fugitive when I arrived. Luka skipped up to the front step at eleven o'clock on the dot. The greeting was a bit awkward. I'd debated a hug or handshake the whole journey there, digging my fingernails into the steering wheel as I'd overthought every possibility. In the end, Luka had gone in for an air-kiss, and I'd put one arm around him, a sort of half-hug. After that shaky start, we'd wandered to the market in Tivat to pick up some fresh ingredients.

'So, tell me again what we're doing today,' he'd asked, leading me towards a seafood stall. I told him all about Mark and his challenge to find something new and innovative for the restaurant.

'So, you thought you'd exploit your long-lost brother for a taste of his culture? I get it.'

I was surprised again by Luka's wicked sense of humour. It felt very familiar. We'd stopped off for a drink before heading back to Apartman Nina. Sipping ice cold beers from glasses straight out of the freezer was the perfect way to rest in the midday sun. It was strange to learn more about Luka's life, like being shown a picture from childhood; you know it's you in the picture but have no real memory of the place.

He'd talked a lot about Rosa and Café Lompar. As a teenager, she worked on weekends as a waitress in a tiny bar in Tivat. The manager of the bar told her not to speak to anyone, simply serve the customers and don't give them a reason to complain.

'But my mother loves to talk to everyone. She could have a three-hour conversation with a cat if you let her.' Luka's eyes lit up when he talked about Rosa. He told me she had a knack of getting customers to linger and talk, and night after night they would come back just for her friendliness and hospitality. The manager made Rosa head of front of house after only two months.

'How did she get Café Lompar?' I asked, wondering if this was the same bar.

'Well, one day she had a fight with the manager because she changed the tablecloths and he didn't like them! Can you believe it? She is so driven and independent. My mother has always hated being told what to do. So she decided to set up her own place next door to show him! All of his longest customers started going to Café Lompar instead.'

'Ahhh, revenge,' I said. A swig of beer slipped down my throat, a reprieve from the burning heat outside. 'Do you mind me asking why called it Cafe Lompar? They weren't married.'

Luka shrugged, 'You don't know what Montenegrins are like. Very old fashioned in their views. It would never have worked if they thought she wasn't married. Mum changed her name for me and for the restaurant.' He smiled awkwardly. 'She always told me that whatever you want in life, you have to go for it no matter what.'

'Is that why you're going to do law this year?' I remembered the plans he'd told us about on the boat.

'Exactly. I would never have got in if it wasn't for her. She never let me give up. Plus, she's such a boss you need a law degree to argue with her.'

I grinned. Luka seemed to thrive on making people laugh. He spoke so fondly of his mother.

'I bet she'll miss you,' I said.

'Yes, I am worried about it. It has been mostly me and my mother for all my life. Although she's independent, she's always had me there. I know she will be fine though.'

It hung in the air, like fog. Mostly me and my mother. Sometimes Dad had been there too.

I'd talked about London and Truffles while we drove back to the apartment. Luka had a knack of listening intently and getting right to the core of an issue. He was intuitive, asking the right questions. I'd ended up talking about how I'd found cooking an escape as an adolescent. Almost a rebellion from my more academic parents, and friends that only seemed to care about drinking and getting laid. Although I did a fair amount of both too.

I remembered the night before my Sociology A-level exam. I'd been banished to the kitchen by Dad, where we had a gargantuan table perfect for family dinners and studying for exams. Unable to focus and stressed out to hell, I'd ended up spending four hours making an elaborate cake. I could still picture the look of disappointment on Dad's face when he came in to find a piping bag in my hand and the table a site of mass destruction with flour and icing sugar strewn across it.

My ailing grades forced him to accept it. I was destined for catering college. Of course, Dad supported me in that; he was always telling everyone he knew that his Kit-Kat could make a four-course meal as effortlessly as others made a cup of tea, but I think he would have secretly preferred it if I'd loved economics and politics like him.

'Passions are what make us human,' Luka said with a shrug.

'That's deep,' I laughed.

'You'll get to know my great wisdom,' he joked.

'And modesty?'

Hours later, we'd cooked up the perfect meal for Truffles. It was a sort of deconstructed stew made using some lamb and Njeguški pršut, a local prosciutto we'd picked up from the market. Montenegro was such a culinary melting-pot, the food typical of Mediterranean diets but with some more traditional Turkish and Hungarian influences. Luka told me how much the cuisine varied with each location in Montenegro.

'The food in the mountains is completely different, heartier. On the coast, it's all about seafood,' he explained.

'I can honestly say I've had some of the best seafood of my life here.'

'That's what everyone says. You will never go back to English food now.' He waved a hand, dismissively.

Luka had shown me the traditional method of cooking the dish, but I'd jazzed it up with rosemary oil, wild garlic fronds and candied peppers.

'You can't do that to my motherland's recipe,' Luka said in mock-horror. I told him to trust me, and the result looked and smelt beautiful. The dish was elegant, simple, perfect for Truffles.

We clinked glasses, sitting opposite each other at the small breakfast bar. Luka lifted a fork up to his mouth and tasted it, his eyes closing.

'Oh my God, you are a genius, Kat. Don't tell her this or she'll kill me, but it's better than my mother's.'

'I knew it would work,' I agreed, tasting the perfect balance of spicy and salty flavours. We both ate a few more mouthfuls in silence, enjoying the eclectic dish. It was a test I always gave myself in the kitchen. The more silence you could create when people were eating your food, the better it was. I loved the cosy feeling when a chatty table at Truffles fell silent into pure enjoyment.

'So, tell me about Adam.' Luka nudged me, looking at the photo of us set as my phone background.

'Well, he's a chef like me.' I sipped my crisp glass of white wine. 'He works in events catering, not restaurants. I think he loves it; he gets to be really experimental.'

'I know he's not as good as you,' Luka said, 'but does he know that?'

I laughed. 'I think he'd argue with you there.'

'He'd have to agree with me. I'm your intimidating half-brother.' Luka had referenced being my brother all day, both jokingly and more seriously at times. It was a little disconcerting at first, but now I liked it. It was starting to feel real.

'And what does he think of you having a brother?'

I looked down at my bracelet, twisting it round until the skin underneath puckered. Luka must have noticed my expression change.

'He doesn't know?'

'I haven't really told him about you and Rosa.'

Luka watched me over the top of his glass but stayed silent.

'I don't know why. When my Dad ... our Dad died, he was really supportive. He came home to Bath with me, rang Mark to say why I wasn't in work, did all that stuff that had to be done. But ... I don't know, it just all seemed to get back to normal very quickly for him. Now when I talk about Dad, he changes the subject very quickly. Like everything is sunny with him and it should be for me too.'

Luka nodded and started refilling my wine glass. I could tell he was taking in my every word. Lately, Adam did less and less of that; he either checked his phone when I was talking or just glazed over. But I did the same to him sometimes. Wasn't that just what happened in a long-term relationship?

'Adam isn't the most sensitive of people, I guess. I feel like he knows everything about me, knows me inside and out... It's nice to have something that's just mine, I think.'

I realised how much I'd told this near stranger. I hadn't opened up to anyone like this for ages. But then Luka wasn't a stranger, was he?

The door opened, interrupting us. Luka gave me a small smile, as if he understood my feelings.

'Hi, Mum,' I shouted.

Luka stood up as she walked tiredly into the room, her bag falling from her shoulder.

'Hello, you two,' she said. It sounded stiff, formal.

'Grace.' Luka gave her a kiss on the cheek.

I hadn't given much thought to how they'd feel about seeing each other again. I tried to read her expression, but she was focussed on Luka, smiling but scrutinising him. I got up to give her a hug, wanting her to feel as comfortable with Luka as I did.

'Something smells delicious,' Mum said, giving me a squeeze.

'We've saved you a plate.' Luka moved quickly to the oven. 'It's delicious. Kat wanted some advice on her cooking so this is something I just whipped up for her.' Mum laughed looking at the plate.

'Hey,' I scolded him.

'Please, I know my daughter's cooking. When a plate's as pretty as this, it's got her name written on it.' Mum sat down, choosing the seat closest to me and leaving the chair next to Luka empty. 'You must have a glass of wine. White or red?'

As Luka poured her a glass, Mum tipped her head towards me in a question. I nodded to convey it was going well. Inside, I felt thrilled.

'That was amazing!' Luka said, taking a huge mouthful and smacking his lips in genuine appreciation.

'Well, you had some input,' I teased, nudging him.

'Why Berlin, then?' Mum asked as we finished the wine. 'It's law you want to study, isn't it?'

'Berlin is a great city and the law department is very prestigious. I've applied for a joint honours in law and politics, and Dad said it was an interesting course...' He trailed off.

And there it was. Dad. The elephant in the room. I glanced at Mum, but her expression gave nothing away.

'We went a couple of years ago,' Luka continued, hesitantly. 'He met me there. Mum couldn't go because of the restaurant. I did consider doing economics in Dubrovnik but Berlin ... it's an exciting city. I can't wait to go in September.'

'Dad must have loved the thought of you studying law and politics. At least one of us has the brains,' I grinned, flapping away their protestations.

'So, I heard you've been to Cetinje today? What did you think of it? My best friend Milo is from Cetinje. It's so beautiful.' Luka's phone started to ring. 'Oh, speak of the devil.' He excused himself and left the room.

'How was it then, Mum?'

'I'll tell you properly after, but it was good. Aunt Sofija is so lovely. I showed her pictures of you.'

'And did she ... know?'

Mum shook her head briskly, then took a bite of the lamb dish.

'You never fail to amaze me.' She kissed the top of my head.

Luka strode back into the kitchen. 'Milo's on his way to pick me up.' Luka's car was being fixed so he'd arranged to get a lift back when his friend finished work. 'I'm so sorry, Kat. I've had the best day.'

'Me too,' I said, suddenly shy, unsure how to end things. I could feel Mum's eyes on me.

Luka saved me. 'My turn next, right? How about a proper boat trip? Outside the bay? For both of you.'

Mum tilted her head in appreciation.

'We'll go on a faster boat ... if you can handle it?'

'Very funny,' I said. 'Let me know when you're next off.'

'Sorry to leave while you're eating, Grace,' Luka said, walking towards the door.

'Pleasure seeing you.' Mum waved.

I got up to walk him out, but he stopped me. 'Stay with your mother. I'll text you.'

I went over to the kitchen window that overlooked the street, wanting to watch Luka go. I could feel the joy radiating from me.

Outside, I saw a red car, and a head of brown hair as the driver opened the passenger door. He waved and gestured for Luka to get in. So, this was Milo. I found myself watching him. He was ... nice. Lean, wearing a plain white T-shirt that showed off muscular forearms, but didn't scream 'look at me' like some other men.

Milo looked up at the window. I backed away slightly, after a glimpse of dark glinting eyes and a hint of stubble. I turned around blushing.

'Spill the beans then,' Mum said.

CHAPTER TWELVE

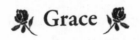 Grace

It was hard not to like Luka. He had a ready laugh and was genuine and attentive. He wasn't the villain here and I tried to separate what I felt about Dan's betrayal from Luka, his son. I could see Kat was happy with him around. It was the happiest I'd seen her in a long time, in fact.

I remembered her nudging and teasing him. I was surprised how quickly they'd developed a rapport. At twenty-four, Kat was five years older than him. She was always so self-sufficient as a child that I didn't think she missed having a sibling. It was taken out of my hands, anyway, as it just didn't happen for Dan and me. I was content with just having one child. Now Kat was positively glowing to have a younger brother. But I wasn't quite sure if I was prepared to play happy families quite yet.

Don't get me wrong, I could see he was making a great effort with Kat, with both of us.

And law in Berlin. I remembered Dan telling me he had a conference in Berlin. He sent lots of photos and even Facetimed me. God, the lies! How did he keep up the pretence for so long? It must have been exhausting.

After Luka had left, I cleared up the dishes and Kat made up the bed in the living room.

'That was a lovely meal.' I paused. 'I'm not sure I'll go on this boat trip, though.'

'Why not?' she asked, pulling the mattress from underneath the sofa.

'You don't need me there. Probably be better, you and Luka on your own, don't you think? I mean, where is this all going?'

'He's invited you and it'll seem odd if you don't go,' she said, glaring.

'He's your half-brother, I get it. But what is he to me? Don't you realise how hard it is for me?'

'You don't have the monopoly on this, Mum. I've lost my father, you know.' Her eyes were suddenly dark and angry. 'What Dad did sucks. He was a shit! A bastard! A lying bastard! But I can't just shut off my feelings for him. And Luka is my link to him. He's my flesh and blood. You can at least try to understand.'

'I think I've tried very hard to understand,' I said, slamming the plates on the drainer. 'Very bloody hard, in fact! For years, your father lied to me, to both of us. When he was away on those conferences of his,' my fingers made air quotes, 'he was shagging Rosa and playing the doting father to Luka. He lied for years.' I could hear my voice rising.

'We can't change that.' Kat sat on the arm of the sofa. 'Don't you see? This is the one good thing to come out of all this. If we turn our backs on Luka now and, yes, Rosa too, then we would be as bad as Dad was.'

I shook my head, 'Of course, I expected you to take his side!'

'What's that supposed to mean?'

'Well, let's not pretend, shall we, that you wouldn't rather it was me instead of your father lying in that cemetery! You always got on better with him than me.' And before I could stop myself, 'You always loved him more than me.'

I regretted the words as soon as they slipped out of my mouth. Kat's face crumpled as she slumped back on the sofa.

'I'm sorry, Kat, I didn't mean that. It was below the belt.' I placed my arm around her, and she sobbed into my shoulder.

'You know that's not true,' she said, between sobs.

I felt appalled with myself. I wasn't handling this well at all.

And so that was how Kat and I found ourselves two days later taking the coast road to Tivat for this boat trip with Luka and his friend.

'Are you sure Rosa is working?'

Kat sighed, 'Yes, Mum. It's just one afternoon, remember.' She almost took the wing mirror off as she navigated around a tight bend too close to a prickly bush. I inhaled deeply. She really wasn't used to driving after being in London so long.

'His friend Milo owns these tourist boats. He's a few years older than Luka and he's been really successful.'

'That's good,' I said, not really listening, keeping my eyes closed.

Luka was sitting waiting on the terrace outside Café Lompar. Despite his wide, toothy smile, I braced myself for the day ahead. He brushed my cheek and, as he leaned in to kiss the other cheek, there was one of those awkward moments as I pulled away too quickly and his teeth crunched into my forehead. He and Kat laughed. Rosa was busy inside with the early lunchtime crowds and she waved at us all briefly, her face unsmiling.

'Milo is ready,' Luka said, pointing to a tourist boat anchored in the harbour. It was quite large with seats arranged under a huge white awning. 'Milo's Montenegrin Boat Tours' was emblazoned in faded gold letters on the side. Milo came to greet us, a tall, handsome, olive-skinned man oozing easy confidence and good humour. I saw Kat's eyes light up. Hmm, perhaps Luka wasn't the only reason for Kat's enthusiasm for the trip. Milo took Kat's hand to help her negotiate the steps and then I followed.

'I'm Milo,' he said with a bow.

'Thank you for inviting us,' I said.

'I take you to the most beautiful parts of Montenegro.' He smiled. 'Places where tourists don't see. You will love it.'

With that, he seemed shy and fiddled about with the motor at the back. Luka helped with untying the ropes from the steel bars at the harbour-side and 'Milo's Montenegrin Boat Tours' pulled gently out of Tivat in the generous midday sunshine.

'My mother has made us a picnic,' Luka said, nudging a large freezer box with his foot.

'That was kind of her,' I said, and meant it. I sat down on one of the middle wooden seats.

'Lemonade, wine?' he asked.

I gave a small sigh of relief when Kat opted for lemonade. She was driving us back later.

Kat and Luka chatted easily as I closed my eyes, enjoying the warm sun on my face. Milo gently hugged the coastline on the tour boat, sailing towards Kotor. Luka pointed to the Lovćen and Orjen mountain ranges and the sheer green valleys, akin to Norwegian Fjords, that plunged precipitously into the iridescent sea. It was a change to see the bay from this angle as we passed Perast on the right-hand side.

'We used to live on the road out of Perast.' Luka pointed

upwards. 'It's a quiet place, not good for a teenage boy. And my mother needed to work. We moved to Tivat when I was twelve.'

As we travelled into the wider sea, I gazed at the houses dotted along the shore and Kat and Luka chatted away, teasing each other and laughing. I wondered about the people living in this utopian bay, with its endless blue skies, sheer cliffs and glistening waters. Lives could seem perfect on the outside, but rarely were. I knew that from experience.

My life with Dan might have appeared idyllic to an outsider. Sometimes I pretended to myself it had been perfect. But Dan was often distracted, even distant. I suddenly remembered that blazing row we had on my birthday two years ago. I'd booked the Michelin-starred Olive Tree in Bath, a treat that Dan said I'd deserved. Kat was thrilled when she heard and made me promise that I'd take a photo of the seven-course taster menu we'd booked. I didn't even question the fact that I'd arranged the taxi and the restaurant. I worked part-time now and Dan had the important job. There was always the unspoken understanding that any family events, meals out and celebrations were organised by me. I reflected on that for the first time: surely for my birthday he could have booked it?

I had gone to the hairdresser that morning and had my layered bob freshly highlighted. I bought a new dress, too, grey linen, and wore it with my silver chunky beads. My trusty firm-control shaping slip was doing its job, a thick, elasticated construction that began below the bra and ended at the top of my thighs. And I'd taken special care with my make-up that night. When I looked in the mirror, for once I didn't shrink back in disgust.

When he was half an hour late and hadn't phoned, I began to

get twitchy. He wasn't answering my increasingly frantic calls. Where the hell was he? I pictured him blood-stained under the wheels of an articulated lorry or administering CPR to a colleague having a heart attack. What could possibly have kept him from my fiftieth birthday? The taxi turned up to pick us up, driven by a sullen, impatient driver, and I rushed out, making grovelling apologies, paying him a fiver for his trouble, and sending him on his way.

'Pick up the blasted phone,' I shouted as I re-entered the house.

When it was eight o'clock, I phoned the restaurant, making up an excuse about car trouble. You couldn't be late for the Olive Tree.

At nearly nine, a good hour and a half after he'd promised to be home, Dan walked in. Staggered, I should say.

'God, I'm so sorry, Gracie,' he muttered. 'Will invited me to the pub and he's worried about funding for this new course. You know what it's like, one drink turned into another and...'

'No, I don't know what it's bloody like! How could you? It's my fiftieth birthday. I've had to cancel the Olive Tree, the taxi. You selfish bastard!'

He grovelled, of course, and spent the night in the spare room. Months later, it became a story we told to friends in the pub, laughing at such a marriage faux pas. I did laugh along with them, but it still hurt. I wondered now if I should have seen the obvious signs of waning interest in me. He'd been with Rosa for years by then, but perhaps the rot had really set in by my fiftieth.

The boat started to slow. Milo had pulled into a rocky inlet. It was so tranquil and idyllic. Kat, Milo and Luka went snorkelling, Kat peeling off her T-shirt dress to reveal her perfect figure, all flat stomach, pert breasts and long legs. She was oblivious to Milo's stares and the general effect she had on the male species.

I enjoyed an hour of peace and read my novel on the deck; a light, unchallenging affair, perfect for summer holidays. I could hear the splashing and shrieks of laughter as they mucked about in the water. This was just what I needed after the intensity of the last few days.

We ate a late lunch that Rosa had prepared. Flatbreads, cheese, prosciutto and grapes. A simple, classy picnic without a sausage roll or prawn cocktail crisp in sight.

'You should have come in, Mum,' Kat said. 'The water is beautiful.'

'Hmm,' I murmured noncommittally.

Milo had opened the wine and handed me a small glass. 'So how long will you stay?'

'Just a few more days now.' I said and felt the atmosphere shift.

'Is this the first time you have visited Montenegro?'

I nodded. 'Yes, it is beautiful. It won't be the last, I'm sure.' That I knew was true. Kat had formed this bond with Luka, and I already knew our lives had changed.

'I have been to London,' Milo said. 'It was great. The London Eye, Big Ben, the red buses.' He laughed. 'Although I could never live anywhere but here.'

Milo spoke to us about his business. He was quite the entrepreneur, buying his first fishing boat at twenty-one and now owning three tour boats in the Bay of Kotor. 'The summer is very busy, but I have time off in the winter.'

As the afternoon wore on, Luka became restless. 'I have to help my mother tonight. We will have to go back soon.'

'Does she have lots of bookings?' Kat asked.

'No, not bookings. It's more relaxed. People come in and it will be, like, crazy,' he said, and we all laughed at the incongruous British phrase spoken in his Montenegrin accent.

It was after five o'clock when we pulled into the harbour in Tivat. It had been a good day and I was glad I'd gone. Kat looked so happy and relaxed. The ever-present dark circles under her eyes had all but disappeared. She seemed younger somehow. The carefree girl of her teenage years. How long could she keep up the high-speed, chaotic life she was returning to? Something had to give.

CHAPTER THIRTEEN

🌿 Kat 🌿

'Luka, what's wrong?' I asked, carrying the empty picnic baskets over to him. He was running his hand through his hair, a gesture I could see was wracked with stress. He'd been speaking to Rosa in muffled tones while Mum and I had helped Milo unpack bags from the boat.

It had been a beautiful day on the water. I'd laughed more than I had in months, well, since Dad died really. It had been pure fun, feeling the ocean spray in my hair as we'd jetted across the bay to the hidden cove this afternoon. I'd even seen Mum relax, kicking off her sandals as she'd read while we went snorkelling. The journey back was calm and serene on the still sea, the setting sun transforming everything to pastel blue.

But I could tell Luka had been tense since we'd turned back. Generally, he joked around in this easy way of his that I was getting to love. But on the way back, he'd stared into the distance, watching Tivat get closer and closer. Milo had let him have that time to himself and kept me laughing with some story about a tourist who'd chartered a boat trip to propose to his girlfriend, but had been far too seasick to go through with it.

Once we arrived at the harbour, Luka jumped out and rushed inside the Café Lompar. Moments later, he walked back to us, looking unsure. Rosa stood in the Café Lompar doorway, looking equally concerned.

'Is everything OK?' I asked.

'I was going to invite you both in for a meal, but we're a bit … thin on the ground here. Mum's head chef is off sick and another one of the staff has had an accident today. It leaves us with just one person in the kitchen and he's only recently started.' He sighed. 'I will help out, but I think Mum's a bit worried. She's been calling the other staff frantically.'

'I will help.' The words were out of my mouth before I could think about it.

'You are on holiday, Kat, you can't do that. Go and enjoy your last few days with Grace. Anyway, I think this is going to be a long-term issue, so don't worry about it. We're going to sort something out.'

I glanced back at Mum.

I didn't want to leave her. I'd felt more distant from her since I'd been spending time with Luka. Things had been a little frayed since we'd argued. I could feel it hanging between us, even in our light-hearted small talk. I was hoping to have the last few nights here with her, close that gap a bit. As soon as I got home, I'd be swept up with Mark and Truffles again; he'd already warned me I'd have to work overtime to make up for this week. I'd never get this time back with Mum. Today had been the first time it was starting to feel normal between us again.

'Luka, let me help. Just for tonight. It will give you time to come up with a contingency plan, and you know I can do it … unless you think my versions of your Montenegrin classics won't be up to scratch?' I was joking but hoped it would push him into a decision.

'Kat, you know that's not it. Café Lompar would be honoured to have you. I don't want you to feel like you have to help out. We'll find another option,' he said, looking skywards.

'It's settled, I'm helping. Don't worry about me.' I touched his arm to show I was serious. 'Just let me find a way for Mum to get home.'

'Milo can take her,' Luka said. 'Thank you so much, Kat, you're amazing. My mother will really appreciate you helping.'

Mum arrived at my side. Her blonde hair looked sun-drenched and curlier than usual from the sea air. I explained the situation to her as Luka went off to speak to Rosa and Milo.

'I'm so sorry, Mum, I know we were going to have a relaxing night in just the two of us. It'll only be for tonight, and Luka needs me. They're desperate. I wouldn't do it otherwise.'

I saw exasperation cross her face, but she covered it quickly.

'If you want to help, Kat...' she said with a shrug, leaving the sentence unfinished.

'I'm so sorry,' I repeated. 'Do you mind?'

'No, I'm just thinking of you. We're going to be back in the UK soon and it's been so nice seeing you relax today. You've got your spark back, darling. I don't want you working hard on holiday.'

Mum's face softened. I smiled and she stroked a strand of hair out of my face.

'This won't be anything like Truffles,' I said, looking at the small handful of diners that were milling around with glasses of wine, taking time over the menus and languishing in the late afternoon sunshine at the outdoor tables. 'Once the main rush is over, I'll be straight back, and we can enjoy a drink together then,' I said to reassure her, but realised I was trying to assuage my own guilt more than anything.

'Don't worry about me. I need to get used to being on my own now,' she said, then reading the horrified look on my face, added, 'I don't mean that, I'm just being silly. Look, I'll call Auntie Claire and get something in for dinner. Don't worry.'

'OK?' I gave her a hug. She assured me everything would be fine and offered to take my bag back to the apartment.

I turned to go into the restaurant. I did feel slightly intimidated at the prospect of cooking in a new place. Despite the gastropub I'd worked at for a few months after qualifying from catering college, Truffles had been the only professional kitchen I'd worked in, Mark the only fire-breathing manager I'd had. I wondered how things would be with Rosa. Apart from a nodded greeting and a few pleasantries, we'd barely spoken to each other.

She eyed me from the bar, with Luka grinning at her side. Rosa was shorter than me, around five foot eight, but there was something about her that radiated power. This was her restaurant and she was in charge.

'Thank you so much for helping, Kat,' Luka said as I approached.

'Yes, thank you.' Rosa simply nodded.

'Anything I can do, I'm happy to help. This view is a lot nicer than in the restaurant I work at in London.' The Café did have an impressive setting, almost touching distance to the seafront, and incredible views to the glittering horizon.

'Have you been working as a chef for long?' Rosa asked. I didn't know if she was truly interested in my culinary background or simply sizing me up as her son's half-sister.

'I qualified four years ago. I've been working at a fine dining restaurant since then — Michelin starred.' I don't know why I added that. I sounded like I was showing off. 'Luka's shown me some amazing dishes from Montenegro, I absolutely love them. Your seafood here is the most incredible I've ever had.'

'Good.' Rosa smiled, but it didn't quite reach her eyes. 'Well, maybe you can just help with some chopping and preparation for now. I'll introduce you to Lovro — he's only been working here for a few months but he's very experienced.' Rosa beckoned me to follow her.

I stiffened. I didn't know if she meant to be rude, but I could do a lot more than chop and prep. Luka knew it too. He looked like he wanted the ground to swallow him up. I didn't correct Rosa for his sake and followed her into the kitchen.

Lovro was a lot younger than me, and his 'experience' was working weekends in his father's gelateria. It was no wonder they were so desperate for extra help.

I got to work, frying off some onions for the stew ordered by the first table of diners. I was pleased to see a decent pot of stock had been left bubbling away on the large stove. The kitchen was partially open, so the stove top had a view out to the rustic tables, each with a single white flower, and the beach beyond. I couldn't help but get into my zone in this atmosphere, much more pleasant than Truffles and with no Mark barking orders at me.

As I put the first dishes out on the pass for Rosa to serve, she assessed them, gave a pleased sniff and looked towards me with a small smile on her face.

'Thank you,' Luka whispered in my ear as I turned round to help Lovro, who was sautéing fresh scallops. 'You're a star, Kat. It's just for tonight.'

Luka's 'just for tonight' turned into three nights in a row. Rosa had struggled to find someone else to cover, and I'd happily agreed to help out again. I enjoyed the relaxed vibe in the Café Lompar kitchen. The food was simple, with none of the gimmicky flourishes or crazy fusion flavours we were pushed to serve in Truffles. Good produce was cooked simply, and Rosa had let me add the meal I'd created with Luka to the menu. Lovro proved himself to be a helpful partner, with a flair for puddings. Whether it was thanks to the the years at the gelateria or not, he could make perfect ice creams. Basil and mint was a personal favourite, the ideal finish to a rich Mediterranean meal.

I think even Rosa started to approve of me. I watched her every night weaving and flirting her way between the tables, attentive with each customer, but never pushy. I was surprised that she let me put my own touch on the dishes, and I even heard her mentioning my name to one of the diners.

Plus, the eye candy that was Milo Martinović didn't hurt either. Every night he came by to drop off some fresh seafood he'd caught. I couldn't believe I had accidentally stumbled into this idyllic way of life, working in this café — sleepy by day and lively and bustling by night — and a tanned hunk coming by with a smile just for me.

'Nice to see you, Milo,' Rosa shouted one night. 'It must be a good season this year, double the amount of seafood than usual.' She winked conspiratorially at me.

Mark had sent me several messages after I sent the recipes across to him. They were a hit. But he kept demanding my return. Adam, as well, kept sending texts: 'Can't wait for you to get home'. My phone felt like a weight in my pocket, dragging me back to reality. I felt guilty at not texting back often, but something inside told me Adam wasn't missing me so much as someone to do the laundry, tidy up and listen to his rambling stories about the events he'd catered for.

Here I felt free, independent, an honorary Montenegrin. Life at Café Lompar was like a sun-kissed dream.

Luka came to dine with us one night and I escaped from the kitchen with two big plates of japraci, stuffed vegetables made with raštan leaves, to sit with him. I enjoyed the pace of this kitchen. Rosa didn't press chefs to work until they were sweaty with burnt fingers, but allowed time to enjoy the sun, a glass of beer, a pause with family.

'Your sister is a genius,' Rosa said to Luka as she stopped briefly near our table. 'Better than our normal head chef.'

'She is,' he beamed.

'I don't know what we'll do when you go back home,' Rosa lamented, a glint in her eye.

CHAPTER FOURTEEN

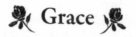 Grace

When Kat left for a third night at Café Lompar, my patience was wearing thin. I couldn't face another TV dinner watching Montenegrin game shows, so I decided to go to one of the local tavernas for a bite to eat.

I slipped on a shirt dress and my gold sandals before I could change my mind. The streets were busy at seven o'clock, families and couples milling around, looking at places to eat or browsing the still-bustling souvenir shops. Most sold the usual tat: fridge magnets, ashtrays and paperweights engraved with images of the Bay of Kotor, brightly coloured beach towels, postcards and guidebooks. Did anyone still send postcards? I looked at a few leather handbags in one shop. Bags were the only clothing I was sure would fit me these days. Even sandals were hit and miss, as my feet expanded in the heat like squidgy Play-doh spreading wilfully between the straps.

I lingered outside some of the restaurants, glancing at the menus, and trying to decide whether I could sit in a corner and get away with people-watching undetected. It still felt strange to be wandering around alone in the evening. I stopped at a café we'd passed a few times called Zdravo. There were just a few tables occupied and it looked authentically Montenegrin. A young waiter rushed over, menu in hand, and a welcoming grin on his face whenever anyone so much as hesitated outside.

'Zdravo,' he said, pointing up at the sign. 'Hello.' After repeating this, it dawned on me that 'zdravo' meant 'hello' in Montenegrin.

'Very clever.' I smiled. He didn't seem to speak much English. He led me to a table for two with a good view of the square, where the sunset cast shades of apricot and orange on the old, grey buildings opposite.

The menu was simple and unpretentious. Dan would have called this place 'rustic' with an accompanying sneer and might even have passed by, looking for somewhere more sophisticated. I liked the simple wooden tables and chairs, the blackboard menu and the large potted plants. It was charming. I ordered a glass of rosé, which arrived ice-cold, the glass clouded with condensation. I sipped it as I perused the menu and ordered some grilled lamb chops with salad and potatoes, feeling quite hungry.

As I waited for my meal, I watched the families passing by, catching snippets of conversation as they bickered about where to eat. I couldn't say Dan and I argued much. He wasn't confrontational and I certainly wasn't. He could sulk, though, for days on end. I hovered continually on the line of least resistance, generally going along with what Dan wanted. There was no chance of me mythologising Dan in death. His long-standing affair with Rosa put paid to that. But perhaps I'd relied upon him too much. Had I been one of those annoyingly clingy wives? God, I hoped not.

I had been a successful businesswoman, I tried to remind myself. 'Gardening with Grace' took off surprisingly well and I had rented and eventually bought a faded shop on the outskirts of Bath with a large greenhouse at the back. I was so proud of it. I had employed two part-time assistants, and our customers enjoyed the personal touch we could give them over the bigger garden centres. I'd loved flowers and plants since I was small when I helped my father in his allotment. It didn't actually feel like work. There's something about digging in the dirt and growing plants that soothed my soul, made me feel connected.

Dan could never understand it and often mentioned my English degree. 'You could teach,' he'd say, 'not waste it.' It annoyed the hell out of me that he couldn't see what I had achieved, that he wasn't as proud of it as I was.

But eventually he got his way. He encouraged me to sell when his work took him away so much. 'It makes sense and I'll look after you,' he promised. He kept saying how he and Kat missed me, how 'tired' I was looking. I made a good profit on the sale, which helped my dignity a little. But selling it had felt like giving up, had eroded my confidence and I'm not sure I'd ever regained it.

Now, after Dan's death, I felt completely lost. When you've been with someone for a long time, it's difficult to know where he ends, and you begin. I did miss him, but I was used to him not being with me long before he died. Even when he was home, he spent long hours in his study, preparing lecture notes, marking essays or researching something or other. We didn't often have days out.

I remembered a May Bank Holiday weekend the year before he died, when Will and Sarah and our neighbours, Steve and Louise, had booked an Airbnb in the Lake District. I was really looking forward to it, a friendly get-together, drinking wine, sailing perhaps, having nice meals out. We were all at that age when the children were grown up and off our hands. I was packing some things on the Thursday night and Dan was in bed reading a book.

'Do you think we'll need waterproofs?' I asked, scurrying about the bedroom.

'Why have you started packing so late at night?' he asked, not taking his eyes from his book.

'I don't want to be rushing tomorrow morning. After work, I had to go into Sainsbury's, stock up on wine. This is the first chance I've had.'

'I'll do mine tomorrow,' Dan said. 'I'll probably have to join you Saturday, anyway.'

'What do you mean Saturday? We've agreed to drive Steve and Lou. You can't go on Saturday. Why the hell can't you come tomorrow?' I could feel my temper rising.

'I've got too much research to do for that paper. It's impossible.' He took off his glasses. 'You take the Audi and I'll follow on Saturday with your car. It's not a big deal, is it?'

'Actually, it is a fucking big deal. Why am I only hearing about this now? You know how much everyone's been looking forward to it. You're unbelievable!' Infuriated, I could hardly get my words out.

'My absence is hardly going to spoil the party,' he said coolly. 'I don't know why you always have to make a fuss.'

'Sometimes I think that work is an excuse with you because you just don't want to go! At least be honest,' I snapped.

'That's not true,' he retorted, without conviction. 'If you want me to be perfectly honest, you're keener to go on this weekend than I am. Will is fine but Steve is an arsehole. He drinks too much and can be so crass.'

'This is so bloody unfair, Dan. You could at least have told me. What am I going to say to them?'

'The truth. I've got a lot of work on and I'll join you late Saturday.'

The weekend was a disaster. I was still fuming at Dan and I hated driving his Audi, but had no choice as there was more room in the boot. I could understand Dan not being overly keen on Steve, but he was harmless, and we'd had plenty of barbecues with them in the past.

When we arrived at the cottage, I could see Will and Sarah's sympathetic glances as I made excuses for Dan. I tried to forget the whole argument on Thursday night, but I felt a spare wheel and we had to make excuses at the restaurant we'd booked for six. When Dan did eventually arrive, late on Saturday, he was morose and quiet, putting a dampener on everyone's mood, refusing to drink because he had a headache. It's not Steve who is the arsehole, I thought to myself, as I rolled over in bed, leaving as large a gap between us as possible, my legs dangling over the side. It rained all day on Sunday, a typical British bank holiday, and when we left on Monday, I was hungover and miserable and couldn't wait to get home. Deep down inside me I knew it was easier when Dan wasn't there, even if I'd never admit it, even to myself. Life seemed to revolve around his needs when he was home. I'd airbrushed all these memories after his death.

The heat of the day was dissipating, and it was pleasant in

Zdravo, unhurried and relaxed. I would have felt awkward sitting in a restaurant alone in Bath, a little bit sad, ignoring the questioning glances. Here, it wasn't a problem. When the food came, it was delicious. I ordered passionfruit cheesecake and coconut ice cream for dessert, persuading myself that it was allowed as I was still on holiday, if you could call this rollercoaster ride a holiday.

Kat arrived back at the apartment after eleven o'clock, beaming.

'How did it go?' I asked.

'It was great. It's such a good restaurant. The food is delicious, and I'm putting my own stamp on some of the dishes.'

'I hope you're not being coerced into this, Kat. You're supposed to be on holiday.'

She brushed my worries aside, 'It was fine, Mum. There's another chef there, Lovro, so there's plenty of help.'

'And how is Rosa?'

'Good,' she answered breezily. 'I think she really appreciates me being there. I don't know how they would cope otherwise. I had something to eat at the restaurant, so I hope you haven't waited.' She rummaged in the fridge for milk.

'How many more nights are you doing there, Kat? We've got our flights booked and before you know it you'll be working all the hours God sends in Truffles. You've hardly had a break.'

'I know,' she paused, 'we haven't spent much time together. I've agreed to tomorrow night and Rosa's invited you to eat there.'

'That's nice of her,' I said, trying hard not to roll my eyes.

Rosa was attentive, explaining what a great chef Kat was. She'd placed me at a good spot looking out at the sunset and brought over a bottle of wine. She was busy all night, weaving between tables, all eager smiles, her hair swept into a loose chignon. Effortlessly chic in that easy European way. This was clearly a successful business and she was very much a woman aware of her own beauty.

I phoned Claire, eager to talk to someone while I waited for my food. She picked up on the third ring.

'Hi Claire. You busy?'

'When am I not?' she sighed. 'But I've always got time for you.'

'Guess where I am? You'll never believe!' I tried to keep my voice down, hastily adjusting the volume of the phone.

'Rosa's place?' she said.

'OK, you're right. Kat's helping out in the kitchen.'

Claire sucked in her breath, 'Ooh, awkward.'

'It's OK. I'm eating here and Rosa is too busy for me to talk to her much. How did Sunday lunch go with River?' I just wanted to talk about something else, think about other people's lives instead of my own.

'Polite, stiff, as uncomfortable as you could imagine. He was well-mannered, full of please and thank yous. But he's so bloody old.'

'Twenty-one, you said,' I reminded her.

'Yes,' she went on, 'but when you're sixteen, those five years are a ruddy great gulf. He's got a wispy beard. Tattoos, of course. A sleeve on his left arm. He explained the Chinese writing in great detail. One saying My life is my art. My art is my life. That I could accept, as he's an art student. But his other one: Too wild to live. Too rare to die. What the bloody hell does that mean? I hate that meaningless, philosophical claptrap!' she said with feeling.

'Oh Gawd,' I sympathised, not really knowing what to say.

'And Laura is madly in love, listening agog to his every word, as if, "Yes, I'll have another spud," is liquid gold.'

'We've all been there.'

'Yes, but when it's your baby...' She sighed. 'You dream of them having a good life, a great job, marrying a consultant at the very least, then having children in their thirties, maybe.'

'Well, I married the high-flier, the university professor. Look how that turned out! Sometimes you have to let them make their own mistakes.'

'Yeah, maybe he should have that tattooed on his forearm,' Claire laughed.

We chatted a bit more before my food arrived and I ate another solitary meal, waiting for Kat. As the diners drifted away, she joined me for a drink and a small bite to eat. Her eyes were glowing, and she talked enthusiastically about Café Lompar.

'No wonder this place has such a good reputation, Mum. The fish is as fresh as it can be, just off the boats. And Rosa isn't afraid to experiment. Montenegrin cuisine is marvellous!'

On the way home, she broke it to me that she was spending our last night working in the restaurant.

'I know it's not ideal, Mum,' Kat said quickly, 'but she's in a real hole. If I don't do it, there's no one and it's getting to the height of the season.'

'Hmm,' I said, not really happy, but not in a position to say anything. 'It's just you I worry about. You need a break.'

'I don't feel as rushed here. People take their time over food and aren't constantly looking at their watches. You feel your work is appreciated. Anyway, I'll make it up to you once I'm back, I promise. The next weekend I'm off, I'll come home.'

On the final night, Kat left early, hoping she could finish in time to pack up before we left for our flight the following afternoon. I sat on the terrace as it grew dark, sipping tea and imagined the inky sea beyond the buildings, the waves swelling rhythmically against the harbour walls. I could hear the chatter of late diners and the clatter as tables were being cleared.

I was glad we came. It had been emotionally fraught, it was true. I wished I had come here with Dan. The reason for his reluctance was all too apparent now. Meeting Rosa had been the last piece of the jigsaw puzzle. It still hurt so much that he'd lied for so long. There was no excuse for the way he'd treated me. Why hadn't he just left? I would have got over it eventually. Now, I had to stomach humiliation as well as the keenness of grief. For Rosa, it was different. She knew about us, was complicit in the lies.

I was blinded by the car headlights as Kat parked in front of Apartman Nina. As she locked the door, she didn't meet my eyes. She looked more tired than usual.

'Come on, love, let's go inside. I'll make you a cup of tea. Leave the packing until the morning. We'll have time.'

I frowned once inside, seeing Kat prepare herself a slice of toast. 'Is that all you're going to have? Let me make you something decent. You just don't look after yourself. You might be twenty-four, but I worry about you, Kat.'

'I'm fine,' she said, with a note of irritation in her voice. It must have been difficult leaving Luka. They'd formed a bond really quickly.

'How was Luka? It must be hard saying goodbye, but you'll see him again soon, I'm sure. You've invited him to stay in a few weeks.' I switched the kettle on. 'I'll help set up the bed now. You need to get some sleep. No doubt Mark will want you straight back in Truffles as soon as you leave Baggage Reclaim.'

Kat turned around to face me. 'I'm not going back, Mum,' she said. 'I'll take you to the airport tomorrow, but I'm staying here, and nothing is going to change my mind.'

PART TWO

CHAPTER FIFTEEN

🌿 Kat 🌿

'The last table has gone,' Rosa called out, bustling through the kitchen doors, empty plates stacked clean in her arms. 'That's the third time I've seen them this week!'

'Thank goodness, I'm exhausted,' I rubbed my neck, feeling the familiar ache from standing over the hob. I was looking forward so much to sitting down and tucking into my own meal, ready to put my feet up. It was not like the war-zone emotion at the end of a busy night at Truffles. This was a satisfied tiredness that came from doing something I loved. I looked around to check Lovro had put the prawns in the fridge to marinate for tomorrow. Maria, one of the waitresses, had nearly finished the washing up. The place looked squeaky clean and ready to tuck in for the night.

I unbuttoned my chef's whites and moved to the door, where I found Luka blocking the exit.

'Kat, I need to show you something in the bar.' He grabbed my elbow and marched me across the room.

'What's going on?' I noticed the nudges and not very subtle mutterings between the other staff. Luka was grinning like a child on Christmas morning.

'Can't I get our new recruit a drink?' He looked accusingly at me and pushed open the old-fashioned saloon doors to the front of the restaurant.

The lights were switched off, the tables illuminated by the silver moon. The handful of staff and Milo had assembled by the bar and were all looking at me expectantly.

'Surprise!' Rosa called out.

I turned to watch her carrying an enormous cake, lit with pretty candles that danced like fairy lights in the darkness.

'Aww!' I was taken aback. 'What's this for?'

'To celebrate.' Luka squeezed my arm. 'One month of you working here.'

'I don't know what to say. I'm speechless,' I breathed.

'First time for everything.' Luka laughed. I rolled my eyes at the totally unoriginal joke.

'Not just that,' Rosa said. 'I want to thank you for being the best head chef we've ever had. To Kat!' She raised the cake so I could blow out my candles. It was such a touching gesture.

Head chef.

The words still didn't sound real. Head chef, Kat Lompar. What would Dad have said?

I marked my first month at Truffles by falling asleep on the sofa after I came in from work, broken, at 2 A.M. I couldn't imagine Mark giving me a cake then.

Milo opened a bottle of white wine, handing me the first glass. 'Your favourite'.

I wouldn't say life at Café Lompar had been entirely easy; it was still work after all. The facilities in the kitchen here were a lot more basic than at cutting-edge Truffles, and I'd struggled to get by on the limited knowledge I had of the Montenegrin

122

language. But after begging Rosa to splash out on an industrial stand mixer and a sous vide machine, things had got a lot easier. And Lovro was helping me with the language, giving me a test every day while we chopped and prepped in the morning.

I still hadn't got used to being the head of the kitchen. It was such a buzz having no one to answer to. I found myself being more creative, dreaming up different recipes and flavour combinations I could use. Although we were still mainly cooking the classics, I was trying to put my own stamp on them. Our squid-ink risotto served with tempura seafood and parmesan tuilles had become one of our bestselling dishes. And I'd introduced a Montenegrin tapas night every Friday — four little taster dishes of our café favourites for ten euros. Fridays were now our busiest nights. Tourists were coming from all over the bay, recommended by their hotels and Tripadvisor.

'Look at all you've done since you started, and it's only been a month,' Rosa said, cutting into the cake.

'I never knew British girls could cook like this.' Maria laughed. She had worked in Café Lompar for two years and was quickly becoming one of my closest friends in Montenegro. She shared the same wicked sense of humour as Luka, and I suspected they had a soft spot for each other. I'd noticed he'd started to turn up at the restaurant at the end of every shift, often with Milo.

'We have a present for you too.' Luka reached behind the bar. 'It took a lot of searching online, like A LOT. I had to make sure I found the right ones, and these are very hard to get shipped to Montenegro.'

He lifted a box of 300 PG Tips tea bags on to the table. Luka had stuck a big gold bow on top.

'Thank God!' I laughed. 'You must have finally got sick of me moaning about the tea in Montenegro.'

'You can't get a decent cup of tea anywhere,' Luka mimicked my English accent. I blushed. Was I such a cliché?

We sat around for the best part of an hour, clinking glasses and giggling. As far as the rest of the staff knew, I was related to Rosa and Luka, which explained why we shared the same surname. It was easier that way. If anyone suspected anything, they didn't say.

My stomach ached from the generous slice of cake I'd had, delicious lemon cream-cheese icing on top. The others started to filter off home for the night.

'Right, Kat, as great as you are, I don't want to see you here tomorrow. You need a day off. It's been six days straight and I haven't seen you take a break once,' Rosa instructed.

'OK. But let me know if it's busy tomorrow or you need help,' I said.

'I certainly won't,' she scoffed. 'Anyway, you need to sort out your visa paperwork.'

Rosa had been helping me with the assault course of bureaucracy that seemed necessary to grant temporary citizenship. I still had another few weeks of being a tourist before I had to be officially registered in Montenegro, but Rosa had warned me several times that I couldn't leave it to the last minute. 'She wants to tie you down officially to Café Lompar,' Luka told me.

'Go get some rest now,' Rosa ushered me out and started to clear away the cake.

Things had definitely thawed between us, with Rosa regularly telling me how many customers had sent their 'compliments' to the chef, and how pleased they were to have me. I always tried to ask how things were front of house and was the first to chat to her when she opened up in the afternoon. Although warmer, things were strictly professional between us. I'd yet to go to her house, always meeting Luka outside on the steps, and I still didn't feel I knew much about her. I think Rosa was wary of me. I wondered if she'd ever let her guard down. I still didn't know how to feel about Rosa. I wanted to get closer but I felt disloyal to Mum. It was all so complicated that it made my head spin.

'Čao, Čao!' I made my goodbyes, turning down a lift back to the flat with Milo and Luka. Outside, the air was still hot; the June days were becoming stifling. I hopped onto my bike, admiring, as I always did, the idyllic peppermint colour and pretty basket.

I set off on my nightly cycle ride back to the flat I was staying at, courtesy of a friend of Luka's. The streets of Tivat were quiet, the last of the tourists strolling to their hotels and the odd cat weaving in and out of restaurant doorways; café chairs stacked upside down on tables, legs in the air. Uphill I went, to the more residential streets, the mountains peaceful except for the whirr of cicadas.

'Home,' I sighed as I got through the door.

But was this really home?

The tiny flat boasted a living room with kitchenette, the units a characterless beige, two small bedrooms just big enough for a double bed, and a bathroom. I'd barely seen Luka's friend who shared the flat; we were passing ships in the night. My room was sparsely decorated — I hadn't been able to buy much of my own furniture yet — and the contents of my holiday suitcase didn't

125

fill much of the wardrobe. Sometimes I missed the tasteful grey and white scheme I'd chosen for our flat in London, the framed pictures of Adam and me, Mum and Dad, and the home comforts, my slippers and furry dressing gown.

I set my gift down on the table. At least now I had tea bags.

I checked the time, working out it was ten o'clock at home, and I could still get away with calling Mum.

My own image looked back at me from the screen as I waited for her to pick up. I looked different – tanned, sun-kissed even. I'd put a bit of weight on from the endless seafood and ice cream I'd been scoffing at Café Lompar, but I looked healthy — the dark bags under my eyes were gone, worn like a badge of honour by Truffles chefs.

'Hi, Kat.' Her picture crackled on to the screen.

'You look nice.' I smiled. 'Have you had your hair done?'

'Yes, I went yesterday. How are you?' We chatted about the last few days. It had been nearly a week since we'd spoken.

Things hadn't really felt right between us since I'd made the decision to stay in Montenegro. I'd been so nervous that night as I walked to Apartman Nina. I'd practised different ways of telling her as I walked back, before deciding there was no good way to say, 'I'm not coming home with you tomorrow, I'm going to stay with your husband's mistress instead.' It felt like a betrayal of her, of Adam, of my old life.

Every sensible part of me told me to go home. But something inside me had shifted during our time in Montenegro; I felt I had a new perspective on life as well as a new family. Surely, I owed it to myself, to the carefree, relaxed Kat I'd found here, to stay and see if life would be better? Montenegro had got under my skin already. It was a part of my DNA and I felt intangibly connected to the place. As soon as Rosa asked me to be head chef, I knew my answer would be yes.

'You're doing what?' Mum's voice still rung in my ears from that night. Her face had crumpled, heartbroken all over again. God, it was agonising. Could I really let her go home and get on with life on her own, without me or Dad?

'I know, I know. It sounds ridiculous, but Rosa's offered me head chef, and I don't know, Mum, it just feels … right, somehow.' I knew I was rambling and probably making no sense. She'd argued but could see 'head chef' had changed everything. She'd seen how much I hated Mark, and how pressured I was at home. I think she'd noticed the shift in me that week too.

'I'm worried you're throwing away everything in the UK for some holiday fling in the mist. What if you miss your life at home?' She'd rubbed her eyes, standing up to face me.

'What life at home?' I'd thrown my arms up. 'I work until I'm sick, I sit cramped on the tube every morning and every fucking night, I have no money left after rent, no social life. I feel about thirty years older than I actually am.' I started to cry.

'But working for Rosa, your father's mistress? You're doing exactly the same as him.' Her face looked pinched, exhausted.

'That's ridiculous!' I sighed. 'Please, Mum, it's not ideal, I know, but I need you to be happy for me.'

'I don't know if I can,' she said. 'I'm going to bed.' And she left me standing in the kitchen feeling like a shit for doing this to her, but unable to stop myself.

We had breakfast together the following day, before I drove her back to the airport, hoping to extend the rental period on the car. We made small talk about the holiday, what she planned to do at home, but didn't mention the job until she got out of the car at Dubrovnik International.

'I can see you're sure about this, Kat. If you think it's the right decision for you, then I do too.' Her voice was tight, unconvincing.

We'd spoken a handful of times since then, mostly catching up about how work was going with me, Claire and the River drama, and this charity night she was organising, but we'd stayed steadfastly away from anything to do with Rosa. I could feel myself constantly trying to keep things light and airy, avoiding the things I couldn't bear to say.

'Are you coping OK there, Mum?' I asked now, hoping to read her expression.

'Of course. Don't worry about me. It's you I'm worried about.'

'I'm fine,' I said, a bit too snappily. There was an awkward pause. Unspoken accusations seemed to dance in the gap between us.

'Shall I let you get some rest?' she said eventually.

'OK.' I showed her the present I'd had from Luka, before saying goodnight and clicking off.

I sat back on the sofa, feeling unsettled. Had I made the right decision? Was this my dream opportunity or was I just running away? Montenegro definitely wasn't my home yet, but London wasn't my home anymore either. I felt torn in two, straddling two countries, uncertain of both.

I had to force myself to get up and go to bed and not sit on the sofa all night worrying. Tomorrow, I had a new start planned, that would hopefully make me feel at home here. Tomorrow, I was going flat hunting.

CHAPTER SIXTEEN

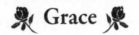 Grace

I lay in bed, listening to the silence. Sometimes, half-awake, I imagined Dan was still here and life was normal. He'd gone out for a run or was up early listening to Radio 4 and Kat was busy in Truffles, worrying about a restaurant critic descending on them without warning. Then reality came crashing in. Dan was dead and Kat was nearly two thousand miles away, working for Rosa. That woman had taken Dan and now she had my daughter.

I rose quickly, shaking the ridiculous thoughts from my head. It was totally irrational. I was trying my best to be happy for Kat, I really was. When I spoke to her, I tried to swallow my jealousy and listen while she talked enthusiastically about the new dishes she was dreaming up. She was thriving at Café Lompar and Rosa obviously appreciated her. It didn't make it hurt any less, though.

'I made pasulj for the first time tonight,' Kat told me at the end of her shift last night, 'and everyone was ordering it. It's this amazing stew with beans and spices. I made it with goat and added my own little twist with avocado oil.'

'Of course,' I smiled.

'We served them in these rustic earthen pots. Rosa was delighted. Did I tell you our bookings are up thirty percent in this last week?'

Her enthusiasm was infectious, and food was always the safest subject. She had her work, and I, shaking myself and getting dressed, had mine, which was something to hold on to.

Sylvie was so relieved I was back from Montenegro. We had Project Child's annual Auction of Promises, our biggest night of the year, coming up, and Sylvie had been flapping about it for the last few weeks. My job was to approach local businesses to donate experiences, products, and vouchers to the auction. It was a welcome distraction.

Project Child UK's offices were on the outskirts of the city above a dusty old hairdresser. We often saw elderly ladies leaving with their blue rinses and tight perms.

Sylvie had started the charity about ten years ago. She used to be a social worker and had seen the pernicious effect of poverty on children. 'The deprivation I've seen,' she told me when I first started. 'I used to cry when I got home. Those kids just don't have the same chances as others and it's not bloody fair!' She always got so animated when she talked about it. She made me feel that I was part of something that was making a difference, even if it was hard work.

A week before the event, I was on the phone, receiving my sixth refusal in a row. It was becoming harder to keep the pleading tone from my voice.

'We're struggling ourselves, love,' said the manager of a local restaurant that seemed packed to the rafters every night. 'I'd love to help otherwise,' he continued, with as much sincerity as a game show host.

'Not much luck, Grace?' Heather sympathised. She was in charge of advertising and brochures for events. That was the deal: the patrons got some advertising and we raised money from the auction. 'Still,' Heather went on, 'you've had some fantastic donations so far. I'm going all out for that Pampering Pooches' voucher on the night. Mitzi would just love a bit of TLC.' Mitzi was her dog, who was fed poached chicken breast fillets nightly and had her own duck down pillow. 'They get a nail clip, ear cleaning, full bath and removal of all matts. I took Mitzi last year and they put this sequinned pink bow in her head. Look, I've got the photos here.'

Sylvie rolled her eyes and escaped, while I was shown Mitzi, Heather's Miniature Schnauzer yet again, along with the aforementioned sequinned bow. I didn't think a week went by without her showing off some photos. 'Mitzi was watching David Attenborough last night and she started barking when the big cats were on. And I told her, "Listen Mitzi, they'd eat you alive." I'm sure she understood. She looked me right in the eye. It did make me laugh,' she giggled.

I smiled and picked up the phone to cut short the conversation, only to be hit with another refusal. 'We'd love to help, but times are hard at the moment.'

I got up to make a cup of tea in the tiny 'kitchen': a sink and drainer, a kettle and mini fridge with room for a half-litre of milk and a couple of sandwiches.

'Frustrating, isn't it?' Sylvie said, startling me as she came into the kitchen.

'God, I'll scream if I see another photo of Mitzi.'

'Well, yes, Heather can be, but I meant having all those rejections.'

I nodded. 'I'm worried we'll have hardly any contributions. It might all fall flat on the night.'

'It'll be fine, you'll see. It's not for another week yet.'

Sylvie was always a calming influence with her unshakeable optimism.

'Do you want a cup?' I asked her.

'Please. How's things going, Grace? You must be missing Kat?'

'I am,' I admitted. 'She's loving it, though, and I can't begrudge her that.'

'That's what parenting is about,' she said. 'You put them first even if it hurts like hell.'

Apart from Claire, Sylvie was the only one I had confided in about Dan. I could trust her. 'All of us have secrets,' she'd said when I told her, as if it was perfectly normal for a man to have a second family on the side. 'Michael had porn magazines in the shed, and stacks of cigarettes. I found them the day after he died. I went into the shed to be close to him. He'd given up smoking twenty years ago, or so he'd told me. But I could smell it on him. I wasn't daft.' She shook her head. 'But the porn mags. Ugh, I don't know. It was as if I wasn't enough for him. Bouncy and Boobilicious was his favourite. He must have had a hundred of them at least. Some wives don't mind it, of course. Even turns them on.'

I tried not to react. It wasn't quite the scale of Dan's deceit, but it did make me feel an eensy bit better. People's lives were never ever straightforward.

'Red or white? We have some orange juice, too,' I offered, as the crowds filtered into the hall for Project Child UK's Auction of Promises the following week.

Sylvie and I were stationed inside the foyer of the village hall.

It was just five miles outside Bath, and it cost two hundred and fifty pounds for the evening. Expensive, yes, but the numbers drifting in meant we would raise a good pot for the charity. Sylvie, Heather and I had spent the whole afternoon blowing up balloons, laying tables and putting place names down. I'd invited everyone I knew and we'd had almost a hundred 'promises'. Claire and Stu were coming as well as my old neighbours Lou and Steve, or 'the arsehole' as Dan used to call him. It was going to be a busy night.

The back of my neck was aching, but I was off the following day and could have a long lie-in to recover. I was wearing my emerald green maxi dress with long, gold earrings and my strappy sandals, and still had a hint of my tan left, to boost my confidence.

Heather stood at the double doors taking the tickets.

'I always get nervous at these events,' Sylvie confessed.

'I'd never have guessed,' I told her. 'You always seem as cool as a cucumber.'

'It's all an act, my dearest.' She smiled. 'Ah, here's Neil Hadley, you remember him, and the golfers I was telling you about.'

I flushed. Neil Hadley was tall, with hair silvering at the temples and that weathered look golfers get from being outdoors all the time. He was very generous to the charity, offering two free lessons and a three-course meal in the golf club afterwards. I remembered him coming in to see us a couple of months after Dan had died. Even then I had registered how good looking he was.

'Well, hello, Grace,' he smiled, offering his hand and holding mine just a second longer than necessary.

I was surprised he remembered my name. Looking into his pale grey eyes, my heart missed a beat.

'Thank you for coming, Neil, and for your generous donation.'

'My pleasure. It's such a worthy cause and, believe me, the golf club can afford it.' He smiled.

'Neil, how nice of you to come along,' Sylvie said, 'and Rob, Tom.' Sylvie knew everyone. 'Do you men have your eyes on anything tonight?'

Neil glanced fleetingly at me and I blushed. Ridiculous. I sucked in my stomach.

As they made their way into the hall, Sylvie turned to me. 'Do you remember I told you we had a large donation a while back? Nearly two thousand pounds. It was Neil. He and his wife lost a child many years ago. So tragic. He's keen to sponsor children's charities.'

'His wife?' I asked.

'Yes, but...' Sylvie turned to a couple approaching us, 'Eve, Derek. I'm so glad you could make it!'

Heather grabbed my arm, 'The auctioneer wants to start.' I closed the front doors, and we made our way into the main hall. The staff table was at the front. I stopped as I passed Claire and Stu.

'Are you two OK? I'll catch up in the break,' I said, leaning over.

Stu turned to me. 'I had the runs before coming.' He clutched his stomach. 'Bad curry last night.'

Claire patted his leg, 'You're such a martyr.'

By the time I took my seat, Sylvie was up on the stage.

'Welcome, everyone, to Project Child UK's Auction of

Promises. It's wonderful to see so many of you here, giving up your evening for this very worthy cause, and a special thank you to those who have generously donated gifts for the auction. Without your kindness and altruism, an event like this could not take place.

'Project Child UK was founded six years ago. As a social worker, I was inspired to help when...'

Sylvie's story was always compelling and she was a confident, charismatic speaker. I glanced at the posters around the room, evocative black-and-white images, photographs of high-rise blocks, the limp washing hanging on tiny balconies, reflecting the deprivation in British cities. In one, a small, emaciated girl hugged her knees. In another, staff at a food bank served a grim-faced mother and her child. They reminded me of why Sylvie and all of us at the charity felt as passionate as we did.

My eyes scanned the tables and I looked directly at Neil Hadley, who was looking straight back at me. I flushed and began to read the programme, which I knew inside out.

Sylvie drew to a close. 'So, I would like you to give a round of applause to Felix Billingham from Somerfield Properties, who's kindly agreed to serve as our auctioneer tonight.'

Everyone clapped politely and Sylvie left the stage and sat next to me.

'Well done,' I said.

'Phew. Let's hope everyone's feeling generous tonight.'

Felix was an eccentric character, wearing a beige waistcoat and red bow tie. He had an extravagant handle-bar moustache and wiry, Einstein-esque hair. 'Good evening, ladies and gentlemen. I was asking my wife before I came here tonight whether I should start with a joke to warm everyone up. She told me to avoid being too charming, witty or intellectual. Felix, just be yourself, she told me.' He laughed loudly at his own joke, his head thrown back. There were polite titters from the audience.

As Felix continued, I wondered if I would bid for anything. Some were going to be more popular than others. Family tickets for Bristol Zoo would be snapped up, as would the overnight stay at a local hotel. The ride in a hot air balloon was likely to be the most popular. That was a real coup, and I was thrilled that I'd secured it from Ballooning Lovely, after much persuasion: 'Think of the publicity it will generate.' Some would be less popular, of course. Morris dance lessons were very niche, and I couldn't imagine there would be a fight for the set of local maps.

The bids came in thick and fast. Lot twelve was the Pampering Pooches voucher: 'An aromatherapy bath and full body massage, followed by a grooming session and haircut souvenir photograph,' I read in the description. Heather was fidgeting in her chair as Felix introduced the lot.

'For the pet lovers amongst you, Pampering Pooches is offering a fantastic grooming session for one pet and a souvenir photo to take home and treasure,' he said, without a trace of irony. 'Who'd like to start us off? Shall we say ten pounds?'

Heather's hand shot into the air. It was surprisingly popular. As it rose to over twenty-five pounds, Heather looked crestfallen. The charity didn't pay much, and I knew money was tight.

'Twenty-six pounds anyone?'

Felix asked, looking over at Heather. She shook her head miserably.

'Going to the gentleman at the back at twenty-five pounds. Going, going, go...'

'Thirty pounds,' I bellowed, my voice carrying across the whole room. The other bidder threw in the towel and the Pampering Pooches voucher was mine.

'I didn't know you had a dog,' Heather said.

I grinned. 'I don't. It's yours.'

'Thank you!' she mouthed, her bottom lip quivering.

Sylvie nudged me. 'You are kind.'

The first half of the auction flew by. Neil Hadley's golf lessons led to quite fierce bidding. 'I've always fancied trying golf,' I whispered to Sylvie.

'Go for it,' she urged.

I shook my head, feeling a bit too self-conscious.

'Two one-hour lessons and a three-course dinner,' Sylvie said. 'When you think, he could have just donated the coaching.' They went for one hundred and fifty pounds. 'That's excellent,' Sylvie said, gratified.

I glanced at Neil and he raised his glass to Sylvie. Or was it me? He was an attractive man, I concluded. Generous, too.

In the break, all PCUK staff were expected to circulate and hand out the canapés and wine. Tickets were ten pounds each, so we willingly did our bit. I stopped briefly at Claire and Stu's table.

'Enjoying yourselves?' I asked.

Claire nodded. 'I'm going to get the spa voucher for two if it doesn't go up too much. Fancy it, Gracie?'

'Need you ask? I'll pay half.'

'Your neighbour Steve is a bit of a knob,' Stu whispered. 'He's been hitting the wine hard. He's smashed already.'

I circulated the room. I saw Sylvie had already got to the table with Neil Hadley and his friends. I was momentarily disappointed but then scolded myself for being silly.

My feet were beginning to ache, so I sat down and ate what was left on the platter, a wrinkly lamb samosa and a devilled egg with an unappetising gloopy-orange filling.

The second half of the auction included the bigger donations and there were some ferocious battles. The competition for the spa vouchers was reminiscent of The Hunger Games, but Claire was determined, and eventually paid one hundred and sixty pounds for them. The hot air balloon ride went for nearly four hundred pounds, people willing to pay over the odds for the charity.

'By my calculations, with the raffle at the end, we'll have made nearly eleven thousand tonight,' Sylvie beamed. 'This has been the best event by far.' She paused. 'By the way, Neil has offered to give you a golf lesson. He said he'll catch you before he leaves.'

'What?'

'Well, I mentioned that you quite fancied a lesson and he offered.'

And with that, she swept up to the stage to thank Felix and give a final speech of gratitude to the audience.

When Sylvie came off the stage with a final round of applause, I continued the conversation as if there had been no break.

'Honestly, Sylvie, I wish you hadn't organised that golf lesson with Neil.'

She looked at me as if I were saying the strangest thing she had ever heard. 'Why? You wanted to try golf; he offered. He likes you and you ob-vi-ously fancy him.' I cringed.

'Is it that obvious? Besides, you said he's married.'

'I didn't say he is married. I said he was married. Oh, for goodness sake, Grace. It's only a golf lesson. Anyway, if you did jump into bed with him, it's nobody's business but your own.'

'But Dan...'

'Dan's not around anymore and he was hardly going to win Husband of the Year. Sorry to be so blunt. Life's for living, Gracie. Neil's an attractive man. Offers like that don't come around often.' She turned abruptly as Felix Billingham left the stage. 'Felix, darling, you were absolutely brilliant.'

I returned to the foyer, to start clearing up and to wish the guests goodbye.

'We're getting a takeaway on the way home,' Stu said. 'Those canapés barely touched the sides.'

'So, the stomach has recovered, then?' Claire grinned.

'I can't wait for the spa day,' I told Claire. 'I'll settle up tomorrow.'

I began to clear up the glasses, and looked round to see Neil crossing over to me.

'I'm seriously uncoordinated,' I began. 'I've got three left feet, I mean two...'

He smiled. 'I've seen it all in golf, believe me. Try it. Perhaps we can have lunch in the clubhouse afterwards?' He was very tall, perhaps six foot. My stomach was doing funny things when I looked into his eyes again.

'Here's my card,' he said. 'Call me.'

CHAPTER SEVENTEEN

❧ Kat ❧

'Happy Housewarming!'

I heard the shout coming from outside my door. Maria stood on the step holding a large plant, its spidery leaves hanging over the terracotta pot.

'That is what you guys say in England, right? Housewarming? I didn't know if it was an American thing,' she checked.

'It is. Come in,' I stepped aside to let her pass. 'You didn't need to get me a plant.'

'Not just a plant!' She reached her other arm out from behind her back, revealing a giant-sized bottle of wine.

'Perfect, I love it.' I kissed her cheek. 'Thank you. You're my first guest. Let me give you the tour!' I grinned as we walked round the new flat.

House hunting had proven to be an exhausting task, made all the more difficult by the Montenegrin heat and foreign language. I'd traipsed round white box after white box, each kitchen more tired and old-fashioned than the last, barely understanding what the barrage of numbers and payments being thrown at me meant. Then just when I was resigning myself to staying in the apartment share with Luka's hotel receptionist friend for another month, I found the one.

It was another flat, but this time in a much smaller and more charming building. There were only six apartments, set around a small courtyard, each with its own entrance. Mine was up a set of small stone steps. The whole building was white-washed and partially covered in vine leaves. Inside, there were floor to ceiling windows in every room (even the bathroom, which would make for some rather odd baths). I loved the cool tiled floors and patches of exposed stone on some of the walls.

When the letting agent showed me the balcony, I knew I was sold. The living room led out to a small platform with wrought-iron railings and a small set of table and chairs. The view over the harbour in Tivat was perfect for people-watching and looking out to sea. I could imagine sipping fresh orange juice here in the mornings in my dressing gown or sharing a sunset meal and bottle of red with someone. Luka or Maria maybe ... Milo certainly didn't come to mind.

'This is the one,' I'd breathed, excited. The letting agent then revealed it was double my budget for rent every month.

'Whaaaat?' I tried not to show my dismay too much, but I felt set-up.

'Well, I think we can get the owner down a little bit.' Haggling had never been my forté, I was much too polite. I'd have to channel some of Rosa's negotiating skills.

I knew I'd take the flat even if I couldn't manage to knock a penny off it, and the fact it was free for me to move in a matter of days was ideal. Not that I minded sharing the flat with Luka's friend — with our opposing work schedules, we'd barely met each other — but it would be nice to have somewhere that was completely my own space. No one to steal my precious tea bags or leave hairs in the shower.

Mum agreed to help with the deposit, and I hoped my Café Lompar salary, would cover the rest. It would be tight, but just about manageable.

'I love it, Kat.' Maria gazed round. I'd invited her over for a celebratory drink at the end of moving day. It would be nice to meet up outside of work and get to grill her about Luka. 'It's very ... minimalist.'

I realised how bare the place looked without my rose-tinted glasses.

'I don't really have much stuff here. Yet. Maybe I need to go shopping.'

Maria made me a list of her favourite furniture shops in Montenegro while we poured two glasses of wine and walked out on to the balcony. It was still balmy late into the evening, and the harbour was bustling with boats docking for the night, tourists flitting between bars and fishermen carrying crates of their catches.

'Wow, it's very brave of you to move here after a holiday.' Maria clinked her glass to mine as she flopped into a chair.

'Well, I think I've always been a bit impulsive.' That was a complete lie really. I was normally so indecisive it took me longer to choose a film than it did to watch it. I suppose my decision to stay had been brave. I'd been so busy with work and finding somewhere to live, I hadn't had time to pause and process it. 'I think Luka convinced me in the end though.'

I noticed Maria's eyes widen at the name Luka. I knew there was something going on between them.

'And how do you know Luka?' she asked with fake disinterest.

'Just ... a relative, a cousin.' I was deliberately vague. 'I have some family in this area, and we decided to visit them. And I hated my job in London, so this seemed like a perfect fit. I guess I just fell in love with Montenegro.'

Maria seemed to buy it, placated.

'Tell me how you know Luka then,' I changed the subject.

'We were in school together. I don't think he took much notice of me then. You know how immature he is now? Imagine what he was like in school?'

I laughed. Luka was such a prankster, it was hard to believe he would one day be studying law.

'But we've had a bit of a fling this summer.' Maria stopped to sip her wine. 'I don't think it'll go very far though.'

I frowned, feeling oddly protective of my little brother. 'Why not?'

'Well, he'll be going to Berlin soon, and I'm off to university in Thessaloniki in September. I don't want to be stuck in Tivat forever. I've never had a long-distance relationship and I'm not sure it ever works. Have you?' She turned to look at me.

'Technically I'm in one now.' It was my turn to sip wine while I gathered my thoughts. Where to start?

Things with me and Adam were ... complicated, to say the least. I thought he was going to spontaneously combust when I told him I was going to stay in Montenegro for a while.

'Why would you do that?' he'd said, staring at me imploringly through the screen. I'd prepared myself for a shouting match, but in some ways his careful words were worse. I'd begun to regret video-calling instead of just phoning; I was forced to see every emotion on his face in minute, pixelated detail.

I had found myself chattering on and on about Café Lompar,

telling him it was run by some distant relative of Dad's, and how I'd been offered head chef. If I'd been expecting a congratulations at that, it didn't come. I went on about not wanting to work for Mark anymore. 'You could come out if you wanted to?'

Adam chose to ignore my question. 'And what does that mean for us?'

I'd let out a long breath. 'I don't know.' It was all I could come up with.

'Six years and that's all you can give me. I deserve more than this, Kat.'

It was true, he did. I knew it was awful of me to expect him to understand. I desperately didn't want to hurt him, and I desperately didn't want him to think it was anything he'd done. God, was I like Dad, shrugging off my commitments at home for a sunny life in Montenegro?

But I wasn't committed to Adam. Six years together and we weren't married, had no children, didn't own a house. The relationship had just lost its spark. Was it really the end of the line? I didn't want it to be, at least I didn't think I did.

'Can we make it work? I still want to be with you. I love you.' Even as I was saying these things, I couldn't see how it would work.

'I don't know, I need to think about it.' Adam was rarely emotional, but I could see the hurt in his eyes. I wanted to hug him. It was horrible being the guilty party.

We'd spoken a few times since then, mostly fraught exchanges about the flat. He asked little about my job in Montenegro and I felt horrendously shitty after each call.

One night last week, he'd sent a text saying I miss you.

I'd replied I love you. I want to see you again.

No response. I didn't know if I had a boyfriend or not. Didn't know if I wanted one or not. Adam and Kat. I'd thought of us as a unit for so many years. I didn't know who I was in the UK without him. Could I really just start a new life here instead?

'God, how much time have you got?' I eventually said to Maria, trying to keep it light and airy. I gave her a very distilled version of events.

'That's intense,' she said, after a while.

I agreed.

'Well, I think Milo's pleased that you're here, with or without baggage,' she smiled.

I fought hard not to blush. It felt wrong after talking about Adam. No, Milo would not be a distraction here, or the reason for the end of my relationship. Adonis or not. I was here for work and family. And myself, nothing else.

We chatted for the rest of the evening. It was nice to have a friend. Although she was a few years younger than me, we shared a similar sense of humour. Maria eventually made her excuses and headed to the door.

'Will you come round tomorrow?' I asked. 'I need help deciding what to wear for this newspaper thing.' I felt embarrassed asking. A local Tivat newspaper had asked to profile Café Lompar and the new head chef, as Rosa had put it. I had to admit it was flattering. I had no idea what to wear and needed advice. Usually I'd ask Mum, but it felt wrong doing that for a photograph I knew would be taken with Rosa.

Maria nodded, 'Of course, you will look amazing. Our incredible head chef!'

After she'd gone, I went back out to the balcony, working up the courage to call Adam. Another glass of wine helped. He didn't answer at first, and I felt relief, but just as I was about to end the call, he flashed up on screen. I braced myself for the icy 'Hello' I knew would be coming.

'Hi,' he called out. He was actually smiling. I instantly relaxed, leaning back in the chair.

'Everything alright?'

We chatted about his work, a minor celebrity whose wedding he'd recently catered for. It felt a lot easier, like having the old Adam back. Not a word was mentioned about my job. Or Montenegro. It reminded me how self-absorbed Adam could be.

'Things are good here too,' I tried, but Adam didn't respond, distracted by something off screen.

'I'm sorry, Kat, I need to go and help Michaela.'

I jolted. 'What's she doing there?' It came out gravelly and annoyed.

'Michaela's lease was up on her flat, so I've let her stay here. It's only fair, I need someone to cover the rent while you're away.' He shrugged, laidback. As if having another woman move in was totally natural.

Michaela was a colleague of Adam's. He often joked she was his 'work-wife'. I'd met her a few times. She was nice, very glamorous for the kitchen, but nice. I'd always suspected she liked Adam. I'd caught her messaging him on days off and sending pictures of food ideas. I was amazed she'd been this bold though.

'That's nice for you,' I said, my voice shaking. 'I bet she's happy.'

Adam gave me a look of triumph. I could tell he knew he had the upper hand here: I couldn't exactly complain when I was the one that up and left.

I still felt the anger thud through my chest. I wondered if this was why he looked so happy at the start of the call. It was all smugness.

'Oh, come on, Kat, don't be like that. She's just taking the spare room. I can't exactly pay this rent on my own, and I can't expect you back anytime soon. You've made that quite clear.'

I didn't know how to feel.

'Makes sense I guess,' I said, aware my tone was more passive-aggressive than I liked. Adam looked amused. I continued, 'Anyway, I'd better go, the local newspaper is doing an article on me tomorrow, so I need my rest.' I shut the phone off.

I knew I was being childish and unfair. It would be difficult for Adam to keep covering the rent in London on his own, especially as I was here indefinitely. What did I expect?

I watched the busy street below. I knew I'd have to make my mind up about Adam soon. We couldn't carry on like this: separated by thousands of miles, bickering and sniping at each other. Could we make it work or did things have to end?

I checked the time; it was much later than I expected. I felt weary, sobering up from the wine and aching from the move. I had to shake it off. I had a big day coming up.

CHAPTER EIGHTEEN

 Grace

'So, what do you wear to play golf?' I asked Claire. Didn't golfers wear 'slacks' like something out of the 1970s? I imagined lots of diamond-patterned jumpers, Rupert Bear-like trousers and a visor. There was definitely a dress code, and I didn't want to arrive wearing something totally inappropriate.

'Something sporty, but not those.' She pointed to my sweaty, baggy T-shirt and leggings. 'He'd run a mile!'

'I've been clearing the spare room,' I said defensively and then giggled.

Claire had called round after school, my house being on her route home. She'd taken to calling around more often lately. She was stressing about Laura and Liam's GCSE exams. She wasn't sure Laura had done enough revision since River came on the scene and Liam was cool as a cucumber about the whole thing.

'River told Liam the other night that the universe has plans for all of us, but we have to trust it, and allow it to guide us on the right path. I'm sure that just gave Liam the excuse not to do any work. I honestly could have throttled him.' Claire pulled a face as she sipped the tea I'd just handed her. 'What the hell is this?'

'Green tea. Don't you like it?' I asked, wide-eyed.

'Oh gawd, when did you start drinking green tea?'

'It's meant to help you lose weight,' I said, as if this would make any difference before my golf lesson tomorrow with Neil.

'You're like the drama teacher in school. I've only ever seen her drink green tea and eat Ryvita with a scraping of Philadelphia. I've seen more curves on a bread stick.' She sighed. 'You're perfect as you are, Grace. Just be yourself and enjoy the date.'

'I'm not sure it is a date,' I countered.

'Of course it is. He's offered the lesson for free followed by lunch. What else is it?'

'What will people think? Dan only died a year ago.' I got up, 'I'll make us a coffee.'

'Stop worrying about what people think! Gracie, I love you to bits, you know that, but you've always been a people pleaser. You've put Dan or Kat before your own needs. Isn't it time you just did something for yourself?'

I shrugged. She was right, of course. 'I just don't know what I want anymore. Besides, you're making me nervous now.' I smiled. 'Do you know that I haven't been on a date since I met Dan? About thirty odd years ago. What will I talk about? I don't think I've got anything interesting to say.'

'Don't be daft,' Claire reassured. 'It's like riding a bike, so to speak. Don't over-think it. Do laugh at his jokes, though. Men love that. Let him pay for lunch. Offer just once and then give in graciously. Ooh, and don't do that self-deprecating thing you do.'

'What do you mean that self-deprecating thing?' I asked.

'Do you know how often you put yourself down? Like then, I haven't got anything interesting to say. He likes you. Accept it.'

He did seem to like me, I had to admit that.

'This is all just first night nerves,' Claire went on. 'If I were in your shoes, I'd be like a dog on heat. You remember Jenny, the PE teacher? She tells me all the golfers swoon when he's around and not just the ladies. I thought he was hot when I saw him at the auction. Don't get me wrong. I love Stu but he's like an old pair of slippers – familiar, comfy and a bit frayed around the edges. Now, if I got the chance to try on a pair of Christian Louboutin heels,' she paused for dramatic effect, 'I'd be there like a shot.'

'That's a terrible metaphor.' I laughed.

She kissed my cheek, 'Promise to tell me all about it tomorrow night.'

I barely slept that night and got up early to shower and do my hair. I opted for a pair of navy capri pants, a pale blue T-shirt and grey canvas shoes, not wanting to look like I'd tried too hard. I was meeting him at eleven o'clock and I couldn't face breakfast. When I'd spoken to Kat last night, I'd mentioned nothing about my 'date'. She might feel some loyalty to her father or more likely, the idea of her mother dating might make her cringe.

When I pulled into the golf course car park, it was just starting to pick with rain. Typical – the curse of frizzy hair. Neil came to greet me almost as soon as I walked into reception.

'Hi, Grace,' he said, his face breaking into a big smile. He kissed me lightly on the cheek.

'Neil. Thanks so much for this.'

'Not at all. I've been looking forward to it.' He ushered me to one of the leather seats in the foyer, his hand resting in the small of my back. 'Another lesson is just about to finish. So, have you played golf at all before?'

'Does crazy golf count?' I asked.

He shook his head.

'No, then I'm an absolute virgin,' I stammered. What? Virgin? I cursed myself. Neil grinned. 'No, I've never played before.'

Gosh, he was handsome. He was dressed in a pair of beige chinos and a navy polo shirt with the club's logo on his chest. Definitely no knitted cardigan draped over his shoulders. His thighs brushed mine lightly.

'Are you nervous?' he asked.

'Is it that obvious?'

He smiled a lot, I noticed. 'We won't do too much today. Just a half-hour session and I'll show you the clubs and a few things on posture. We'll start with a few basic shots around the green. It's good fun. You'll enjoy yourself. Come on, let's get going. The lesson should have finished by now.'

Thankfully, the rain stopped as Neil led me to the green.

'Now, it's probably best to start with three clubs, a driver, a putter and sand wedge. We don't want to over-complicate things,' he said.

'Three?'

'Many golfers carry up to fourteen. If we opt for wood, with more loft, it can reduce sidespin, so shots fly straighter.' He grinned at my puzzled face. 'Don't worry about the details, just relax.' He turned around and took his time choosing the right club from the caddy, as if he were sampling a fine wine. 'Yes, this one will suit you.'

'So how long have you been playing golf?' I asked.

'I started playing with my father when I was eight. I love it!' he said.

'I'd never have guessed.' I smiled.

'Ah, sarcasm. Let's see how clever you'll be when you've tried a few shots.' He was fun to be with and the banter made me relax. I loved his passion for golf. It was infectious.

'Now I'm going to just get you to hold the club first,' he said. 'Are you right-handed?' I nodded. 'Hold the club aloft and put the pad of your little finger around the top of the club. Close your hand, and the knuckle of your first finger should be placed there. Your right thumb to the left of your grip.'

'What?' I laughed. I'd never felt so uncoordinated in my life.

He came over and placed his hand over mine, his grip tight and his hands warm. A thrill shot through me.

'Now for your posture. Let your arms hang straight from your shoulders, so your hands are below your chin. With your knees slightly flexed and shoulders over toes. That's it.'

I mirrored his movements, as far as I could.

'Now, do you mind?' he asked, politely, as he put his hands on my hips. 'Just relax your pelvis so you stay centred.'

My heart was beating fast in my chest and a sudden image of him flashed in my mind, Neil holding my hips as I writhed on top of him in bed.

'Are you OK?' he asked.

'I think I'm getting it,' I breathed. 'Definitely.' I willed myself to concentrate.

We spent the next half hour practising putting small shots, me constantly missing the ball and displaying the coordination of a two-year old. He was very patient.

'Come on,' he said at last, after my fifth miss in a row, 'let's go in and have a bite to eat.'

'I'm hopeless,' I said, then bit my lip as I remembered Claire's advice to stop putting myself down.

'No, really. Everyone is the same. Did you enjoy it?' he asked. 'And you can be honest.'

'I did, I really did.' I didn't tell him that most of my enjoyment came from being close to a very attractive man.

The clubhouse was bustling with the early lunch crowd as we entered the restaurant, 'The Nineteenth Hole'. Neil knew everyone and people nodded and called his name as he led me to a table by the window giving us panoramic views over the course. The table had 'reserved' on it, so Neil had obviously planned for us to sit in the best seat.

'The food is nice here. I know the menu inside out,' he said, ruefully.

He ordered a steak sandwich and I went for the grilled halloumi and olive salad, trying to show some decorum.

I did have a small, chilled glass of rosé Pinot Grigio. The conversation flowed easily, which surprised me. He asked me about the charity and how I was involved.

'It's a great charity,' he said. 'I don't know if Sylvie told you, but I lost my son Max when he was eight. A car knocked him off his bike. I can't begin to describe the nightmare Cass and I went through. The strain it put on us. It broke us, really.' He shook his head. 'We have an older son, Ollie. Poor Ollie. We neglected him at the time, for years. Enveloped in our own grief.'

He stopped. 'Anyway, that was fifteen years ago, now. I still think about him every day and what he'd be like at twenty-three.

I don't suppose you ever get over something like this.' His grey eyes had a faraway look.

'Gosh, I'm sorry, Neil.'

'It's fine,' he said. 'Well, not fine. Sorry, it's not the thing to talk about on a first da—' He stopped himself. 'Anyway, you've been through a loss, too.'

And because he was being so open with me and it seemed natural, I told him about Dan and Rosa and Luka.

'If you'd asked me last year, I would have said I had a good marriage. But now, I honestly think I was kidding myself. It's not just the whole other family. It's the way we were. I'd suppressed everything I wanted. He was quite a dominant man. Nobody guessed that, though.'

Neil listened, really listened and we got on well. I didn't feel awkward at all.

'Have you had many relationships since you and your wife divorced?'

'Short term. Nothing special. One of them was so high maintenance, she kept asking what I was thinking every two minutes. If I was quiet, she kept pestering to know if I was OK. It was exhausting,' he said.

'I'll try not to be too needy, then.' I laughed.

'It did put me off dating for a while and you kind of get used to your own company.' He smiled. 'Look, Grace, I've really enjoyed myself today. I'd like to do it again. A proper date. Would that be OK?'

'I'd like that.'

'Let me get this,' Neil said, 'I insist. I'll call you tomorrow and we'll book somewhere for Friday night, if you're free.'

When I left the club, he kissed my cheek again. I felt like skipping with happiness. If this were a Richard Curtis movie, an Ed Sheeran song would be playing in the background and Neil would have chased after me, pinned me to the car and kissed me passionately. Instead, as I reached the incline to the car park, the rain, that had been holding back all morning, suddenly came down in a torrent. I was drenched by the time I slid into the driving seat, my hair stuck to my forehead. It didn't wipe the smile off my face.

I stopped in Waitrose on the way home and treated myself to some nice flowers and a bottle of wine. Claire phoned almost as soon as I was home.

'Well, how did it go?' she asked without any preamble.

'Amazing! I really enjoyed myself. He was so attentive. I was absolutely crap at golf. Just as I suspected. But I might go again.'

'Of course you'll go again,' said Claire.

'He was very touch-feely. I felt like a teenager.'

'Aw, it's so exciting at the beginning of a relationship. When everything they say is so interesting and all you can do is think about having sex with them.'

'Hmm,' I agreed, lost in thought.

'Enjoy it while you can. Then all you end up doing is picking up their dirty socks and pants or hoovering up their toenail clippings. Stu has got this snorting habit. Every morning he goes into the bathroom and snorts like a distressed pig. He says it's his sinuses. Disgusting!' Claire shuddered. 'If only they stayed like they were at the beginning, the airbrushed version of themselves.' She sighed, 'Then, I suppose I have one or two disgusting habits of my own. He hates the way I pick my teeth after a meal.'

'I snore,' I admitted.

'You do. So, are you seeing him again?'

'Yes, Friday. Anyway, what's the news with you?'

'Well, Laura and Liam had their English language exams today. Liam said it was easy and Laura just said it went as expected. Make of that what you will.'

'I'm sure they'll be fine.'

'Look, I'm going to have to go,' Claire sighed. 'It's all very well living vicariously through you, but I've got a pile of essays discussing whether Wolsey's failure to gain an annulment for Henry VIII was the reason he fell from power.'

'I'd better let you get on, then.' I laughed, feeling lighter than I had felt for a long time.

CHAPTER NINETEEN

 Kat

I looked around the spotless kitchen with pride. I'd come to Café Lompar earlier than usual today, wanting to make sure the kitchen was sparkling. I'd moved some of the clutter to the store cupboard and shifted the stand mixer to pride of place on the countertop. Today was the big day.

I heard glasses smashing from the front of the restaurant. Sticking my head over the top of the door, I saw a frowning Rosa bent over between two tables. I could tell she was swearing, even though it was in Montenegrin. I stepped through, not wanting to startle her.

'You're in early too?' I asked.

She looked up briefly, barely noticing me, and wiped her brow.

'Just trying to tidy up.' She leant over, flicking an invisible spot of dirt. 'I thought I told my staff to make sure it was clean every night before they go home.' She muttered something else under her breath. I'd never seen Rosa stressed before; she was usually the queen of cool, everything under her control. I wondered if she too had been up all night worrying about this article.

Newspaper reviews and critic visits were commonplace in Truffles, but Mark would have every member of staff in two hours early, treating it like a military operation, barking orders,

157

shouting expletives and undermining everyone. It always felt like punishment, not the celebration of our good work that it should have been.

Here, I felt a different kind of nervous energy, knowing it was me, as head chef, under the spotlight. I couldn't tell if the sickly feeling in my stomach was a good or bad thing. I'd carefully laid out my outfit, wanting to look professional. The photographer was coming first, to get some pictures of Rosa and me before service began, candid shots of the Café in action. I'd chosen a black T-shirt and long brightly coloured skirt, hoping it would look casual but put-together. I'd curled my hair for the first time in months. I'd even chosen a bright red lipstick, a tip I'd read on a website about how to look good in professional photos. I worried now that the lipstick would smudge in the heat of the kitchen and make me look more Joker-esque than red-carpet siren.

'You look nice, Kat,' Rosa said, looking up at me for the first time.

'So do you.' I gestured to the half-up half-down style she had done with her hair, a departure from the usual sleek bun.

'Yes, I thought I'd try something new.' She carried a brush and pan over from the corner for the broken glass.

'Here let me help.'

'No, no,' she batted me away. 'I need to get this right.'

I picked up her abandoned cloth and cleaned a few tables. It was superfluous; the restaurant was gleaming. Luka had told me Rosa was a control freak when it came to the business. I hadn't seen it so far myself; she always seemed happy for me to make changes in the kitchen. The way she was now, forensically positioning the miniature potted plants on each table, chimed with Luka's assessment.

'I like these.' I indicated the new linen napkins she'd laid out.

'They don't look old-fashioned?' she asked, frowning.

'Not at all. I was going to say they look really modern.'

She carried on rushing around.

'Have you had many newspapers come here?' I asked, tentatively. I didn't want to sound patronising.

Rosa finally paused and looked at me. 'Well, not recently. We did when we first opened, but I think Café Lompar became ... more like a family favourite. You know, always there, always the same. But now things are different.'

'In a good way?' I asked, unable to read her expression.

'In a great way. You've been such a good addition to the place, Kat. You know I think you're wonderful,' she carried on, cleaning as she spoke. It felt there was a but coming.

'What are you worried about then?' I asked. I hoped I wasn't pushing it.

Rosa didn't answer for a beat and then sighed. 'Me. I'm worried it was boring because of me. I'm getting old now. What if people think, We don't want to go to that place where the boring old woman will talk our ears off?'

I sat down and pulled a nearby chair out for her. I was glad she didn't leave me hanging and perched herself down.

'You know that's ridiculous, don't you?' I said. 'You're not old at all.'

Rosa scoffed, 'Please, my boobs fall down to my waist now when I have no bra on.' A smile broke on her face.

'At least you have them. This is all bra with me.' I pointed at my own chest. We both laughed. 'Rosa, the customers come here because of you. Food is one thing, but you make this place so special. It's such a beautiful place to work, I love it. I feel so relaxed here and I think the customers do too. That's because of you.'

She smiled and touched my arm.

'You remind me so much of your father. You looked so much like him then.'

I froze. It was the first time she'd mentioned Dad to me, and I still felt that if I showed Rosa any sympathy, I'd be betraying Mum. But today she seemed almost vulnerable. Everyone has insecurities, no matter how much they deny it or put on a brave face.

I wondered how losing Dad had made her feel, whether she'd had these worries before or not. Losing Dad had made me feel less like myself, less confident, as if I was just going through the motions in life. I wonder if it affected Rosa in the same way.

I was starting to talk about Dad more to Luka too. He'd tell me his memories, and it was strange to hear about a man I was so close to from someone else. The other day he'd told me that Dad sent him a new bookmark on the first day of every month without fail, because of some in-joke they'd had years ago. That was so Dad, but must have been very time-consuming for him.

'Did you even use all those bookmarks?' I'd asked Luka in disbelief.

'Not really, but he'd write some goofy message on the back. I've kept them all.'

'Can I see them one day?' Luka had agreed, and we'd hugged. It must feel strange for him too, talking about Dad to me.

'It's funny,' I said, 'people always saw Dad as stuffy and earnest. With me, he never was.'

'Earnest?' Luka had looked puzzled.

'Serious.'

Luka nodded.

Now Rosa had opened the door to a conversation about Dad, and I did want to understand how she felt, but I just wasn't ready and I changed the subject, aware I was dangerously close to crying.

'I'm worried that people who read this will stop coming because of me,' I said.

'Why?'

'Well, the food is so amazing in this country. I don't know, people might think, who is this English girl trying to change our recipes? I feel I have to prove myself today.'

'Nonsense.' Rosa waved her hand. 'Now that is ridiculous. You're the best thing to happen to Montenegrin cooking since we discovered you could cook prawns in wine.' We both laughed. I knew she was trying to reassure me, but I still felt the same. Today was judgement day: my future in Montenegro hung in the balance.

'Come on, I have more cleaning to do,' Rosa stood up, her energy relentless. 'Do you want to help me carry in the new glasses? I'm a disaster on my own.'

The photographer was a bit gruff, and we struggled to communicate. He resorted to acting out where he wanted me to stand and what he wanted me to do. He seemed unhappy, constantly moving me and Rosa to various spots in the restaurant, before looking at the images and shaking his head. It was not a great start. When the journalist arrived, I was so relieved she spoke English.

He lurked in the background, snapping various objects in the restaurant and occasionally crouching down to get a picture at table-level. It was distracting, but I left Lovro preparing the ingredients while I sat down and spoke to the journalist. She was a woman in her thirties and was very smiley, which instantly put me at ease. I tried to remind myself that this wasn't a story of huge national importance, as my heart pounded.

'So, obviously we've heard great things about the restaurant and the work you're doing,' she smiled encouragingly. 'My friends have raved about the tapas nights, so I've been very excited to come here, especially on seafood night. The piece will be mostly about the food, but I want to get an idea about your background. How did you get in to cooking? Where did you work before?'

I relaxed as I relayed the rehearsed story about my interest in cooking. I got in early that some of my relatives were Montenegrin and I'd always been fascinated with the food in the area. She was sympathetic when I talked about a death in the family, and wanting to visit 'my roots'.

'I fell in love with the place. Montenegro is such a beautiful country and the food just suits it perfectly. I love the inspiration it takes from its neighbours and the combination of rich meats and light flavours is perfect. Good food done well, that's all I've ever wanted to cook, and here I get to play around with that.' God, I was impressed with my answer. I hadn't planned on that soundbite coming out. Take that, Mark Douvall.

'And how well do you know Rosa?' the journalist asked, pen poised over her neat notebook. Her scribblings looked indecipherable. I wasn't sure if it was shorthand or a different language.

'Erm...' I faltered. I hadn't prepared for such a direct question. The journalist furrowed her brow a little.

'She was a relative of my father's. Through marriage.' Shit, could that sound any dodgier? 'I got to know her well while I was out here, and we just clicked. I offered to help out in the restaurant one night and...' I was babbling.

Luckily, she breezed past it and asked about my favourite recipes. This was my strong point, and I started talking about our sesame calamari, when I saw Lovro walk over, a grave look on his face.

'I'm sorry. Chef, can I speak to you?' he interrupted.

'I'll be coming to help in a few minutes,' I reassured him, knowing Lovro could be a bit of a flapper. He sometimes panicked about minor details, but he was such an efficient help in the kitchen.

'I need to show you something.' He looked more and more terror-stricken.

'Please go ahead,' the journalist smiled. 'I think I've got everything I need anyway. Thank you so much, Kat. I can't wait to try the seafood specials.'

'Yes, we'll get them sent over promptly. I do hope you enjoy them.' I waved, calling Rosa over to offer her a drink. I felt Lovro's desperation, like a child pulling on my arm.

'What is it?' I hissed as we got in the kitchen. Things were going well, but Lovro's concern was starting to frighten me.

'It's the seafood fridge.' He motioned me over, eyeing the machine as if it was some dangerous animal.

I swung open the door. The salty smell was pungent, and I didn't need to pick up the food to know it was decaying. I touched one of the sea bass.

'It's warm,' I confirmed. 'What happened?' I turned to Lovro. He looked dumbfounded.

I was sure I checked the fridge when I got in to work this morning. Only a fool wouldn't check. But I was preoccupied. Had I checked it?

Milo had brought a double order of seafood after a trip on the water yesterday, ready for our seafood spectacular night. He was out on his boat on a tourist charter all day today. The floor was falling away beneath me and a whooshing feeling rocked my stomach as the reality sunk in.

'Someone turned the fridge off.'

CHAPTER TWENTY

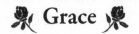 Grace

I hurriedly loaded the dishwasher before work, a family-sized one that I only filled every three days. Since I'd returned from Montenegro, I was acutely aware that everything about this house was family-sized, far too big for one. I rattled around in it like a rogue lipstick top in an over-roomy handbag. Four bedrooms, three bathrooms, a study, two reception rooms and a snug. All that cleaning! I'd taken to racing upstairs when I wanted the loo, so I didn't have to clean more than one toilet every week.

I'd started browsing through Rightmove in the evenings, fantasising about a cosy cottage just big enough for me, and Kat when she visited. Did I need a place in the city anymore? I only worked part-time and Project Child's offices were on the edge of town. All that traffic when I just wanted a few things from the shop? All those fumes?

I saw the cottage in the estate agent's window when I went for a walk during my lunch break at work. It was halfway between Cheddar and Bath. In the photos Willow Cottage was picture perfect, with a lavender-flanked path, pink geranium-planted baskets and wisteria growing around the front door. Dan would have hated it. He preferred steel and glass structures, clinical and minimalist, with all the charm of a dentist's surgery. Last year, our neighbour's house had sold within a week, so I felt confident I could start looking. Town houses in Bath were at a premium for those who could afford the property prices and astronomical council tax. The cottage was about twelve miles from Bath, but the commute wouldn't be too long if I left early and it looked worth the compromise. Wasn't that the word Jules Hudson always used in Escape to the Country? Compromise.

On the way back from work, the evening light was mellowing into pastel shades of coral and rose. The little church where Dan was buried was on the outskirts of the city. At first, I had gone almost every day after the funeral. Since I'd returned from Montenegro, however, I hadn't been and now I felt guilty. Dan's parents were buried in Montenegro. We had spoken about it once, where Dan would be buried. Morbid perhaps, but it was when we were much younger, when death seemed remote, untouchable, something that happened to other people. Dan said he felt more British than Montenegrin and wanted to stay here, to be with us.

The typically English medieval stone church stood proudly in rolling countryside. Dan's grave was in the shaded western corner and the limestone headstone had only been erected a month before we left for Montenegro:

In memory of Danilo Lompar

Beloved husband and devoted father

Died 5th May, 2018

Much loved

It was simple but what Dan would have wanted. I had tissues in my pocket and a bottle of water in the car. I set about cleaning the rain-spattered headstone and wished I'd brought some flowers. An elderly couple was visiting a relative's grave a few rows away and they nodded – the camaraderie of grief.

I tried to picture Dan under the earth and shivered, despite the still warm day. He should be living and breathing and in bed with me. I was struck anew by the sadness of it all. He was taken far too soon, and it was unfair. It was trite but true. I had always assumed we'd enjoy an old age together and I'd worried how he would cope if I went first. Tears pricked my eyes.

Did Rosa want to visit Dan's grave? I couldn't feel too sorry for her. It was the price she had to pay for being the mistress, the other woman.

I kneeled down beside the grave. I was too self-conscious to talk aloud to him with that elderly couple close by. I looked up to see the woman carefully placing pink and white peonies inside the lid of a cemetery vase.

I got back in the car, feeling subdued. I would have a glass of wine tonight and send Kat the estate agent's photographs of Willow Cottage. It felt odd to think how life was already moving on.

That Thursday night I booked a viewing, but Claire had a parents' evening and couldn't come with me. I was half-tempted to postpone it, but got a grip of myself. I could do this. There was no one else who had to like this place, just me, and that was quite exciting.

This is idyllic, I thought, as I passed a corner shop and post office, a church and two village pubs. Down a little country lane stood a row of honey-stoned cottages with a 'For Sale' sign posted in the front garden of the end one. I could imagine Jules telling me that it was not too rural and had a great community feel.

The estate agent was waiting in her car outside and came out as I approached. She wore a navy suit and had sky-high heels. She thrust out her hand. 'I'm Jasmine from Utopian Estates. Mrs Lompar?' Her eyebrows were unconvincingly over-arched, giving her an odd, quizzical look.

'We've had a lot of interest in the cottage,' she said. I knew this might be a line she gave everyone, but I could imagine that I wasn't the only one enamoured with Willow Cottage.

I was determined to play it cool but, once inside, I couldn't help myself. It was both cosy and airy, with stripped back beams and exposed brickwork. I was already imagining Christmas there with a tree next to the wood burner.

'It's over two hundred years old,' said Jasmine, 'but it is spacious and modern.'

'Oh my God, I love it,' I gasped, as we entered the kitchen, then, remembering I'd promised myself not to be too keen, said, 'Hmm, the kitchen is nicely refurbished.' The sleek, duck-egg blue units and the island in the middle looked like they came from the pages of an interior design magazine. French doors led to the pretty, walled garden outside.

'The garden is very manageable,' Jasmine said walking through the French doors.

'It's perf ... perfectly manageable,' I agreed, following her outside.

The garden was brimming with foxgloves, alliums and penstemon. A rustic style pergola was planted with wisteria, clematis and fragrant roses and honeysuckle, the top adorned with fairy lights. I would love enhancing this space, awakening my inner gardener that had slept for too long.

By the time we saw the two pretty bedrooms upstairs, all decorum had been abandoned and I all but squealed with delight.

Jasmine smiled widely, clearly recognising she was on the verge of a sale. 'It is decorated to a very high standard,' she said superfluously, her hand sweeping round the pale-sand coloured carpeting, the creamy walls and floral bedding.

I gasped when I saw the spa-like bathroom. I envisaged myself soaking in the bath, ivory candles lit, and pan pipes tootling away as I was transported to some Zen-like state of ecstasy.

I was practically ready to sign the dotted line as Jasmine locked the door behind us. I could imagine her telling her husband later, 'We can afford a holiday this year. I've just sold that cottage in Meadow Ponsbury.'

'It was perfect,' I told Neil, as I sipped a chilled glass of Chardonnay at lunchtime in Le Jardin, a newly opened restaurant in town. 'I'm waiting to see if my offer is accepted, but Jasmine, the estate agent, said that as it was only five thousand below the asking, it should be fine.'

Neil smiled. 'It's exciting finding a new place. A new start.' He gazed into my eyes. He'd insisted on picking me up earlier from my place and I'd agreed, knowing I could then have a glass of wine. I felt ridiculously nervous.

'So what's your place like?' I asked, hoping it didn't sound as if I was angling for an invite. Everything you said was loaded with double meaning in this awkward dance of dating. I felt a complete novice.

'It's a two-bed apartment on the other side of town. Cass got the house when we split four years ago. Ollie was still in uni then and it seemed more practical. It's a nice place. Ground floor with a little terrace at the back. It suits me.'

'I've been wanting to try this place since it opened,' I said, as the waitress brought over the sea bream, clams and samphire. Neil had opted for the same and the conversation flowed as easily as the wine.

I looked out through the bifold doors at the back of the restaurant and the eponymous cottage garden of Le Jardin. Rambling roses decorated the archway to the lawn beyond, where peonies with voluptuous white, pink, coral and magenta petals vied for position in raised beds, midnight-blue delphinium and irises peeping out shyly behind.

'It's almost like a Monet painting,' I told Neil. I could gaze at gardens like this for hours. 'Do you like gardening?'

'I'd like to learn more about it, but mine is postage-stamp-sized at the apartment, I'm afraid.'

'I used to own a garden nursery,' I confessed.

'Wow, a woman of many talents,' he teased. 'What happened? I take it you no longer have it.'

He listened intently as I explained about Gardening with Grace and why I gave it up. 'I'd like to start a business again. The charity work is enjoyable, but I've been there a long time now and it's not really fulfilling.' I paused, realising it was the first time I'd admitted this to myself, and how relaxed I was feeling. 'You're very easy to talk to.'

'You look sensational in that colour,' he told me and I blushed. I was wearing a light blue linen shirt and white jeans. It was so long since a man had paid me any compliments. Dan barely noticed how I looked. Despite my protestations to Claire that his absences meant we had a great sex life, the truth was it had dwindled to almost nothing. I hadn't known I was competing with the voluptuous Rosa, the Eva Mendez lookalike. I should be grateful for small mercies!

Neil, though, seemed to genuinely think me attractive; either that, or he was an Oscar-worthy actor. I felt heady with the wine and the compliments.

'Come to mine for coffee,' he said, and I nodded. He ordered a taxi. My head was spinning as we walked outside, and I loved the feeling of his strong hand as it gripped mine. In the back of the taxi, I leaned my head on his shoulder and he kissed my hair gently. Sex was on the agenda and I was excited.

That was until we pulled up outside a Georgian townhouse, and my stomach flipped over. I felt as if someone had thrown ice-cold water into my face. Bloody hell, was I really going to do this?

I hadn't had sex with another man for thirty-odd years. This was terrifying. I thanked the Lord I had put on matching underwear – my ivory lace knickers and bra. But I couldn't kid myself I had a good body. It was middle-aged and it sagged in places, dimpled in others, and looked decidedly creased and crumpled, like a linen dress that had been worn too long at a wedding. As Neil leaned over to pay the driver, I thought about how athletic he was. Lusted by everyone in the golf club, Claire had said. Oh God, oh God! I smiled but felt sick with nerves.

Once inside the hallway, Neil pushed me back against the door

171

and kissed me hard, passionately, on the lips. Then he pulled me by the hand into his bedroom. My heart pounded with nerves and excitement as we fell back onto his bed. His kisses were slow now, tender and sensitive.

Then he stopped. 'Is this OK? There's no rush, but I've been thinking about doing this all through lunch.'

I nodded and kissed him again, as he undid my shirt and I slid my jeans down my legs. I felt self-conscious and it was as awkward and ungainly as first-time sex always is. But it felt so good to be desired. He stirred feelings in me I had forgotten I had, feelings I had buried for a long time, devoted to a man who didn't really love me.

Afterwards, I lay in his arms, listening to the hum of traffic and laughter and chatter of people as they walked along the pavement outside. I was grinning. It was over and almost a relief. I had just had sex with a hot man, who was not my husband and it wasn't a disaster. Quite the opposite.

Suddenly, my phone vibrated on the bedside table. I leaned over and saw 'Utopian Estates' light up the screen.

'Is that Grace Lompar?'

'Yes.'

'It's Jasmine Allen here, from the estate agent. It's good news, Grace.'

CHAPTER TWENTY-ONE

❧ Kat ❧

My mind whirred as I stared into the very dark, very silent fridge, in total disbelief. How could this be happening? Today of all days?

There were so many possibilities. Had Lovro turned it off by accident? Had someone else done it — sabotage, maybe? Or was it just me? I'd been playing around with the fridge yesterday, maybe I pressed something. Whatever the reason, the fact was I hadn't checked the bloody thing this morning. I could have kicked myself. I'd cleaned pretty much everything else to within an inch of its life.

'Oh my God,' I was almost hyperventilating, adrenaline shooting through me. What was I going to do? Could this possibly be salvaged?

'Do we keep seafood anywhere else?' I asked Lovro, although I knew the answer. I felt like the worst head chef on the planet. I could hear Mark scoffing from two thousand miles away.

'What should we do?' Lovro looked terrified. I didn't know what to say.

I leant on the open fridge door, contemplating the options. Run away, cry, hibernate? Get a last-minute flight to England before anyone noticed?

No, I was a fighter; Dad had made me this way. I pictured his hands on my shoulders, like it was his fiftieth birthday all over again. 'You do what you have to do, Kit Kat.' There had to be a way to salvage this.

'OK, two options,' I said to Lovro, sounding my thoughts aloud. 'Either we find some other way of getting seafood at the last minute, or we'll have to announce we're changing the menu for tonight. We've got enough lamb, haven't we? Good. Maybe we could do a lamb main and some tapas-style starters.'

I looked around. We'd been gearing up for seafood night all week, our other ingredients were limited. The food at Café Lompar was all fresh; we didn't keep a massive store cupboard, but surely I could think on my feet and cobble something together?

'Everything alright?' Rosa stuck her head into the kitchen and frowned when she saw us. It was time to own up.

'Not really,' I was desperate not to let her down. But this was her restaurant, she needed to know about the impending disaster. 'Rosa, I'm so sorry, I've made a terrible mistake. The fridge is off, and all our seafood is rotten. I don't know what happened. I can't think why I would have turned it off, but I didn't check it was on.' I felt tears work their way up to my eyes. 'I'm so, so sorry, I don't want to ruin our review.'

To my astonishment, Rosa smiled.

'Don't worry, Kat. We've weathered worse storms than this.' She walked over to the fridge and started playing around with the back of it. 'Hmm, it looks like it should be on. I wonder if it has a fault. I will get my electrician to come round tomorrow,' she said matter-of-factly.

I exhaled. It was a relief to know I hadn't caused the problem, but I still should have found this out earlier, and I was left with no menu for tonight.

'I don't know what to do, Rosa, the whole meal was based on seafood. I can try and adapt the dishes, do something with the lamb maybe, but it won't be what our diners expect.'

Rosa thought for a moment. Lovro watched us both anxiously. I realised I was biting my nails, an awful habit for a chef, and stopped myself. My T-shirt felt damp with sweat. I peered out into the restaurant.

Service had not started and we had no customers yet, but some of the wait staff had started to filter in. Maria waved at me as she put on her Café-Lompar-branded apron, then must have read the concern on my face because she mouthed, 'Are you OK?'

I nodded and turned back.

Rosa said, 'I have an idea. Do you think you and Lovro can prepare a starter without seafood? Buy us some time? I might be able to get some more, ask our other suppliers. Jasna and Gordana may be able to get some at the last minute.'

'Of course, we can pull something together.' I was relieved to have something to focus on, to dampen down the guilt I still felt. 'Thanks, Rosa, this is going to cost money, I know.'

'Don't worry about it – these things are sent to test us. I'm meant to be speaking to the journalist now. We need someone to stall her,' she said, casting her eye around.

I winked at Rosa, and shouted, 'Maria!'

'How long left on the dolmiades?' I called out to Lovro.

'Two minutes, Chef.'

'Perfect,' I fished my arancini out of the fryer, before drying the oil off the golden-brown risotto balls and balancing each one on top of the spots of tomato gel I'd piped on to each plate. The starter was beginning to come together: a gorgeous trio of vine-wrapped roasted vegetables, arancini (the risotto originally meant to be filled with mussels and scallops), and a pea and mint gazpacho. It wouldn't have been my first choice to serve to the critics but with the minimalist plating we'd gone for they actually looked quite impressive. I resisted the urge to high-five Lovro. He was really improving. I'd noticed he had an eye for presentation. He might have even got a job in Truffles with a bit more experience.

I called for service, as the first plates were finally ready, and I could hear the relaxed chatter of diners mixing with the trickle of pouring wine and clinking ice. It was my favourite sound: a happy restaurant. Maria was keeping the journalist occupied with a wine-tasting session at the bar; I don't how she'd pulled that out of the bag, but it seemed to be going well as I noticed the two women giggling.

'Make sure these go to table five first.' I gave one of the waiters a knowing look, as he came to collect the starters.

Rosa had managed to get her hands on a carton of fresh tuna, a result of a begging Facebook message to her supply chain. It was arriving imminently. I knew I wouldn't have time to do anything incredibly fancy with it. I was planning just to grill the steaks and serve with plenty of garlic, parsley and lemon. It was a shame I wouldn't get to make my sesame calamari and stuffed sea bream. I'd been planning it for so long I was starting to have dreams about it. I'd even drawn a picture of the plates to stick up on the fridge in the new apartment as inspiration.

As I moved around the kitchen, I felt happy and sharp, in my element. I loved not having rigid menus, and the freedom to create whatever I wanted. It was invigorating. Now the panic had left my body, the adrenaline helped me work faster and more efficiently. Every now and again the photographer would take a snap of us cooking, and I felt a swell of pride.

'Kat!'

I heard the familiar Montenegrin voice and spun round to see Milo. He almost filled the doorway to the kitchen with his broad shoulders and the crates he was carrying.

'What are you doing here?' I asked, hurrying over to help him.

'Delivery for you.' He held out the crates. I saw the shiny scales of bream and the curled tentacles of the squid. The salty smell almost made my heart burst. I couldn't believe it.

Milo shrugged as he read my delight. 'I saw Rosa's message on the Facebook group.'

'I thought you were busy with that tourist trip today?' Lovro came over to help us unpack.

'Luckily, some of them were interested in catching fish. They agreed to make an unscheduled stop in Tivat, provided they got to try some of it – the freshest seafood they will have ever tasted.'

I noticed the group of ten queuing up at the front of the restaurant.

'You're quite the salesman. Tell them their meal is on the house,' I said instantly.

'They've agreed to half price.' Milo grinned. God, I'd never felt such an urge to kiss someone. Yes, the man was an absolute knock-out, but the way he'd come to help so readily made him even more attractive. I looked away, overwhelmed.

'Thank you so so much! I don't know what to say, Milo.'

'Well, I wouldn't mind a meal on the house if I'm going to be staying here for the next hour or two,' he teased.

'I'm on it,' Lovro ran back to the kitchen.

'Thank you,' I said again, impulsively touching Milo on the arm.

I perched a chair for him at the end of one of the units so we could chat while Lovro and I worked, although having him there was very distracting. I met Milo's gaze for what felt like the hundredth time in minutes. Those dark, glittering eyes.

Rosa popped in as things were slowing down. She gave me a thumbs up. 'I just heard the newspaper staff calling the food delicious. Great job, you two!'

She looked surprised to see Milo in the room, but then gave me a sly look. 'Look, it's your hero, Kat.'

I put my feet up on the sofa next to me. I didn't think I'd ever felt so exhausted after a shift, even after the gruelling pace of Truffles. There'd been so many ups and downs today. I was too tired to contemplate what the review might say, and I was glad I had a few days to decompress before it was due to be published.

I appreciated the silence of my little flat. If I held my breath, I was convinced I could hear the sea outside. It made a nice change from London: Adam's moaning about his job every night, and the constant headache of traffic.

I felt another pang of guilt. I knew I had to make a decision about Adam. I checked my phone.

'How did it go today?' A text message from Mum. Nothing else. I knew I'd told Adam about the newspaper as well, but clearly it hadn't stuck in his mind.

I texted back straight away. 'Lots of drama but good, I think. Will tell you all tomorrow. I'm too shattered to remember my own name now. How's the packing going?'

Mum had sent me a flurry of pictures of her new house. It looked like the pages of a Cath Kidston catalogue. I couldn't believe I'd be spending Christmas in a different house this year. No Dad, no more Truffles and now my childhood home gone. Who would have thought it? It felt very odd that Mum would be living somewhere new. Both of us moving on.

'Claire's been helping – even dragged Liam in. Laura's too busy snogging her new boyfriend though!'

'Gross,' I messaged back, laughing to myself.

'Doesn't seem that long ago that it was you and Adam.'

'Don't remind me.'

I pictured a teenage Adam, back in our catering college days. I felt a swell of affection for his boyish face and cheeky charm. But when I thought of him now, that warmth just wasn't there anymore. I couldn't see us ever being that couple again. Didn't I deserve someone that would put me first? Above everything?

When Mum didn't reply, I messaged again, 'I think I'm going to break up with Adam.'

CHAPTER TWENTY-TWO

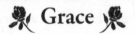 Grace

The kitchen looked like one of those TV programmes where hoarders squeeze through tiny corridors between mounds of rubbish. I was moving in a couple of weeks and had been trying to clear a room every week. Easier said than done when you've been living in a house for over twenty-six years. I found a tin of butter beans going back ten years and packs of flour I'd forgotten. There were some cupboards that I was almost too afraid to open.

It probably wasn't the best time to invite Neil over for lunch, I thought, surveying the chaos around me, but just thinking of him made me smile. I'd put on a simple jersey dress and bright red lipstick and felt younger than I had in years.

I rushed to the door as soon as it rang. 'Well, hello, Mr—' I said in a husky voice.

The rest of the sentence caught in my throat as Laura flew into my arms. I looked over her shoulder and saw a pink, sparkly suitcase propped up behind her.

'Auntie Grace,' she sobbed into my ear, her face streaked with mascara. 'I can't stand it any longer. She's such a bitch to me!'

'Come in, sweetheart.' I tried to drag her into the hall as she clung to my shoulder. I glanced discreetly at my watch. Neil was due in less than ten minutes.

'Can I stay with you, please? It'll only be for a little while until River finds us somewhere to live,' she said, breathless with all the crying.

I gulped. This wasn't good. I wondered what catastrophe had occurred. Claire hadn't said anything last night. She had moaned about Laura and River spending too much time together, but no more so than usual.

'Come in and have a cup of tea and tell me all about it.' I looked in despair at the wet patch on my shoulder of my dress.

Once Laura was sitting in the armchair in the lounge and she'd had a few sips of tea, she seemed to calm down.

'Have you got any biscuits? I was too upset to eat breakfast.'

I watched as she dunked a chocolate digestive into her tea, a soggy corner slipping unnoticed into her mug. Her blue glittery fingernails were bitten and uneven. She was a pretty girl, her blonde wavy hair tied up in a top-knot high on her head, and her large, blue eyes watery with tears.

It reminded me of the days I would comfort Kat over some boy when she was Laura's age and I felt a dull ache in my heart for those times. It was complicated with Kat at the moment, working with Rosa and being so far away. She had a right to her own life, to make her own decisions, but I missed her and wondered if we'd ever be the same with one another again.

'So, what happened?' I asked.

'You know what Mum's like,' she hiccupped. 'She just overreacts to everything. River had dinner with us last night and it was all fine. He went home, but...' she hesitated, 'he sneaked back in.'

'Ah. How did your mum find out?'

'She came in this morning. She swore she knocked.' Laura rolled her eyes. 'Well, I didn't hear her. Or River. When she saw him, she went completely apeshit. I've never seen her like that before.' Another fresh bout of sobbing. 'She told me I was a selfish cow. I was disrespecting her and Dad. I'd changed since I'd met River. Blah blah blah.' She looked at me all wide-eyed and innocent. 'I mean, she knows we're sleeping together. I'm sixteen, for God's sake. I'm an adult!'

I could picture the scene and didn't quite know what to say, so I kept quiet as she went on.

'It was so embarrassing. And poor River had just woken up and couldn't get out of bed. He was naked.' She gave a little smile at the memory. 'Then she turned on him, telling him he was a lazy, good-for-nothing layabout and a slob! That he'd never amount to anything.'

'What did River say?'

'He's so sweet-natured, he just took it. Dad was in work, otherwise he would have calmed her down. My arse of a brother found it amusing. He's such a pig.'

'She just had a shock,' I argued, trying to defend Claire. 'I'm sure she'll calm down soon. And it was a bit naughty of you.'

'But Auntie Grace, what harm are we doing? We love each other. I don't think Mum has a clue what it's like to be in love, I really don't.'

'Well, actually, your mum and dad were crazy about each other.' I thought about Claire and Stu when they first met and how they couldn't keep their hands off each other, how I'd often walk into the kitchen and they were snogging each other's faces off. Claire had a permanent red rash around her mouth.

She held her hand up as if to block what I was saying. 'Ugh, just don't go there, pur-lease! Anyway, I saw red,' Laura went on, trying to retrieve the biscuit remains from the bottom of her mug. 'I told her she was just jealous. She couldn't stand to see me happy. That it was obvious she never liked River. Which she didn't deny, by the way.'

'She only wants the best for you,' I said.

'Does she? What's so wrong with River? She keeps banging on about him being older than me, but it's only five years. There's three years between her and Dad, but of course she never sees that as a problem. What a bloody hypocrite!'

Would there be any point telling her that they met when Claire was older than Laura, and that the gap isn't so wide as you get older? Probably not.

'Anyway, I packed a suitcase and told her I was leaving. Please can I stay a little while until I figure out what to do? River's finished uni and he's hoping to sell his paintings. We can find somewhere to rent.'

The doorbell cut into her conversation.

'If that's Mum, tell her I'm staying here.'

'I'm expecting a friend over,' I told her, hurriedly. 'I'll just say I'm busy. Don't do anything rash. Stay here and I'll talk to your mother. Does she know you're here?'

Laura shook her head. 'She might think I've gone to River's place, but his mum has had another baby. There's seven of them. They're really crammed. River has to share his bedroom with his brothers 'cause it's a three-bedroom house. That's why it's easier at mine. Can't Mum see that?'

Neil stood at the door, his face full of hope, holding a bouquet of white roses and green hydrangea. He stepped forward and I blocked the entrance.

'I'm so sorry, Neil,' I whispered, 'but my niece has just turned up. It's a family crisis. Can we do this again?'

Hurt briefly crossed his face, 'Uh, yes, yes – of course,' he stuttered.

'I'll explain later.' I was too flustered to give more reassurance.

He stood there for a moment and I tried to read his thoughts, but he turned abruptly away. Damn. I'd really been looking forward to this lunch and what was on the menu afterwards. I just hoped he would understand.

I needed to phone Claire as soon as I could. At least Laura would be safe with me.

She insisted on showing me some of River's paintings on her phone. 'He's so talented,' she said. I scrolled through the images of a haggard, red-faced man, his eyes hideously over-sized in a scarlet face; another of a naked woman, her face stretched, and her mouth elongated into a scream. Her body was painted lilac with darker purple legs.

My mind searched for something positive to say, 'They're very ... interesting.'

'Aren't they?' Laura didn't pick up on my hesitation. 'They depict the horror of modern-day life and how people struggle mentally to cope. They're really thought-provoking.' I don't profess to know much about art, but I didn't think River was going to display his work in any galleries soon.

'He likes purple and red, doesn't he?' I said, seeing yet another 'character' with a purple body. 'Has he had much interest in his work?'

'His tutor said that he was really talented. He did get a third-class honours, but that's because his mother had just had his sister. He found it hard to concentrate.'

She had a point, I thought. 'Look, you take your things upstairs and I'll phone your mum, tell her you're safe.'

I went to the garden, so I was out of earshot, and phoned Claire. She picked up on the second ring.

Before I could speak, Claire launched into a tirade. 'Oh, Grace. I've had a hell of a morning! I've had a massive fight with Laura, and she's gone. Packed her bags to stay with River! That arsehole. I've phoned Stu and he just told me to calm down, which was very helpful. I don't know what to do.'

'Well, she's not with River. She's here with me.'

'What! Send her home immediately!' Claire ordered.

'Don't you think it would be better for her to stay a few days until you calm ... until she sees sense.' I was treading on egg shells with both of them.

'I thought you at least would be on my side!' she shot back. 'She's talking about going to live with him and not taking her A levels. She's going to ruin her life for that waste-of-space!'

I spent the next few minutes soothing Claire until she finally agreed to let Laura stay for a while.

I looked forlornly at the Asian chicken salad I had made for Neil and me. I knew Laura was vegetarian and was trying to become an all-out vegan. I needed to do a shop.

'How do you fancy an omelette?' I asked her.

She giggled, 'I don't eat any dairy products, Auntie Grace.'

'I've got some pasta. I could make a tomato sauce. Are you allowed to eat cheese?'

She shook her head vigorously. 'You are a case,' she said patronisingly. 'Is it OK if River comes to dinner tonight, Auntie Grace?'

I nodded.

I thought about texting Kat for vegan meal inspiration, but never felt I could when she was working. Luckily, the supermarket came to the rescue and I stocked up on some vegan meals. We'd have Malaysian vegetable laksa with rice noodles, followed by pineapple and coconut ice cream. I just hoped that this arrangement wouldn't be for too long, as I had so much to do with the house move. When I saw the bill at the end of the shop, my eyes watered. The cost of vegan food was daylight robbery.

When I got home, I could hear the television blaring as I walked up the path. Laura and River were sprawled on the sofa watching Netflix. River stood up when I entered the lounge. He was very tall and gangly, his dark hair caught up in a man-bun.

He thrust out his hand, 'Nice to meet you, Mrs Lompar.'

'Grace, please,' I said. 'You two relax here. I've got a few jobs to do and then I'll make us some dinner. What are you watching?'

'Black Mirror. Fancy you having Netflix!' Laura said, as if I was ninety. 'It's the second series. Have you seen it?'

'No, I haven't. Would you turn the volume down just a tad?' I pleaded. It was so loud it was giving me a headache. I had texted Neil in the car outside Waitrose trying to explain about Laura, but he still hadn't replied.

The kitchen table was piled high with sheets of paper and paints messily strewn on top of some kitchen roll. River had obviously been painting that afternoon.

After a while, Laura came in the kitchen. 'Anything I can do to help?' she asked. She seemed eager to please.

'He seems very nice,' I told her.

Her eyes sparkled, 'Do you think so? He's just so interesting and when he chats about his paintings, I could listen to him for hours.' She caught me glancing at the purple smudges on my walnut kitchen table. Laura rubbed at them hurriedly. 'It'll come off. Mum manages to get it off.'

Claire often moaned about it to me, but I didn't let on.

'Are we eating in here or in the dining room? I could lay the table.'

'Thanks. We'll probably go in the dining room. It'll save clearing the table now.'

'It's strange without Uncle Dan here?' Laura said. 'Do you miss him?'

'Yes, of course.'

'Auntie Grace, can River stay tonight?'

That was a swift change of subject, I thought. 'I'm afraid not, Laura. I have to abide by your mother's rules. It's only fair.'

She pouted, 'Just for tonight. He can't sleep at home.'

'Laura, no,' I said firmly. 'Now lay the table, please.'

She trotted out of the kitchen, no doubt rolling her eyes. It must be very wearing for Claire, I thought for the umpteenth time.

At dinner, Laura and River sat opposite me, holding hands under the table and eating with just a fork, not easy with noodles. He wore a collection of leather bracelets and his forearms were covered in tattoos. His hair flopped over his eyes, but he smiled a lot.

'So, what are you doing at the moment? Laura says you've just finished uni.' I hoped it didn't sound too much like an interview.

'I thought I'd have the summer off. Take stock.'

'Laura showed me some of your work. Interesting,' I said. 'It's about mental health, she told me.'

'Yes, that's right. I want to portray the effect modern society has on the mind. The colours reflect the inward agony. Purple and red to signify bleeding inside. It just came to me one day. No one seems to be doing this. I think art is a visceral thing. It comes from deep inside, if you're lucky enough to listen to it. Really listen to it.'

Oh, gawd, he was a bit pompous about it. 'Do you think it'll sell?'

'Auntie!' Laura protested.

'It's OK,' he said, looking up at me. 'It's not about selling.'

'River and I will clear up,' Laura offered.

'No, it's OK. It's only filling the dishwasher.'

'I'll make us a cup of tea then,' Laura said and they retreated to the living room, Within seconds, Black Mirror was once again blaring at two hundred decibels from the tv. I took my cup of tea to bed, hoping Claire and Laura would make up soon.

As I got into bed, I phoned Neil. I wondered why he hadn't answered my text. It rang a few times before he eventually picked up.

'Hi Neil,' I said, 'I want to apologise for earlier.' I realised I sounded a bit stiff and formal.

'There's no need, I understand. Family dynamics and all that.' Was he irritated? I didn't know him well enough to tell. Surely not. He had his own family. He knew what it was like. These early days were a minefield.

'My niece Laura has had a huge argument with my sister Claire. It's over this new boyfriend of hers. I've agreed to let her stay a few days.'

'It's fine,' he said. I was sure he sighed.

'I'm disappointed, too, but it will only be a night or two and I could come over to you. I texted you earlier.' God, I hoped I didn't sound too desperate.

'Honestly, stop worrying, Grace. I was teaching a lesson on the course late afternoon. Julia Hurst, the owner of the florist Blooming Lovely.'

I felt a stab of jealousy. This was ridiculous. He was bound to teach lots of women.

'Look, I've got an early start tomorrow. We'll rearrange soon.'

'Fuck,' I said aloud as I ended the call.

CHAPTER TWENTY-THREE

❦ Kat ❦

The television presenter was speaking a stream of Montenegrin I didn't understand while I rushed round the apartment. I threw on a T-shirt and denim shorts, searching for the right pair of sandals. I checked my make-up in the mirror, knowing it would have to do. I was too excited to put more effort in. I grabbed my bag and sunglasses and headed for the door, swearing as I almost forgot my keys.

Today was the day the review came out.

We'd been nervously anticipating it all week. I was simultaneously dreading it and electrified. I'd agreed to meet Luka at the restaurant so we could read the review together and he could translate if needed. We were then planning a day out together – Luka was finally taking me to Dubrovnik, to either celebrate or commiserate.

'Definitely celebrate,' he'd said, earlier in the week.

'I'm not so sure. With the whole seafood debacle, I don't think I was on my best game. I didn't have time to properly marinate my calamari and get the right balance of flavours on the bream.' I shook my head. I'd gone over the night's events again and again, berating myself for fridge-gate.

'Yeah, you're right, it was disgusting actually,' Luka grimaced.

I hit him on the arm, 'Are you ever serious?'

'Not when you talk such nonsense! You know it is going to be a good review.'

I wish I'd felt as confident as him. Even Rosa had seemed quieter than usual yesterday, more brisk when I tried to make conversation over the pass. As I hurried along the pavement, dodging market stalls and tourists lazily strolling along, I kept my eyes peeled for newspapers. Eventually I found the right stall.

Mine and Rosa's faces were on the front cover – the front cover! In a column of teasers for the main stories inside. Grainy but definitely us. I handed over the money for five copies of the Pobjeda, the national paper, one to send back to Mum, one I was tempted to send to Mark as a fuck you, and the rest for me. My first review as head chef! Although I couldn't read it all, it had to be good if we were on the front cover, surely?

I started to run to Café Lompar, when I spotted Luka heading towards me, his arms full of copies. He grinned widely as he saw me and held them up in the air.

'Is it good?' I asked, as we reached each other.

'Good? It's fantastic!' Luka flung his arms around me, causing a few of my copies to go tumbling.

The relief was intense. It was strange knowing there was a whole newspaper article written about me that I couldn't read. I couldn't wait to find out the details. The journalist had told us there would be an abbreviated article posted online in English as well so I'd be able to send it to Mum later.

I followed Luka into the empty restaurant, quickly pulling out two chairs at the front, no time to marvel at the glittering Adriatic and pink sky ahead of us. I opened one of my copies, smoothing the paper out so it didn't crinkle.

'Read it,' I ordered Luka, reminding myself of Mark every time there was a press release about Truffles. Maybe the pressure of being at the head of the kitchen would turn me into a female version of him. I hoped not.

'OK, OK,' he laughed, leaning over my copy. 'Who would have thought it would take an English chef to cook some of the best Montenegrin food in the Bay of Kotor? Head chef Kat Lompar, 24, of Café Lompar, has proved herself as a master of flavours and elevated some classic dishes to fine dining standard.'

Luka read on, a detailed piece about the quality of the meals and exciting twists on traditional dishes. It felt like listening to music, and my head was so full of joy I almost couldn't take in the rest of his words.

I felt absolutely and thoroughly relieved. This move had been such a big step in my career and such a gamble, I felt it was all hanging on the line. And more importantly, I felt personally responsible to Rosa. This was her restaurant after all, and I had been so scared to let her down.

I realised I was clutching my other copies so tightly one of the corners was started to tear. I let out a huge breath and put them down, determined to soak up every last ray of pleasure from this.

'Kat proved herself to be unflappable as a chef, even with a last-minute change of menu, and provided plates that not only looked stunning and tasted divine, but came from the heart of this family-run restaurant. A must-visit in Tivat.'

'Thank God for that.' I let my head drop back.

'Mum will be so thrilled,' Luka said, patting my arm. 'Are you happy now?'

'Yes, extremely.'

I noticed Luka looked tentative, like a puppy about to get a telling off.

'Please don't kill me, but I can't come to Dubrovnik with you today. I know, I know, I'm so sorry. I need to get some paperwork done in prep for uni. I didn't realise when the deadline was until this morning,' he continued with his biggest puppy dog eyes, knowing I couldn't protest if it was for his university course. To be honest, I felt so elated after the review, I didn't mind.

'Don't worry, we'll go another time.' I was quite happy with the prospect of a day relaxing on the beach, maybe a celebratory cocktail with Maria.

Luka shook his head. 'No, no, you will be going to Dubrovnik today. I have an alternative arrangement.'

I didn't have time to work it out myself, before a smiling Milo stepped into the restaurant. He was wearing a cool blue shirt, unbuttoned just the right amount, and fixed me with that gaze that caused my pulse to quicken.

'I hear congratulations are in order,' he said as I stood up to greet him. I caught a whiff of his aftershave, masculine, but not a hint of Old Spice, as he leaned in to kiss my cheek. 'Well done, Kat.'

'Thank you.' I noticed Luka smiling at us, puppy dog eyes now replaced by an impish grin. I wondered how long this had been planned, and cursed myself for not putting more effort into my make-up.

An hour later I found myself on the boat, heading out of the bay towards Croatia. It would be the first time I'd left Montenegro since I'd arrived, but so many friends had told me about

Dubrovnik, I'd always been desperate to see the city. It was so close by – just under two hours by car and even faster by boat, I was promised.

The sun was starting to get stronger as we whizzed across the water. Milo turned her up to full throttle and the boat pitched back and gained speed.

'Not too scared?' he asked, checking my face.

I sat just behind him, relaxing. 'Bring it, Martinović,' I laughed.

I hadn't been out on Milo's boat since that glorious day with Mum and Luka. That was the day I'd started working at Café Lompar, when I'd filled in for their previous chef. The day that changed everything. I couldn't believe how much had happened since then. I felt like a different person.

I was glad the engine on the boat was so loud; it was difficult to speak over the roar. My stomach fizzed with nerves at spending the day with Milo. I didn't want us to run out of conversation or for him to think I was boring. I was scared he'd realise how fragile I felt inside.

I watched his profile, steering us past a small island dense with lush green forest. This was so beautiful. Milo reminded me of a singer Mum liked called Jack Savoretti, with his strong Mediterranean features and dark curly hair. I couldn't help but stare at him, blushing when he glanced back at me. I'd been so busy in Café Lompar, I don't think I'd realised how much I fancied him until now. It burned inside me. Had I ever fancied Adam this much? We'd been together so long, it was hard to remember.

It felt wrong to think about Adam today. Although I'd made the decision to end things between us, I hadn't told him yet. I'd sat on the sofa every night this week, my phone in my hand, psyching myself up to do it. But every night I'd found an excuse. I was too tired, or worried my phone would run out of battery, or didn't want to disturb him at work. All pathetic, I knew. I knew the conversation would be so much gentler, so much better in person. Adam and I just didn't communicate over the phone, never really had. Still, I didn't exactly have a choice, living in Montenegro, unless I went over for a weekend trip. As things stood, I was in a relationship, but here on the boat with Milo Martinović, that was hard to remember.

'Wow, it's beautiful,' I breathed as we rounded the corner and the red roofs of Dubrovnik came into view. I couldn't believe I was staring at the city I'd seen in photographs and on TV shows so many times. 'How often do you come here?' I asked Milo, the engine now quieter as we slowed down.

'Many times. Dubrovnik by boat is one of our most popular tours.'

'Oh.' I was momentarily disappointed. This wasn't the special day for him that it was for me. Was it just another work day? My excitement slipped away a little. Then the way Milo looked at me with his long lashes and dark eyes brought it back.

'I've never really explored the city though, always been here with work,' he said. 'I think it will be ... fun today.'

I smiled. God, I felt hungry for him. This was like an out-of-body experience: being on a boat, in Croatia's most famous city, with a gorgeous man and a rave review as head chef. I felt light, floating, for the first time since Dad's death.

Milo docked the boat at an empty space in the harbour, tying it to one of the posts. It gave me a chance to glance at myself in my pocket mirror. The power of a tan meant I didn't look quite as washed out as usual without my foundation. My hair had been ravaged by the boat journey and looked a tangled mess. I didn't have a brush, maybe I could stop and buy one somewhere, pretend I was going to the loo? I told myself off. I must try not to ruin this day with anguish and nerves.

Milo was saying something to a man on the stone harbour wall. I couldn't tell whether it was in Croatian or Montenegrin. I asked Milo as he turned round to help me out of the boat, trying to ignore the pleasure I felt with my hand in his.

'Croatian,' he shrugged. 'But it's very similar to Montenegrin, very easy to understand.'

'I don't think I'll ever understand the language,' I said, impressed.

'Do you speak any other languages?'

'No.' I felt totally inadequate. 'Us Brits usually expect everyone else to be able to speak to us.' Luckily, Milo laughed.

'I think you probably understand more Montenegrin than you think.'

We strolled along the harbour towards the city. The city walls were much higher and more imposing than in Kotor, a gentle sandy colour in this light, and the red roofs cut a dramatic skyline. The place was crawling with tourists. We had to dodge to the side every few paces to avoid being in other people's photographs, like doing a secret dance. We carried on into the heart of the city, past thriving restaurants and tacky tourist shops. Shouts came from all directions, inviting us to 'Join for a walking tour' or 'Game of Thrones Museum this way'.

'Are you a Game of Thrones fan?' I asked Milo, remembering

the way Adam would be glued to the screen every week, the curtains drawn to shield the TV from any sunlight. Every time I caught a glimpse of the show, there would either be a naked woman or blood-filled battle.

'No, not really,' Milo shrugged. 'Dubrovnik has really capitalised on it, though.'

He was right, the programme was everywhere. From shops selling merchandise to tour operators advertising the 'full G.O.T experience', it was unavoidable. There was even a re-enactment going on further down the street, the crowd cheering, their cameras held high to catch it all. Milo and I got swarmed by a Game of Thrones walking tour, pressing us together. I was acutely aware of his bare forearm against mine and had to prise myself away.

Dubrovnik was such a beautiful, historic city, and yet the streets were so crowded, I was beginning to feel I was overheating. The hot air was suffocating.

'Come on,' Milo pulled my elbow, 'there's a lookout point on the City Walls just up here.' He steered me to the side before I was swept away by the crowd.

'Yes, get me off this street,' I murmured, as we climbed the narrow steps between two buildings.

Reaching the top was like entering another world. We were on top of the city walls, stepping onto a platform with views over the whole city, framed by mountains and dazzling sea. Away from the main street, I could breathe.

'This is much better,' I said to Milo. He looked as relieved as I did. 'Can we stay up here?'

Milo pointed towards a small rooftop bar a little way along the walls.

'Perfect.'

'As a London girl, I thought you'd be right at home in the crowds,' Milo said, once we were sitting down. Fairy lights were strung from the trellis above our heads, with just a few occupied tables around us. The crashing waves made a nice backdrop as we chatted, sitting next to each other.

'I think Tivat has changed me,' I said, sipping my ice-cold wine. 'I used to love how busy it was when I first moved to London, but now I can't wait to get back to peace and quiet. Have you always lived in Tivat?'

'I grew up in Cetinje,' Milo told me, 'with my father and sister. My mother died when I was eleven so my dad looked after us.' He looked down.

'That must have been hard for him?'

'It was. He worked a lot and drank a lot. He wasn't always there for us, but he did his best. I had to ... grow up quickly and help care for my sister. We didn't always have a lot of money, so I moved to the coast, to Tivat, to set up the business. My sister looks after my dad now, so it helps that I can send them money.' He paused, wiping the condensation from his glass. 'I am sorry, I don't normally tell people this.'

'No, I want to hear it. Your family are very lucky to have you,' I said. It was touching.

'It's hard being away from them, but I think that's why I've got so close to Rosa and Luka. He's like a little brother to me.'

'An annoying one.' I smiled. I didn't know how much Milo knew of our situation, but right then I didn't want to hide it from him, especially after he'd been so honest with me.

I took a deep breath. 'I don't know how much you know about

me and Luka, but he's my half-brother. After my father died, we found out he had this other family and...'

'I know,' Milo said. I didn't know how to feel at this, but Milo was so gentle and encouraging. 'I met your father a few times when he came to visit Luka. He was such a nice man, although it doesn't excuse what he did to you. You know, Luka talked about you for years. He begged your father for information about his sister, but was told nothing. He was desperate to meet you.'

'I had no idea Luka existed,' I said, enraptured. Luka had never told me this. I wondered if he'd seen pictures of me before, but decided he couldn't have as he didn't recognise us on the boat.

'When he died, Luka didn't know what to do, whether to make contact with you or not. He didn't know if you knew about him or what you'd say. He was so thrilled when you came over, he called me in the middle of work!'

I smiled. I loved Luka, in a strange way. He was family to me. Despite Dad's betrayal I was unbelievably happy to have him in my life. Why couldn't Dad do this when he was alive? I didn't think I would ever understand.

'Well,' I smiled at him, 'I'm happy I'm here too.'

I stumbled out of the bar, still singing Dancing Queen. As the fresh night air hit my face, I could tell I'd had too many. Milo and I had been bar-hopping all day, weaving our way between rooftop bars across the city, our own private tour. We'd eaten a meal, but I'd since topped up with a few more glasses of wine before I'd coerced Milo into a cheesy tourist bar on the seafront blaring out Abba songs. He'd protested, but eventually I'd had him shimmying to Waterloo.

He laughed now, putting his arm around me. 'Why did you make me do that?' We'd become a bit more touchy-feely as the day had gone on, our legs touching as we sat together. The wine had ended my resolve to keep it platonic between us. I couldn't help it when Milo looked so handsome.

'How should we get back?' I asked, gesturing at the harbour. 'Will you be all right to sail?'

'I think so. I didn't want to tell you, but I've been drinking water all day, secretly filming you for a documentary about drunken chefs,' he joked.

'Stop it,' I said. 'Seriously?'

'Yes, I'm fine, honestly. I wouldn't sail the boat otherwise. I've spent too much money on it.' He paused. 'Are you OK?'

I looked up at him, feeling warm all over. I wanted Milo. Now. I leaned close.

'I'm more than OK,' I said. 'I've had a great time today.'

Milo leaned in towards me, his hands on my waist.

'Me too,' he said. 'Although I've been distracted for hours, thinking how much I want to kiss you.'

I pulled him in closer to the wall, not caring about the tourists milling around us. 'Milo Martinović, let me show you.'

CHAPTER TWENTY-FOUR

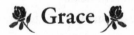 Grace

It was my day off. I sat up in bed, propped up by my pillows, listening to the silence. My bed was angled to face the window. Birdsong filtered through, the most optimistic soundtrack to start my day. I had moved in nearly a week ago, the house sale going through surprisingly quickly, and Meadow Ponsbury was living up to its promise. Boxes were still stacked in the spare room and kitchen, but it was already feeling like home. I had chosen this place myself and I didn't realise what a joy that would be. I felt like a butterfly emerging from a cocoon.

I wasn't unhappy with Dan, but I could see now that I had suppressed my own feelings and opinions. I hadn't even realised it was happening.

Laura had left after a couple of days, finally realising that I wasn't any more liberal than her mother. Things were strained between her and Claire, and Stu didn't seem to be much help. The GCSE results were due this morning. It had been bad enough waiting for Kat's results – having twins must be double the angst.

I'd always remember Dan's disappointment when Kat didn't have straight A grades. He was careful to hide it from her, but she knew. He was such an academic snob.

'Since when did GCSE grades reflect the measure of a person?' I'd argued that night as I took off my make up before getting into bed.

'She won't get into top universities with those grades. Grade C in maths!' He shook his head.

'Dan, perhaps she doesn't want to follow your path.'

'Have you been putting ideas into her head?'

'Like what? That she can choose her own future, that she can study what she wants to? Ideas like that, you mean?'

He retreated to his book. That was his default position: pout and ignore me. I was glad Kat stuck to her guns.

Kat had Facetimed a few nights ago, anxiously waiting for the review the local newspaper had written about Café Lompar. Her skin was biscuit-coloured and she was more relaxed than I've ever seen her, drinking wine on the balcony with the picture-perfect indigo sea beyond. I had a feeling it wasn't just the restaurant giving her that sparkle. Her eyes lit up whenever she spoke of Milo. I was relieved she'd decided to give Adam the heave-ho.

Things between Neil and I were back on an even keel after I had practically barred him from entering my house when Laura was with me, and I had seen him a couple of times since. The sex was even better and I smiled whenever I thought of him.

The phone ringing punctured my reverie.

'Well, the twins have had their results,' Claire began. I was trying desperately to read her tone, but she was staying bland.

'And?' I asked.

After a beat, Claire burst out, 'They've both done brilliantly! Well, Liam did better than I expected. Two 7s, four 6s and five 4s.' She laughed. 'I know, it sounds like a bloody Chinese takeaway order. So, he's going to sixth form college next year. And Laura has smashed it. Two 9s, three 8s and six grade 7s. How she managed it with all her dramas, I'll never know!'

'God, that's fantastic!' I sighed with relief. 'I bet Stu's delighted, too. Where are they now?'

'Liam's gone into town with Josh and Matt. The three Musketeers. No doubt he'll come back pissed. And guess where Laura is?'

'With River?'

'Yep. I could see her mind ticking over today, though, with her friends all chatting about college. I hope she can see she'll miss out if she doesn't go. She wants to do the sciences and maths. The world could be her oyster if she sees past the love goggles!' Claire sighed, 'I don't know, you get them through the toddler age without them getting run over or drowning in a paddling pool and you think it'll be plain sailing after that. Anyway, how're you settling in? Have you met any of the neighbours yet?'

'Only the ones next door. They're both retired. She brought round a homemade red velvet cake on Monday.'

'Sounds good,' Claire said, 'I do feel a bit flat. I was hoping we'd all be celebrating as a family at lunch. Well, we are all at Noir tomorrow. I've never been before so I hope it's not too fancy. River's coming. I'll need you there as reinforcement.'

'Thanks for booking there. Kat wants us to try out the menu and report back. You know what she's like – never off duty! Why don't you come to Zumba with me this afternoon?'

'I'd rather have a root canal! I'm going to have an early gin to celebrate doing something right as a parent at last.'

After lunch, I tried on a few sporty outfits ready for the

Zumba class. I'd bought some patterned Lycra leggings a couple of years ago in my last aborted foray into fitness. When I tried wiggling them over my knees, they wouldn't budge. Could you put weight on your knees? I was regretting eating the rest of the red velvet cake at lunch. I opted for black stretchy leggings and a voluminous T-shirt, hoping it would hide a multitude of sins.

As I approached the village hall, I could hear Ricky Martin's 'La Mordidita' blaring from the hall. I loved the song, but the fast beat did make me feel a bit nervous. Perhaps I should have practised for a while first with a few YouTube videos in the living room. Two women were bouncing in ahead of me, jiggling their narrow hips as if they couldn't wait to get started. I was about to turn back, but another group was heading in behind me. I was trapped.

The hall was surprisingly packed. A woman in her forties was on the stage, wearing an orange vest top and grey leggings tighter than cling film. Her long black hair swayed as she twisted her hips and lifted her legs to touch her elbows in time with the music. She waved and beckoned us in. It was another five minutes before the class began. Why on earth had everyone already started?

'Come on in, ladies. Let's get this par-tay started!' she yelled above the music.

Was there no gradual warm-up? I sidled as close as I could to the back wall.

Without stopping, she shimmied over to turn the music down. 'Welcome, everyone and especially the newbies. I'm Rach. Let's start with a few gentle warm-ups,' she said, doing box steps and rolling her arms at the same time. Gentle?

God, why hadn't I joined tai-chi or yoga? I was wheezing and puce by the end of the first song, which segued without stopping into the next. I caught the eye of the woman next to me, and she smiled sympathetically. After about forty minutes, I gave up, collapsing on to one of the chairs at the back. The woman who'd caught my eye earlier was also sitting the final couple of songs out and we smiled at each other again. Meanwhile, Rach was still pounding on the stage, barely breaking into a sweat.

My legs ached as I made dinner later, last night's leftover lasagne with a salad that had seen better days. I wondered what I could watch on TV. Grantchester or Lewis perhaps. Even choosing what I wanted to watch on television was a revelation. Dan preferred thrillers that were bloodier and faster paced, where the body count was ridiculously high and working out the killer was more complex than Einstein's Theory of Relativity.

It was nice to relax a little. Maybe tomorrow I could go into Bath and buy a new outfit for the meal with Claire's family. The house sale had left me a bit of money in the pot as Willow Cottage was smaller and cheaper. I could afford to treat myself.

Grantchester started. Robson Green was leaning over the body of a middle-aged woman found next to a toppled-over bicycle. It was an old episode with James Norton playing the vicar. 'Can you see this, Sidney?' Robson Green was saying solemnly, revealing bruises on her neck. 'This was no accident!'

The phone rang and I saw Sarah's name flash up on the screen. God, the wife of Dan's colleague, Will. I hadn't seen her since I returned from Montenegro. What could she possibly want? I contemplated not answering but knew I would have to talk to her sooner or later. I muted the television.

'Hi Grace,' she said. I could tell she was keeping her voice light and breezy. 'I feel so guilty that I haven't been in touch for ages. I heard that you've moved. Why didn't you say? Will and I could have helped. I hate to think of you organising all that on your own.'

'I managed,' I told her, tightly.

'So, where have you moved? Do tell all!' she urged.

I filled her in about the cottage and then mentioned that we had been away to Montenegro and Kat had decided to stay there. I paused. Was it worth telling her I knew about Rosa? That I knew she and Will had lied to me all these years, had colluded with Dan in keeping his secret?

'I've heard that you've been seeing Neil Hadley. It's the talk of the golf club,' she said.

Ah, so that's why she had phoned. Just for the gossip.

'Look, Sarah, I'd love to chat, but I'm really busy with unpacking,' I said. I realised I was trembling as I put the phone down.

I met Claire, Stu, the twins and River at Noir, as they couldn't fit all of them and me in their car. I didn't mind. I was picking Kat up early in the morning from Bristol Airport. She was coming home for a few days and I couldn't wait for her to see the cottage. I'd made up the spare bedroom for her with fresh flowers and candles. She intended to see Adam on Monday, so she'd probably only spend the day with me before going on to London. I didn't envy her that conversation. It was typical of Kat, though, to see him face-to-face and not take the coward's way out.

I parked in the small car park at the back of Noir. It was quite an expensive place. Claire and Stu were really pushing the boat out. I wondered if they were paying for River, but there was no way an out-of-work artist could afford to eat in a fancy French restaurant. The late August nights were drawing in, the air decidedly autumnal, and I pulled my silver cardigan tighter around me. My black jersey dress was off the shoulder and quite daring for me. Michael Kors. A real indulgence but I could wear it when I next saw Neil. Dan would have had kittens at the price – it made me giggle to think about it.

I was greeted at the door by the maître d'. 'Madam, let me show you to the table. The other diners have already arrived,' he said, with a little bow, sweeping ahead of me as he carried an awkward, over-sized menu.

The interior walls of the restaurant were painted black and one wall was entirely mirrors. It was terribly distracting. No one wanted to watch themselves eat. Extravagant gold chandeliers cascaded like waterfalls from the ceiling. A single ivory pillar candle in a pewter holder, sitting on a white linen tablecloth, was the only decoration on each table. No plastic IKEA plants in tin pots in this restaurant.

Claire waved as soon as she saw me. She hugged me and Stu kissed my cheek.

'Well, I must say, Laura and Liam, you two have scrubbed up well,' I said, as I handed over an envelope to each of them. 'Just a little something to say how proud I am of you both.'

'Thanks, Auntie Grace,' Liam beamed, as he pulled his collar awkwardly away from his neck.

'That's so kind of you, Auntie Grace,' Laura said. She looked gorgeous in an eye-catching red dress, her long, blonde hair falling down her back. Sitting next to her, River was gangly, awkward, hair dyed an implausible soot black. He wore a black T-shirt and black jeans, with a loose grey jacket that Claire told me Stu had loaned him for the night.

'You look nice,' Claire asked. 'New?'

She knew everything in my wardrobe, as sisters do. I mouthed, 'Cost a fortune!' as I sat next to her. 'So, have you lot decided what you're having?'

Stu shook his head, 'I don't understand half of it and the waiter has been translating it for us. I'm having the con-fit dee can-ard,' he said, pronouncing it phonetically. 'Duck in plain English. My stomach's being playing up, so I'm worried about having anything in a rich sauce.'

Claire gave me a knowing look. Stu's hypochondria was legendary. 'There's nothing bloody wrong with him,' Claire would say. 'Even when I was pregnant, he had sympathy pains. He kept quoting this Oxford University study claiming men could have mood swings, tiredness, depression, morning sickness. Honestly, I could have swung for him. I was the one carrying twins.'

As much as she moaned, they were very close and he adored Claire. Stu was salt of the earth, a straightforward guy, football every Saturday, drinks in the pub with his mates. He and Dan didn't have much in common.

'They do chicken and French fries,' Liam said. 'I'd prefer Nando's. It's tastier.'

'How on earth can you say that before you've tried it?' Claire rolled her eyes.

'I just know.' Liam laughed good-naturedly.

I knew Laura and River would struggle with the limited vegan options. In French cooking, anything without meat usually had lashings of cheese. River had ordered ratatouille with garlic potatoes and Laura, a tomato tart with salad. I couldn't wait to tuck into my pork tenderloin medallions in a creamy mushroom sauce.

'So, what are the plans for sixth form college?' I asked, as we waited for the meals.

'I'm going to do maths and computer science, probably geography,' Liam said. 'I want to do game design at university.'

Laura shifted in her seat. This was a set-up, of course. Claire wanted me to ask as Laura got all narky whenever she broached the subject.

'Laura?'

'I haven't quite decided,' she said, glancing quickly at River. 'I might take a year out and save up a bit of money so I can buy a car. They're looking for staff at Tesco.'

Claire stiffened beside me.

'Have you thought about seeing a careers' advisor?'

Laura played with her rings, 'I might do. I've got a place for sixth form at Abbeyfields. I'm going to think about it over the next couple of weeks.'

As the night wore on, I became more and more convinced Claire didn't have to worry too much. I caught Laura glancing across at the handsome, young waiter a few times. River was the embodiment of Laura's rebellion. The relationship would fizzle out, I was sure of it. Stu was more laid-back and even listened with what looked like mild interest to River's latest project.

'It's my biggest composition yet,' he said earnestly. 'Each figure represents different aspects of mental suffering. Guilt, envy, loneliness, sexual deviance. Universal issues like that. The deeper the suffering, the darker the colours, to suggest the troubled inner recesses of the mind.' He seemed to have no self-doubt. It must be nice to have that conviction, I thought, feeling a bit sorry for him.

The conversation got onto safer territory when the food arrived. Noir was busy on a Friday night. As the waiter wheeled over his trolley, I glanced at the couple behind him.

God, that looked like Neil. I blanched. It couldn't be.

'Oh, I wish I'd ordered the medallions,' Claire said, as the waiter placed my meal in front of me.

She stopped. 'Are you OK? You look like you've seen a ghost.' She turned around to look where I was staring. 'Shit, is that Neil Hadley?'

Stu turned around too, as Laura and River giggled about something or other.

Neil was there with another woman. Cass. His ex-wife. I recognised her from the photograph I'd seen at his place. They were gazing at each other intently and then he reached across and took her hand. There was no mistaking their closeness.

Claire looked at me sympathetically. 'I'm sure there's a simple explanation.'

I shook my head. 'Like what?'

Was there any man I could trust? I jabbed at the food with my fork, but my appetite had deserted me. I felt heartsick and angry. Every time I looked over, Neil was staring into Cass's eyes. How I got through the meal, I'll never know.

'How am I going to get out of here without him seeing me?' I looked pleadingly at Claire.

I could see Neil beckon the waiter for the bill. As they stood up, he helped Cass into her jacket and he looked over. Confusion suddenly filled his eyes. I looked away, trying to seem engrossed in my food. When I glanced up, Neil was heading for the door. I saw him glance back again, but then he was gone.

As we left the restaurant later, Claire looped her arm in mine. 'It might not be what it seems, Gracie. Not all men are like Dan. Listen to what he has to say, at least. You owe him that.'

'Do I?' I asked.

As I headed back to Meadow Ponsbury, tears of frustration rolled down my cheeks. I felt such a fool for believing he could genuinely be interested in me.

By the time I was ready for bed, I saw I had three missed calls from Neil. I just couldn't face speaking to him right there and then. Kat was home tomorrow and I was looking forward to it. I had to learn to stand on my own two feet. I don't need a man in my life, I thought as I put the light out.

CHAPTER TWENTY-FIVE

❦ Kat ❦

I was worried coming back would make me homesick for my old life in London. In a way I did miss the familiarity of it, the comfort of knowing everyone speaks the same language as you, the places tied to a lifetime of memories.

This trip was last-minute, hastily arranged. Rosa had given me some time off to celebrate the review, leaving Lovro and another chef, Ivan, in charge of the kitchen. The flights had cost more than I'd paid in rent that month, and I'd had to take one with a three hour stopover in Charles De Gaulle on the way back. But it seemed like the right thing to do; I'd get to see Mum's new house and do the dreaded deed with Adam. I'd felt guilty since the kiss with Milo. I needed to put things right.

It was a joy to see Mum. The new house was incredible. I'd never thought of Mum as a village-dweller, always connecting her and Dad to the limestone of Bath, but the little flower-filled cottage was a delight. She looked so much more at home there. Even though I hadn't grown up in the house – I didn't have any height markings on the door frames or boy band posters stashed under the bed – it still felt like my family home. Mum beamed with pride as I looked round.

'Are you sure you didn't spend a shedload on an interior designer?' I joked as we shared gin and tonics.

'Amazing what a new start can do,' Mum agreed.

'I need you to help with my place,' I said. 'It still feels like a holiday let.'

'You'll get there, darling; you've only just moved in.' Mum sipped her drink. 'You just need some time, and catalogues for inspiration!'

It was strange not seeing Dad's stuff there. His worn leather armchair had a new floral piped cushion, and I found his philosophy books, which had once had pride of place in the old living room, lending it a shabby charm, on the upstairs landing. I wondered where Mum was keeping the rest of his stuff: pictures and old newspaper clippings, fussy professor-style jackets. He'd had so much of it. I didn't feel I could ask if she'd thrown it, didn't want to know the answer. After she went to bed, I plucked one of his books from the landing. Coffee-stained, with well-thumbed pages. It reminded me of Dad as I sniffed the cover.

'You're coming to a new home now,' I whispered, wanting to keep a piece of him with me. I buried it in my case, hoping Mum wouldn't spot it had gone.

The next morning, as I sat on the train, watching the ubiquitous greige tones of crammed-in buildings and overcast sky as country gradually became city, I realised I didn't miss this. I missed the technicolour life I had in Montenegro. It was the confirmation I needed that I was making the right decision with Adam.

My stomach lurched as the train pulled out of another station, another stop closer to Adam. A man got on, talking loudly into his phone, 'Gary, it's a fucking nightmare... yeah... yeah.... I'll be in the Horse and Hound tonight...' His voice was like a pneumatic drill. The train was getting more crowded now, and I moved my bag for an elderly woman to sit down. She ignored my saying, 'Hi.' I was back in London, all right.

My morning commute was a lot more pleasant these days, cycling down the streets of Tivat with the sea as a constant backdrop. The stuffy train reminded me of long tube journeys, the non-existent personal space, and the exhaustion of going home after a shift at Truffles, unsure if I would find the energy to climb the three flights of stairs to our apartment.

'Peckham Rye,' the train's tannoy system crackled over the bustle and noise of Mr Pneumatic Drill. Oh God, one more stop and I was there.

Adam knew I was coming. I'd told him I'd only have a couple of hours and made up some excuse about an early flight. He'd sounded frosty on the phone, as he had in all our recent contacts, but eventually said he was looking forward to seeing me. I had no idea if he'd guessed the real purpose of my visit.

Was it too much to ask for, just to get through today unscathed? Minimal tears? In sixth form, when I'd tried to dump Ezra, he wrote me a song and performed it in the common room to a crowd of mocking teenagers. I still cringed thinking about it. Would today be even worse? But I didn't run away from Ezra then, and I wouldn't run away from Adam now.

I paused as I got to the door of our flat, not knowing whether I should knock or let myself in with the key. I did both in the end, shouting 'Adam!' as I stuck my head round the door.

It was subtle, but the atmosphere had definitely shifted since I was last here. Pink flip-flops by the door that weren't mine. A new reed-diffuser on the sideboard. The sideboard that I had chosen at an antiques shop. It looked as if Michaela was here for the long run. I didn't have time to investigate further before Adam materialised in the doorway.

He stopped in front of me. We took each other in for a second, before Adam seemed to soften. He pulled me towards him. It was a surprisingly tender moment.

'You look different,' he whispered.

'So do you,' I said, although he didn't. Adam was tall, like Milo, but thin and pale. A hazard of spending too much time in the kitchen; I remembered my own pasty complexion in the pre-Café Lompar days. Adam had his mother's deep-set eyes and slim nose, but I'd never noticed before just how much he looked like her. He was wearing the same old faded jeans and cartoon T-shirt that I used to joke was his 'house uniform'. It was nice to see he hadn't changed while Michaela was living there.

'Have you had your hair cut?' He looked at me.

'No, just a tan,' I smiled, 'but very attentive of you.' He laughed.

'Cuppa?'

'Go on then.'

I followed him to the kitchen, peeking briefly in each of the rooms off the hallway of the flat. Our old bedroom, the sheets still unmade, was next door to Michaela's spare room. Her door was closed. I stood in the kitchen, fiddling with a loose chip of nail varnish, as I let Adam make me a cup of tea. It felt awkward, like I was a guest in my own house. We'd lost the easy way we used to move around each other in the kitchen, the old tea-making ritual gone. The place was clean, except for two mugs in the sink, and a few plates drying on the rack. Adam would be happy to leave them out until they were next required; putting dishes away had always seemed an unnecessary task to him.

'Is Michaela here?' I asked, not hearing any noise coming from her room.

'No, she's in work today. We've got a new client who's ordered catering for a weekend break.' Adam started going into the brief in great detail, and how the client had preferred his plan for the meal. I was so relieved that we had the place to ourselves, I was hardly listening. I had no right to dictate whether she was or not, but I had been worried about having the conversation we needed to have with someone else there.

'Sounds good,' I said, accepting a tea from Adam. We made our way to the living room. The flat was partially furnished when we moved in, and one of the reasons we took it was the massive U-shaped sofa that dominated the room. We'd spent so many hours lazing on it, the cushions were practically moulded to our backsides. I tried not to look at the pack of cigarettes and open window in the corner of the room, or the empty packet of crisps on the coffee table. All reminders of a previous life I didn't want anymore.

'So, I said to Beth and Michaela that even though doing a celebrity wedding would be great for business, we don't want to get too big for our boots, don't want to lose our authenticity just to meet greater demand. But Beth's gone ahead and done it anyway. It's fucked up,' Adam swore.

I'd often heard this line about greater demand. I wondered if he didn't want the business to get bigger out of laziness or pure spite for the manager, Beth, who he hated. Adam carried on talking about some menu he'd designed that Beth touted as 'not ambitious enough'.

'I mean, can you believe it? Me? Not ambitious enough?' He shook his head.

It occurred to me that I'd been here twenty minutes already and he hadn't asked a word about Montenegro.

'Mmm.' I wondered how best to move the conversation along. 'And how is Michaela getting along here?' I hoped I sounded nonchalant.

Adam tilted his head, in a pitying way. 'Don't worry, Kat, she's got a boyfriend. There's nothing going on between us.'

He looked so smug, I wanted to tell him that I wasn't worried at all, but swallowed it down.

'David's round here most nights. He's a good bloke, I let him beat me on the PlayStation every night,' Adam carried on. I felt a flicker of remorse for him then. Despite his brave front, it couldn't be easy for Adam having another couple here. A wave of guilt came over me.

'Are they going to get their own place?' I asked.

'Well, I guess they'll have to when you come home.'

Adam stopped talking and stared me down. As if it was a challenge, as if he knew what was coming. I took a deep breath. Here goes...

'Adam, I'm not coming home,' I started. He began to laugh.

'Not this again, Kat. I know you're having a great time in Montenegro with the Café and your tan and everything, but when are you going to come home to the real world?' His tone was harsh.

'Montenegro is my real world now. I love it so much there. The Café's doing well. I've got a flat there, friends, family. I'm going to stay.'

'Yeah, I know you're happy there running round with Rosa and Luke, but you're wasting your skills as a chef, Kat. You had real potential in Truffles...'

'Luka.' Whether the mispronunciation of his name was deliberate or not, it really got under my skin. As did potential. 'And I don't need potential at Café Lompar, I'm head chef. You have no idea how well I'm doing because you never listen!'

I realised I had raised my voice and took a breath. How had it escalated this quickly?

'So, what – you come home just to check in on me and Michaela, flaunt your new life and fuck off?' Adam snarled.

'I came here to...' I felt tears starting. 'I came here because I wanted to tell you I think ... we should break-up.' Once the words were out, there was no going back.

Adam nodded.

'That's pathetic, Kat, even for you. I helped you through catering school, I helped you get that job at Truffles and I've supported you through your dad dying. And now what, have you met some European waiter that's taken you out on his moped?'

'It's nothing like that,' I said, but I felt my face flush. Adam laughed, vindicated.

'Well, you shouldn't have bothered coming back,' he said, arms crossed.

'I came because I thought I owed you an explanation.' I stood up. 'But I don't owe you anything.' I could feel tears streak my face. This really wasn't how I wanted to leave things. I tried desperately to think of something to say that would ease this horrible tension.

'Well, just don't come back here when it all goes wrong with you and the waiter, and you realise you're going nowhere in that crappy restaurant. You've made your own bed. It's over, Kat.'

I took one last look at his face, red with frustration, and left.

I hated confrontation, hated leaving things this way, but if Adam wouldn't listen, I had no choice. I ran down the stairs, sobbing quietly. As the door to the apartment building shut behind me, I realised I hadn't had the chance to pick up any of the stuff I meant to get, and I could never go back again.

I started off down the street, feeling like a very small person in a very big, unfamiliar place. I picked up my phone as soon as I got to the train station, knowing there was only one person who could make me feel better. My call was answered straight away.

'How did it go sweetie?'

'Mum,' I sobbed with relief. 'I need you.'

CHAPTER TWENTY-SIX

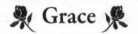

Grace

Neil was waiting in the window seat at The Fallen Angel in the village. He nodded and waved as I entered. It was eleven-thirty and we'd agreed to meet for brunch. We hadn't seen each other since that fateful night at Noir and when I did eventually pick up one of his calls afterwards, the tone between us was strained, to say the least.

'Look, Neil, I understand it was Cass, your ex-wife. All of us come with baggage, but I'm not sure how much I want to take on right now.'

He'd sighed, 'Can't we just meet? I'd rather explain to you in person.'

I hadn't told him I was going to Dan's delayed memorial service in a few days, and I didn't want to. I had been surprised when I returned from work a couple of weeks ago to see the Bath University logo on an envelope lying on the mat, amongst all the bills and junk mail. A formal invitation to a service in honour of Dan. It had set off a flood of memories and left me feeling confused and brittle. It had been held up because of staff changes in the department and a new Vice-Chancellor, and I really wasn't sure I could face the old memories.

Neil rose and kissed me on the cheek as I reached the table.

The previous intimacy between us had definitely diminished. This felt awkward, almost formal.

'What do you want to drink? I'll get it,' he said.

'Tonic water and a dash of lime, please. I don't feel like drinking anything alcoholic this early.' I thought of our boozy lunch only a few weeks ago where we'd ended up in bed.

I gazed at the shoppers in the small high street. The Vintage Gallery, a small antiques shop opposite, was bustling with browsers, and tables had been placed on the pavement outside the little café next door.

When Neil sat down, we both spoke at the same time.

'I know what it looked like the other night,' he started.

'You don't have to explain...'

'I think I do, Grace. I told you about Max. It was his twenty-fourth birthday on Friday. Cass and I meet up twice every year — on his birthday and on the anniversary of his accident. Olls is usually with us, but he's gone off to Majorca with some friends.'

'I do understand, of course I do. It's just that I'm not sure where I fit in all this.' I sipped my drink, pausing before I spoke again. 'I've got my own problems at the moment and I don't know if I'm up to taking on anything else.'

He looked annoyed. 'I didn't realise you saw me as a problem. I thought you would understand more than anyone.'

'And I do. It's just that I'm finding it hard to trust anyone. Surely you can appreciate that? I was lied to for years by someone who said they loved me. It's not something you can get over quickly.'

'Not all men are like your husband, Grace! You have to start trusting again. Cass and I will always have a connection. We lost our son. She's the only one who feels the same way I do. And we are divorced, for God's sake.'

'I know, I know, but...'

'I thought this was going somewhere,' he said.

'I'm scared. It's not the right time.'

'OK. I get it,' Neil said testily. 'That's it then.' Anger and disappointment flashed across his face.

We finished our drinks in silence. As I walked away, I felt empty. I liked Neil, really liked him. I couldn't shake the feeling I'd made the wrong decision. But this way, I couldn't get hurt again.

I felt uncertain about going to the university and seeing Dan's colleagues again. I had met several of them over the years, particularly when he first started work there. However, as the years went by, I went to university events less and less. I knew he'd relax more without me. They were a stuffy old bunch, anyway, talking about some dusty research paper like it was the funniest thing they'd ever heard. In the same way, I wouldn't have dreamt of taking Dan for drinks with my charity colleagues. Sylvie often brought the talk around to the menopause and night sweats. Dan would have been horrified.

Debating what to wear for the memorial service, I'd opted for a grey jacket and black skirt. I kept my make-up light, just a taupe eyeshadow and a nude lipstick. As I slipped on my heels, which felt unfamiliar and already pinched at the toes, I wondered how I would survive the day. Claire had agreed to come in Kat's place. I understood that Café Lompar was too busy for Kat to take another weekend trip so soon after the last one.

I heard the toot-toot of Claire's Volkswagen Beetle outside.

Lime green with a daisy bobbing on the dashboard, it wasn't the most inconspicuous of cars. 'It annoys the hell out of the twins. That's why I keep it,' she told me once, half serious.

'Hi, hon. How are you feeling?' she asked, as I got in the car.

'Shit scared,' I admitted. 'It's worse than the funeral. I can barely remember that.'

'You'll be OK,' she soothed. 'I'll be right by your side. I suppose it's thoughtful that they're doing this. Although it's a long time after a death for a memorial service.'

'They had to fit it in with the holidays, I think, and there's been a lot of reshuffling of staff. I'm glad it wasn't too soon after, in a way.'

'Bloody traffic!' Claire cursed, as we joined the rush-hour mayhem.

'We've got plenty of time.'

'How did things go yesterday with Neil?'

'Strained. I think it's over. He told me that it was his son Max's birthday, you know, the son who had the accident. That they meet every year. I do believe him. It's just that I don't know if I can trust again. Perhaps it's better if I have some time on my own for a while.'

'There's never a perfect time, though, Gracie. You two seemed to click and... Move it, twat!' she suddenly shouted. 'Did you see how that idiot tried to cut me up?'

After a moment, she went on, 'You know best, of course. But you have to take a chance sometimes. There's never much fun in playing safe.'

'I hate town at this time,' I muttered, wondering if I had been stupid to give up on Neil so easily.

Continuing at a snail's pace, we reached the university twenty minutes later and it took Claire an age to park the car. We made it to the service with five minutes to spare.

'I'll be glad when this is all over,' I said, as we entered reception. The pungent smell of white lilies filled the air and I sneezed.

'I'm Grace Lompar, Danilo's wife,' I told the receptionist. 'We're here for the memorial service.'

'Take a seat,' the receptionist said, with that sympathetic tilt of the head I hadn't seen for a while.

I glanced down the corridor to the right where Dan's office was. I hadn't visited him there for a long time. When we were first married, I often came to the office. We even had sex on his desk once, Dan hurriedly closing the blinds as he unbuttoned his trousers. I knocked over his spider plant, creating a terrible mess on the carpet. Dan didn't give two hoots. It had felt illicit and exciting. He'd never have dreamed of doing that as our marriage went on. He became far too uptight.

But perhaps he wasn't so uptight with Rosa.

'Grace, darling, how lovely to see you. We're all in the seminar room waiting for you.' Will swept into reception and Claire and I rose together. I'd dreaded seeing him today, knowing what I knew now.

'The Vice-Chancellor, Professor Tarquin Kirby, will be saying a few words. I don't think you've met him. He's only been here eight months, but he'd met Dan at conferences before then, of course.' But barely knew him, I thought. Why didn't the old Vice-Chancellor return to the service? It seemed disrespectful to me. 'And a few students from last year will be speaking.' I noticed a damp patch on Will's upper lip. 'The canteen has prepared a light buffet afterwards.'

I braced myself as I entered the seminar room. A CD played 'Somewhere Over the Rainbow' as we walked slowly in. Solemn students and staff filled the room. There were leaflets placed on the seats reserved for Claire and me at the front. I picked one up and put my reading glasses on. On the cover, there was a photograph of Dan at his desk, looking very earnest. Inside, it had an order of service, the hymn we would sing, 'Morning Has Broken', and some quotes from students and staff.

'Professor Lompar was passionate about his subject and I really enjoyed his lectures.'

'I was in Professor Lompar's tutor group. He knew all there is to know on European Politics.'

I read one written by a colleague. 'Professor Lompar was a highly respected colleague whose quiet generosity, vibrancy and commitment made him immensely popular with staff and students alike. He will be sadly missed by his present and past students and all of us who have worked, laughed and spent time with him.'

It seemed terribly sad. Did I even recognise the man in the obituary comments? Popular? Someone to laugh with? In the early years of our marriage, perhaps, but even then, he was often solemn and preoccupied. Yet Kat and Luka saw a completely different side to him. A loving father, fun. He was a complex man. I wondered how many here knew about Dan's parallel life. Was it just Will? I couldn't imagine many of his colleagues knew that this respected professor was an adulterer.

As the Vice-Chancellor began his address, his lack of intimacy with Dan became all too apparent. 'Although I hadn't known Professor Lompar for very long, he seemed to inspire his students with his in-depth knowledge of...'

Everything was discussed third-hand: 'I heard Professor Lompar was... His colleagues say he was dedicated to the job... Professor Lompar appeared to be a most conscientious colleague.' It was torturous.

The buffet afterwards consisted of curling egg-and-cress sandwiches, some pork sausages on sticks and a Battenburg cake sliced up on a large ceramic cake stand with a domed lid, which was far too fancy for it.

'Jeez, I feel like we've returned to the seventies in a time machine,' Claire whispered.

I grabbed a glass of sherry and swallowed a large gulp as Tarquin Kirby moved purposefully towards me.

'Mrs. Lompar, I am so glad you could make it. What did you think of our little ceremony?' he asked, patronisingly.

'What can I say?' I said, which he obviously took for gratitude. After we exchanged a few insincere pleasantries, I made my excuses to go to the toilet.

I passed Dan's office on the way, realising it would be the last time I would see it. Pausing, I looked at the name plate, 'Professor Emily Taylor-Brown.' It was like being dowsed in freezing water. But what did I expect? It was over a year and a half since he died. They wouldn't have left his office empty all this time.

As I washed my hands in the sink, I looked in the mirror. What had it all been for? The long nights Dan stayed up working on his research, the papers he wrote, the essays he ploughed through. Now he was gone and people had moved on. For the first time since I had found out about Rosa and his cheating, I felt sorry for Dan.

As I left the toilet, I almost ran into Will, startling him. He looked as if I was the last person he wanted to see.

'How have you been, Grace? Today must be terribly difficult for you,' he said.

I grappled with what to say. 'Yes, it's been tough,' I mumbled.

'Sarah told me you'd been to Montenegro.' I could see his life flash before his eyes. Did I know about Rosa and Luka? Did I know that he knew about Rosa and Luka?

'Yes, Kat and I wanted to see where Dan grew up.' I toyed with the idea of telling him I had found out about Dan's other family, then changed my mind. I wouldn't be seeing Will and Sarah again. Times like this made you realise who your friends were.

Down the corridor, Claire came walking towards us. 'Are you ready to go?' she asked, reading the awkward situation expertly.

'What a bloody hypocrite that man is!' I said as I got in the car. 'Thanks for rescuing me.'

'What a bunch of pompous pricks!' she said, releasing the handbrake of the car as she reversed out of the university car park, and after the solemnity of the day, it was a relief to laugh.

Kat Facetimed that night to ask how it went. I was in my pyjamas watching an old episode of Downton Abbey with a cup of tea.

'It was fine, love, quite emotional,' I said.

'I bet. I'm shattered tonight.'

'Have you heard from Adam?' I asked.

'No, thank God! He's definitely in the past now.'

As we rang off later, I wondered if Neil was in the past too, and if so, how did I really feel about it?

CHAPTER TWENTY-SEVEN

🌿 Kat 🌿

I walked up to the detached one-storey, whitewashed building feeling strangely nervous. Weirdly, I'd never been to Rosa and Luka's house before. We always seemed to be at the restaurant, and Luka had been to my apartment dozens of times, but I'd never even seen Rosa's place. The invitation had come from Luka, saying it would be a 'welcome back dinner' to make sure I wasn't too homesick since my return from the UK. If I was being honest, I felt anything but. I couldn't wait to get back to Tivat after the Adam debacle.

'Kat!' Luka flung the door open before I had a chance to knock. I hoped he hadn't noticed me stopping to adjust my dress on the path. I was regretting the choice: floral, green, bought in Charles De Gaulle airport when I'd been so bored I'd have bought anything, and a bit hippy for my style.

'Thanks for having me over.' I kissed his cheek. I'd seen Luka only fleetingly at the restaurant since I'd been back. It was nice to see his dimpled smile again.

'Isn't that the wine from the restaurant?' Luka asked, as I held out a bottle. I slapped him on the arm.

'As if! I'll have you know this is a fine wine I spent many hours choosing.' I acted offended.

'Charles De Gaulle?' Luka asked.

'You know me too well.' Maybe I had moaned a little too much about the connection.

'Welcome to my humble abode,' he feigned a posh accent. It sounded hysterical with his Montenegrin undertones. We stepped into the house.

'Did you decorate this yourself?' I teased, already able to tell he had nothing to do with it. The living room was pared back and elegant, with the same rustic charm of Café Lompar. It had Rosa written all over it. Was there anything she couldn't do?

'Of course,' Luka said. 'Follow me for the grand tour.' As he turned, I noticed for the first time that Luka looked a bit ... weird. I couldn't put my finger on it but there was something flat about him. Perhaps I was imagining it.

'Okay.' I wasn't sure if I should bring it up or not.

'Thank you for coming.' Rosa entered, distracting me. She looked radiant as ever, her dark eyes sparkling and a wide smile on her face. I went over to greet her.

'Thank you for having me,' I said into her mass of lustrous curls. 'What a gorgeous house.'

'I can't believe you haven't been here before.' Rosa gestured for me to sit down. Luka went off to the kitchen to pour some wine. 'We've missed you so much at the Café. Don't tell him I said this, but even though Ivan's worked with us for years, he's not a patch on you.'

'You should have seen him, Kat.' Luka stuck his head back round the door. He mocked the previous head chef, covering while I was away, in a thick accent, 'I don't understand how this girl can crisp up the bureks like this.'

'Wine!' Rosa dismissed him as I rolled my eyes. 'Please don't tell me you're moving back home. I don't know what we'd do without you.' She laughed but there was something serious in her voice.

'No, no,' I assured, 'I missed Café Lompar so much while I was away, although it was nice to see my mum. Ooh, I had a great idea while I was there for a rose and pistachio mousse with Earl Grey biscuits. Sort of a blend of the two cultures.'

'Well, I can't wait to try it,' Rosa said. 'Everyone's been raving about the article, Kat. Well done.'

Luka came back in carrying three full glasses in one hand, the contents nearly spilling over the edges.

'Watch out,' Rosa shouted. 'I despair sometimes. How is this man supposed to cope at university!'

I laughed along but Luka shot Rosa a grave look. They both fell quiet.

'You've definitely got Dad's clumsiness,' I said. I'd expected more of a laugh from Luka than the tight smile he gave me in return.

'How is your mother?' Rosa asked.

I told her about the new house and how beautiful it was. I felt I was rattling on, to fill the silence. 'Then I just popped to London, which was grey, miserable as always. I spent the last night with Mum before coming back. The flight was OK.' I was almost on the topic of Charles De Gaulle airport again, when Rosa seemed to brighten.

'We're not the only ones that have missed you. I think Milo's been pining.'

I was embarrassed to feel my cheeks heat up. For God's sake, I was like a teenage girl with a crush.

'I don't know what you're talking about.'

'Then why was Milo giggling like a child when you got back from Dubrovnik? It was pathetic.' Luka laughed. 'I told him to be a brotherly stand-in for me.'

'Please, that excuse was more rehearsed than a Shakespeare play,' I snorted.

'Wait, I want to hear all about Dubrovnik,' Rosa stood up, 'but I need to get the chicken out of the oven. I'm sorry, it's not going to be patch on yours, Kat.'

'I think you need a new job,' I toasted Rosa after we finished eating. 'Forget front of house. That was incredible!'

'Delicious as always, Mum.' Luka wiped his mouth on his sleeve in a child-like gesture.

I clocked Rosa's motherly hand on his arm, and for a second felt a sharp sadness, thinking of my own mum. I still felt a little like I was betraying her by being here, even though she'd assured me otherwise. I couldn't help it. I was getting closer to Rosa, and I found I was starting to think of her as a friend. Family, even, like Luka.

'I hate to say this, Kat, but even when you're a celebrity chef in Montenegro with an army of followers, you still won't beat my mother's roast chicken.'

'I agree with you.' I laughed. The chicken was delicious, cooked simply in a lemon dressing with roasted sweet potato and a red pepper salsa.

'Right, let me clean up.' Rosa stood, waving away my offers to help. 'I don't want to hear a word of it.'

'Mum.' Luka rose to his feet opposite her, taking the heavy metallic tray from her hands.

'I can do it,' Rosa said, pulling back.

'Mum,' he said again, his voice heavy with warning. 'Let me carry it.'

'You sit and enjoy time with your sister,' she said.

'NO!' Luka practically barked.

I didn't know why there was such tension between them, something more serious than a normal tussle for the washing up.

'You need to take it easy,' he said, then followed with something else in Montenegrin.

'Yes, Rosa. Let our generous waiter do the work,' I tried to joke, but neither of them looked at me, their eyes locked in a silent stand-off.

'Is something going on?' I asked, looking from one to the other.

Silence.

Luka raised his eyebrows at his mother, as if to say, The ball's in your court.

'Oh, Kat,' Rosa eventually sighed. 'I didn't want to tell you tonight.'

'What?' I asked, frowning.

Luka sat back down, this time next to his mum instead of me. He covered her hand with his. I didn't like where this was going.

'So, it's nothing major, but a few weeks ago I noticed a ... lump in the shower. Just a small lump, honestly tiny.'

I didn't know where to look. I felt as if the floor was moving beneath me.

'I wasn't even going to go to the doctor, but I did. The biopsy confirmed it. Breast cancer. Early-stage breast cancer.' She shook her hair back behind her shoulders, defiant.

'Oh my God,' I breathed. 'When did you find out?'

'Just before the journalist came,' Luka answered for her. 'But she didn't tell anyone until afterwards. Not even me.' He tried to joke but his voice sounded wobbly.

'Rosa.' I didn't know what to do, what to say. My instincts were to hug her, but I felt frozen to the chair. We were all quiet for a moment. The cool night breeze swirled in through the patio doors.

'You said it's early stage?' I asked.

'Very.' Rosa nodded. 'But it needs treating.'

'Chemotherapy?' I asked. A word I never wanted to say.

'Yes, and radiotherapy. They said a combination is the best chance. I have to have the lump removed first.' Her voice shook for the first time.

'It's starting in October,' Luka took over, 'which is fine. I'm going to delay the start of university. It's not a big deal.'

Rosa's back straightened. 'Kat, I have told him he's doing no such thing. I don't need anyone here to look after me, I will be in hospital when I need to be and at home when everything's fine.' I admired the strength in her voice. I still felt unable to move.

'Mum, I can't leave you,' Luka said. I understood the redness beneath his eyes now. What a terrible thing to have to deal with.

Rosa gently stroked his hair. 'You've worked so hard for this, my darling. I'm going to be fine.'

'You have to be,' Luka sighed.

'I'll be here,' I said.

They both looked up at me, as if they'd forgotten I was there.

'Whatever Dad did, however this family was formed, I don't care. We're family now. I'll be here to help.'

'You're so sweet, Kat.' Rosa took a sip of wine. 'I'm more

worried about what will happen to the Café. The doctors said I'm going to be so tired, it's not likely I'll be able to work for six months. I don't know what to do.'

I hadn't even thought about the Café. It would be torture for Rosa not being able to work; the restaurant was her safe haven.

'Can anyone run it while you're away? I can try but obviously I'll be in the kitchen most of the time. I'm sure Maria could help?'

'Maria's going to university in October as well,' Luka said, 'in Thessaloniki. She was accepted last week.'

'Most of our staff are moving on. It happens this time of year, but I'm always around to find new ones. Getting wait staff is easy enough, but finding someone to manage the place is a different matter.' Rosa rubbed the back of her neck. 'I don't know what I'm going to do.'

'You shouldn't be worrying about this now,' I said. 'I'm sure we'll sort something.'

Rosa nodded, but I could see her real feelings in her eyes. Fear. She must be terrified. I couldn't imagine how she must feel, knowing the hell she was about to go through. My chest was heavy, my throat dry.

'We've got, what, two weeks to sort it? We'll figure something out.' I sounded more certain than I felt. The atmosphere was grim. I wanted to cry but didn't feel I could.

We all stared at the centre of the table, lost in thought. The empty wine glasses glinted in the half-light.

Rosa had poured her whole life into Café Lompar. I hated to think of her worrying about her business on top of everything else. I wanted so much to solve this problem for her — but I didn't know who I could ask.

'I'm sorry,' Rosa said. 'I don't mean to upset you, Kat.'

'That's nonsense. Come here.' I walked round the table and gave Rosa a hug. She held my arm.

'Well, now I feel left out,' Luka joked, and I pulled him over to pile on top. We stayed this way for a few minutes.

It was strange, being a thread in this family that I didn't even knew existed a few months ago. Life changed in the strangest ways. Giving you connections when you needed them most. Perhaps I was destined to be here, for Luka and for Rosa.

We pulled apart, and Luka got up to clear the table. 'Do we have dessert?' he asked.

'I was just going to serve some fruit,' Rosa called, 'but I think we need chocolate.'

I added, 'And more wine.'

We tried desperately to talk about other things for the rest of the night, but it hung over us all, tormenting us. I watched Rosa and Luka; the bond between them undeniable. I made a promise to myself: I had to find someone to look after Café Lompar. I would do it, for Rosa, for Luka, and for Dad.

CHAPTER TWENTY-EIGHT

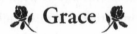 Grace

I was reading up on one of the Project Child UK's recipients. Six-year-old Jaden Darling's single mother had social anxiety and depression and wasn't able to work. They lived on the fourteenth floor of a council tower block in Bristol. In April, the charity had provided a box of presents for Jaden's birthday. I clearly remembered the conditions they were living in when Sylvie and I visited. The lift was out of order and, although the flat was clean and neat, it was spartan and there were no curtains up, not even in Jaden's bedroom. He was in school when we visited and his mother, Madison, was so grateful.

'That poor woman,' Sylvie said, as we descended the stairs afterwards. 'Imagine not having enough money to buy your kiddie a few birthday presents. It's so easy to judge people like that. She's only twenty-three.'

I nodded, thinking that she was just a year younger than Kat, who was head chef at an up-and-coming restaurant. I'd have hated to see her struggling like that. I later found out that Sylvie had bought curtains for the Darlings out of her own pocket and had gone back two days later to help Madison hang them up.

I was reading over the notes and was going to phone Madison that afternoon to do a follow-up interview for the charity's newsletter. Heather had called in sick, so it was just Sylvie and me. Work was keeping my mind off Neil, at least. Stories like this reminded me why the work was worthwhile, but I did feel a bit bored. Sometimes, I felt the charity work didn't fulfil that creative side of me that gardening once had. I loved when someone visited the nursery and asked for advice on re-designing their garden. The whole process of advising them on resourcing, building and aesthetic planting was so satisfying, especially when clients were thrilled with the results. I could see the difference in Kat now she was allowed to be imaginative with her recipes, 'adding a little twist' as she called it. No wonder people were flocking to the restaurant.

The morning was drizzly and grey. Kat had told me that in Tivat, the late August temperature was still over 30 degrees and she couldn't sleep without the air con on. I felt a bit envious as I looked at people with their umbrellas up in the bustling street outside.

'Do you want a coffee?' I asked Sylvie, stretching as I stood up.

'I'm fine, thanks.'

As the kettle rumbled noisily in the tiny kitchen, I could hear Sylvie speaking animatedly to someone.

'There's somebody to see you,' she said, poking her head through the door.

I saw Neil hovering behind her. His hair was wet and I don't know whether it was that or the dark rings under his eyes, but he looked so forlorn, almost desperate.

'I had to see you,' he burst out over Sylvie's shoulder. 'Have you got time for a coffee?'

'My lunch break is at twelve-thirty.'

'Go now,' Sylvie said. 'It's quiet here. Come back around two.'

The Starbucks nearest the office was quiet when we arrived, and we managed to find a cosy corner with two armchairs.

'Just hear me out,' said Neil, once we were sitting down. 'I'll get us a coffee in a minute, but I haven't slept well for the last few nights and I've missed you.' Reaching for my hand, he went on, 'There is nothing between Cass and me, I promise. And I was a complete oaf to put pressure on you like that. Your husband was a bastard to treat you as he did, but not all men are like that. I can understand you've been hurt and you're reticent about starting a new relationship, but we have to give it a try. Please.' He brought my hand to his mouth and kissed my fingers.

I wavered, knowing I shouldn't give in so easily, but he looked so earnest and I had to admit I had been miserable without him too. Had I reacted too quickly? Blown things out of proportion?

'I've missed you, too, Neil. I'm sorry. I was stupid to back off like that. It's just that when I saw you and Cass...'

'I know,' Neil said. 'I should have told you that we were meeting. There was nothing to hide. I'm prepared to wait for you, Grace. We can take things slowly.'

I smiled. 'I'd like to try again, start where we left off.'

Neil went to get us coffees and he placed a slice of carrot cake in front of me. 'You told me this was your favourite once.'

'You remembered.'

'You haven't tried internet dating, have you?' Neil asked, his voice getting less strained as we both started to relax. 'Ollie persuaded me to try it once saying everyone was doing it.'

I shook my head. 'And what was it like?'

'I went on a few dates before I gave up. Well, I've told you about the high maintenance one but, invariably, the women were nothing like their profiles and it seemed such a clinical way to meet someone. It just didn't work for me. Then I came along to the charity and saw you there. You were so natural and confident and yet kind. I thought you were hot.'

'You're making me blush, Mr Hadley,' I joked.

I felt like I was walking on air as I came out of Starbucks. I had invited Neil over to the cottage for dinner. For the first time in ages, I felt hopeful about the future.

I bought two duck breasts for us and thought I'd rustle up a quick stir fry with plum sauce. I called Claire as soon as I got home.

'Guess what? Neil called in work today and we're giving it another try.'

'Thank gawd for that,' Claire said. 'I thought you were a bit mad to give him up, to be honest. He's so much more your type than Dan ever was.'

'Do you think so?'

'I never told you this, but Stu and I both thought Dan was controlling, in that sort of passive-aggressive way. I always thought you could do better.'

'Why are you telling me this now and why are you whispering?'

'Laura is breaking up with River. They're downstairs and I think I could hear him crying earlier. I almost feel sorry for the poor bugger.'

'What's brought this on?'

'She went out with that waiter last night. You remember the one from Noir. And she's enrolled in college at last. Finally come to her senses!' Claire whistled with relief.

'Well, she's her mother's daughter. You went through that rebellious stage before you met Stu.'

'Was I that bad?' She laughed. 'Stu is crowing of course, saying I had taken it all too seriously. I'll let him have his moment of glory. He's rarely ever right, bless him.'

When Neil came around later, he handed me a bottle of Prosecco and gave me a long, lingering kiss on the doorstep.

'You look gorgeous,' he said.

'I could say the same about you.'

I showed him around the house, proud it was something I had chosen. It would have been different if we were in the house in Bath. As lovely as it was, that house held too many memories of Dan. In the cosy kitchen of Willow Cottage, the air was filled with promise and I felt giddy with excitement. Neil sat on the stool at the island watching me cook and sipping wine.

'I'm looking forward to this,' he said, and I wondered if he meant the meal or what came afterwards.

'This won't be a patch on what Kat can produce,' I said earnestly. 'She's a genius in the kitchen.'

'Does she know about us?'

'I haven't said anything yet. I will do.' I meant it. 'She wants me to be happy. What about Ollie?'

'He's staying with me on the weekend. He'll be fine about it. He's actively encouraged me to meet someone else. Cass is in a serious relationship now and he worries about his old dad.' He laughed. 'Did I tell you Olls is as mad about golf as I am?'

I nodded but turned back to the vegetables smoking in the pan, praying they wouldn't set the smoke alarm off.

'Do you think they'd get on, our two?' Neil asked.

'Yes, I do. Ollie is only a year older than Kat and I'm sure they'd have a lot in common.' I grinned. 'They have lovely parents for a start.'

The meal was perfect. I realised I had to stop over-thinking this relationship and just enjoy Neil's company. It was wonderful to flirt with such an attractive man and my stomach flipped when I looked in his eyes. Why did the young feel they had the monopoly on sex? I hadn't felt like this for years and it was every bit as thrilling as when I was younger. If Dan hadn't died, I wouldn't have met this man, felt this way.

I pushed the thought aside. I deserved happiness. And good sex!

When I poured a second glass of wine for him, I said, 'Stay tonight.'

'Let's take this upstairs,' he told me, holding my gaze.

As we fell back on the bed, my phone buzzed in my pocket. I slid it out and Kat's name flashed up on the screen. She didn't usually call just before a shift. She was always in a rush.

'I've got to take this,' I said, as Neil let his body sag onto the bed.

'Hi, Mum,' Kat started. She sounded flat, miserable.

'Are you OK, darling? What's up?'

'Oh, Mum. It's Rosa. She's got breast cancer.'

'God, that's awful.' I sat bolt upright.

Kat let it all tumble out of her. 'She's being very brave, but Luka has taken it really badly and he's threatening to not go to uni. She's got to have surgery and chemo and she won't be able to work. The business will go under. There's no one else who can manage it and do front of house. All those years she's built it up.' Kat sobbed, 'It's the best job I've ever had, head chef. I love it and now it's all going to end.'

'I'm sure she'll find someone,' I soothed. 'There must be someone.' She might have been Dan's mistress, but I felt sorry for her, as a woman. I wouldn't wish it on my worst enemy.

'The thing is, Mum,' Kat said, after a minute, 'I've been thinking and thinking about it. I feel I have to sort this out for Rosa, she's got too much to deal with, and the only way I can think of saving Café Lompar is if you take over.'

'You can't be serious, Kat. I know nothing about hospitality! I'd be hopeless and I can't speak the language. How could that possibly work?'

'You have run a business before, Mum, and that was a success. You miss it, I know you do. Maria can speak English and Lovro is quite good. I wouldn't ask if I wasn't desperate.'

I was aware that Neil was hearing the gist of the conversation and I could see my misery reflected in his face.

'Hasn't Rosa got anyone she can ask? Someone more suited to it?'

'She has friends, of course, I'm sure we could find a manager if we had more time, but we need someone straightaway. Her treatment has to start soon, and anyway, you know what she's like. She's fiercely independent.'

'I don't know if I can have the time off...'

Kat pleaded, 'Please, Mum, just till we find someone else. Two weeks, that's all. Come out here as soon as you can.'

CHAPTER TWENTY-NINE

❧ Kat ❧

'Good luck, from your family at Café Lompar.' Rosa stood in the doorway and read out the card I'd carefully written in my best handwriting.

'Do you like them?' I asked, handing over the bouquet.

'They're absolutely beautiful. I'm not sure I have a vase big enough though!'

I'd clubbed together with the other staff at the restaurant to buy a gift for Rosa to wish her luck for her treatment, and I'd brought the flowers over to her house. She was having the surgery to remove the lump today. Luka was taking her over to the specialist oncology centre at the hospital in Podgorica later that morning.

'How d'you feel?' I asked her.

'Fine.' Rosa smoothed back her hair. Her eyes betrayed her real emotion. I would have been terrified if it were me. Her mane of dark hair was groomed back into a sleek ponytail and she was wearing a postbox-red lipstick. Her perfectly manicured hand gripped the door.

'You look far too glamorous to be going into hospital.' I tried to lighten the mood.

'That's the plan,' Rosa said. 'Surely cancer only affects ill people in hospital gowns? Not a fabulous woman in high heels.' She showed me the killer pair she was wearing.

'Exactly!' I admired her spirit. 'Let me know how it goes, won't you?'

A look of defiance crossed her face. 'No, you let me know how it goes at the Café.' She pointed at me.

'OK, deal.' I hugged her, squeezing tight, before letting go and turning to leave.

'Don't forget to sign off the orders,' she called after me, 'and make sure you check the bookings. Don't overbook the place!'

I turned round at the bottom of the garden path and waved. We'd been over things a hundred times. Rosa had written me a list of front-of-house jobs that had to be prioritised.

I did feel apprehensive, though, as I started walking to Café Lompar. I hoped the first day without Rosa would run smoothly. I didn't want to give her any worry when the restaurant should be the last thing on her mind.

It was a beautiful morning, mild and sunny, but with a hint of autumn in the air. A couple of days ago I had noticed the first tinge of yellow on the trees lining the pavement.

The stream of tourists hadn't slowed yet, spending the last of the sunny days in beautiful Montenegro. I'd noticed an increase in local customers as well, now the tourism industry was starting to slacken for winter; more and more Montenegrins were returning home to see family and friends. Rosa told me this would happen and stressed how vital it was that we served them well; they would be our main customers through the changing seasons.

Could I really do this? Rosa's set of restaurant keys weighed heavily in my pocket. I loved this job so much and I was desperate not to let her down. I resolved to take things one step at a time, not get overwhelmed, and focus on the food, which was central to our success, as well as helping out wherever I could with the front of house.

It would be a miracle if Mum said 'yes'. Perhaps I'd been wrong to ask. She sounded ruffled on the phone, to say the least, but this was important to me and I was desperate.

I unbuttoned my chef's whites for a second to fan myself down. The heat of the kitchen could still be ferocious, even in the milder weather. Thank God, it was nearly the end of service. I peeked out to see the last few tables finishing up their meals.

'I think we've done it.' I turned to Lovro, who was sprinkling raspberry dust over a white chocolate panna cotta. 'That looks fab,' I told him.

'Thanks, Chef.' Lovro smiled to himself.

'Last ones.' Maria came to collect the plates at the pass.

'Do not offer them coffees. I need an early night,' I tried to joke, but it fell flat. The atmosphere in the Café had been sombre all day. Things had run fairly well: the orders Rosa promised me would come in the morning had arrived on time and been signed for, the chalk boards changed to reflect the evening's menu, and we'd had a steady stream of happy diners from five, all leaving healthy tips and compliments to the kitchen. I usually thrived on days like these, but today I was forcing a smile.

Everyone felt Rosa's absence. The chatter that usually passed between kitchen and restaurant staff was gone. I'd checked my phone pretty much every ten minutes throughout the day, but there'd been no updates from either Luka or Rosa. I felt tense, waiting to hear, my stomach in a knot.

'Delivery,' I heard a thick voice call out. Milo strode into the kitchen, smiling.

'Mr. Martinović,' I said, formally, bowing my head.

'I would have brought more but it's been a lot busier than I expected on the boat today,' Milo explained.

I hadn't seen much of him lately; Milo was trying to eke out the last of the tourist trade before summer faded, and had been working double shifts on the boat. We'd stolen odd drinks after work, kisses in the kitchen at the end of service, our fingers lingering together. I still felt a little awkward after what had happened with Adam, but I was a free woman now, free to enjoy Milo as much as I wanted. But I didn't want to dive straight into another relationship, wasn't sure if it was wise. Although every time I looked at Milo, I couldn't help but melt a little bit. I paused to watch him unload things into the fridge for me, his plain white shirt stretched tight over his muscular forearms.

'How's it gone today?' he called over his shoulder.

'Not the same without her,' I sighed, joining in to help him. 'Things have been quiet. I'm worried the customers are feeling it too.'

'I'm sure not. It looks like it's been busy to me.' He glanced out at the messy tablecloths with stacked plates.

'I just worry what will happen long term, what if ... Rosa can't come back again? How will this place survive?' I shook my head, as if trying to shake the thought away.

'It's been a long day.' Milo pulled me into the empty back room when we'd finished unloading. 'Things will be sorted in the end. Maybe I can help when it's quieter, who knows. You just concentrate on the spectacular food you do.' He pulled me against his chest. I felt enveloped in warmth; it was both comforting and sexual.

'Can we do something soon?' I asked.

'Tonight?' Milo returned my hungry gaze.

I looked around. 'No, I need to stay and help the others. Can you wait a bit?'

'No,' he said, "I have to be up early for tomorrow's trip.'

I groaned, 'This is so frustrating.'

'I know,' he said into my hair. 'But we will soon.'

I took a furtive glance around to make sure no one was watching, before kissing him straight on the lips. It felt like a firework bursting through my body.

'Night, Milo.' That would have to do for now. I buttoned my white jacket up, and went back to the kitchen.

Did all head chefs do this? Snog in the back room? I doubted it, but it was a nice distraction from today's worries.

I was just about to grab my bag and head off, the tables now set ready for tomorrow and the last of the wait staff gone home for the night, when I heard a voice call out.

'Kat?'

'Luka, what are you doing here...?' I started to ask, before I saw him.

He was standing on the doorstep of the restaurant, his eyes red and glassy. I'd never seen him look so forlorn. It was like being hit in the stomach. I walked straight over to hug him. When he didn't pull away, I realised he was crying. I rubbed his back.

'Shall we sit down?' I asked. 'You need a good British cup of tea.'

Luka rubbed his eyes, not making eye contact yet. 'Cappuccino for me.'

I left him sitting at a table while I went inside to play barista. The coffee machine was another thing I would have to learn while Rosa was away.

Coming back in with something that, at least, looked like two cups of coffee, I saw Luka had stopped crying, and was staring out over the beach. I sat down next to him and just stayed quiet.

'It was awful today,' he said at last, turning to me.

I drew in a sharp breath. 'What do you mean?'

'No, not like that. Just seeing Mum go through this.' He shook his head. 'I kept thinking, I can't believe this is happening to us.'

'Tell me about it.'

Luka started at the beginning: how they'd struggled to find a parking space at the hospital, how they'd registered on the ward. 'She had to have all these blood tests and sign all these forms. It was really intimidating. Then she saw a different doctor who talked us through the surgery. And then we just sat there. For hours. It was actually kind of boring.' He gave a gentle laugh.

'How's your mum doing now?'

'The operation went well. She's a bit sore because they took lymph nodes from under her arm. She's very tired and she told me to go so she could sleep. I could see she was trying to hold it together for me – like I'm a child – but she's afraid. It was frightening there today. The other patients were much further along than her. They'd lost their hair. They looked … ill. I'm scared, Kat.'

Luka looked on the brink of tears again. My heart ached for him. We watched a couple strolling along the water's edge, the dark sky illuminated by a still moon. I wondered if Luka would have felt any different if Dad was still around, how supportive Dad would have been for him. Would this have been the trigger to get Dad to tell us the truth? We'd never know.

'She'll get through this, Luka. Your mum's a strong lady. It's at an early stage and I bet the doctors deal with this all the time. Yes, the treatment's crap, but it will be worth it, and she will be fine.' We both knew that I had no way of saying this for certain, but it was comforting to believe it.

'How on earth am I meant to leave her for university?' Luka sighed, running his hand through his hair.

'Luka...' I started.

'Would you leave your mum?' he asked me. 'What if something happened while I was away? I'd never forgive myself. I want to be here with her, so desperately.'

I couldn't say anything because he was right. I knew I would feel the same way as him if it was my mum. But Luka had to go to university.

'Will they let you defer?'

'Like, push back a year? I haven't asked because Mum is dead set against it. I don't care anymore, Kat. This is way more important to me. I can reapply for law next year.'

'You have to start university,' I insisted. 'You can't lose your place. What will you do if you stay here? Sit around and comfort your mum? I know that's what you want to do, but there's no reason for it.'

'No reason?' Luka said, his tone harsher.

'What I mean is, it won't help your mum knowing that you're sitting round worrying about her. She'd prefer you to be there, starting your course, making friends, wouldn't she?'

He didn't answer, knowing I was right.

'And look, it's only Berlin, it's not the other side of the world. I'll be here all the time. If anything happens to your mum – not that it will – you'll be able to get here in a matter of hours.'

He nodded, but his brow was still knotted.

'I know this is a shit situation, and not how you imagined starting uni at all, but it's your life. You have to do it for Rosa.' I hoped I'd made a convincing enough speech.

'They did say I could study from home every Friday so I could visit Mum on the weekends.' He looked down at his cup.

'There we go, see, the university will understand. You need to do this, Luka.'

He nodded again. I felt relieved that I'd managed to help. We were quiet again, the air heavy.

'I love you.' The words came out before I'd even thought about them.

'I love you too,' Luka said, a tear in his eye again. I felt emotional as well. I couldn't begin to fathom the bond we'd formed in such a short time. From when we were absolute strangers on a boat – to this. I felt like my whole life was here with Luka, in this café.

'Do you want me to come and stay with you tonight?' I offered, realising how late it was.

'No, you get your sleep,' Luka said. 'Thank you.' He smiled. I stood up, getting ready for the walk home. Luka stayed there, sipping his drink.

'Kat?'

'What?'

'This coffee's vile.' He grinned at me, that wicked streak still alive and kicking.

'Odjebi,' I said. I may not be fluent in Montenegrin yet, but at least I could swear.

PART THREE

PART THREE

CHAPTER THIRTY

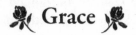 Grace

I must be mad, I thought, as I tried to stretch out my legs on the plane to Montenegro late on a Sunday afternoon. I looked out from the window and could just make out the corrugated navy-blue sea below, no land visible. The man next to me was snoozing, the muffled shouts from the film he'd fallen asleep to drifting from his headphones, the stale smell of chicken chasseur still hanging in the air.

I closed my eyes, just to calm my muddled thoughts. Kat was so distressed whenever we spoke over the last few days, worrying about the future of Café Lompar. So here I was, unable to bear her being in trouble.

I had to frame it as that – helping Kat, rather than helping Dan's mistress. I still didn't like the woman. She had known he was married, known he had a family. It wasn't good enough to say she loved him and ignore the rest of it. Although time had healed the initial shock, it still hurt.

'Would you like a drink? Wine, tea, coffee?' the flight attendant asked, leaning over.

'Tea, please.'

My fellow passenger woke up and ordered a double whisky. He kept leaning over me to look out of the window. I wasn't feeling very sociable and closed my eyes to avoid conversation.

It's only two weeks, I told myself.

Was I being a mug? It was so frustrating. I had just settled into the cottage. And Neil was now in the equation. I couldn't stop the smile spreading on my face whenever I thought of him. He was so different to Dan: more outdoorsy, more fun, more spontaneous. He looked gutted the other night when I spoke to Kat and it dawned on him what she was asking. Two weeks wasn't that long, but was our fledgling relationship too fragile to last? He'd told me he'd wait but we hadn't long got back together. Perhaps time apart would kill us off completely?

Kat was waiting for me at arrivals. She looked tired and I hated the fact that eighteen months after her father died, she had to face such an emotional time again.

We hugged tightly. 'Are you OK, darling?'

She nodded, 'Thanks for coming, Mum. I can't tell you how relieved I am to have you out here. I've really missed you.'

'It's been pretty grim then?'

'Let me have your suitcase,' Kat said, taking it from me. 'Rosa is doing OK. She's due to start chemo next. It's Luka who's falling apart.'

'Poor kid. It's just been the two of them for so long. He's lucky you're here.'

Once in the car, Kat chatted about the restaurant and filled me in on some of the things I would be doing. 'Rosa keeps meticulous records. In Montenegrin, of course, but Maria is helping to translate. You'll just need to greet the guests, make the orders, perhaps serve some drinks. Only until we find someone else. Two weeks max!'

'So, how did Rosa find out about the breast cancer? She's young for a mammogram, isn't she? Forty-two?'

'She found the lump in the shower. It's early stages – well, grade two. She said it's localised, so it hasn't spread. The lumpectomy was straightforward.'

'Poor woman,' I said.

'She's very upbeat. I think she's trying to hide her fear from Luka. She's worried about the business, too.'

Darkness was drawing in, the traffic thinning out as we left Dubrovnik. Kat negotiated the roads more confidently than she had when we arrived. I thought about how much had changed since then, for Kat and me. We sat in comfortable silence as we drove to Tivat. Some of the roads seemed familiar, and I felt buoyed by the scenery surrounding us.

'Sylvie was OK about you having time off?'

'Yes, she was very good. Her friend Liz has agreed to help out. Sylvie says she's been a godsend, so I don't feel quite so bad about leaving her in the lurch. It was a bit of a wrench leaving the cottage. I love it there. I can't wait to see your place, though.'

'The views are amazing, but it'll feel a bit small for the two us.'

'We'll manage.' And then, because I was feeling brave, I added, 'I've met someone recently. He's a professional golfer.'

'Oh.'

'Is that OK?'

Silence hung in the air.

'It's not for me to say whether it's OK or not. I don't know how I feel about it, that's all.'

I could have kicked myself. It was too soon, and she was already stressed.

The conversation was stilted and uncomfortable until we finally pulled up outside Kat's apartment. Its position facing the harbour was idyllic. The moonlight cast a silvery path on the water, and humble fishing boats vied for position with opulent yachts. Kat carried my suitcase upstairs and let us into the apartment.

'Wow, it's lovely, Kat,' I exclaimed. She'd left a small light on and its shadow danced on the exposed stone wall in the lounge. The modern kitchen with its granite tops and sparkling, white units was Kat's minimalist taste to a tee. Her bedroom was spacious and light with whitewashed wood flooring and a huge creamy rug.

'You have my room,' she said. 'The second bedroom is tiny.'

'No, it's fine,' I insisted. 'It's only for two weeks.'

The other bedroom had one single bed and a chest of drawers. I'd be living out of a suitcase for two weeks, I thought, my heart sinking.

Kat made us hot chocolate and we took it outside on the balcony. We could hear a dog barking in the distance and the cicadas thrumming in the bushes below.

'Do you want something stronger?' Kat asked. 'I just thought you might be shattered after travelling.'

I yawned right on cue. 'This is just what I need.'

Kat rested her feet on the railing, her long, slim legs golden brown.

'I've just spoken to Luka. Rosa has slept most of the day.'

'How far is their home from here?'

'About two miles,' Kat replied. 'It's in a lovely, secluded spot and it's got a sea view. Montenegro is a spectacular country. It really gets into your heart. I'm sorry Dad kept this from us.'

'Have you felt lonely?'

She shook her head. 'I've been too busy. It's been mad. And it's been lovely getting to know Luka. And Milo.' She smiled.

We fell silent as we watched the bats weave frenetically between the lampposts on the promenade.

'Mum, I'm sorry for earlier.'

'It's OK.'

'No, it's not,' she insisted. 'I was wrong to make you feel guilty about dating again. What Dad did to you was utterly shitty. Most women would have called him all sorts, but you've resisted. You deserve to be happy. And I know that you agreed to come out here just for me.'

I didn't say anything because it was true, of course.

'Tell me about this professional golfer, then,' she invited, smiling.

'Well, he's very different to your father. Very sporty. He's divorced and has a son just a little older than you. He lost another son in an accident fifteen years ago. His name is Neil.'

'He sounds lovely.'

I nodded, 'He is. He's really kind and I like his company. It's early days, though.'

'I'm genuinely glad you've met someone else.'

'I'm shattered,' I said, getting up and kissing the top of Kat's head. 'I'm going to bed.'

I Facetimed Neil as soon as I got into bed.

'Hi darling,' he said, as soon as he picked up. 'You've arrived safely then. How's it going there?'

I smiled. It was the first time he had called me darling. I told him about Kat's apartment. 'It's a bit cramped in here but comfortable. God, I'm not sure helping in the restaurant is a good idea, though.'

'You'll be fine,' he reassured. 'Olls came over today and I told him all about you. He was chuffed to bits.'

'So was Kat.' I didn't tell him about her first reaction, wanting to keep things light.

'He's gone for a few beers from the offy round the corner. We're going to play golf tomorrow.'

I laughed. 'I would never have guessed.' I liked how straightforward Neil was. There was no hidden agenda with him.

We chatted for a while and once I went to bed, even though I felt nervous about the next day, I fell asleep almost immediately, soothed by the unfamiliar sounds drifting through the open window: the rhythmic breath of the sea as it swelled against the harbour wall, and the street noises further away in the town.

CHAPTER THIRTY-ONE

❧ Kat ❧

'I'm sorry I have to go to work today,' I said, 'I wish I could stay and enjoy Tivat with you.'

'Don't worry about it,' Mum smiled, sipping her coffee. 'I'm just going to relax, have a read through some of these documents Rosa's given us, and enjoy the sunshine.'

'Are you sure you'll be OK?' I asked.

'Don't worry, Kit Kat. I'm happy being left with these bureks.' She held one of the crumbly pastries up as a toast. I'd kept some of the dough back after my shift yesterday to pop in the oven for our breakfast. Buttery and flaky, with a gooey centre, they were quickly becoming my new addiction and a Café Lompar favourite. We sat on the balcony, enjoying the gentle heat of the morning sun. It was my favourite thing to do, sit out here in the morning, watching the world go by. I loved picking out whichever new boats had docked the day before, pretending I was one of the wealthy owners.

'I have to say, I feel very glamorous sitting here,' Mum laughed, lifting her sunglasses to raise an eyebrow at me.

'So do I. Most days I'm outside in an old dressing gown, so it makes a nice change to be dressed for once.'

'You can't come out here in a dressing gown! You're like those people shopping in Tesco in their pyjamas!'

'I might have been guilty of that once or twice too...'

'No!' We both giggled.

It was nice to have Mum here, like having my partner in crime back again. I felt guilty for the way I'd reacted yesterday. I knew I had no right to comment on Mum's romantic life; it was her decision and it was great that she felt ready. It was just the last thing I expected her to say. I never really thought of Mum as someone who would be dating, she was always just ... Mum. One half of Mum and Dad. But it was wrong of me to think of her like that. Especially after the betrayal she'd been through.

'I'm sorry again about yesterday.'

Mum shook her head, brushing it off.

'You didn't tell me last night how you met this Neil.'

'Well...' She took a breath. 'I never had any plans to date again. But Sylvie introduced me to him at that auction and he's visited the charity office once or twice. I thought I looked frumpy, squeezed into that new dress. Neil was so lovely, though. It felt nice to be noticed.'

'You never look frumpy, Mum. Neil's a lucky man.'

She touched my hand. 'Look, I don't know if it will go anywhere, but he's easygoing and funny. You'll like him.'

'I'm sure I will,' I said. Inwardly, I was glad that I was unlikely to have to meet him anytime soon. 'Did you say he's a professional golfer? He must be loaded!' I had images of a greying man with a preppy cardigan tied around his shoulders, the full cliché.

'I wouldn't know anything about that,' Mum laughed. 'He did give me a golf lesson on our first date.'

'You? A golf lesson? You're a dark horse! Were you any good at it?'

She lifted her sunglasses to look at me again. 'What do you think?'

'Well, you do Zumba, now golfing. You're like a new woman!'

'And tomorrow I'll be a restaurant manager,' she said.

I gave her a hug, a gesture I hoped would convey some of my gratitude.

'Speaking of which, I'd better get going to work.'

'Hi, you must be Ivan?' I held out my hand.

'And you must be the famous Kat.' He took my hand. 'My pleasure.'

I'd been apprehensive about meeting Ivan, as I'd essentially taken over his job when I came here. Since working at Café Lompar, I'd heard lots about the original head chef. People had described Ivan's hearty Montenegrin food fondly, although Maria called it 'bor-ring'. She told me he hadn't changed the menu in the whole twenty years he'd worked there, sticking rigidly to the classics. I'd imagined an older, overweight man with a receding hairline.

Ivan was anything but. I guessed he was in his fifties, and he looked well for it. Tanned and lean, he had the appearance of someone who spent all his spare time in the gym. He had a natural air of authority that came from self-confidence.

Ivan had fallen off a ladder when tending to the vine leaves on his villa, breaking his fibula so badly it needed pinning and weeks in plaster. That was when I'd arrived. Ivan had started the transition back to work, first by covering when I travelled back to England, then working a few hours here and there helping with lunch services. But now, plaster off, he was back in earnest.

'I've heard lots about you,' I smiled. 'I'm looking forward to working with you.'

He sniffed and gave me a look as though he was sizing me up. 'Is your leg better now?'

'Much better. It's been agony being away from the kitchen. Especially knowing there've been so many ... changes while I've been off.' A grimace flickered across his face, so fleeting I didn't know if I'd imagined it.

'Well, I've enjoyed working with your recipes. It will be nice to have your expertise on board.' Flattery might work.

'Yes, expertise is a good combination with youthful daring. Hopefully, we can work well together.' He smiled, but it didn't quite travel to his eyes.

I bristled at hearing my skills boiled down to 'youthful daring'. Oh dear, I could feel my worst fears coming true. Ivan was blatantly less than excited to work with me. Rosa had assured me that he had been talking about taking a back seat for years and was happy to have a new head chef. I didn't feel so sure.

He immediately got to work preparing vegetables, without checking with me first. I didn't know whether to butt in and tell him our usual plan of getting the dessert pastry made first, before moving on to mains. As he chopped away, Lovro looked at me, unsure of himself.

I tried a subtle approach. 'Lovro, shall we get on with pastry as usual, before helping Ivan with the veg?'

Ivan didn't look up. Hmm, this might be difficult. I enjoyed the creative freedom that came with being at the head of the kitchen, but I hadn't needed to put my management skills to the test yet. Lovro was so easy-going and enthusiastic, keen to soak in anything I had to teach him. I hoped Ivan wouldn't challenge me too much.

Lovro and I carried on doing our own thing while Ivan kept to himself. Every now and again, I heard him sigh and mutter something as he read my recipes.

'Shall we pause to think about tonight's specials?' I asked.

Lovro immediately sprung to my side. I was grateful to have him there.

'I found some amazing fennel this morning at the market,' I started. 'I was thinking we could do something with crab meat, some kind of linguine?'

'Roasted tomato and chilli might be nice with that,' Lovro offered.

'That sounds great.' I nodded at him. 'A simple white wine sauce.' I was sold on the idea. I enjoyed our daily brainstorming sessions: it kept the menu fresh.

Ivan came over, scratching his forehead. 'I don't know about chilli with that. It might be overpowering.' He scrunched up his nose as if it were the most disgusting suggestion he'd ever heard.

'True,' I said. 'But I worry it might be a bit plain otherwise. Do you have any ideas?'

'You're the boss,' he said, unhelpfully.

'Well, if I make the sauce and put a hint of chilli in, you can taste it and let me know if it's too much?' I tried to be diplomatic and involve him in the decision.

Ivan shrugged, then said something to Lovro in Montenegrin. Lovro looked at me uncomfortably. I tried to ignore the prickly feeling on the back of my neck.

The three of us carried on working in silence. The kitchen was a lot quieter than when it was just Lovro and me, humming along to the radio and chatting about nonsense. I found Lovro easy company, and his insights into Montenegrin cuisine were invaluable.

'So, Ivan, how long have you known Rosa?' I tried to strike up a conversation.

'Since we were children.' He moved over to the hob. I watched out of the corner of my eye as he started throwing vegetables into the pot. 'I've worked here for twenty years, seen Rosa raise it from the ground. She's very determined. And careful. That's why I was a little ... surprised to hear she's taken on someone new. Especially someone that doesn't know our culture well.' He stirred the pot with his back to me, nonchalant. I considered my response but decided there was nothing I could say that wouldn't sound passive aggressive.

'How exactly do you know Rosa?' he asked.

'Family ... on my dad's side,' I gave the practised answer.

'She never mentioned you before.' He looked at me. If he knew Rosa as well as he made out, I wondered if he knew the real backstory, and whether he was testing me. His eyes certainly held a challenge.

'Rosa's wonderful to work with.' I tried to change tack. 'I used to work in London in a restaurant called Truffles.'

'I've never heard of it.' Ivan made it sound like I was trying to name-drop. We really were getting our wires crossed.

'No, I'm not surprised. It's only a few years old. But it was so stressful there. Working in Café Lompar is beautiful. I'll never get tired of that view.' I looked at the endless stretch of sand and sea.

'Yes, it's perfect really for a traditional Montenegrin café,' Ivan agreed.

'Hello,' Maria greeted us as she started her shift. 'Ivan, how are you?' She widened her eyes at me. I got the impression Maria wasn't too fond of him either. I couldn't wait to have a good moan with her later.

'Ooh, careful!' I called out, watching as Ivan poured nearly a whole bottle of red wine into his risotto stock.

'What?' He stared at me, confrontationally.

'Well, we've been using the same red wine to make the gel with the risotto. We won't have enough left if we use it all in the stock.' I tried not to sound too bossy, but I was desperate.

'Gel?' Ivan asked.

'I can show you after, if you'd like, it really elevates the dish.' I smiled.

Ivan shook his head, turned around and poured the rest of the bottle into the stock.

'OK, I get it,' I said to Maria, 'it must be hard for him. He must feel I've stolen his job. But does he have to be such an arsehole?' It felt nice to let off steam. I needed this snatched conversation in between courses.

'Well, yes, you have stolen his job from him – because you're so much better at it! I've always thought he's an arsehole! I love these British words you're teaching me!' She laughed.

'I have a lot more where those came from to describe him,' I sighed. 'What am I going to do?'

The service had gone disastrously. Ivan was refusing to adhere to the plating and finishing touches I'd worked so hard to finesse, so in the end our dishes were inconsistent. His plates weren't fine dining so much as moderately OK dining. It broke my heart. I'd put so much work into the quality of our food. I really wasn't the confrontational type, but I knew I'd have to do something.

Ivan was challenging my position as head chef, knowing I didn't have Rosa to turn to. Things had been going well for me here, but it all felt at risk now.

'Kat, you need to show him who's boss,' Maria said. 'Don't let him walk all over you because you're younger than him – and a much nicer person.'

'Maybe he's just nervous about being back. Shouldn't I give him the benefit of the doubt?'

'Don't let him take advantage of you,' Maria said, stopping as Ivan strolled back in from his break. 'Oh, by the way, that journalist who wrote your review is back in. She's on a table with other women, looks like she's having the night off.'

'Oh great,' I muttered. It was nice to know that she deemed Café Lompar worthy of a meal with friends, and that the praise in her review hadn't been just empty words. Knowing there was any kind of press with us tied a knot in my stomach. Added pressure I didn't need tonight. I prayed she hadn't chosen one of Ivan's courses. 'Make sure we look after her. I'll come out to say hi soon.'

'OK.' Maria headed back out front.

'Kat?' Lovro called me over.

'What is it?' I asked.

He pointed to my handwritten recipes, which were lying in the bin.

I gulped. Ivan had really laid down the gauntlet now.

CHAPTER THIRTY-TWO

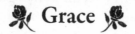 Grace

'So, we only have these bookings so far,' Maria explained. 'Most people just stroll in from the street.' Her English was very good. She smiled. 'You will soon get used to it. If it's quiet, you can stand on the terrace and try to get customers, but it won't be. We will be very busy.'

'Oh, I hope I'll cope,' I said.

'You will,' she assured me. 'Remember you are the boss. Ana is very good and works hard, but Dav takes long breaks and he smokes out the back. Then there's Ivan. He'll be in soon. I'm sure Kat has told you about him.'

Kat had spent most of the night complaining about the pig-headed Ivan and I was not looking forward to meeting him. I had spent yesterday getting to know the menu. Kat changed the specials every day, but I had tried to learn the core menu inside out – what the dishes consisted of, any allergy warnings, and which wines suited which meals. My head was spinning by the time Kat got home and she was ratty and tearful.

'He's such a bastard,' she'd moaned, as she slipped off her shoes. 'He obviously sees me as a threat, yet Rosa told me he didn't want the head chef role long before he went off with his accident.'

'He sounds a bloody nightmare.'

'He grumbled about every new recipe, and then ignored every instruction I gave and went his own sweet way. It was infuriating. I'll have to tell Luka when he's back tomorrow, but we can't tell Rosa, obviously. I don't want her worrying that there's a clash of egos at the restaurant.'

'What do Lovro and the others think of him?'

'Well, they hate him, but he can be quite intimidating. I'm just so relieved you're here, Mum.'

How could I live up to Rosa? She had built that restaurant up, knew all the locals, and was an expert schmoozer. I felt the responsibility on my shoulders. What did I owe this woman? Nothing. But I would be true to my word to Kat and see out the fortnight.

I had packed a couple of black shift dresses I could alternate and some black, flat pumps. There was no way I could swan around in skyscraper heels as Rosa did.

It was a bit of a squeeze in Kat's apartment as we both wanted the bathroom at the same time this morning, but we ate breakfast outside again, which was lovely, something I could easily get used to. We watched the harbour creak to life and saw the fishermen returning with their catch, the early morning dog walkers and joggers, and delivery floats making their rounds before the cafés and restaurants opened their doors. It was very much a tourist town, but it still retained its Montenegrin charm, with its cobbled side streets and terracotta-roofed houses. Even at nine in the morning, the cobalt Adriatic shimmered like a jewel.

'I don't think I'll ever tire of this view,' Kat said, sipping her coffee, before we had to leave for the restaurant.

All the wait staff, Maria, Ana and Davor, came in around ten o'clock. They put menus on the tables, filled bread baskets and set out single white peonies in vases, in preparation for the lunch service. Rosa obviously paid a lot of attention to detail.

'Where's Ivan?' I asked Maria.

'He's always late.' She rolled her eyes.

Ivan eventually strolled in at ten-thirty. Maria said, 'Here he is,' under her breath.

He barely glanced in my direction as he headed to the kitchen. 'Uh, Ivan.' He ignored me — or pretended to. 'Ivan!' I bellowed.

His hand on the kitchen door, he slowly turned around. 'Yes?' Quite tall, he could look down the length of his nose at me.

'I'm Grace, the new manager.'

He shrugged.

'You're Ivan, yes? You're late.'

'I had trouble getting my moped started this morning.' He strode into the kitchen. No hint of an apology.

Unbelievable! No wonder Kat found him so infuriating. Before I could stew over it, a couple of customers drifted in asking for coffee and cake.

'Zdravo,' I said, smiling warmly. I'd been practising the pronunciation the day before. 'Govorite li engleski?' Or go-VOR-i-teh lee ENG-les-kee.

Alone in the apartment yesterday, I kept repeating words phonetically from Kat's phrase book. I was impressed with the number of words Kat could understand. 'Dobro' was 'good', 'Da' was 'yes' and 'no' was 'Ne'. That much I could manage and I had Ana and Maria if I needed help. I couldn't see Dav anywhere.

Luckily, the couple who came in was British. But at twelve,

just as I was getting into my stride, a huge party of fourteen Montenegrin customers flooded in, including six children. They pointed to a table outside and, flustered, I started pushing tables together.

Maria and Ana came to my rescue. 'Where's Dav?' I whispered to Ana.

'On his break.'

'At twelve o'clock?' I made a mental note to speak to him later.

They began to order, when another group of four came in, followed by a young couple. The lunch service was soon in full swing. I felt was juggling so many balls in the air, and I felt they were all about to come crashing down. I brought the wrong wine to the Montenegrin group and spilt a bottle of Coke over a pristine white table cloth. 'Izvinite!' I said, changing the cloth, as one of the women rolled her eyes. I replaced the drink and didn't charge them for their drinks or the bread in recompense.

'They're good customers,' Maria told me, just as my stress levels were at fever pitch and I could feel the sweat patches under my arms. At least Dav had returned.

'What are the specials?' a young woman asked me.

'It's buzara today or musaka od krtola, a potato moussaka with minced lamb.'

'What's buzara?'

'A fish stew. It's delicious,' I said with confidence. Kat had cooked me this one night when we stayed in Kotor. 'It has prawns and cod. All freshly caught this morning. It's cooked with wine, tomatoes and herbs. The chef adds fennel seeds and her own touches. You'll love it.'

'I've heard great things about you,' her husband said. 'This is the first time we've come to Montenegro and everyone is talking about this place and the new chef.'

My heart swelled with pride, especially when they both took my recommendation and ordered buzara.

When I was getting drinks for another table a little later, I saw Maria taking the two fish stews to the young couple. I was quite taken aback. They didn't look as neat as usual. How Kat could make a fish stew look sexy, I really didn't know, but she had an artistic eye and knew exactly how to position food on a plate. 'It's as much a feast for the eyes as the stomach,' she always told me. I had barely seen Kat since we'd started, and when I entered the kitchen, she was absorbed in putting the final flourishes to the food on the pass.

It eventually quietened down at two-thirty. I was tired but I was getting the hang of how things worked. I glanced at my mobile, the first chance I'd had in the last two or three hours, wondering whether Neil had sent me a message. Instead, there was a text from Claire. 'Hi hon. Good luck for today. Off into town for some retail therapy! Let me know how u get on xx.'

I sat down and ate some ćevapi – little lamb kebabs – and salad. Kat joined me. The restaurant only needed a skeleton staff until it became busy again at seven. Kat had planned that we'd eat together and go back to the apartment for a few hours before the evening service.

'How did you find it?' she asked.

'Hectic! When that huge party came in, I was running around like a headless chicken.'

'You've done brilliantly, Mum,' Kat said.

'Were you making the buzara today?'

'No, Ivan. Why do you ask?'

'I thought so. It didn't look like your food. Perhaps a bit scruffier.'

Kat sighed. 'I know. If I'm not careful, Ivan will undo all the good I've achieved. He seems to be awkward just for the sake of it. I honestly wouldn't serve some of the things he does. He has no professional pride.'

Just then, Luka appeared at our table and Kat rose to hug him. Their closeness was obvious. I wondered what the other staff thought. He hugged me too, then flopped down into a seat.

'How's Rosa?' Kat asked.

'OK,' he said. 'Well, not really. She's sleeping a lot and barely eating. She's on some anti-sickness meds but still pretty nauseous.'

Kat touched his knee gently. 'She'll get through this.'

'It's strange to see her like this,' Luka went on, stealing one of Kat's lamb kebabs. 'She's always so strong. And of course, when I ask her, she says she's fine.'

'She's lucky she has you, Luka,' I said. I bit my lip, remembering the agony he felt about starting university.

'Her wig arrived this morning. I saw it by the side of her bed. I know Mum. The thought of losing her hair will kill her.' He shook his head. 'It's part of who she is. That long, wavy, dark hair.'

'It will grow back,' Kat said. But we all fell quiet, knowing how difficult the road ahead was going to be for Rosa. How would I feel if it were happening to me? I'd hate Kat to go through this. Luka was usually so happy-go-lucky. Now, there was an undercurrent of sadness about him.

'Sorry I couldn't be here this lunchtime,' Luka said. 'I didn't want to leave her. How has it gone?'

I nodded. 'Good. Busy.'

Kat interrupted, 'Why didn't you warn me about Ivan? He's been awful, truculent and bloody-minded.'

'Truck?' Luka looked puzzled.

'He doesn't listen to a word I say. I can't believe he was head chef here. He'll destroy Café Lompar's reputation, Luka. I'm not kidding.'

Just at that moment, Ivan emerged from the kitchen, his face solemn. He walked out to the street without even saying goodbye.

'Lovro is on duty this afternoon,' Kat explained, as we watched Ivan leave.

'I've had to speak to Dav today too,' I added. 'He takes long breaks at the most inappropriate times. He disappeared for half an hour at twelve!'

Luka shrugged. 'Dav is Ivan's nephew.'

'Well, that makes sense,' Kat said.

'We were hoping that Ivan wouldn't come back. His heart has never been in the job. He was becoming more and more difficult before his accident: arriving late and there were complaints about the food. Mum always says the worst thing about running a business is managing the staff. I haven't told her that he's back. She has enough to worry about.'

'I'll handle Ivan,' Kat said firmly.

Luka laughed. 'I think you are bossier than my mother.' Kat hit him on the arm, lightening the mood momentarily.

'Listen, you two,' I said, rising from my seat, 'I'm going back to the apartment to put my feet up for a bit. This old woman needs a break.'

'Thank you, Grace,' Luka said. 'I am so grateful to you for agreeing to this.'

Outside in the afternoon sunshine, the heat was gruelling, and I couldn't wait to get into the air-conditioned apartment. I felt my mobile ping in my pocket. Looking at the screen, I could just make out Neil's name, and my stomach flipped over. Frustratingly, the sunlight was too strong for me to read his message.

As soon as I was inside the apartment, feeling like some giddy teenager, I read Neil's message: 'Hi Grace. How's things going there? It's my day off today and I've been thinking of you. Perhaps we can have a quick chat tonight if you have time xxx.'

Three kisses. One kiss was non-committal. Two kisses were what my friends and I usually sent each other. I tried to stop interpreting this.

I quickly texted back: 'Hi Neil. My first shift was hectic today. I'm back tonight and should be home by eleven. It would be lovely to speak to you. I've been thinking of you too xxx.'

I pressed send before I could change my mind, then reached for Kat's store of PG Tips, to inject a little bit of home into my day.

CHAPTER THIRTY-THREE

❧ Kat ❧

'My biggest cooking disaster? Oh, I don't know, there's been so many!' I rested my chin on my hand, trying to think and then shuddered when I remembered. 'Well, we used to have a lot of proposals in Truffles, and sometimes they'd call ahead and ask us to be involved. One time, this man asked me to write Will you marry me, Katie? on a cake, but he forgot to tell me she was allergic to hazelnuts...'

I stopped to sip my wine and watch realisation dawn on Milo's face. 'Oh no, oh no. You didn't, did you?'

'Yep, chocolate and hazelnut! It was one of our most popular cakes in Truffles! She was all right, I promise. But that's not all... The poor man had a strong accent- from Liverpool I think- so I misheard his fiancée's name. It was actually Adie but I wrote "Marry me Katie"' in big fancy letters. I was mortified. As was she. And that's before she needed to seek medical attention.'

'Oh, Kat, that's terrible. Do you know if they got married in the end?'

'A year later. Of course, they didn't ask us to cater their wedding.'

Milo gave a big snorting laugh, causing a few other tables to glance over at us. It felt nice, watching the creases form at the corners of his eyes, making him even more attractive. We'd been laughing non-stop for the whole day.

'I still don't think that beats your work disaster, though – falling off the boat in front of a full group of customers. I wish I'd been there!'

'I'm glad you weren't. I had to spend the rest of the day with my top off while my clothes dried.'

'I'm sure the female tourists didn't mind too much,' I grinned.

'Well, I'd only just started working then so I was maybe eighteen. I was really skinny back then. Weedy, as you'd say.' I laughed at his attempt at a British colloquialism, which sounded awkward but charming in his accent. Besides, I didn't believe a word of it, willing to bet a younger Milo was every bit as handsome as the twenty-seven-year-old version.

It was bliss to have a day off from Café Lompar, knowing my mother was taking care of it. If I hadn't had Milo to distract me, I was sure I'd have spent the time worrying what damage Ivan was creating in the kitchen – and to my reputation. The wine was definitely helping too!

For our first official date, we'd come to Lake Skadar and spent the day wandering along the shore, before stopping for a leisurely meal at a waterside taverna.

The lake was beautiful, the sapphire blue waters and lush green hills reminding me of the Italian Lakes. I'd been to Lake Maggiore on holiday with Adam a few years ago – although he spent the whole week moaning about the noisy air conditioning unit in our room and Facetiming Michaela about an upcoming event they were catering. Looking back, I couldn't believe I'd put up with him. I was always making excuses: he was stressed at work or worried about the business. Why hadn't I believed I deserved more attention and care than that?

Milo had been so effortlessly attentive today, focusing on our conversation and asking me interested questions. The way he stared into my eyes made me weak at the knees. The whole day had been filled with anticipation, knowing we'd have the flat to ourselves tonight.

'Mmm, this is incredible.' I chewed on some rustic bread, enjoying the light texture and cracked surface. 'What is it?'

'I think it's pšenični, a wheat bread, although I'm not an expert like you.' Milo flicked his eyes up to me, a tiny smile on his face. 'My mother used to make bread like this. I've still got her recipes somewhere. She wrote them all down in a book for my sister and me. I'll have to show it to you.'

'I would like that. Maybe I could include some of her recipes in the restaurant?' I was tentative, not knowing if he'd want to talk about his mother.

'Now, she would have loved that. She always fancied herself a bit of a baker. You know we used to come here on the weekends. My mother loved the lake. She used to tell me stories about a princess that lived in a castle at Vranjina, looking out on the water.' He ran his hand through his hair and looked across the lake.

'Tell me more.'

'It's stupid. Every day the princess would watch out for her prince to come to her by boat, waiting for years. But he never came, and she burnt the castle to the ground in her rage.'

'That's not the ending I expected!' I laughed.

'My mum used to say: never keep a girl waiting, never play

games. When you find your princess, you must treat her well, and buy a big castle for her on the lake.'

'Your mum's right,' I said.

'Tell me about it.' Milo sipped his wine.

'You must miss her?' I asked, slowly, carefully.

'Of course.' Milo then took my hand, turning it over in his and tracing the lines in my palm with his finger. 'Do you miss your dad?' he asked eventually, looking up at me.

'Every day,' I gulped, hoping I wouldn't cry. 'Finding out that he was hiding this big thing from us, another family, well, it changed everything, but at the same time, it changed nothing. He's still my dad. I think about him all the time, what he would say, what he'd think about everything I'm doing. I'm sorry...' My voice broke. Milo gave my hand a gentle squeeze.

'He'd be very proud of you, putting everything aside and getting to know Luka and Rosa. I didn't know him well, but I think he would have loved that.'

I kept forgetting that Milo had met my father. 'Dads are strange, aren't they?' I remember Milo telling me about the struggles he'd had with his when he was growing up.

'I think I'll be a good one, one day,' he grinned.

'Well, they would be very lucky children.'

We fell quiet as our mains arrived. I paused, enjoying the sharp citrus flavour of my sea bass. I loved coming to other restaurants, taking inspiration from their menus. But I was struggling to focus today, feeling the heat from Milo's leg pressing against mine under the table. I slid closer, so my inner thigh pressed against his knee. He looked up at me, hunger in his eyes. I knew I wanted him tonight. We couldn't go to Milo's flat, his roommate worked from home and we would have no privacy there. I knew Mum would be out late.

'You look so beautiful, Kat,' Milo said, sincerely. It took me by surprise.

I usually felt anything but beautiful, spending most days in my chef's whites, spattered with sauce. Today, I'd channelled my inner 'siren' in a flowing red floral dress. I could tell Milo liked it by the way he'd looked at me when he picked me up earlier.

I blushed. 'You're not too bad yourself, Mr. Martinović.'

'Mmm, you're doing something to me.' He shook his head.

'What?'

'Maybe we should eat quickly and get home?'

I nodded, but took a slow bite of my food, our eyes locked in a secret game.

Milo was gorgeous, all six foot two of him. He drew the eye of every woman in the room. But for me it was more than that. He was so thoughtful ... mature. It was sexy and comforting at the same time.

I knew it was early days, but I could feel myself falling for him. I couldn't help it. It was terrifying but electric.

We parked and walked along my street, too excited to even contemplate another drink somewhere. The sun was setting earlier in the evening now. Milo's arm was draped across my shoulders, so close I could smell his faint aftershave. We arrived at my building, the courtyard thankfully quiet, illuminated by shallow pools of light outside each apartment. I led Milo by the hand up my small set of steps. I was glad there was no one around. Mrs. Janković usually loved to sit on her terrace, watching out for gossip and other people's business, but there was no sign of her tonight. We paused as I got my keys out of my bag.

'Are you sure about this?' Milo gestured inside.

I appreciated his checking, but there was no way I was going to stop now. I'd waited long enough, ever since our drunken date in Dubrovnik. The hidden kisses in Café Lompar and snatched coffee breaks together had made me desperate for him.

I kissed him hard to show him how sure I was. He kissed back, pressing me into the wall next to my front door. It felt incredible.

Until the door opened.

'Kat? I thought I could hear... Oh, sorry.' Mum's head peered out. I didn't know who looked more embarrassed, her or Milo.

'Hi.' I caught my breath, feeling like a teenager caught kissing behind the school bike sheds. 'You're here?' I smiled, trying to cover my surprise.

'The restaurant's been quite quiet today, so we closed early tonight,' Mum explained, her arms wrapped around her body. I noticed she was wearing pyjamas, and realised she probably felt as mortified as we did.

'We were just coming in for a drink?' My voice sounded high-pitched and defensive.

Milo looked at the ground, as if it couldn't swallow him up fast enough. 'Nice to see you again, Grace,' he recovered, leaning down to kiss my Mum on the cheek. 'I'll just head off...'

'No, no, come in,' Mum protested. I was grateful, knowing Mum would really want her privacy.

'Are you sure?'

'Yes, the kettle's just boiled.'

She stepped aside, ushering us both in. Milo walked ahead of me, his tall frame filling the hallway. This was not the end of the night I'd envisaged.

We reached the living room, and I could see Mum's meal steaming on the coffee table, untouched.

'Oh God, we're interrupting. You carry on eating,' I told her. The situation was getting worse by the second.

'I'll have to call you back,' Mum told her phone, giving a small wave at the screen. She clicked off, flustered. 'Just Claire.'

I knew it wasn't Claire. We'd clearly interrupted her video call with Neil.

Milo stood awkwardly, scratching his head.

'I'll get us a drink,' I said to him. 'What do you want?'

'I'll come and help.' He followed me into the kitchen.

'I'm sorry, I thought she'd be home much later,' I whispered, redundantly, once we were alone.

'Don't worry,' Milo laughed. 'We wouldn't have much luck at my flat either. I'll just have to wait. It'll make me want you even more.'

Disappointment ricocheted through me. I reached to open a bottle of wine, but he tipped my chin up to look in his eyes.

'I'll be right here ... waiting,' he mouthed. I wanted to melt into him.

'Ooh, sorry!' Mum came in again. 'Just needed to get cutlery.' To reach it, she had to pass us and Milo had to step out of the way. I wanted to put my face in my hands.

'I won't disturb you again,' she said, trying to make a joke of it, as she held the cutlery in the air. 'I can eat in my bedroom.'

'No, don't be silly,' I said. Milo's eyes danced with amusement.

'Come on, I'll make you a cuppa? Unless you want a glass of wine too?'

We sat around on the sofa, Mum awkwardly eating her dinner, and Milo with his hands folded neatly on his lap. I was pleased he was such a good listener, getting Mum to tell him all about her job and the new house.

'And how are you finding Café Lompar?' he asked.

'It's amazing, seeing all that Kat's done.' She beamed. 'I'm enjoying getting my hands dirty too, but Ivan's been a bloody nightmare again today.'

'Oh, not again.' I rolled my eyes. 'What's he done now?'

'So today we had this snooty table in. They were annoying, don't get me wrong, and they sent the mains back saying they weren't hot enough. I took their plates in to the kitchen and Ivan just threw his towel down and refused to do anything about it. I felt so embarrassed, I didn't know what to do.'

Milo and I recoiled in horror.

'What did you do?' I asked.

'Poor Lovro had to make them again behind Ivan's back. And I had to take the mains off the bill because they took such a long time.'

'He's worth his weight in gold, is Lovro,' I said, my blood boiling at Ivan's behaviour. I had to do something. 'I wanted to give him the benefit of the doubt, honestly, but he's just impossible to work with,' I spat out.

'And he's ruining all your hard work. I can see some of the customers look surprised by what we're serving them,' Mum admitted.

'Look, I know Ivan's family well,' Milo said, leaning on his elbow. 'I bought the boat from his brother. He used to work hard in the restaurant, he really did, but I think things went downhill with his son and everything.'

'Why? What happened with his son?' I asked. Milo gave me a look as if he wasn't sure if he should be gossiping or not, but he answered.

'A few years ago, he was caught shoplifting. Ivan and his wife had to pay a lot of money to bail him out, but things spiralled out of control from there. I think it was very embarrassing for Ivan. His son was in a bad way, taking drugs and gambling, getting in debt.'

'Awful for them,' Mum said.

'It was. Ivan and his wife got divorced.' Milo sighed.

'That's so sad,' I said. I'd been so focussed on how difficult Ivan was to work with, I hadn't considered what might be going on behind the scenes.

'His son is in prison now. It changed Ivan. And in a town like Tivat, everyone knows everything,' Milo explained.

We all fell silent.

'Maybe I should give him another chance,' I said.

'I wouldn't say it if I didn't think he was worth a chance.' Milo leaned towards me. 'He might improve once he sees how amazing you are.'

I sighed, but resolved to give it a go.

'Ivan was great before all this, really cooked from the heart.' Milo patted his chest.

Mum looked at me. 'Well, I need you and Ivan to get on,' she said. 'I've had a great idea for the restaurant.'

CHAPTER THIRTY-FOUR

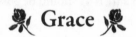 Grace

I was a bit nervous Kat would think I was telling her how to run the Café, but I was excited about my ideas, so I decided to just go for it.

'Look, I know I haven't been here that long, Kat, but I think that Rosa could capitalise more on the morning trade. It's quite slow in the mornings. What about brunch? The pastries you make are amazing. Your bureks with chocolate and hazelnuts are incredible. Your filo pastry is so light and crumbly and oh, those priganice doughnut things you do. Heavenly!'

Milo nodded in agreement. He was so smitten with Kat and I could see she felt the same. He was so different to Adam, who could be so negative and anti-change he'd knocked all the confidence out of her.

I carried on, 'Ana and Maria could take samples on trays around the harbour to draw in the crowds. Dav and I could hold the fort.'

'That's a brilliant idea, Mum. I've seen you organise this kind of thing at the charity events you do.'

'And I was wondering about a cook book. I've been googling cook books to see if anyone does any sort of fusion Montenegrin and British cuisine. There's no one but you, Kat. Think what that could do for the restaurant and your career.'

'Wow!' She obviously liked the idea. 'But would anyone buy it?'

'Of course they would!' Milo and I protested together.

'I wouldn't have a clue how to go about it.' Kat smiled.

'Leave that to me. Your head is always full of recipes, Kat. That's all you ever think about. Well, not all you think about.' This time Milo smiled. 'It's just an idea and will take time, but it's something you could look into in the future.'

Milo's hand rested on Kat's knee and they kept stealing secret glances. It made me wish I could see Neil again. We'd Facetimed earlier on, but the conversation was a bit stilted.

'So, how is the restaurant going?' he'd asked, looking as handsome as ever.

'Hectic. There are quieter times, of course, but it's a good business and Kat is gaining a great reputation as a chef. You'll have to visit some time.' Was that too forward? Meeting in person, you had all sorts of clues – body language, nuances in tone – to indicate how the other person was reacting. On screen, it was so much harder, especially as we were still getting used to each other.

'How's work going with you?' I asked.

'Not too busy at the moment. Olls came over again yesterday and we had a game and some lunch afterwards. It was great to see him. I'm sure you'd get on well with him.'

I nodded and contemplated telling Neil about Ivan, but I didn't in the end, and the conversation fizzled out. I hoped our budding relationship wouldn't go the same way. Then Kat and Milo came in and I had to cut the conversation dead. I felt sad and very far away from him. I comforted myself thinking that we'd be together again in just over a week's time.

Rosa's place was about two miles from the restaurant, in a stunning location, on top of a promontory. Kat had told me it had floor to ceiling windows to make the most of the views of the dazzling Adriatic Sea. Luka asked us to visit, just to cheer Rosa up. She'd had her first round of chemotherapy and she hadn't seen anyone apart from Luka. I wasn't sure she'd want to see me, but Luka insisted she did and was keen to hear how the restaurant was carrying on without her. He was like an enthusiastic Labrador. Rosa had done something right in bringing up such a good-natured young man, I decided. There wasn't much of Dan in his temperament, although they looked so alike. Rosa's illness had knocked the stuffing out of Luka. If only for his sake, I agreed. In the car, Kat and I agreed to downplay the whole Ivan business.

'The summer season will be winding down soon,' Kat said, as she swerved round a sharp corner, revealing the wooded valleys dropping down to the picturesque coastline below. 'I think Rosa is worried how she'll be able to sustain the restaurant. She's not likely to be up to working for a while. The chemo has a cumulative effect and she'll probably feel shittier as time goes on.'

'Is there any progress with finding a new manager?' Kat's little Toyota didn't have air-conditioning and my legs were sticking to the seat.

'Luka has put the feelers out. He knows lots of people in the restaurant trade. The only thing is that she's not sure she can afford to pay someone for too long. They still get some trade from locals in the winter, but the restaurant is nowhere near as lucrative as in the summer. Finding a new chef is difficult enough. That's why Ivan, chef-extraordinaire, managed to hold on to his job for so long.'

The incline continued to rise, until Rosa and Luka's place was visible on the top of the headland, a modest stone cottage from the back, with its terracotta roof and black wrought iron gates leading into the small driveway. As we walked towards the side of the cottage, the sight of the Adriatic made me catch my breath. The cottage enjoyed 180° uninterrupted views of Tivat to the left, with its huddle of hotels, villas and restaurants around its bustling harbour, and untouched, emerald green valleys to the right. The glittering sea lay gem-like below.

'Do you think she will mind me being here?' I asked as Kat tapped the door and walked into the kitchen. Kat shook her head.

Luka welcomed us as effusively as ever, giving Kat a hug and then me. 'Thank you for coming.' He smiled. 'Mum is a lot brighter today. Coffee? Go into the lounge. I'll bring it in.'

Rosa was in an armchair facing the windows and she turned to us as we walked in. My shock caught in my throat. She was always very slim, but her lack of appetite was already taking its toll. Her usually glossy hair looked thin and lifeless, and her make-up-free face was getting hollow.

She stood up and Kat folded her in her arms. 'Rosa, how are you? I've been longing to see you.'

Rosa turned to me and it felt natural to hug her. My heart went out to her. 'Hello, Rosa.' I sat beside her.

'It's lovely to see you both. And poor Luka needs more than his mother for company.'

'You're always thinking about Luka,' Kat scolded her gently. 'It's time to think about yourself for once.'

'He's my boy, my sweet boy.'

Luka came in with the coffees.

'He's not always sweet,' Kat teased.

'Your house is beautiful,' I told her, taking in the muted beige and cream décor, the candles and huge white hydrangeas in glass vases. I spotted the photograph that I had found in the study after the funeral, the one with Dan, Rosa and Luka. It seemed incongruous to see Dan in this house. Rosa caught me looking and I glanced away quickly.

'You're back at the hospital next week? How many times will you have to go?' asked Kat.

'I have six rounds, so another five to go. I felt awful, really terrible a few days after the first sessions. Exhausted. But I can cope. I'm strong,' she said.

'Mum, you need me to look after you for once, please.' Luka frowned.

Rosa touched her hair, looking embarrassed. 'Luka has agreed to shave my hair at the weekend. He's a good boy. I don't know what I have done to deserve him.' Luka looked tearful.

'It's only hair,' she admonished. 'It will grow back. It's my way of feeling in control. I might even keep it short. Is it "elfy" they call it?'

Kat and Luka laughed, breaking the tension. 'Elfin,' Kat said.

'Tell me all about the restaurant,' Rosa asked. 'Don't miss anything. Is it busy? Is Ivan working hard? How do you find him, Kat?'

Rosa was too astute to miss the glance that passed between Kat and Luka.

'Don't worry. I'm keeping an eye on him,' I told her.

'Mum's had some terrific ideas for developing the restaurant,' Kat said.

'You two go and make lunch. Please help him, Kat,' Rosa said. 'We will just end up with eggs and toast if it's left to Luka. Grace can tell me all her ideas.'

I ran through the things I'd discussed with Kat and Milo the night before. Rosa's eyes lit up with excitement.

'You are like a breath of fresh air there, Grace. Just like Kat. I always go with my gut instinct and when I tasted Kat's food, I knew how much she would bring to the restaurant. She's done more than I could ever have imagined. She's very driven, just like Dan.' There was a moment of silence, before Rosa continued, 'You two are a great team. But I have little to invest in making too many changes. Once you finish, I will have to pay someone to do front of house and it will be difficult as the summer season draws to an end.'

'I realise that. I've looked at ways that you could develop it without it costing too much.'

'You are very creative.'

We lapsed into silence once more and I looked out at the cobalt blue sky, cloudless and perfect, like the most exquisite painting. We could hear laughter coming from the kitchen.

'I am sorry, Grace. I have hurt you so much. Meeting you and getting to know you and Kat, has brought home to me the devastation Dan and I caused you. In the abstract, I never thought about you too much, never felt too guilty. I was wrong.'

The protestation caught in my throat. This interaction was so different to our first one.

'Can you hear those two?' Rosa smiled suddenly. 'Dan was a bastard and I was selfish, but it's brought Kat and Luka together, brother and sister. It was meant to be.'

I nodded, not trusting myself to speak, but I took her hand in mine.

'Listen, Grace, before Luka comes in again. Will you and Kat try to encourage him to go to university? He's an intelligent young man. If he doesn't go this year, I am afraid he will never go. Please.'

Kat and Luka burst into the lounge. 'Are you up to eating on the terrace, Mum?' Luka asked. 'I've put up the umbrella, so it won't be too hot.'

'I've made a fresh tuna salad and a few sides,' Kat said. 'Let's just say it's rustic.'

We sat outside on the terrace enjoying a long lunch. Luka poured us glasses of chilled rosé and Kat squealed, 'No, Luka, not too much for me. I'm driving.'

'Please,' I joked, 'don't add drink to the mix. Her driving is dodgy enough as it is.'

'Dodgy?' Rosa asked, puzzled. We all laughed. The atmosphere was light-hearted.

I noticed Rosa sipped water and ate little: some tuna, olives and bread. Her wrists were stick thin.

'So, Luka, is it general law you'll study?'

'Yes, it is only in the third year you get to specialise.'

'Do you have any idea what you want to do?'

'I find corporate law quite interesting. I'm not sure yet.'

'A big shot lawyer, eh? You will remember us when you're making your millions?' Kat laughed.

He sipped his wine. He would be starting uni in a matter of weeks. I could understand his reluctance to go. Rosa would find it difficult to cope on her own here. I wondered if Aunt Sofija would agree to look after her. I made a mental note to mention it to Kat in the car on the way home. Sofija was in her seventies but she was fit and healthy and she drove. I had no idea what she would think of caring for Dan's mistress. It was a long shot but worth a try.

After lunch, I carried the dishes inside as Kat and Luka cleared up the kitchen. Rosa went for a lie-down in her bedroom.

'This treatment has really taken it out of her. I dread how she'll be after the next one,' Luka said solemnly.

'She's tough, Luka,' I said, 'tougher than you think.' He didn't look convinced.

'Shall we go for a walk around the cliffs, Luka? Mum, do you want to come?' Kat asked.

'No, you two go. I'm going to have coffee on the terrace, and I might call Auntie Claire. She's off today.'

'Hi hon,' Claire greeted me in her usual way. 'How's things going there?'

'Good. Well, busy. Kat and I are here having lunch with Rosa and Luka.' I made sure Kat and Luka were far in the distance and I was out of earshot of Rosa's room.

'Jeez, that must be awkward.' Claire blew out a long breath.

'It's not, actually. I feel sorry for her. Going through chemo is hellish. And she's worried about the restaurant. Life throws these horrible things at you.'

'What a setup,' Claire said. 'You having lunch with Dan's mistress and his son!'

'Weirdly, I'm not thinking about it too much. And even more weirdly, they feel a bit like family.'

'A therapist would have a field day working through that! Still, I suppose all families are fucked up in some way or other.'

'That's true. You have such a wonderful way with words! How's things with you?'

'Great, to be honest. Laura and I went shopping. We haven't done that for months. I feel like I've got my daughter back. Having said that, teenagers have a way of making you feel as if you're ninety. Everything I picked up to show her, she either wrinkled her nose and said, "Really, Mum, I wouldn't be seen dead in that," or smiled patronisingly and said, "Hmm, for you maybe."'

'They think they know it all and you were never young.'

'So, have you booked your flight back?'

'Not yet. I need to. Sylvie phoned last night and she's putting the pressure on. The charity's got a couple of big events coming up. I just don't want to leave Rosa and Kat in the lurch. She can't really afford to pay someone else. I'll have to decide soon.'

'You'll have to come back sooner or later,' Claire said firmly. 'Have you heard from Hadley the Hunk?'

'Is that what you're calling him now? Yes, I spoke to him last night. It's not the same over the phone, though.'

'That man ain't gonna be single for long,' Claire teased. 'You better hot-foot it back home soon before he's snapped up!'

I knew she was only teasing but I thought about what Claire said all the way back to Tivat.

CHAPTER THIRTY-FIVE

🌿 Kat 🌿

'A cookbook?' Luka asked incredulously.

'I know, it would be a dream come true, a dream I didn't know I had until now.' I smiled. Luka and I were walking side by side up the narrow mountain path. It was nice to have some alone time together, and to get Luka out of the house. He'd been so caught up in the stress of his mum and what to do about uni, I don't think he'd left Rosa's side since she'd had the diagnosis. He looked paler than usual, and almost as slim as she did.

'Go for it.' Luka smiled. 'You can put Montenegrin food on the map! I can totally see it now. Just make sure you dedicate it to your brother.'

'I will, I'll write: To my annoying little brother.' I grinned. Luka humoured me with a laugh. I could tell he wasn't himself though, he'd been subdued and thoughtful throughout our visit.

'Do you know what you're going to do yet?' I asked.

Luka kept his eyes firmly down on the path.

'You'd better not be giving me a lecture as well, Kat. It's all I hear, Go to uni, Go to uni. Even Milo sent me a text to tell me that, and I thought he was too busy kissing you to think of anything else.' I rolled my eyes.

295

'Well, that's because you should go to uni. But I don't want to lecture you. Let's just sit for a moment.' I gestured to a bench.

We both flopped down side by side. I tried to ignore the heat of the metal bars on my bare thighs. It was another gorgeous day, Montenegro certainly wasn't short of them, and the view here stretched across the whole of Tivat and the narrow fjord-like bay.

'This used to be my favourite place to sit as a child,' Luka said. 'The number of times I'd tell Mum I was running away, and I'd come and camp here with my rucksack packed.' We both laughed.

'God, I can't imagine you and Rosa arguing.'

'We did. She was quite protective when I was a child. I couldn't go to parties, couldn't go out on the boat.'

'Actually, I can imagine you were a nightmare as a child,' I laughed. 'You two seem so close, though.'

'So do you and Grace.' He nudged my arm with his elbow.

'Believe it or not, we weren't always. I was closer to Dad growing up,' I explained. 'Mum was always flying off the handle, but Dad was the calm, logical one. Mum and I clashed too much. We're too similar.' I couldn't believe how much things had changed since then. We'd been through more pain than I could have ever imagined. And now we were a team. When Dad died, I'd worried it would shake our already fragile relationship, but I was glad the opposite had happened. Mum and I needed each other.

'Do you think we would have got along growing up?' Luka tipped his head to the side to look at me.

'Me and you? God no, we're both used to being spoilt only-children. You would have got on my nerves being a smart-arse and I would have got on yours talking about boys all the time.'

'That's true,' Luka agreed. 'I'm sad we didn't get to find out, though.'

'Well, we have each other now.' I nodded slowly. 'And we'll always be close, even when you're miles away in Berlin.'

'Shut up,' Luka said, but I could tell he was laughing. I was starting to get through to him.

'I can see why you like it here, it's amazing.' I gazed at the view. 'Divno!' I'd learnt the Montenegrin for 'amazing' from Lovro, who loved to exclaim it loudly in the restaurant.

'Impressive,' Luka said, 'but your pronunciation really needs work.' It was nice to see him making jokes again.

'Smart-arse. Come on, let's go back to our mothers. We've run away long enough,' I said.

The look on Lovro's face when I walked into Café Lompar told me everything. He walked straight over to me, gesturing for us to go outside. He glanced round for Ivan, who could often be found smoking out the back of the café with Davor.

'It's been a nightmare,' Lovro said, eyes wide.

'Oh no, why? Don't tell me Ivan...' I started.

'I don't think he can cope. We had three complaints by one o'clock, and Ivan refused to do anything about them.'

My heart sank. Three complaints were no coincidence. Ivan's shoddy work was dragging us down.

I opened my mouth to speak but Lovro cut in. 'That's not all.' He took a big gulp as if steeling himself for something big. 'He refused to cook the buzara. Just refused. He wouldn't let me do it either.'

'Why not?' I felt equal parts confused and outraged.

'He said he didn't want to make it your way and,' Lovro paused and looked sheepish, 'he said he didn't want to ruin our national dish.'

It was like a blow to my heart. I'd worked so hard to stay authentic to Montenegrin dishes and treat them with the care they deserved.

White hot rage built up inside me. That stubborn bastard! He was pig-headed and too lazy to change. Too scared to change.

Too scared to change.

Milo's words came back to me. There was no excuse for his temper or rudeness, but Ivan had been through a lot. I'd promised to give him a chance. I looked at Lovro's nervous face.

'Well, Ivan probably wants what's best for the Café,' I sighed.

Lovro looked betrayed.

'Ivan's worked here so long, he knows the dishes well. It must be hard for him to have us making changes all the time. Who knows, he might be able to help develop our dishes,' I explained. 'Maybe we can find a way to work together?'

'Sure,' Lovro said miserably.

I wanted to tell him the real reason for my change of heart, but didn't want to sound like someone who would fall for a sob story. The truth was Ivan had been through a hard time, but that didn't excuse his behaviour. I had to find a way to create harmony in the kitchen.

'I've had an idea,' I said.

'Rustic night?' Ivan frowned.

'Back to basics, back to the roots of Montenegrin cooking,' I explained. 'You can take the lead tonight, go back to the old

298

dishes of Café Lompar. We'll serve thick pšenični bread to go with every meal, and offer a reduced menu of the classics done well. I'm excited.'

'And we'll play traditional music front of house,' Mum said. I'd got her on board with my idea earlier: to trial the authentic menu, on Ivan's terms, to see if that would soften him.

'What were your best-selling dishes before I came in?' I asked him.

'Balšića tava,' Ivan said thoughtfully.

I tried not to show my reaction. I wasn't a big fan of the fried veal dish. But this experiment was my idea and I had to take a back seat tonight.

'Also, Čorbast Pasulj, gužvara pastry...'

We drew up a quick menu and Mum copied it down on to a chalkboard to display outside, before agreeing on a price for the set meal. I hoped our loyal customers wouldn't mind the change of menu and our carousel of small taster classic dishes would work well. Lovro looked as unsure as I felt. But this was Ivan's chance to prove himself.

I wasn't convinced that the old-fashioned stew was up to our usual standard, but I carried on cooking with Ivan at the helm. Mum kept poking her head round the kitchen door, no doubt worried that she'd be the one dealing with any unhappy customers out the front.

Lovro's priganice fritters for dessert were delicious. I pinched another one from the sugar-dusted tray, as I watched Ivan going about his business. There was none of the continual tasting and checking of the balance of flavours that I'd had drummed into me when I was in college. He didn't seem to put much care into the food at all. This was just a job to him, whereas to me it was everything. But I knew I couldn't say anything. Dealing with Ivan was like walking on eggshells, any hint of criticism and you'd get a grunt or smarmy comment.

Mum came back in carrying a tray of bowls.

'Table three enjoyed their dolmades, but table four said the broth was a bit bland,' she said, eyeing Ivan carefully. I sighed. 'Is there anything we can do to change it?' she asked, tentatively.

'Have you tasted it?' I asked Ivan, knowing he hadn't. There were a million ways of elevating the broth.

'The soup is fine,' he huffed, then mumbled something in Montenegrin.

'I think it needs more seasoning,' I suggested, coming to stand beside him.

Ivan looked at me with total disgust in his eyes. His line had been crossed. Again. He started to walk away, but not before I heard him mutter, 'Idiot,' under his breath.

'What did you call my daughter?' Mum demanded, outraged.

Ivan held a hand up. The three of us watched his retreating back as he walked out.

'This isn't working, Kat,' Lovro said. 'What can we do?'

I crossed my arms, feeling overwhelmed. It was clear Ivan was never going to change. Was he even going to come back today?

'Let's stick with the same menu, but do it our way,' I instructed him.

Lovro smiled back.

'I'm sorry, Mum, please can you tell the diners there's going to be a delay on the next courses.' I hated saying it but knew honesty was the best policy.

'Can we make some kind of nibble to take round in the meantime?' Mum asked. I smiled. She really did have business acumen. Milo and I had been impressed by her ideas for the restaurant.

'I can make some punjene paprike quickly,' Lovro suggested.

'They're these amazing stuffed peppers Lovro makes,' I explained to Mum. 'Let's go.'

'I don't know what I'm going to do about him,' I moaned to Maria and Ana at the end of the night. Ivan had come back twenty minutes after his tantrum but proceeded to sulk at the back of the kitchen. Every order I gave him was met with a grunt or a stream of Montenegrin. I hated the way he undermined me. I hadn't loathed anyone this much since Mark at Truffles.

'Just get rid,' Maria said. 'He's been like this for years. I'm sorry, Kat, but that man will never change.'

'I know, I know,' I sighed.

'Anyway...' Maria drained her cup of coffee. 'I'd better get going or I'll miss the last bus to Kotor.'

'See you tomorrow,' Ana called after her.

'Tell her all about your date with lover boy,' Maria shouted as she left the Café. I turned to Ana. I didn't know her as well as Maria. She'd only just started in Café Lompar. But she seemed nice enough and Maria had been friends with her for years.

'Who's lover boy?' Ana asked, leaning in towards me.

'Isn't it obvious?' I'd seen the nudges and wolf-whistles Maria and the other staff made whenever Milo visited us. 'Milo.'

'Milo?' She looked away, grimacing into her coffee cup.

'What?' I asked, sensing there was a story behind her expression.

'Well, it makes sense — you are new here. I think every new girl in town has been out with Milo Martinović.' She must have seen my appalled expression because she covered up quickly with, 'I'm sorry, I shouldn't say that. He's a nice guy really.'

I didn't know how to react, so I just sipped my coffee. There was an awkward silence.

'He is a flirt,' I said eventually, wondering if I could make light of this. 'Isn't every guy in Montenegro, though?' Luka was an awful flirt. He couldn't keep away from Maria. I'd even seen Lovro batting his eyelashes whenever Dav came in the kitchen.

'All I'm saying is be careful.' Ana touched my arm. I could feel my happy buzz fading quickly. 'Don't let him charm you, and do not fall in love with him ... because he'll just move on to the next girl.'

'Right,' I said, trying to act casual, when really I wanted to exit this conversation as quickly as possible and cry into my pillow.

Maybe Ana didn't know him well? Milo certainly seemed trustworthy. Maybe she was jealous? I decided to bite the bullet.

'Have you been out with him?' I asked.

She tipped her head back and gave a laugh. 'Oh God no!' She shook her head. 'My sister was unlucky enough to date him a few years ago. They went on a few dates. He took her out on the boat, then after she invited him back to meet our parents, she found him sleeping with one of the tourists. On his boat, of all places!'

The disappointment was crushing. I just didn't see Milo as a sleazy guy. It didn't sound like the man I knew. Maybe he'd grown up since then?

'I shouldn't say this. I don't want to ruin things between you. I just don't want you to get hurt like she did.' Ana looked sincere.

'OK,' I said. I didn't know how to feel. Should I believe her? I didn't see why she would tell me this if there wasn't some element of truth to it. Ana started talking about her own boyfriend, but I couldn't concentrate on what she was saying.

My phone vibrated in my pocket. I checked it and saw Milo's name. I suddenly felt less excited to read it than I usually did.

'I'd better head off,' I said to Ana, getting up.

'OK, me too. Hope you have a good night.' She looked apologetic.

'Night.' I started the walk home. I wondered if I'd feel this sad if I'd just decided to go back to London after all.

CHAPTER THIRTY-SIX

 Grace

Kat was really subdued when she got back to the apartment. I could tell something was up as soon as she walked in. I'd gone straight back after finishing at the restaurant, and Kat had stayed on as she sometimes did. The waiting staff often stayed behind for a drink or she, Luka, Lovro and Maria would go into town to a late-night bar. Luka hadn't been out for a while, of course. Kat needed to let off steam. The hours were long in the restaurant and I worried that she worked too hard. She would tell me I was fussing too much.

Tonight, though, Kat looked really tired and down. She had a shower straight away and then we had a hot chocolate on the balcony.

'Very rock and roll,' I joked as I handed her a mug. She barely mustered a smile. 'I think that Ivan is really crossing a line, you know,' I told her. 'We can't keep covering for him. You should have heard the complaints tonight. It was embarrassing.'

'I know, Mum. Let me handle it, OK?'

We lapsed into silence. A motorbike puttered past, a girl on the back, her arms snaking around the rider.

'Are you all right, Kat?' I asked after a while.

'I don't know,' she sighed. 'I'm wondering if I've taken on too much. Trying all these new recipes, the newspaper columns for Pobjeda.' After the interview had gone so well, Kat had secured a weekly slot in the oldest and one of the most prestigious newspapers in Montenegro. She had written one column so far, on her fusion concept for Café Lompar. She also included a simple-to-follow recipe. 'Then there's the cook book. It's exciting, but ... am I up to it? Perhaps Ivan's right and I shouldn't be messing around with traditional recipes. They were successful long before I arrived.' She stared at the sea.

'Rubbish. This is just self-doubt. See it for what it is, Kat. You deserve this success.'

'Everything's happening so fast. In Truffles, I knew what I was doing and was slowly gaining a reputation.'

'Yes, and you had to put up with that knob of a boss, who took all the credit for your hard work. I've never seen you so happy as you are here. You're so passionate about cooking and you can taste it in your food. You're the best chef around!'

She gave a reluctant smile. 'I think you're a little biased, Mum.'

'It's not just me, Kat, and you know it. Everyone loves your food.'

'Ana told me something about Milo tonight.' She hesitated, and I could see her eyes fill with tears. 'Basically, he's slept with most of the women in Tivat and he cheated on her sister.'

'Oh.' Now I didn't know what to say.

'I'm really falling for him,' she said, wiping a tear away. 'I thought I could trust him.'

'Look, don't rush to conclusions. Ana's sister might have an axe to grind. You don't know Milo's side of things. He's probably like every attractive young man his age. Of course he's had lots of girlfriends.' I smiled. 'Let's be fair, you've had your share of boyfriends too.' I thought about Claire's words to me after I had seen Neil with his ex-wife Cass. 'Not every man is untrustworthy. There are good ones out there.'

She went to bed soon after and I tossed and turned all night worrying about her.

Simply Delicious? Café Lompar's Fusion Recipes? Cooking Kat Style? I had to work on that one. Montenegrin Recipes with a British Twist?

I was doodling possible names for cook books. I'd already contacted a few publishers and one or two had shown an interest, although they suggested we should get Kat an agent. Kat had lots of recipes and I was trying to collate some of them before she came home last night.

The restaurant was pretty quiet in the mornings and Ana and Maria had gone to the square with some samples, Ana with the sweet tray, the delicious priganice, mini doughnuts and the chocolate and hazelnut bureks, while Maria carried the savoury dishes, Kat's homemade bread with mashed avocado, some with feta and mint, and others with chorizo, pepperdew and smoked paprika. They looked delicious and would certainly draw the crowds. We were also giving out two-for-one vouchers for brunches. If we did this for a week or two, I was certain that the tourists and locals would starting coming in earlier. Ana and Maria were so excited. It was fun for them to get out of the restaurant for an hour.

We all needed cheering up. The tension between Ivan and Kat was really souring the atmosphere. He was a liability. He seemed to me to be purposely trying to ruin the reputation of Café Lompar. Kat was willing to give him another chance, but here he was, late again today. I would have fired him on the spot for walking out yesterday. She was far too soft.

Ana and Maria walked in, hooting with laughter.

'Hey, Grace,' Ana said excitedly, 'they've all gone!'

'Within ten minutes,' Maria talked over her. 'We walked once down the promenade and they'd all been eaten.'

'Did you give out the vouchers?' I asked.

'Yes.' Ana put down her tray. 'Some people will be in soon and others said they'd try it tomorrow. They were very keen.'

Oh Lord, I did hope that Ivan would turn up soon. It was all very well pulling in the extra customers, but Kat and Lovro would struggle to cope on their own.

Ana and Maria were wearing black polo shirts with Café Lompar across the chest. I wondered whether the place needed rebranding — if calling it a café was really appropriate for the kind of food we were serving. It was fine dining standard. Kat had, after all, come from a Michelin-starred restaurant.

But I was getting ahead of myself. And I had other responsibilities apart from Café Lompar.

I thought back to the conversation I'd had with Sylvie last night. She had always been very supportive, especially since Dan had died. We had an affinity because we'd both lost our husbands. But she was decidedly cool to me last night and had asked me outright if I'd booked my flight back.

'I was going to ring you, Sylvie, to ask for an extension.'

I heard her sigh. 'Has no one been found to replace you yet?'

'Well, the advert has gone out,' I lied, 'and there are interviews this week.' I felt terrible. The truth was that with Rosa's hospital appointments, me getting used to all the systems at the restaurant and all the upset with Ivan, I'd had no time to even think of finding a replacement.

'Heather's been working on the Tower of London trip, but you know it's not her forté organising events like this. Liz has said she can help out, and she's angling for more work. You'll have to decide where your loyalties lie, Grace. I don't mean to put pressure on you, but we are struggling.'

'I'm sorry, Sylvie. I'll book the flight tomorrow and return in the week. I'll catch up with everything and put in extra hours,' I promised.

I thought about Sylvie's question. Where did my loyalties lie? To tell the truth, I was really enjoying myself at the restaurant. It was frustrating at times, especially with the mistakes I was making with the language. The way the Montenegrins rolled their r's was difficult to replicate. I was trying to listen to YouTube clips, but it was challenging. It could also be embarrassing. I tried to say, 'Excuse me' yesterday to a customer who had left her hat behind, and the way I pronounced 'Oprostite' sounded awfully like 'prostitute,' and drew some very strange looks from a nearby table of British tourists.

But, yes, I was enjoying getting my teeth into the front of house and dreaming up ways to promote the restaurant. I loved thinking creatively and being with Kat was great, not that I saw much of her in the day. This place challenged me far more than the charity events. The restaurant really needed some investment if it was going to grow and I worried about that, but it also made me want to help. I could see Kat in the future with cook books and tv appearances. It was exciting, all the potential for her and the restaurant. I'd mooted the idea of having wine tasting evenings in the winter months or cocktail-making parties. Dav had been all over that, showing more enthusiasm than he had in a long time.

But I missed Neil. Deep inside, I worried I was sacrificing a promising relationship by staying. How often did a woman over fifty meet someone they fancied, someone single and interested in her? One of my neighbours in my last house had divorced in her fifties. She often came over for coffee and told me how she was trying various dating sites: Plenty of Fish, Match.com. She met someone perfect for her in the end, but it took so much time it was like having a second job.

Neil and I had just clicked. I would be a fool to let him go. I missed the way he looked at me, his touch. But our conversation was drying up now that we weren't seeing each other. If I didn't return soon, it would be over.

Ivan strolled in.

'Afternoon, Ivan,' I said, sarcastically.

He looked at the trays the girls had taken out and his lip curled. He ignored me and waved to Dav, who was re-stocking the fridges with wine bottles.

Outside, the sky had darkened into a bruised purple. Since I arrived in Montenegro, the weather had been gloriously and achingly sunny, but now a storm was brewing. I loved Café Lompar, more than I thought I would, but I wondered if Kat and I had bitten off more than we could chew.

CHAPTER THIRTY-SEVEN

 Kat

I took a deep breath when Milo came into view. The cut of his tanned jaw stood out against the cool blue of his linen shirt. He was clean shaven, a new look for him, even more distinguished than his usual sexy stubble. I didn't want to feel this way. Why couldn't he be less handsome? No wonder he'd had his pick of women.

I watched at the window as he climbed the steps up to my apartment. Was I being silly? I'd spent the last two days going back and forth, changing my mind from Milo's side to Ana's. Should I tell him today? Mum had told me not to, just take Milo at his word and enjoy my time with him.

He knocked. My heart was pounding as I paused before opening the door so that he wouldn't know I'd been waiting next to it.

'Hi.' He leaned in to kiss me on the cheek, opening his arms wide. 'You look stunning.'

'You look nice too. I'm nearly ready.' I beckoned him inside.

'Your mum's not here this time?' Milo teased. I gave a weak laugh.

'She's at the restaurant.'

Milo's smile lowered a little. No doubt if I hadn't had the conversation with Ana, I'd be all over him like a rash now.

'Are you alright?' he asked, concern in his face.

'Yeah,' I answered, not meeting his eyes.

'Has the restaurant been busy?'

'As always.'

There was a small awkward pause. I grabbed my bag. 'Shall we go?'

Milo and I walked to his car in silence. I felt I was being a bitch. It was becoming clear I wouldn't be able to pretend nothing had happened. I decided to talk to him when we got to Kotor.

'So, you've not been back to Kotor since the first week you came with Grace?' Milo asked. The car snaked around the coastal road.

'No.' I realised I couldn't leave another awkward silence. 'It will be nice to see it again with you.' Milo seemed to cheer up at my hint of encouragement.

'Look,' He pointed across the bay to the harbour, dotted with tourist noticeboards. 'That's where we first met.'

I looked across the azure bay. I wondered if he met many women here. Should I have run the other way that first day? Not allowed myself to fall for his charm? Would that have saved me this heartache?

We parked, not far from Apartman Nina. How much had changed since we'd stayed there!

Milo put his hand on my thigh. 'If you don't want to go out today, don't worry. We can do something another time?'

Any other day I would have appreciated his attentiveness, but today I bristled. 'I'm fine, honestly. Let's have a coffee.'

We strolled in through the city walls, and I marvelled once

more at the ancient stone architecture and narrow streets. It was such a romantic place, despite my torn feelings. Milo kept my hand in his. We found a little café, walking up a set of narrow steps to a rooftop terrace. It reminded me of the place we stopped at in Dubrovnik, where I first started to fall for Milo.

I couldn't pretend. I had to talk to him, and decide if I was being led right into heartbreak, or if this was the start of something important.

'Look Milo, I know I've not been myself today,' I started.

'I think I know why.' Milo put his menu down. 'It's Ivan, isn't it? He's really getting to you. I've heard from Luka and Maria what a nightmare he's been.' He paused to order two cappuccinos and a plate of baklava to share. 'I know I said all that stuff about his past, but I didn't mean to make you feel guilty, Kat. You're an excellent chef and it's clear that Ivan's intimidated by you. You do what you have to do.' He waved his hand, as if flicking Ivan into the Adriatic.

I smiled. It was nice to have the validation from Milo, even if it wasn't what I wanted to discuss. And he was right: Ivan would have to be dealt with, and I was starting to see how.

I took a breath, still unsure if I should go down this rabbit-hole or not.

'Ivan is an issue,' I admitted. 'And so are you.'

Milo looked dismayed. I didn't mean to sound so dramatic.

'What do you mean?' His voice was unsteady.

'I spoke to Ana the other day,' I said, wondering if he would connect the dots to her sister.

'Ana Ivanković? What did she say?'

'She told me what happened with you and her sister.'

Realisation started to dawn in his eyes. 'Oh no. She still hates me.'

'She does.' My heart was sinking. There was clearly some truth to Ana's words. Milo wasn't denying it. 'She said some other things as well. About your reputation. I didn't realise you offered other services ... on your boat.'

Milo looked affronted. 'I don't know what she told you. But I know it's one side of a very twisted story. I did some things wrong, but can I tell you what happened?'

I realised I was sitting with my arms crossed and my body tilted away from him. There'd never been this distance between us before. It was painful. I owed it to Milo to listen to him.

'I've told you about my childhood. But I haven't told you how bad things got with my father. He was a drinker, and it got hard for us at home. His temper when he'd been drinking... He obviously missed my mum, but he took it out on my sister and me.' Milo sighed.

I touched his arm, wanting to show I was listening. I didn't see quite how this connected to Ana's story, though.

'I was desperate to leave that house, and I was very young when I came to Tivat. Young and stupid. Of course I had some ... flings.'

I took my hand back, although I knew I had no right to judge Milo's love life.

'It was the wrong time to meet Ana's sister. She wanted more than I could give. I was busy, setting up my business, travelling back on the weekends to check on my sister. My heart wasn't in it. I was a terrible boyfriend, but I never promised her more. She was frustrated and we had massive fights.'

'And you slept with someone else?' I asked.

Milo nodded slowly.

'I did. I don't want to say it, but it's true. I saw how upset she was and I realised I had to grow up. But that was years ago, another lifetime. I'm a different person now.'

He paused as our food arrived. Although it was unpleasant to hear, I appreciated his honesty.

'Kat, you're the first person I've met in a long time who's made me feel this way.' He looked in my eyes. 'If you're worried that you're just another fling, that's not true. Ask Luka and Rosa. I'm crazy about you.' His voice went quiet, almost as if he were shy.

'I feel the same way,' I said, my voice small too.

'I know you haven't known me long enough to trust me, but I really think this could go somewhere.'

'So do I.'

I hoped I wasn't being naive. Would I just end up heartbroken? I'd never have thought Dad capable of cheating. And here Milo was, telling me he'd cheated on someone. Was it bound to happen again?

Even so, I couldn't help the way I felt.

'I'm not one to judge your past. We've all made mistakes.' I smiled. 'I'll get past this. Just give me a few days to brood.'

Milo laughed. 'I'll do it for you.'

'Good. And let me have all this baklava. I'm starving.'

He kissed me hard. It felt nice.

The rest of the day passed quickly. After a long, leisurely coffee, we strolled around Kotor and some of the art galleries. I couldn't say if I'd made my mind up about Milo, but I was enjoying walking hand in hand with him. It felt right.

'I'd better get back. I've got an early shift tomorrow,' I said, checking the time on my phone.

'Can't you just skip it?' Milo teased, knowing full well I would do no such thing.

'It's busier than ever before now.' I pulled him along the street towards the gates to the old town. 'I think Mum's doing something right. She has so many fantastic ideas.' The shimmering ocean blue came into view.

'Thanks for a lovely day,' I said, when we pulled up outside my flat. 'I need to go in and get an early night.'

'Maybe I could come in and join you?' Milo joked. I was tempted, but I didn't have much time.

'OK, at least I'll walk you to your door.' Milo offered me the nook of his elbow like an old-fashioned butler.

'Thank you, kind sir,' I giggled, slipping my arm through his. 'I've really enjoyed today ... honestly.' I emphasised the word, even if I didn't feel fully back to normal.

'Good,' he said. 'I'm glad. If you ever need to talk about something again, just tell me. I'm not going anywhere.'

I looked into Milo's eyes, gentle and sincere.

'OK.' I'd made my mind up. I trusted him.

We walked across the courtyard together. As my eyes adjusted to the shade, I realised there was someone sitting on my steps.

'Adam?'

'Kat!' He stood up, holding onto the railing.

'What—? What are you doing here?' My whole body tensed and I saw Milo look at me. I thought I was going to be sick.

'I wanted to surprise you,' he said in a meek voice.

'I'll leave you be,' Milo whispered, giving my hand a squeeze

315

before backing away. I turned and he gave an understanding smile. I'd only given him little details about Adam, but he'd obviously put two and two together.

I gripped on to the railing to steady myself. I felt a trickle of sweat drip down the back of my neck.

Adam moved towards me, keeping one eye on Milo's retreating back. 'Who is he? Is he the reason you're still here?'

I heard a door opening in one of the flats below, no doubt Mrs. Janković coming out to hear the gossip.

'Let's go inside,' I told Adam, not wanting a full showdown on the steps. We went inside to the living room and I gestured for him to sit down. I could not believe my eyes.

'How did you find me?' I asked, knowing I hadn't given him my address.

'Your Aunt Claire,' he answered. 'Kat, let me talk. I know things didn't end well between us, but please hear what I have to say.'

'All right.' I nodded. I was too stunned to say anything else, still feeling close to vomiting. An hour ago, I was in Kotor with Milo's arm round me. Now I was with Adam. It was surreal.

He sat on my sofa. I mirrored him, sitting at the other end.

'The last month has been the worst of my life, Kat. I didn't want to admit it to myself, but I miss you. Me and you ... we're just right together, aren't we? Have you missed me at all?' he asked, trying to meet my eyes.

There were things I had missed about Adam. The way we knew each other inside out was comforting. Sometimes when I'd had a hard day in London, listening to Adam talk through his issues made me feel better. And he did love me in his own way.

'In some ways ... but, Adam, I'm happy here.'

'Are you really? As happy as at home?' he pleaded.

I certainly was happy in Montenegro. Getting closer to Luka had been wonderful; it felt like I was closer to Dad. And I was doing my dream job, although Ivan had been a roadblock recently. Then there was Milo. Things hadn't been all rosy lately, but the idea of being back in London with Adam, taking the tube to Truffles every day, was unthinkable.

'I am. I want to be here,' I said, although I didn't sound as convinced as I wanted to.

'I could make you happier. I know I wasn't the best boyfriend, and you deserve much more. You're so beautiful and funny. I didn't appreciate how amazing you are. But I want to change that. If you come back, I promise you a better life.' He shuffled closer.

I didn't know why but I had an urge to touch him, to feel the warmth of his hands again. I held back. This was confusing.

'And you're an amazing chef. I ran into Mark the other day and he actually told me he misses you in Truffles,' he said.

This was a surprise. I couldn't believe he'd actually grown enough to admit that. Today was too much to digest; I could feel a headache coming on.

'He didn't say it explicitly, but I'm sure he'd be interested in having you back.'

'I'll stop you there,' I said, shaking my head. 'I don't want my old job back. You never listened to me saying how much I'm enjoying this job. I'm head chef here, and they appreciate me.'

'Well, can't you apply for head chef somewhere in London?' Adam asked, tipping his head to the side.

'I don't want to leave Café Lompar. It's in my blood,' I said, then stopped, remembering Adam didn't know my true connection to Luka and Rosa.

'Well, I could come out here. I've been thinking about taking the next step for a while. I'll find a job here. Couldn't we make it work?' Adam looked desperate.

I imagined Adam replacing Ivan. Something told me he wouldn't be problem-free in the kitchen either; I doubted he'd give me the respect I needed.

Why was I even considering this? The last thing I wanted was for Adam to be here. What right did he have to turn up and interrupt my life like this? I hadn't invited him. I hadn't spoken to him in weeks. My confusion started to turn to anger.

'What is this really about?' I demanded, standing up.

'What do you mean? I just want you back.'

'No,' I said. 'I know you too well, Adam. I know you wouldn't go to this effort for nothing. What's happened at home?' His mock innocence didn't fool me.

'Nothing's happened.'

We both locked eyes, neither of us moving. I knew from the flicker at the corner of his mouth that I'd landed on something. And then it all made sense.

'Michaela,' I said.

Adam pressed his lips together, tightly. I knew it.

'I want you, Kat.'

I stayed silent. Adam stared at me, before he let out a sigh and flopped back on the cushions.

'OK,' he said. 'Fine. We slept together a few times. After you left that day, I was so upset, and when Michaela came home ... she wanted to make me feel better. We didn't plan it. It wasn't a big deal, but they caught us at work.' He ran his hand through his hair, pulling the skin on his forehead taut.

'What happened?' I asked, trying to be gentle. I sat down next to him.

'We've been fired. Both of us.'

'Isn't this something you should be sorting out with her?'

'She doesn't want to know me anymore. She said the whole thing was a big mistake, and she's gone running back to her boyfriend. She wants me to move out and him to move in. How fucked up is that?'

I tried not to smile. I honestly felt bad for Adam, losing his job. 'What are you going to do?'

'I don't know.' He lay his head back against the sofa. 'I just don't know. My life's a mess.'

'Do you know what you need?'

'What?'

'A holiday.'

'With you?' he asked, hopefully.

'No,' I said. 'Alone.'

CHAPTER THIRTY-EIGHT

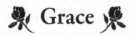 Grace

I couldn't believe it when I walked in and Adam was in the apartment. Kat had had the day off, out with Milo. I'd worried all day. She was so hurt and I'd prayed they'd make it up. I knew Kat was mad about him. So, when I walked up the steps to the apartment and heard voices, I'd assumed it was Milo.

They were both sitting at separate ends of the sofa, Adam with his tousled hair and self-pitying eyes, and you could cut the atmosphere with a knife. He looked startled to see me.

'Hello, Adam. How are you?'

'Fine, thanks. You?'

'Good.' He never did make much effort with me. He was so narcissistic and self-absorbed. I wondered what possessed him to come here. Kat was so over him and she told me after seeing him in London that the relationship was dead in the water. He didn't seem that bothered, she'd said at the time.

I looked at Kat. Her eyes were trying desperately to transmit some message to me.

'So, are you staying in Montenegro?' I asked him, putting my bag down and switching on the kettle.

'That's up to Kat,' he said, stealing a quick glance at her.

'Well, I'm going to take my tea to the bedroom,' I said. 'I need an early night. I'm shattered.'

I was settling down with a book when Kat crept in.

'Oh, my God, can you believe Adam's here? I came back from Kotor with Milo and he was waiting on the steps like some abandoned puppy,' Kat whispered.

'What the hell does he want?' I said, a bit too loudly.

'He's lost his job and been kicked out of the apartment in London and, basically, he's been begging me to go back with him. Telling me Mark is missing me too.'

'What have you said?'

Kat shot me an appalled look. 'What do you think? I'm letting him stay tonight but he's got to go in the morning. He's only here because Michaela threw him out.' She flopped on the end of the bed. 'Milo saw him when we came back. I'm going to have to ring him to explain.'

'Did you make up?'

She shrugged, non-committal. 'I'm going get a blanket for the sofa. God, what a mess it all is. Life's so bloody complicated sometimes.'

When I crept into the kitchen the next morning to make some toast and coffee, the living room was in darkness. Adam's feet were sticking out of the blanket, dangling over the edge of the sofa, and the smell of coffee, body odour and stale food from the night before lingered in the room. Ugh!

My phone was buzzing as I tiptoed back to the bedroom. It was a phone number I didn't recognise and when I pressed accept, I could hardly make out the voice.

'It's Rosa,' she said, pausing to take a breath. My stomach

flipped over. I couldn't think why she was calling me. 'I need to go to hospital. Luka is not home.'

'I'll be right there, Rosa,' I said, before hanging up.

Kat caught the end of the conversation as she came out of her bedroom, heard the panic in my voice, and insisted she was coming with me when I explained.

'No, Kat. You need to go to the restaurant. Maria can do front of house, but we'll never get a replacement chef in time and Ivan needs to be watched. Lovro can't cope on his own with him.' I was acutely aware that Adam was a chef, but knew Kat was desperate for him to go. He was a control freak in the kitchen and we didn't need any further complications. 'The hospital is in Podgorica. I'll have to take your Toyota. At least I've got my licence with me.'

'How did she sound?' Kat asked.

'Terrible. Weak. She thinks she's got a temperature.'

'It had to be when Luka is flat-hunting in Berlin. This will just prove to him that he shouldn't go.'

'We're here, though, and we'll manage. How long will it take me to get there, do you think?'

'It's about an hour and a half away. The traffic will be bad in the morning. I'll come across this afternoon if I can. Or tonight.'

'Do we tell Luka?'

'No, he'll be back tomorrow. There's nothing he can do.'

'What about him?' I whispered, pointing to the living room.

'I'll order him a taxi to the airport. He's not staying any longer than he has to, believe me.'

'I thought he might want to see Café Lompar?'

'He hasn't mentioned it. Typical Adam, really.'

As I drove to Rosa's, my stomach was churning. It was already warm, and I had the windows wound down. I wasn't sure of the roads, and some of the corners were precariously close to the edge of the steep valley.

I was worried about her. I felt differently towards Rosa now. No matter how hurt I'd been when I first found out about her, she was beginning to feel like family. Kat loved Luka and she was close to Rosa too. I was becoming more and more entangled in their lives. It was a bizarre set-up, but whose family was perfect? I couldn't think of a single one.

When I arrived at Rosa's, she looked a lot worse than the previous time we'd been there. She was in the armchair again, but her skin was deathly pale and waxy. She managed a weak smile as I entered the lounge.

'Hello, Rosa,' I said. 'How are you feeling?'

'Not good, Grace. I'm washed out and something is wrong.' Her voice was thin, as if she were speaking from far away.

'Come on, I'll take you to the hospital. You'll be fine. I'm going to take care of you.'

'I didn't know who to call. I don't want Luka to know.'

'Don't worry. We haven't called him. But you need to go to the hospital.' I placed my arm under hers and half-carried, half-supported her to the car.

'I'm too weak to dress,' she said, as her dressing gown slid across her legs in the car.

'That doesn't matter. You try and rest.'

She closed her eyes as I drove the distance to the hospital, guided by satnav. We crossed the Millennium Bridge, with its huge steel pylons soaring above us. I'd never been to Podgorica.

It was a bustling city, with traffic nose to tail in the busy streets of high-rise apartments and office buildings. This was a modern city which still retained its sense of the past. I felt stressed as we inched forward, desperately trying to search for the hospital signs amongst the Montenegrin street names.

'Take a left here,' Rosa said, her eyes opening momentarily. 'It's not far.'

The hospital was a grey, concrete, utilitarian building that seemed to stretch for miles. I remembered Dan telling me once that the Montenegrins had a similar health care system as Britain, with contributions taken from salaries. I parked the car and headed for reception to get a wheelchair for Rosa. I helped her into the chair and I followed the signs for the oncology department. The staff were helpful, even answering in English as I tried to explain Rosa's condition.

'Rosa Lompar. She is very ill,' I said, pointing to her. 'She comes for treatment here. She's got a really high temperature.'

'Please take a seat. We will find her records and call you as soon as a doctor becomes available. Are you next of kin?'

'Uh, no.' I hesitated. 'A cousin.'

'The doctor won't be long.'

Rosa just sat quietly, almost asleep. I didn't try to make conversation, just let her rest.

Ten minutes later, a doctor appeared. He led us into a cubicle. He still looked a teenager, younger than Luka even. He began speaking in Montenegrin.

'Govorite il engleski?' I asked.

He nodded. 'I'm Doctor Nikac Popović.' He turned to Rosa. 'I have your records. You had your last chemotherapy treatments seven days ago?' Rosa nodded, almost imperceptibly. 'You are not feeling well, is that right?' He didn't need to confirm this. It was obvious she was struggling.

Rosa raised her eyelids. It struck me how ill she looked. Was this really the vibrant woman I'd met just a few short months ago, a woman running a very successful business? The deterioration was breathtaking. I held her hand as the doctor spoke.

'I think you have an infection,' he told her. 'I will have a nurse take your temperature and do some tests. If this is the case, then we will give you intravenous antibiotics, but you will have to stay in, I'm afraid.'

Rosa had a series of tests. Her PICC line was infected, a nurse explained to me. The middle-aged nurse was bustling and efficient and even brought me a coffee.

Once on the ward, Rosa slept for most of the day. Kat came in late afternoon after the lunch service. We went to the cafeteria, deep in the hospital grounds.

'I bet you haven't eaten yet,' I told Kat.

'Nor you,' she said. 'How long are you going to stay?'

'I'll probably stay until after visiting tonight. They don't seem to mind me being there. They asked if I was next of kin or family. I had to lie and say I was her cousin.'

'We kind of are,' Kat said with a small smile.

The cafeteria looked onto a large courtyard and the doors were open. There were picnic tables outside. We both grabbed some sandwiches and sat in the garden.

'Do you think she'll be OK?' Kat asked.

'Yes, one of the nurses told me that patients pick up relatively quickly once they are on antibiotics. She looked terrible this morning. She'll be out tomorrow or the day after. When is Luka back?'

Kat nibbled her sandwich. 'Tomorrow, quite early. He'll be horrified, of course. This will make him doubt going away.'

'I can understand that, but Rosa's adamant he'll go this year. I feel sorry for both of them.' I looked up at the windows of the hospital. 'Illness like this is terrifying. You lose control of your life.'

We were both quiet.

'How was the restaurant at lunch time?'

'Busy,' Kat said. 'Almost as soon as we opened. That brunch idea of yours has taken off. You're really good at ideas like that.'

I hesitated. I had all these ideas for Café Lompar, that I'd been turning over and over in my mind, but I had ignored them, because of what Rosa represented in my life. Dan's betrayal.

But today, after seeing her so vulnerable, after she'd let me help her, somehow none of that mattered any more. Rosa was more to me now than 'Dan's other family'. Luka and the Café, Kat's life here, were more important than the past.

'I've been thinking,' I said, after a while. 'After buying the cottage, I've got quite a bit of money left over. And there's your dad's insurance money, and the money I made when I sold my business. It's just sitting there in the bank. The restaurant could do with an injection of cash. The kitchen is too small for the business to grow any bigger. The newspaper column is likely to draw more crowds in. You're really putting the place on the map.'

'Well, not just me. What are you thinking, Mum?'

'Becoming a partner with Rosa! Am I mad?'

Kat grinned widely. 'What? How—?'

I interrupted her. 'It's got such potential. The location is fantastic. It just needs refurbishing.' My words were coming out in a tumble. 'The core menu is great, and it gives the restaurant a real identity. A consistent message. The specials, if we keep to just one or two, I think that works. The fusion between British and Montenegrin is really interesting and delicious, of course.' I hardly paused for breath. 'You were saying the other day how you'd like to try foraging. Well, I've been reading and there's vine kiwis that could be used in mains as well as desserts. Not that I know much, but you do!' I laughed at myself.

Kat's eyes were sparkling. 'When I went for a walk with Luka the other day, I tasted loads of wild herbs and a nettle that would be great to make a tea. I was thinking that we could make a really unusual ice cream or panna cotta with it.'

'See, what I mean?'

'But what about Neil? You're keen on him, Mum. I can tell.'

'If it's meant to be, it will work,' I said with more conviction than I felt. 'I don't want to move to Montenegro, but I could spend some time here and then help with the finances and marketing from home. It would still be Rosa running it with you. It could work, but I'm not sure how Rosa would take it. The restaurant's her baby. Would she want to loosen the reins?'

'Luka said that she was worried if she'd ever be able to run the restaurant in the same way again. And illness makes you re-evaluate your life. Oh, Mum, I think it's a great idea.'

'I'm going to have to hand my notice in at the charity. It's only fair on Sylvie, and she'll be relieved – she was telling me that Liz is keen to do more at the charity and she wished she had a job for her. Realistically, I can't do both and I've loved getting involved more here. I feel as excited as I did when I had my gardening business. I'll have to go back in a few days to help out with these big events Sylvie has planned, but I'll tell her then.'

'Wow, you've really thought about this.' Kat shook her head.

'That's not all. I'm thinking of buying an apartment or house here for you. Something with an annexe perhaps, where I could stay over when I come to Montenegro. I wouldn't interfere with your plans, of course.'

'Really? Oh, Mum, that's fantastic!' Kat came round the picnic table and squeezed me tightly.

'Let's not get ahead of ourselves. Rosa has to agree first.'

'She will, I know it,' Kat said firmly.

After visiting hour was over, we got back to the apartment around eight-thirty. Both Kat and I were exhausted, but I couldn't miss another day at the restaurant.

We visited Rosa the next day late in the afternoon. Luka had landed in Dubrovnik at eleven. Kat had told him about his mother before he boarded the plane and he'd gone straight to the hospital.

Rosa was sitting up in bed when we arrived. She looked a lot brighter and even had her trademark red lipstick on. Luka was holding her hand. He rose and hugged us as we came in.

'Thank you so much,' he said, 'for looking after Mum. I'm grateful. I feel so guilty I wasn't here.'

'Nonsense!' Rosa exclaimed.

Kat kissed her gently on the cheek. 'How are you feeling?'

'A lot brighter.' She told us that she'd slept well and would probably be home tomorrow. 'The PICC line was infected. I'm

328

fine, though. Counting down the rounds of chemo I have left,' she sighed.

'I'm glad you're both here,' Luka said, turning to Kat and me. 'I've arranged with the uni that I can study remotely this semester. That way I don't have to delay my course and I still get to be with Mum.'

'But…' Rosa protested.

'It's all been arranged, Mum.' Luka picked up her hand and kissed it. 'I knew if I told you first, you'd never agree to it. But I spoke to the tutors yesterday and they were very understanding.'

Kat and I sat down. 'Well,' I began, 'seeing as we're all being honest, I've got a proposition to put to you, Rosa.'

CHAPTER THIRTY-NINE

🌿 Kat 🌿

Mum nudged my hand as we sat at Rosa's bedside. Through the thin pane of glass at the door we could see Milo. He knocked before sliding it open and presented a large bouquet of white roses.

'That's so sweet,' Rosa smiled sleepily. I squeezed her hand, worrying that our visit was tiring her. 'Come in.'

'I didn't know you were coming,' I said to him.

Milo shrugged. 'I might have had a panicked phone call from someone at the airport.' He motioned to Luka with his head, setting the simple bouquet down on Rosa's small bedside table.

'Luka, you shouldn't worry like this.' Rosa smiled. 'Now, I've got a full crowd.'

'Will we all be allowed to stay?' I glanced round, eyeing the rather matronly nurse's back.

'Uh, Milo and I will charm them, if it's an issue.' Luka grinned.

'I don't doubt it.' Mum laughed. It was nice to have the group of us here. Something felt right about it. This strange family we'd formed. 'I'd better be heading off, anyway.' Mum started getting up to put her jacket on. 'Someone has to run this restaurant,' she joked.

'Oh yes, that reminds me.' I turned to Milo. 'You're looking at the new co-owner of Café Lompar.' His eyebrows shot up in surprise.

'My business partner, Grace Lompar.' Rosa presented Mum. I was pleased she'd been so on board with the idea. The restaurant had been her baby for years, we weren't sure how easily she'd share it. Fortunately, Rosa could see the opportunity and promise Mum brought with her.

'Well,' Mum said, 'we won't make any agreements till you're feeling stronger. We'll wait to make sure this is what you want to do when you're feeling yourself.'

'I'm sure,' Rosa said. 'I've had it to myself long enough. I can see it needs work. Having both of you, Kat and Grace, for even a short time, has made such a difference. I'm all for it. The Lompar girls are stronger together.' Rosa had looked serene, quietly sure of her decision. The unspoken words – that she might not be around in the future – floated between us. This infection had given us all a real scare. It made sense to plan for the unthinkable and if we could get the restaurant on a more solid footing as well, then it was truly the best thing possible.

But luckily it didn't look like Rosa was going anywhere any time soon. I had felt sick all day, hearing the worry in Mum's voice on the phone. Thank God Rosa had pulled through. The way Luka had held her tight when he finally arrived back from Berlin had brought a lump to my throat. This was it now. We were family. And family was everything.

'Are you going to be staying around Montenegro then?' Milo asked Mum, leaning against the wall.

'Not full time. I'm thinking of working mostly online at

home, still having my life there, and spending part of the year out here. We might get somewhere for Kat to live where I can stay in when I need to.'

'What did we say? Montenegro gets under your skin,' Luka said smugly.

'Shame about Montenegrin men though,' Mum joked.

'Mum!' I gasped, indignant on their behalf.

She winked at me. 'Right, I'd better get going. I can come back tomorrow if you need me to bring anything?' Mum leaned over Rosa's bedside.

'You've already done more than enough.' Rosa patted her hand. 'Thank you, Grace, for everything.' A knowing smile passed between them.

'Hope you have a good rest tonight. Take care.'

I waved her off, knowing I'd need to join her in the restaurant soon, but hoping to get a lift back with Milo. Although Lovro was taking care of Café Lompar today, I felt uneasy about leaving him alone with Ivan. I wanted to have a good talk with Ivan tonight, show him that I wouldn't put up with his behaviour anymore. If he wanted to stay, then he would have to play by my rules.

'Why don't we grab a drink in the café and leave you two to have some time together?' Milo gestured to mother and son. I followed him out, feeling nervous about being alone with him. I hadn't managed to speak to Milo since the Adam fiasco. He hadn't answered his phone when I tried to call and explain. Things still weren't quite right between us and I was worried he thought I was going back to my ex.

As if I would! When I'd seen Milo at the hospital, any doubts about him were resolved. Ana had understandably been hurt on behalf of her sister, but I knew in my gut that Milo was a good person. I couldn't wait to spend my future with him.

We stood in the queue at the little hospital café, the leather sofas and stained carpet incongruous against the clinical white surroundings. It dawned on me that Rosa's illness was the first time I'd set foot in a hospital since that awful day I'd had to rush from London to see Dad for the last time. I'd had no way of getting to Bath, other than on the train, which was frustratingly slow. I had sat in the carriage sobbing, my phone gripped in my hand, unable to believe a day that had started so normally, with a bowl of cereal and a sleepy episode of Friends, had turned out to be the worst day of my life.

And yet, in a way that terrible grief had led to this: a whole new life.

'Are you OK?' Milo asked, noticing me shudder. I blinked away tears.

'Yes, I just don't like hospitals.' I slid my little finger into the palm of his hand, and we shuffled forward in the queue. Milo kissed my hair gently. I leaned my head against his solid shoulder.

He ordered two cappuccinos.

'Let me pay for this,' I said when we got to the till. 'Let your girlfriend buy you a drink for once.'

Milo's mouth twitched. We'd never said the words before. I didn't know what he'd think. Boyfriend sounded an immature term to describe Milo.

'Well then, let your boyfriend do this.' He put his arms round my waist and pulled me up into a kiss. The masculine smell of him filled my senses and I realised, with absolute certainty, that I loved Milo Martinović.

'I'm sorry, I'm sorry.' I dumped my bag in the corner of the little room, shouting as I ran into the back entrance of Café Lompar. 'The traffic from Podgorica was ridiculous. I'm here now.' I stopped in the middle of the kitchen, needing to catch my breath.

Lovro's face was redder than the spicy tomato salsa smeared all down his apron. The ding of a timer sounded and he hurried past me.

'Let me get that.' I went over to rescue the filo tarts from the oven. Lovro carried on rolling our salmon fillets in their marinade. 'Where's Ivan?' When there was no answer, I frowned at Lovro. He gave me a dark look.

'He's not here?'

Lovro shook his head.

'Was he here at lunch?' I asked, already knowing the answer. 'Lovro, why didn't you call me? I could have come back from Podgorica early.'

'Well, the morning service was fine, but it's getting busy now.' Lovro wiped his brow. 'I haven't had time to start on the specials yet.'

'Don't worry about them, we'll just play catch up.' I went over to help him prepare our skewers for the lamb. We roasted the lamb on skewers first to enhance its smokiness; a trick I'd learnt from Truffles that really added je ne sais quoi. It was then served in a sticky sauce with a hint of rakija brandy. It was a new dish, and needed a lot of work, plus a third pair of hands in the kitchen. Ivan's absence was totally unacceptable.

After some effort, Lovro and I managed to catch up, even starting to think of a seafood special. We chatted while we worked, peeling prawns and shelling oysters, and I brought Lovro up to date on what had happened with Milo.

'So it's official then?' Lovro asked.

'Yep.'

'I'll be calling you Chef Martinović soon,' he joked. I threw a shell at him, thankful that the atmosphere in the kitchen had relaxed since I'd arrived. Lovro was getting better and better as a sous chef, but a service alone was too much to handle for anyone. Plus, with Café Lompar's growing popularity, we were feeling the tiny size of our kitchen more than ever. I promised myself that one of the first things I'd do when Mum put in her investment was ask for a raise in Lovro's pay. We couldn't afford to lose him.

'You never tell me about your love life?' I prompted him, trying to be nosy and casual at the same time.

'Well, there's not much to tell. The gay scene in Tivat isn't exactly thriving,' he said, keeping his head down.

'And there's no one you've got your eye on?'

'Not really.' He paused, as if unsure whether to tell me more. I held my breath, hoping he'd open up about Dav. I saw the looks that passed between them every night.

'Evening.' Ivan strolled in. Lovro and I looked up in surprise. My initial confusion quickly turned to anger. I didn't know how to play this, whether to give a British passive-aggressive 'Nice of you to join us' or go straight to shouting. I felt my hand shaking as I slid the knife down the back of a prawn.

'What?' Ivan snapped.

'You're three hours late.' My voice sounded shaky.

'So?' Ivan shrugged. 'Lovro was here. He was fine, wasn't he?' He turned his back on me, slowly taking his jacket off to put on his chef's whites.

'Do you not care about this job? Or are you really that lazy?' I asked, my voice rising. I hadn't expected to go from zero to a thousand this quickly.

Ivan turned, his nose wrinkling as if I was a bad smell. 'You weren't here either. Why is there one rule for you and another for me?' He gestured to himself nonchalantly.

I put my knife down and gripped the side of the kitchen counter. This man made my blood boil. I couldn't believe he was such a bastard. I took a breath, not wanting to say something I regretted.

'Because this is my kitchen. Because I was visiting Rosa. Because I care about this place.'

'Hey, I used to be head chef too.' Ivan drew close to me. 'And there was none of this extravagant rubbish then. It was real Montenegrin food. And we had real customers back then. Now the customers care more about what they can Instagram than what they can eat,' he snarled.

'And so what, as long as they have a good time,' I practically shrieked. I hated confrontation. I was always more likely to back down than to have a stand-off. But I wanted this man out of my kitchen. He was the worst person I'd ever worked with. Even worse than Mark!

'Ivan, I've tried so hard to make things good for you here,' I attempted to level with him. 'I know you've not had it easy and I know things have changed a lot in Café Lompar. But you need to start treating me and this restaurant with some respect.'

He held my eyes for a second. I didn't know if he was going to back off or hit me. Lovro stood at my side, quiet, watching us both.

'I only respect real chefs.' Ivan grimaced. 'I don't want to cook this bullshit fusion anymore.'

Even though I knew he was scum, the words still hurt. I tried not to show it.

'It might be popular now, but one day everyone will see how twisted this place is.' He smacked his hand down on the countertop, giving us one last glare before grabbing his jacket.

'Ivan, I really mean this,' I said at his retreating back. 'Never come back here.'

He turned round. 'My pleasure, Chef.'

The sound of the door slamming reverberated around the room. Lovro and I turned to each other. I was shaking. I'd never had a face-to-face shouting match before. I hated the feeling, but I was so relieved I'd seen the back of him.

'Are you OK?' Lovro asked, wide-eyed.

'I think so.'

He pulled me into a hug.

'I think I need a drink,' I said.

'I'd better carry on with the prawns,' Lovro said at the same time. We both giggled.

'Please remind me never to be late.' Lovro grinned.

'Oh my God! Was I really that bad?'

'This is my kitchen,' he mimicked, emphasising the my. We both laughed. I knew the whole conversation with Ivan would play over and over in my mind, but for now I felt nothing but relief that he was gone.

'We can cope on our own tonight, can't we?'

'I think we can do anything,' he smiled.

Mum popped her head in, concern etched on her face. 'I heard shouting. Is everything all right?'

'Fine,' I answered, smiling, 'but I think we'll be needing a new chef.'

CHAPTER FORTY

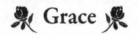 Grace

Sordid Set-Up at Top Restaurant in Tivat!

A local community was reeling in shock yesterday when it learned that one of Montenegro's top restaurants is being run by a wife and a mistress! A source close to the proprietor revealed that Café Lompar, owned by Rosa Lompar, a well-known business woman in Tivat, was mistress for many years to British-Montenegrin Danilo Lompar, a Professor of Politics and Economics at Bath University in England.

The Professor died suddenly eighteen months ago of a heart attack. Rosa and Danilo had an affair for almost two decades and had a son, Luka Lompar, who is nineteen. Rosa Lompar, whose real name is Rosa Lazović, assumed her lover's surname to convince people they were married.

An ex-employee, who wishes to remain anonymous, said, 'Suspicions were aroused weeks ago when another woman took over front of house. When we learned her name was Grace Lompar, we started putting two and two together. They concocted a story about being cousins, but it didn't add up.'

Up and coming chef, Kat Lompar, is Danilo and Grace Lompar's daughter. She has been creating quite a stir in the restaurant industry in Montenegro for her creative and unique dishes, a fusion of Montenegrin and British cuisine. She has a column in this newspaper and is planning to write a cookbook.

Montenegrins are famed for their pride in the concept of family, so this sex scandal has rocked the town. Another restaurant owner has stated how disgusted people were when they heard the news. 'To carry on an affair for years with a married man shows a complete lack of morals and respect. Rosa Lompar ought to be ashamed of herself!'

The ex-employee added, 'Grace Lompar is inexperienced in the trade and doesn't speak Montenegrin. Most staff feel she is incompetent, and the atmosphere has changed since her arrival. Her daughter is ruthless in her determination to make a name for herself and has sacked long-standing members of staff.'

It remains to be seen whether customers, who have been flocking to Café Lompar in recent weeks since the appointment of avant-garde chef, Kat Lompar, will continue to patronise this popular restaurant.

Luka marched in, grim-faced, and slapped the Pobjeda in front of me as I was sitting at one of the tables, checking over the receipts for the deliveries we'd had earlier that morning.

There on the right-hand side of the page, under a story on the president's recent economic cuts, was the article about Café Lompar.

'Has your mother seen it?' I asked.

'No, and she can't!'

'I'm surprised it's newsworthy enough to print.'

'Is that all you can say?' Luka paced back and forth. Then he called Kat from the kitchen.

Kat read the article, her eyes widening. 'Oh my God! Well, it doesn't take Sherlock Holmes to guess who's behind this. The bastard!'

'It's slanderous!' Luka blurted. 'It makes my mother sound like a slut. It's not true. They were in love. Yes, she never married him, but she took on the name as she knew how narrow-minded people are. She didn't mean for any of this to happen.'

Kat said, 'Calm down, Luka. It doesn't matter what people think. We know the real story. Is it such a scandal?'

'Yes, you don't understand how old-fashioned Montenegrins can be. They are not as liberal as British people.'

'Well, they might not be as open-minded, but I'd say the Montenegrin press is about on a par with the British in making a story out of nothing!' I said.

'What they say about us is hardly flattering,' Kat sighed. 'Mum, you're not incompetent. Quite the opposite and Ivan knows it. And I'm ruthless in my determination to make a name for myself!' she read again.

'Mum will be devastated,' Luka said, grimly. 'She doesn't need this. Not now, especially. This could ruin us. Do you think we should make a counter-statement?'

'Definitely not,' I insisted. 'It will show we're rattled.'

'So, what can we do?' Kat asked, as she slumped down next to me. 'It's really below the belt when Rosa is so ill. How could he? She's given him so many chances.'

'Well, he's gone now, and he should have been sacked a long time ago,' I said.

We were all distracted by a rattle behind us. Dav had been to the cellar and was returning, cradling wine bottles in his arms. We lapsed into silence.

'Come on, let's go outside,' I said. 'Ana and Maria can hold the fort for a while. You can join Lovro in a bit, Kat.'

We must make a subdued picture, I thought, the three of us sitting on the patio at the back, as we debated how to handle this latest storm.

'It's so unfair,' Luka brooded.

'Right. I think I know what we should do,' I said, suddenly.

'What?' Luka and Kat asked in unison.

'Nothing.'

'Nothing?' Luka snorted.

'Hear me out first. Look, the news or, more to the point, the gossip is out there. So, rather than hang our heads in shame, what if we embrace it? People were going to find out eventually. It was only a matter of time. Let's take pride in our connection. Let's have photos over the wall of us with Danilo. My wedding photos. You as a child, Kat, with us both. Rosa and Dan. Luka as a child. We could even put a sign up saying Families are complicated. Everyone is welcome at Café Lompar. OK, the wording needs some working on, but do you see what I mean?'

Kat grinned.

'Let's not hide this. It's part of us, what makes us us and, you know what, it works!' I said, quite pleased with myself.

Luka looked dubious.

'Come on, Luka. What else can we do? You'll have to go home and tell Rosa before someone else does. But what the hell does this matter? Tell her what I propose to do and, if she agrees to it, we'll start the display straight away. We've got to fight this with love, because that's what glues us all together. If it doesn't sound too cheesy.'

He brightened. 'You're right. I'll go home now. Thanks, Grace.' He kissed my cheek.

'Remember all publicity is good publicity. It's called a top restaurant in the article and you're an avant-garde chef,' I said, turning to Kat. 'I mean, some people will come here out of sheer nosiness and then when they taste your food, they'll keep coming back.'

'Do you know what, Mum? I'm really really proud of you.' She stood up and hugged me.

'Come on, we've got a lunch service to run and I'll need to go back to the apartment this afternoon to pack. Tonight is my last night here, for a while at least. Let's go out with a bang.'

I was distracted a little during lunch as I bustled about. We were as busy as usual, although a lot of the customers were tourists. We'd have to survive the long winter months by getting locals in. Rosa had agreed to my proposal and now I felt this place was as much mine as it was hers. We'd need to hammer out the final details and then get started on extending and modernising the kitchen. I had the wine-tasting events to organise and we needed to advertise for weddings, christenings, even supper clubs with taster menus. And the place did need updating. The décor was tired, but simplicity was best. I wanted this to have a quality feel to it. Kat's cooking was worthy of it, that was for sure.

The location was unbeatable: the Adriatic, a constant, reassuring presence, rhythmically murmuring as it swelled and ebbed against the harbour wall. It sparkled in the midday sun, a bright sapphire blue. I'd miss this back home, as I faced the leaden skies and cold winds of a rainy British winter.

But I had missed Meadow Ponsbury and Claire and Stu and the twins. And I needed to see Neil. Was our relationship going anywhere? Who knew? But I owed it to myself to find out.

I headed back to Kat's apartment to pack. I wouldn't miss this room, I thought to myself as I tidied my suitcase.

Kat had booked to see a few houses and apartments next week in and around Tivat. She was very excited and promised to keep me updated. An annexe was a must. The way things were going between her and Milo, it wouldn't be too long before they moved in together. The little blip between them seemed to have brought them even closer and they were crazy about each other. It was so different to how she was with Adam.

I ate my lunch on the balcony, the sun burning my legs. I watched the crowds of tourists pass, people eating ice-creams on benches and the sunbathers stretched out on their yachts. It was a glorious place, yet I was under no illusion that part-owning a restaurant was going to be hard work. Rosa wouldn't be up to work for months. Luka would help out when he could, but he would have assignments to do. Milo was open to doing more in the restaurant, as his tourist boats would be redundant for the winter months. He could do the front of house. He was a charming and likeable man. Ana was an asset, too, if she and Milo could settle their differences. She had offered to help me set up an instagram account for Café Lompar, knowing the importance of developing a social media presence. She was a very good photographer.

Kat hadn't come home for lunch. She was interviewing two new chefs and they were each going to cook a dish for her and Lovro. They both sounded quite promising, one more experienced than the other, but Kat was keen to mentor new chefs. It was important we factored in some breaks for Kat, so a quality chef was essential. And Lovro was great; he was thriving under Kat's tutelage.

As I walked back to the restaurant, I wondered what to do about Dav. He was young and lazy, but I had a feeling with his uncle gone, he could improve. Maybe we could develop his experience with wine? Perhaps I should send him on a course at one of the wineries near Lake Skadar. Montenegrin wine was very distinctive. The red wine was deep and heady. I'd been reading about vranac, the dark grape used to make red wine here, and krstač, for dry whites. We'd see. I was becoming as obsessed as Kat with the restaurant.

When I returned to Café Lompar at six, Kat was buzzing with enthusiasm about the new chefs.

'They were both promising,' she said. 'The older one, Bojan, said that he was desperate to come here as he had heard about me and he was keen on the idea of British-Montenegrin fusion. He was really knowledgeable. You won't believe this, but the younger one was called Ivan.'

'Oh, God, I hope that's not a bad omen,' I laughed.

'That's what Lovro and I said. But his dish was gorgeous. He made grilled squid, with the crispy tentacles coated in wild garlic and olive oil. Simple but delicious and he loves foraging.'

'So, when do they start?'

'Ivan at the end of the month, as he has to work his notice in his current place, but Bojan starts next week.'

'That's good, Kat, but it's going to be time-consuming training up new chefs, no matter how good or experienced they are.'

'True, but it means that we can lighten the load eventually and not have to work so hard. When the tourist season ends in October, we can close on Mondays, too.'

Luka entered the kitchen, looking far brighter than earlier. He raised his eyebrows, as if to hint we should go outside. Lovro was prepping vegetables for the night's service.

'It's all right,' Kat said. 'I filled Lovro in on what's happening. He has a right to know. It's in the paper, anyway.'

'How did Rosa take it?' I asked.

'Better than I thought,' Luka sighed. 'Well, obviously she was upset at first. But then I told her what you'd suggested, and she agreed we should face it head on. She even said it was a relief.' He removed something from his rucksack. 'She's given me some photos to put up.'

Kat and I took them outside, with Luka trailing behind, and we sat on the patio at the back of the restaurant. There were about ten photos, some with just Rosa and Danilo and others with the three of them. One was of a birthday party with Luka blowing out the candles on a birthday cake, the flickering flames reflected in his excited eyes, Dan and Rosa standing proudly behind.

'I was five there,' Luka explained. 'He never spent a Christmas with us. I never asked why. Mum said he had an important job in England. It was just the way it was.'

It was a sobering moment and Kat reached for my hand.

'Let's put these in frames,' I said, 'and I'll post ours as soon as I get a chance when I get home. I'll be back in a few weeks.'

I was right that we'd be busy. That night the crowds kept coming. It was just as well that Luka was there to lend a hand and

Milo turned up about seven and helped in the kitchen and front of house, wherever he was needed.

Kat had spoken to Ana, Maria and Dav before service started. She wanted to clear the air. She told them about the newspaper article and how we were continuing regardless. They had the good grace to pretend they didn't know about the article, but it was the talk of the town. I watched Dav behind the bar and serving the wine at the tables. He was subdued, but that was to be expected. He seemed keen to keep his job and now Ivan had left, the toxic atmosphere had gone with him. I'd tell him about my idea before I left tonight.

Once service had finished, I left the others to clear up. I had an early flight in the morning. Kat and Milo were lingering, anyway, enjoying snatched moments together. She wouldn't be late, I knew, as it was our last night before I went home. Earlier, she'd thanked me for coming and told me that she was proud of me, and my heart was bursting with pride at all she was achieving here. We were the closest we'd ever been.

When I arrived back at the apartment, I combed my hair and reapplied bright lipstick. I hadn't spoken to Neil in a couple of days. I hoped it wouldn't be awkward. It was now or never.

He picked up on the second ring. He smiled widely as soon as he saw me.

'Hiya, Grace,' he said.

'Hi, Neil. I'm coming home.'

EPILOGUE

🌿 Kat 🌿

Seven months later

I brushed my hair, cursing the way it frizzed in the humidity. It was only April, but Montenegro was starting to heat up. The only respite was the cooler nights when you still needed a jacket to walk around. I was hoping to create a chic chignon for tonight, but it was clear my hair wasn't going to play ball. I didn't mind. I smiled at myself in the mirror anyway. A slightly more casual effect might work better with my green linen dress and ankle boots. Besides, no one would be looking that closely at my hair when I showed them ... the rock.

My left ring finger twinkled in the gentle light. I still couldn't believe I was engaged. I'd done nothing but stare at the ring, catching it glistening every time I was chopping something or whenever I picked up my phone. It was gorgeous, just what I would have picked out myself. Nothing too fancy or ostentatious, just a simple pear-cut diamond on a silver band. Classic and perfect.

I was determined not to be one of those showy-off fiancés or soon-to-be bridezillas. Just being engaged to Milo was enough for me. When he'd proposed two weeks ago on my twenty-fifth birthday, it was completely out of the blue. We'd been out for a celebratory birthday dinner in Perast, the whole clan in tow of course: Luka, Rosa, Maria, Lovro, and Mum had flown out especially for me. Milo didn't make some fancy proposal at the restaurant or on one knee at sunset, but back at the house we'd been sitting out on the balcony, just the two of us, finishing a bottle of Prosecco when he'd looked across at me and said, 'I want to spend the rest of my life with you.' It was perfect.

'We're going to be late!' I heard Milo's muffled shout coming from downstairs.

'Come on then, Bella,' I sighed. The ginger and white cat jumped up on my dressing table, completely obscuring the mirror. 'Fusspot.' She purred appreciatively as I rubbed her neck, and paced back and forth on the tabletop, nestling into my hand.

Bella had turned up at the door one day, about a week after I'd moved in. She'd looked thin and a little worn then, and I could tell she was a stray. It wasn't long before I'd been charmed into feeding her, and now she was plump and shiny and had taken to curling up in bed next to me at night. I wasn't sure who'd adopted whom, but now I was more besotted with Bella than Mum's old colleague Heather was about her dog Mitzi.

'I should have known I'd find you two in here.' Milo turned up at the door, leaning on the frame. 'I don't know who you love more, me or Bella.'

I stood up, hooking my hoop earrings through at the same time. 'Hmm, it's a very close call, but I think Bella wins by a sliver.'

'I hope that's not true,' Milo laughed. 'You look absolutely beautiful.' I went over and slid my arms around his neck.

'Do we have to go?' I asked him, batting my eyelashes.

'We can't miss our own engagement party!'

'I know. I told Mum and Rosa not to make a fuss. I hope they haven't gone to too much effort.'

'Rosa's hardly been taking it easy, has she?' Milo said, stroking my back.

'I knew she wouldn't. I found out the other day she's been making dinners for Luka to take back to uni; he takes them on the train in a cool box. I don't think he's cooked once since he started in January. And she still does all his washing!'

'When will he ever grow up?' Milo rolled his eyes, laughing.

'Rosa, you look amazing.' I greeted her at the door. She really did, her shiny dark hair in a perfect pixie-crop. It was strange thinking that just eight months ago she still had her thick mane of dark curls. She'd been through the mill since, but the old sparkle was definitely back in her eyes.

'You don't think it makes me look old?' She tucked a strand of hair behind her ear.

'Don't be ridiculous!'

Rosa ushered me inside. I whispered to her, 'Have you met her yet? What's she like?'

'She's inside,' Rosa said. 'She seems nice, very quiet. I don't know if she can handle our boy.'

'Luka and Leonie, it's got a certain ring to it.' I hoped Leonie, Luka's new German girlfriend, wouldn't be overwhelmed. She'd only known him a few months — they were on the same course in uni — and this was the first time he'd brought her to Montenegro. Luka was obsessed, talking about her non-stop and sending me daily pictures from Berlin. I wasn't sure if bringing her to a family party, where she was likely to meet Maria, also back from uni in Thessaloniki, was the best choice, but Luka insisted.

'Here we go!' Milo said, pushing through the door. We were met with a barrage of familiar faces, everyone milling around with glasses of champagne in hand and laughing convivially. It was such a lovely sight, I felt my heart swell. I spotted Mum in the corner, who came over to give me a big hug. She looked gorgeous in a coral shift dress. Rosa went to sit down next to Aunt Sofija, who was perched at the buffet table, watching the action. Auntie Claire and Uncle Stu were beaming at me, Laura already eyeing up one of the waiters and Liam on his phone.

The restaurant looked incredible, fresh from its facelift and extension. After planning with Rosa, Mum had worked hard on the decor, sourcing the classiest furniture and lighting, and kitting me out with a wonderful kitchen, fit for a professional team like ours. The whole restaurant was simple and white, with one wall of completely exposed stone: the perfect mix of modern and rustic. We'd painted the bar area black for a stark contrast. The staff had all been given uniforms with our new branding. I still marvelled at the place every time I came to work.

It was proving to be a real hit in Tivat, our popularity having only grown since that damning article in the Pobjeda. Bojan and Ivan (or Saint Ivan, as we'd taken to calling him to distinguish from the previous one) had been wonderful additions to the team. For the two months we'd closed over the winter to work on the extension, the entire kitchen staff had worked together to create an arsenal of recipes that really showcased our skills and talents as a team of four. Our Skadar Lake carp, smoked with foraged truffle and dill oil, was my personal favourite and the most successful dish in the restaurant. Our core menu was gaining quite a following, and we'd even been featured on Italian MasterChef. I couldn't believe how far I'd come from timid Kat, the sous chef at Truffles under Mark's thumb.

We'd had so many compliments from tourists and locals alike on the classic setting of the restaurant and our wall of family pictures. 'You could linger for hours looking at their gallery of love,' one wonderful review had said on Tripadvisor. I'd developed a habit of poring over our reviews in bed at night, a little bit sad I knew, but the feedback was invaluable. Mum did it as well from home, messaging me, 'Have you seen the comment about our new sexy wine connoisseur? They surely can't mean Dav, can they?'

The restaurant's name had been the most difficult decision. Mum and Rosa were constantly chatting about whether to keep Café Lompar or change to something more upmarket. We wondered if Café gave us an informal feel, but I personally liked the contrast between our fine-dining setting and more familiar name. In the end, we'd given Rosa the decision, to celebrate her getting the all-clear.

'Neil, thanks for coming tonight,' I said, as he bent down to kiss me. He moved to Mum's side, his hand on the small of her back. 'How are you finding our beautiful country?'

'I can't believe I haven't been before,' he smiled. 'It's such a well-kept secret. We went to Šćepan Polje today because Olls wanted to go rafting.'

He gestured to his son, who was busy chatting up Jela, one of our most recent recruits for front of house. She was such a straight-talking person, I was sure she'd eat him alive, but it was funny to see Olls casually touching her arm, trying to make a good impression.

'On the Tara River?' I asked Neil, remembering when I dragged Milo there. He'd been all confident on the journey, but completely freaked out when we boarded the raft with an experienced team and some tourists. I joked it was the only boat that didn't come naturally to Milo. He'd held onto the ropes so tightly his hands cramped for days afterwards. But I loved the adrenaline rush as we flew down the river, bumping off rocks and taking in the fleeting views of Montenegrin countryside.

'I didn't go on, of course!' Mum laughed.

'No, we sat on the banks and had a picnic. It was gorgeous being with this one.' Neil was gazing at Mum, all moon-eyed and swooning. I'd met him a few times, the first time when I went home for Christmas. It still felt very new, but he clearly adored Mum.

'They're going golfing tomorrow.' Mum smiled.

'Of course,' I laughed. 'Hope you've packed your diamond sweater,' I teased Neil, knowing he could take it.

'And my corduroy trousers.' He winked.

Milo and I mingled in the restaurant. It was strange seeing the staff off duty, especially Lovro, who was wearing a T-shirt and the skinniest black jeans I'd ever seen. I was used to seeing him in chef's whites; I didn't have him pegged as a skinny jeans and bling kind of guy. I felt pleasantly tipsy by the time Mum called me outside.

'We thought we'd take a picture the four of us,' Mum said, gesturing to Rosa and Luka.

'You've managed to drag yourself away from Leonie then?' I

teased Luka when we got outside, his lips smeared pink with Leonie's lipstick.

'Please, this is the first time I've seen you not waving your ring in front of everyone's faces,' he jibed. I ruffled his hair. It was great to see Luka so carefree, no longer worrying about his mum. It had been such a hard few months, watching her become sicker and thinner with the chemotherapy. I used to hate Thursdays, knowing what Rosa would be going through. Luka didn't leave her side once, fitting all his work around her treatment. Cancer seemed so random, ripping apart normal lives and damaging futures. I saw the pain in his eyes, haunting him relentlessly.

The only time I saw him cry, really cry, big heaving sobs with gasps for breath, was in January when Rosa came from the hospital shell-shocked. 'It's over.'

'What?' I'd asked them both.

'The treatment.' She looked spaced out, as if she didn't quite believe it herself. 'It's done.'

Of course, Rosa was still reeling. She looked fragile, but she was coming back stronger, wearing the new uniform proudly and working with Mum on our publicity part-time. We really did feel like a family, the four of us.

'Right, big smile.' One of Rosa's cousins worked as a photographer in Nikšić and had come over for the evening. We stood in a line, arms around each other's shoulders. It was cheesy, but we needed a new picture to display proudly on our wall: Mum and Rosa beaming in the middle, Luka towering over us all on the end.

'Let's take a few more,' the cousin said, pointing his camera. I went to move but the heel of my boot slipped into the sand, and I nearly tripped over.

'Right, these are coming off,' I said, kicking them off and loving the feeling of the cool sand between my toes.

Mum teetered in her heels. 'Mine might have to come off, too.'

'Let's all do it,' Rosa said.

We all laughed, holding our shoes up in the air. The photographer clicked away.

'Imagine if Dad could see us now,' Luka said, trainers in hand.

'I wonder what he'd think?' Mum whispered.

'He'd be surprised.' Rosa smiled.

'Surprised, more like horrified,' I joked, although I knew it wasn't true. 'I think he'd be proud ... of all of us.'

Rosa pulled me in tighter. The four of us looked at each other. I felt tears prick my eyes.

'Don't tell me you're crying again,' Luka laughed. 'Let's see these pictures.'

The photographer came over with his camera. We all crowded round, flicking through them.

'Oh no, not that one. My eyes are shut.' Mum grimaced. We flicked through, laughing at our faces in the ridiculous barefoot pose.

'OK, that's the one,' I said as he came to the last photo. It was us as we'd been talking about Dad, each gazing at each other with pure love. We looked so relaxed, so happy. A real family.

And we were perfectly positioned under the new and improved restaurant sign, the name still in pride of place as 'Café Lompar'.

'We have to frame that for the wall,' Mum said.

'Kat, that might make a nice cover photo for the cookbook,' Luka suggested, smiling at me.

'Yes!' He was right. I could imagine the photo enlarged, with some of the recipes pictured along the bottom.

'Have you thought of a name for the book yet, by the way?'

'I agreed it with the publishers yesterday,' I said.

'Well, go on then,' Mum laughed.

'Love at Café Lompar.'

KAT'S BUZARA SEAFOOD STEW

Perfect for a summer evening with wine and a gorgeous sunset! A light and popular Montenegrin dish with the classic Café Lompar twist.

Ingredients
Olive oil
2-3 cloves of garlic, finely chopped
2-3 shallots, finely chopped
2 tablespoons of sun-dried tomato paste
3 large tomatoes, roughly chopped
Pinch of chilli flakes
1 teaspoon of paprika
Pinch of saffron strands
200ml of dry white wine
150ml of fish stock
250g of cooked prawns
150g of mussels, scrubbed and debearded
2 tablespoons of fresh white breadcrumbs
1 tablespoon of finely grated parmesan
1 tablespoon of chopped parsley, plus extra to serve
Crusty bread
Salt and pepper to season

Note
Steps 1 to 4 can be completed in advance if cooking for guests. When ready to dine, simply heat the sauce and add the seafood and breadcrumb mixture.

Safety – if you have not cooked mussels before, do please look up how to clean, debeard them and be sure they are safe. There is a lot of good advice online if you're unsure. Wash them thoroughly and discard any that are open and don't close when tapped or that have broken shells. After cooking, they should all be open – discard any still closed.

Method
1. Heat a splash of olive oil in a frying pan set over a medium heat. Add the garlic and shallots and sauté for 1-2 minutes.
2. Stir in the sun-dried tomato paste, chopped tomatoes, chilli flakes, paprika, saffron and a pinch of salt. Cook for 5 minutes, stirring often.
3. Add the white wine and stir for a further 1-2 minutes, before adding the fish stock and bringing to the boil.
4. Stir then reduce the heat and simmer for 15-20 minutes, to allow the sauce to thicken.
5. Add the mussels to the pan and cook for 4-5 minutes until they have opened. Stir in the cooked prawns, and any other seafood you wish to add.
6. Meanwhile stir the breadcrumbs and parmesan together in a separate bowl with chopped parsley. When thoroughly mixed, stir in to the stew.
7. Cook for a further 2 minutes, tasting for seasoning, before serving in the frying pan with crusty bread.